Carol Marinelli recently filled in a form asking for her job title. Thrilled to be able to put down her answer, she put 'writer'. Then it asked what Carol did for relaxation and she put down the truth—'writing'. The third question asked for her hobbies. Well, not wanting to look obsessed, she crossed her fingers and answered 'swimming'—but, given that the chlorine in the pool does terrible things to her highlights, I'm sure you can guess the real answer!

Natalie Anderson adores happy endings, so you can be sure you've got happy endings to enjoy when you buy her books—she promises nothing less. She loves peppermint-filled dark chocolate, pineapple juice & extremely long showers, plus teasing her imaginary friends with dating dilemmas! She lives in New Zealand with her gorgeous husband & four fabulous children. If you love happy endings too, come find her on facebook.com/authornataliea, Twitter @authornataliea, or natalie-anderson.com

CLAIMING HIS HIDDEN HEIR

CAROL MARINELLI

PRINCESS'S PREGNANCY SECRET

NATALIE ANDERSON

MILLS & BOON

First Published in Great Britain 2018
by Mills & Boon, an imprint of HarperCollins*Publishers*
1 London Bridge Street, London, SE1 9GF

Claiming His Hidden Heir © 2018 by Carol Marinelli

Princess's Pregnancy Secret © 2018 by Natalie Anderson

ISBN: 978-0-263-93532-5

Printed and bound in Spain
by CPI, Barcelona

CLAIMING HIS HIDDEN HEIR

CAROL MARINELLI

For my great friend Frances Housden

An inspiring woman and wonderful writer.

Love always

Carol xxx

PROLOGUE

HE WOULD NOT be hiring Cecelia Andrews.

Property magnate Luka Kargas had already decided that Candidate Number Two would be his new personal assistant.

'Ms Andrews is here for her interview,' Hannah, his current PA, informed him.

'There's no need for me to meet her,' Luka responded. 'I've decided to go with Candidate Two.'

'Luka!' Hannah reproached, a little braver now that she was leaving. 'At least have the decency to see her. She's been through two extensive interviews with me, and as well as that it's pouring outside. She had to come across London in the middle of a storm.'

'Not interested,' Luka said, because he didn't buy into sob stories. 'It's a waste of my time.'

And a slice of Luka's time was precious indeed.

But then Luka suddenly remembered that Ms Andrews had been personally recommended by Justin, a contact he wanted to keep onside.

'Fine, send her in,' Luka said, deciding to see her briefly but then to get rid of her as soon as he could.

Impatient fingers drummed the desk as he waited, and then Candidate Three was shown in.

'Ms Andrews.' Luka stood and shook her right hand, noticing that on her left she wore an engagement ring.

Nothing would induce him to hire her, for she would have to have the most patient fiancé in the world to tolerate the ridiculous hours she would have to devote to him.

And *everyone* knew his reputation.

He just had to give her a few minutes of his time so he could tell Justin that he had interviewed her but gone with another candidate.

'Please,' he said. 'Take a seat.'

Cecelia knew that although he had called her Ms Andrews he was awaiting correction and an invitation to call her by her first name.

There would be no such invitation to do so.

Ms Andrews would do just fine, Cecelia had decided.

She had read about him, thoroughly researched him, and even been told by his current PA during two prolonged interviews about his bad-boy ways.

'You would have to deal with his girlfriends, or rather his exes,' Hannah had explained. 'It can be quite a juggling act at times. Luka works hard all week and then works just as hard breaking hearts at the weekend.'

Cecelia had seen it all before, and not just through her work. She abhorred the rich, debauched kind of lifestyle he led and with good reason—her mother, Harriet, had lived and died the same way.

Still, Luka Kargas's morals were his own concern, not hers. Cecelia had her sights set on working for royalty and he was a step in the right direction, that was all.

'He has a yacht, currently moored in Xanero,' Hannah had said.

'That's where he's from?' Cecelia checked, although she had found that out in her research.

'Yes, though you won't be expected to travel there with him and you won't be involved with the family business there. Luka keeps that strictly separate.'

She would not be falling for him, Cecelia had reassured both his incumbent PA and herself. The only thing the career-minded Cecelia wanted from Luka Kargas was his name on her résumé and the glowing reference that, after a year's hard work, he would surely provide.

But now she had finally met him, and as his long olive fingers had closed around hers, the very sensible Cecelia's conviction that she would not be attracted to him in the least had wavered somewhat.

'Hannah said you got caught in the storm,' Luka frowned.

The skies had darkened just over an hour ago.

Luka, from his vantage point of the fortieth floor, had watched the black clouds gather and roll over London.

Candidate Two had arrived drenched and had asked Hannah for a ten-minute delay before proceeding with the interview.

Usually that would have been enough to ensure a black mark against her name but, having watched the storm himself, Luka had accepted the excuse and the rather bedraggled candidate.

Cecelia Andrews was far from bedraggled, though.

She wore a dark grey suit that was immaculate, her blonde hair, worn up, was sleek and smooth, while her make-up was both discreet and in place.

Hannah had insinuated that a drowned rat sat in the entrance yet the woman who sat before him was far from that.

'I got caught up in the storm,' Cecelia said, 'but I wasn't caught out—I heeded the warnings.'

And she might want to start heeding them now, she thought, for the impact of him on her senses was like nothing she had ever known.

He wore a dark suit and tie and his crisp white shirt accentuated his olive skin; he hadn't shaved that morning.

The air in the room had changed, as if the charge that had lit the sky for the past hour had joined them.

Luka Kargas was everything her aunt had warned her about, and though she had told herself she could handle it, and that there was no way she could ever be attracted to someone like him, Cecelia hadn't allowed for the impact of Luka close up.

They skipped through the formalities, both determined to get this over and done with and move on with the day.

'Hannah will have explained that the hours are long,' Luka said.

'She did.'

'Sixteen-hour days at times.'

'Yes.' Cecelia nodded.

'And there's an awful lot of travel,' Luka said. 'Though for all that the working week is hell, you do get every weekend off.'

She smiled a tight, slightly disbelieving smile.

'You do,' Luka said, as he read those full lips. 'Come Friday night, the entire weekend is yours.'

'Though I'm guessing I wouldn't be out of here by five p.m.?'

'No,' he said. 'Usually around ten.'

So not really the entire weekend to herself, Cecelia thought as his black eyes scanned through her paperwork. 'Why are you finishing up with Justin?'

'Because I didn't want to live in Dubai.'

'I go there a lot,' Luka said, 'which would mean, by default, so would you.'

'That's fine. I just don't want to live there,' Cecelia said, and she knew, she just knew, he was alluding to the fact she had a fiancé whose needs would have impacted on her decision.

He was right.

Gordon wouldn't consider it.

'Do you speak Greek?' he asked.

'No,' Cecelia said, suddenly hoping it was a prerequisite for the role and that this torture would therefore come to an end. It was torture because her stomach seemed to be folding in on itself and she all of a sudden could feel the weight of her breasts. She had never had such a violent reaction to another person, though of course it was one-sided.

Luka Kargas looked thoroughly bored.

'Do you speak any other languages?' he asked.

'Some French,' Cecelia said, even though she spoke it very well and had both lived and worked in France for a year.

Anyway, he didn't want her French, whether a little or a lot of it, for he screwed up his nose.

Good, because Cecelia had now decided that she did not want this job.

She liked safe, and for very good reasons.

Cecelia liked her world ordered, and ten minutes alone with Luka Kargas had just rocked hers.

His black eyes were mesmerising and his brusque indifference had her re-crossing her legs.

Until this moment, sex had been a perfectly pleasant experience, if sometimes a bit of a chore.

Now, though, she sat across from a man who made her think of it.

Actually sit and think about torrid, impromptu sex at two p.m. on a Monday afternoon, and that could never do.

'Ms Andrews…'

'Cecelia,' she corrected, but only because she didn't want to sound like some uptight spinster.

And she wasn't.

She was engaged to be married, and right now she found herself desperately trying to hold onto that thought.

Oh, this really would never do!

'Cecelia.' He nodded. 'I see that you don't have any real experience in the hospitality industry.'

'No, I don't,' Cecelia said. 'Not a jot.'

'A jot?' His black eyes looked up and met her green ones and she saw that his were not actually black but the deepest of browns.

'I don't have any experience in the hospitality industry, none at all.'

'And I note that you wear an engagement ring.'

'Excuse me…' Cecelia frowned '…but you can't comment on that.'

He waved his hand dismissively.

Luka read her emergency contact and saw that it wasn't her fiancé but, in fact, her aunt.

And she intrigued him a touch. '*Are* you engaged?'

'Yes.' Cecelia bristled. 'Not that it's any of your business.'

'Cecelia, if you are considering working for me, then you might as well know from the outset that I am not known for my political correctness. I'll tell it to you straight—I don't want a PA who is in the throes of planning a big wedding, neither I don't want someone who is going to have to dash off at six because her fiancé is sulking.'

Cecelia's jaw tightened because at times Gordon did just that.

'Mr Kargas, my personal life is not your concern and, let me assure you, it never will be.'

Never, because she was not taking the job!

He heard the double meaning behind her words and almost smiled but then checked himself.

'Come over here,' he said, and stood up and headed to the floor-to-ceiling windows.

It was like no interview she had ever experienced before, Cecelia thought as she stood and walked over to join him.

Gosh, he was tall.

And he smelt as if he had bathed in bergamot with a testosterone undertone.

'See the view,' Luka said.

'It's amazing.' Cecelia nodded, looking out across a gleaming, wet and shiny London. The grey skies were starting to clear and black clouds were lined with silver but there was no rainbow that she could see.

'It's all yours,' Luka said, and Cecelia frowned. 'When you finish on a Friday, right up to Monday morning the world out there is your oyster.' Then he looked over at her. 'But when you're here…'

He expected devotion. Cecelia got his meaning.

'When can you start?' Luka asked.

Before she declined, Cecelia took a deep breath and thought of the perks of this job—a salary that was almost twice her current one, endless travel and the Kargas name on her résumé for ever.

And then she thought of the pitfalls.

Sixty-hour weeks spent beside this stunning man.

Her attraction to him was as unexpected as it was unsettling.

She actually didn't know what to do.

'I'd like some time to think about it,' Cecelia said in response to his offer.

'Well, I'm looking for someone who trusts their own instincts and can make prompt decisions.'

Luka now wanted her working for him.

She had impressed him when he had not expected to be impressed, yet something told him that if she walked out of the door Cecelia Andrews would not be coming back.

He could *feel* her hesitation.

And because he was Luka Kargas he knew when to push, and how. 'So, I'll ask again, when can you start, Cecelia?'

Never! Her instincts screamed.

Yet she had so badly wanted this job and the challenge it would bring and, though he was undoubtedly attractive, Cecelia knew herself well enough to be certain she would never get involved with anyone at work.

'Now,' Cecelia said, shocked at her own decision. 'I can start now.'

'Then welcome aboard.'

And as he shook her hand, Cecelia told herself she could handle it.

CHAPTER ONE

LUKA, AFTER CAREFUL consideration I've decided...

Waking just before her alarm went off, Cecelia lay listening to the hiss of bus doors opening on the street outside her London flat and working out how best to resign.

And when to do it?

Did she get it over and done with in the morning? Or wait until the end of the day to tell him that she would not be renewing her contract?

Most people would say she was mad to quit.

The pay was amazing, the travel wonderful, if exhausting, but in the eleven months she had worked for Luka, Cecelia had hit the limit on her primness radar.

He was a playboy in the extreme.

And that wasn't some vague, unsourced opinion.

It was fact.

Cecelia ran his diary after all!

Quite simply, she couldn't do it any more and so on Friday, as Luka had headed to the rooftop to swan off in his chopper for a debauched weekend in France, Cecelia had reached for her phone and accepted a six-month contract as personal assistant to an esteemed and elderly foreign diplomat.

While the money and perks would be worse in her

new job, the peace of mind it would bring was, to Cecelia, worth its weight in gold.

Only as she reached for her phone to check the time did Cecelia see the date and remember that it was her birthday.

There was never much fuss made of it and she had long since told herself to get over that fact. Her aunt and uncle, who had raised her since the age of eight, simply didn't bother with such things and before she had died, neither had her mother.

She saw that a message had come in overnight from Luka.

Shan't be in today, Cece. Cancel my meetings and I'll call you later.

Cecelia ground her teeth at the annoying shortening of her name that she had repeatedly asked him to stop using. But then she frowned, because in the eleven months that she had worked for Luka he had never taken a day off. Luka had a phenomenal workload yet never missed a beat. But now, on the one day she really needed to speak to him, he wasn't going to be there.

Cecelia wanted her resignation handed in and sorted, and for her time with Luka to be over. As well as that he had an important meeting with Mr Garcia and his entourage in NYC later today. Although it was an online meeting, it had been incredibly hard to set up and it was going to be extremely messy to cancel.

Despite the absence of her boss—in fact, *because* of the absence of her boss—today was shaping up to be an exceptionally busy one, and so Cecelia forced herself up and out of bed.

She showered quickly and began to get ready.

Her routines were set in stone and, despite the extensive travel and odd hours required by her job, there were certain things that never changed. She could be in Florence, New York, or home in London but these things remained—her clothes were set out the night before, as was her breakfast, which she ate before tackling her hair.

Routines were vital to Cecelia's sense of well-being, for during the first eight years of her life, when she had lived with her mother, chaos had been the only certainty.

The reddish fire to Cecelia's strawberry blonde mane had, courtesy of foils, been dimmed to a neutral blonde. She smoothed and sleeked out her long curls and then tied them back into a neat, low ponytail.

Next, Cecelia applied her make-up.

She didn't wear much, but as Luka's PA it was expected that she was always well turned out.

It wasn't always the case. A famous actress she had once worked for had insisted that Cecelia wear no make-up whatsoever as well as extremely plain clothing. With another employer, for practical reasons, her wardrobe had mainly consisted of boots and jeans.

Cecelia's skin was pale and needed just a dash of blusher to liven it up. She added a coat of mascara to her lashes, which enhanced her deep green eyes, but, as she did so, a rather bitchy voice coming from the radio caught her attention.

'What on earth did she expect, getting mixed up with Luka Kargas?'

Cecelia stabbed herself in the eye with the mascara wand at the sound of her boss's name.

It wasn't so much that it was a surprise to hear Luka mentioned, more an annoyance that even at seven a.m.

and alone in her bedroom *still* there was no escape from him.

Luka was extremely prominent and, although his name often graced the finance reports, his antics and bad-boy ways were regularly discussed in the tabloids and on the news.

They were having a field day discussing him now!

It would seem that he had used every last second of the weekend to create his own particular brand of havoc. A wild party had taken place aboard his yacht, currently moored off the coast of Nice, on Friday.

Cecelia sat at her dressing table, lips pursed as she heard that the raucous celebrations had continued on to Paris, where Luka and selected guests had hit the casinos. Now it was a case of tears *after* bedtime for some supermodel who had hoped that things might be different between herself and Luka.

Well, more fool her, then, Cecelia thought.

Everyone knew Luka's track record with women.

But they didn't really know Luka—there was a private side to him that no one, and certainly not his PA, had access to.

From what Cecelia could glean, Luka had led a very privileged life. His father owned a luxurious resort in Xanero. The famed Kargas restaurant there was now the flagship venue of its own very exclusive brand in several countries. Luka, though, focused more on expanding the hotel side of things and lived life very much in the fast lane. He dated at whim and discarded with ease and all too often it was Cecelia mopping up the tears or fielding calls from scorned lovers.

Yes, he was a playboy in the extreme.

And he unsettled her so.

Cecelia had once glimpsed that life.

Her mother Harriet's death had been intensely embarrassing for her well-to-do family for she had died as she'd lived and had gone out on a high—knickers down and with the proverbial silver spoon up her nose.

Harriet had left behind a daughter with whom no one had quite known what to do. Her father's name did not appear on the birth certificate and Cecelia had glimpsed him just once in her life.

And she never wanted to see him again.

Cecelia's staid aunt and uncle, who had always sniffed in disapproval at Harriet's rather bohemian existence, had, on her death, taken in the child. With tangled curls and sparkling green eyes, little Cecelia had been a mini replica of her mother, but in looks only.

The little girl had craved routine.

In fact, it had been a very young Cecelia who had kept any semblance of order in her mother's life.

She had put out her own school uniform and taken money from her mother's purse to ensure there was food, and she'd always got herself up in the morning and made her own way to school.

After an unconventional start, Cecelia now lived a very conventional life and was efficient and ordered. Even though she travelled the globe with her work, she was generally in bed by ten on weekdays and eleven at weekends.

She had perfectly nice friends, though none close enough to remember her birthday, and this time last year she had been engaged.

Gordon and the break-up had been the only problem she had caused for her aunt and uncle, who could not fathom why she might end things with such a perfectly decent man.

It hadn't been Gordon's fault, and she had told him so when she'd ended it.

It was bloody Luka's!

Though of course Cecelia hadn't told Gordon that.

Still, there wasn't time to dwell on it this morning.

She pulled on her flesh-coloured underwear and then glanced out of the window where the sun split a very blue sky, and found she simply could not face putting on the navy linen suit that she had laid out last night.

To hell with it!

Given that Luka wouldn't be in the office today, and that she wouldn't now be sitting in on meetings, Cecelia made an unplanned diversion to her wardrobe.

She wasn't exactly blinded by colour. But there was the dress she had bought to wear to a friend's wedding she had recently attended.

It had been a rare impulse purchase.

It was a pale cream halter neck, which Cecelia had decided as soon as she'd left the boutique was too close to white and might offend the bride.

She loved it, though, and, maybe because it was her birthday, she decided to wear it.

While it showed rather too much of her back and arms, she took care of that with the pale lemon, sheer, bolero-style cardigan she had bought on the same day.

The dress was mid-calf-length so she didn't bother with stockings, and then she tied on some espadrilles.

Yes, perhaps because Cecelia knew she would soon be leaving Kargas Holdings she was finally starting to relax.

As she closed the front door to her flat, Cecelia decided that despite Luka's absence she would still be giving in her notice today. It would be far easier to do it over the phone or online.

'You're looking very summery,' Mrs Dawson, her very nosy neighbour, said as she passed her in the hall. 'Off to work?'

'I am.'

The pale lemon bolero didn't even make it past the escalators to the underground. It was hot and oppressive and as she stood, holding a rail, she saw that Luka's weekend escapades had made headlines on the newspaper a commuter held.

She looked at the photo beneath the headline. It was of Luka on the deck of his yacht moving in on a sophisticated, dark-skinned beauty. His naked chest and thick black hair were dripping water over the woman and though their bodies did not touch it was an incredibly intimate shot.

Cecelia tore her eyes from the picture and stared fixedly ahead but that image of him seemed to dance on the blacked-out windows of the Tube.

Having left the underground, Cecelia walked towards the prominent high-rise building that housed Kargas Holdings. She smiled at the doorman and then entered the foyer and took the elevator. She had a special pass that allowed her to access the fortieth floor, which was Luka's in its entirety.

There weren't just offices and meeting rooms, there was also a gym and pool, though Cecelia couldn't recall him using them—they were more a perk for the staff.

And there was a suite that was every bit as luxurious and as serviced as any five-star hotel. When in London, Luka often slept there when he chose to work through the night or had a particularly early morning flight.

Yes, it was his world that she entered, but knowing that he wasn't there meant Cecelia breathed more easily today.

It was just before eight and it would seem that she had beaten Bridgette, the receptionist, to work. There were a couple of cleaners polishing windows and vacuuming and the florists had arrived, as they did each morning to tend the floral displays.

Cecelia made a coffee from the espresso machine before heading to her desk that was housed in a large area outside Luka's vast office.

The gatekeeper, Luka called her at times, though she felt rather more like a security guard at others.

As well as greeting his clients and guests, Cecelia was the final hurdle for his scorned lovers to negotiate if they somehow made it past the security in place downstairs.

Occasionally it happened, though generally Cecelia fielded them by phone.

And there it was again, springing to mind—the sudden image of him, wet from the ocean and dripping water, and Cecelia shook her head as if to clear it.

She hung her little cardigan on a stand and was just about to take a seat when his voice caught her completely unawares.

'Is that coffee for me, Cece?'

Cecelia swung around and there, strolling out of his office, was Luka. Apart from being unshaven there was little evidence of his wild weekend on display. He wore black pants and a white fitted shirt that showed off his toned body and his thick black hair, which, though perhaps a little tousled, still fell into perfect shape.

And he was not supposed to be here.

'I thought you weren't coming in today,' Cecelia said.

'Why would you think that?'

'Because you texted me in the middle of the night and told me you weren't.'

'So I did.'

He looked at the usually poised and formal Cece caught unawares. To many it might seem no big deal— she was simply holding a coffee and wearing a summer dress. Usually she was buttoned to the neck in navy or black, but it wasn't just her clothing that was different today.

'Thanks,' he said, and took from her hand the coffee she had made.

'It's got sugar in it,' she warned as she took a seat at her desk, 'and, please, it's Cecelia, not Cece.'

'Habit,' he said.

'Well, it's a very annoying one.'

Good, Luka thought.

Her cool demeanour incensed him.

His choice of name for her was deliberate, for he loved to provoke a reaction, even if it was only mild.

'How was your weekend?' she asked politely, pretending of course that she had heard nothing whatsoever about it.

'Much the same as the last,' he answered, and then came over behind Cecelia's desk and, to her intense annoyance, he lowered himself so that his bottom was beside her computer. 'Do you ever get bored?' he asked.

'Not really,' Cecelia lied, for she had realised she had been bored with Gordon.

He had also worked in the City and they had fallen into a pattern of meeting for drinks on Wednesday, allowing time to catch up with friends on a Friday. It had generally just been the two of them on a Saturday, followed by a vague hint of an orgasm that night and generally a boring drive on Sunday with a pub lunch somewhere.

And then perhaps another anti-climactic tryst that night.

It hadn't been Gordon's fault.

Cecelia held back in sex just as she held back in life.

In fact, the fault lay with the man now lounging against her desk, for he had opened her eyes to sensations that should surely remain unexplored.

Oh, she should never have taken the job, Cecelia thought as Luka persisted with a conversation she would rather draw to a close.

'But don't you ever get tired of doing the same old thing?' he asked.

'I like the same old things,' Cecelia answered.

He glanced at her neat, ordered desk and knew that the inside of her drawers would look exactly the same.

And then, just to annoy her, just to provoke *some* reaction, he picked up her little pottery jar that held her pens and things and moved it to the other side of her desk. 'Live a little.'

'No, thank you.' She smiled grimly and moved the jar back where it belonged. As she did so he got the scent of freshly washed hair.

That was it.

Cecelia didn't wear perfume; there were no undertones that he could note, and not just in her scent.

She was impossible to read, unlike any woman Luka had ever met. He had long ago given up flirting with her—the disapproval in her eyes kind of ruined the fun.

And as reckless as he was, Luka only ever played with the willing.

'You look nice,' he told her, and he felt the scold of her slight frown for daring to comment on something personal. Cecelia kept things very strictly business, yet she responded politely.

'Thank you.'

But Luka did not leave it there. 'You're wearing a dress.'

'That's very observant of you, Luka.'

'I'm just mentioning it because you don't usually.'

'Well, it's been a long, warm weekend. I couldn't face wearing a suit.'

'No, but—'

'Luka,' Cecelia interrupted him, 'if you have an issue with me dressing more casually than normal, then please just say so and it won't happen again.'

'I have no issue with you wearing a dress.'

'Then there's nothing to discuss.'

'Are you sure about that?' Luka said. He hadn't intended to address this today but clearly the moment was upon them.

'What I wear—' Cecelia started to say, but then Luka cut in.

'Do you have another *dental appointment* today, Cecelia?' His voice had changed and he delivered his words with a threatening edge by using her correct name. 'A final interview perhaps?'

He was rather certain that she was leaving, and more certain now because to her pale cheeks there came a very rare flush.

PAs came and went.

Luka was very used to that.

He was an exceptionally demanding boss and was aware that few could keep up with his impossible schedule for very long.

Usually all he required was for the incumbent PA to train the next one to standard before she left and ensure that the handover was seamless.

That Cecelia might be about to leave, though, brought a sense of disquiet like nothing he had known.

He liked her in his life, Luka realised, and he didn't want her to be gone. But three prolonged dental appointments in recent weeks had served as ominous signs, and he'd been certain of it when she had avoided discussing the renewal of her contract.

'Is there something you've been meaning to tell me?' he asked.

'Actually, yes.' She took a breath and then glanced over at the sound of the elevator door opening and saw that Bridgette had arrived.

Cecelia did not want an audience for this.

'Would it be possible to have a word in private?'

'Of course,' Luka said. 'You know my door is always closed.' When she didn't smile at his little joke he stood from the desk. 'Come on through.'

Luka decided he would have to talk her out of it.

And he knew just how to do it.

CHAPTER TWO

IT FELT LIKE a very long walk to his office.

Luka led the way and Cecelia actually felt a little sick because she still wasn't certain that it was the right thing to do.

Cecelia was very career minded and knew that by resigning she was throwing an amazing role away— Luka's empire was rapidly expanding, with hotels in New York City and Singapore on the cards, and to be a part of it would be amazing on her résumé.

But as he held open the door and she walked in, Cecelia knew she had little choice but to leave.

She could feel his eyes on her back.

On her skin.

They most certainly were.

Cecelia had the drabbest wardrobe he had ever seen.

Granted, she was always groomed and elegant, but Luka had long ago decided that she could make a modest outfit out of a handkerchief.

Not so today.

On the day she would tell him that she was leaving, he got the first glimpse of her spine.

Her back was incredibly pale, and he wondered if she should check her Vitamin D levels because he was sure that body rarely, if ever, saw the sun.

Luka had run into her out of work once and she'd been dressed in much the same monotonous, drab tones.

It had been at a museum exhibition a couple of weeks after she had started working for him, and not *quite* by accident. Luka had heard her discussing going with her fiancé and he'd wanted to see what made Cecelia tick, sexually speaking.

Pale English men, with skinny legs apparently.

They hadn't even been holding hands and had stood as politely as two strangers while admiring an incredibly erotic work of art.

She'd jumped when she'd seen him, though! And blushed just a touch as she'd introduced Gordon to him.

And all the more Luka had wanted to know her in bed.

'Please,' he said now. 'Take a seat.'

Luka gestured to a chair and then went around his desk while Cecelia took her seat.

And then she faced him.

He really was a very beautiful man.

Aside from fancying him rotten and everything, Luka Kargas really was exquisite to look at.

Those velvet eyes awaited hers but she could not quite meet them and she took in the high cheekbones and full plump mouth.

Cecelia liked mouths.

Gordon's had been a bit small and pinched but she had only really thought that after she had seen Luka's.

No, she should never have taken the job in the first place.

The very second she'd entered his luxurious office and he had stood to greet her, Cecelia had known she should turn and run.

Until that point, she and Gordon had seemingly ticked

every box, yet that had changed the moment she'd shaken hands with Luka.

She had known that she *had* to end her engagement the night she had come back from the museum and while being intimate with Gordon had found herself imagining Luka instead.

It had been the best orgasm of her life!

Luka was everything that her aunt had warned her about.

Despite somehow knowing it could only end badly, and that she should leave now, instead she had taken the job.

And now she was here.

About to resign.

'There is something you wish to discuss?' Luka said, and she nodded.

It was all very formal and deliberately so, for Luka was not about to make this easy on her.

Quite simply he had never known a better PA and he did not want that to change.

He wanted Cecelia to stay and Luka *always* got what he wanted.

'So?' he invited. 'What is it that you have to say?'

It wasn't the first time she had handed in her notice and Cecelia was about to deliver her well-rehearsed lines yet she just sat there in strained silence. For when he held her gaze, as he did now, there felt like a limit on the oxygen in the vast room and superfluous words were rather hard to find.

'I'm leaving.'

'Pardon?' Luka checked, and cocked his head a little, as if he hadn't heard. He would make her say it again, and more explicitly this time.

'I shan't be renewing my contract.' After such an appalling start the words now came tumbling out. 'I've given it considerable thought and though it's been an amazing year I've decided that it's time to move on.'

'But for all your *considerable thought*, you haven't discussed it with me.'

'I don't need your permission to resign, Luka.'

Oh, this wasn't going well, Cecelia thought as she heard the snap in her voice.

Yet she was almost at breaking point and that was verified when Bridgette buzzed.

'There's a woman called Katiya down in Reception, asking to see you, Luka...'

He rolled his eyes. 'I'm busy.'

'She's very insistent. Apparently you'll know why.'

'Tell Security that whoever lets her up will be fired.'

He looked over at Cecelia. 'Why can't women take no for an answer?'

'Why can't my boss?'

'Touché,' he conceded and then decided to play the sympathy card, 'Cecelia, *one* of the reasons I changed my mind about taking the day off was that I have just found out my mother is very unwell.'

'I'm sorry to hear that.' Cecelia said. 'If there's any...' She stopped and then she closed her mouth rather than continue.

'You were saying?' Luka checked, and when she didn't respond he spoke for her. 'Because actually there is something you can do for me. Cece, I am going to be away a lot in the coming months. My mother has cancer and will be undergoing extensive treatments...'

She felt her own rapid blink.

Luka never spoke of his family.

Ever!

'I am going to have to spend a lot of time in Xanero.

You're an amazing PA and I hope you know how much I appreciate you.' He saw the swallow in her throat and went in for the kill. 'At this difficult time, I don't want to deal with someone new.'

'Luka, I am sorry to hear that your mother is unwell but it doesn't sway my decision.'

She really was as cold as ice, and yet, and yet…as he looked across the desk he could see tension in her features and that those gorgeous green eyes could not meet his.

'Can I ask you to stay on for another six months? Naturally you'll be reimbursed…'

'Not everything is about money, Luka.'

He saw her green eyes flash and knew full well she thought him nothing more than a rich playboy.

She knew nothing about his start in life and Luka certainly wasn't about to enlighten her.

No one knew the truth.

Even his own parents seemed to believe the lie that had long been perpetuated—that the resort on Xanero Island and the original famous Kargas restaurant housed within it had given Luka his start in life.

Well, it hadn't.

Sex had.

Affluent holidaymakers looking for a thrill had first helped Luka to pave his way from near poverty to the golden lifestyle he had now.

The more sanitised PR version was that the first Kargas restaurant had given Luka his start.

Lies, all lies.

Not that he had any reason to tell Cecelia that.

Luka did not have to explain himself to his PA.

'What if I offered more annual leave?'

'I've already accepted another role.'

And so, when being nice and accommodating didn't work, Luka grew surly. 'With whom?'

'I don't need to answer that.'

'Actually, Cece—'

'Don't call me that!' she reared. 'Luka, on the one hand you tell me how much you appreciate the work I do and yet you can't even be bothered to get my name right.'

Finally he had his reaction.

'So you're leaving because I don't call you by your correct name?'

'No.'

'Then why?'

'I don't have to answer that.'

'Actually Ce-cel-i-a—' he drawled every syllable of her name '—if you look at your contract you cannot work for any of my rivals for a period of a year and you cannot—'

'Don't.' She halted him. 'Luka, I am allowed to leave.'

She was.

'Of course you are.' He just didn't like that fact.

'I've got four weeks left on my contract and naturally I'll start looking for my replacement straight away. Unless you have anyone particular in mind?'

'I'll leave all of that to you.'

'Sure.'

He flicked his hand in dismissal and Cecelia read the cue and headed out, though she did not return to her desk.

Once alone in the quiet of the bathrooms she leant against one of the cool marble walls.

She'd done it.

Possibly it was the worst career move she would ever make, but soon sanity would be restored to her mind.

No longer would she stand on a busy Tube in rush hour, wishing that somehow she was the woman lying beneath that depraved, beautiful face as he leaned in for a kiss...

No more would she have to breathe through her mouth when he was close just to avoid a hit of the heady scent of him.

Finally, the clenching low in her stomach at his lazy smile would dissipate.

Order would be restored to the chaos he had made of her heart.

Not yet, though.

It really was an awful day.

Flowers were delivered for Luka that Cecelia signed for, and then stupidly she read the card.

Oh, the offer from Katiya was very explicit.

And if he would just give her the elevator code then Katiya could come right up now, it would seem, and get straight on her knees.

Cecelia returned the card to the envelope and took them in to him.

'A delivery for you.'

'From?'

'I have no idea.'

He opened the card and then tossed it.

'Have them if you want,' he said, gesturing to the flowers.

'No, thank you.'

'Then put them somewhere that I can't see them.'

In case you get tempted? Cecelia wanted to ask.

But of course she didn't.

And then the downstairs receptionists messed up and a call was put through to Luka, but thankfully she was in his office at the time and it was Cecelia who answered it.

'I just need to speak to him…' a woman, presumably Katiya, sobbed.

'I'm sorry, Mr Kargas isn't taking any unscheduled calls,' Cecelia duly said.

Luka didn't even look up from his computer.

'What time do you have to finish today?' he asked when she ended the call.

'Any time,' Cecelia said, surprised by the unusual question, because Luka never usually bothered to ask. 'Why?'

'I want you to move the meeting with Garcia to the close of business there.'

'I'll see what I can do.'

'And I need you to sort out my flight tomorrow to Xanero. I'll be away for a couple of weeks.'

'A couple of weeks?' Cecelia checked, because for him to be away for that length of time was unheard of. Luka used his jet the way most people used public transport.

'I already told you,' Luka said and his voice was curt. 'My mother is ill.'

With his flight arranged, Luka rang Sophie Kargas and told her that her only child would be back tomorrow.

'One thing,' Luka said. 'I shan't be there to hold your hand and watch you give in. You're going to fight this.'

'Luka, I'm tired, I don't want any fuss. I just want you to come home.'

He could hear the defeat in her voice and he knew only too well the reason. The treatment would mean regular trips to Athens and Theo Kargas liked his wife to be at home.

Yes, it was a very long and difficult day spent avoiding each other as best they could but the tension hung heavy in the air at the office.

'I have your mother on the phone,' Cecelia said as afternoon gave way to evening.

'Tell her I'm in a meeting.'

'Of course.'

He really was a bastard, Cecelia decided as she relayed the message to the feeble-sounding woman.

'But I just need to speak with him for a moment.'

'I'm so sorry,' Cecelia said. 'Luka can't take any calls right now. I know he's busy trying to clear up as much of his schedule as he can today.'

Luka sat with his hands behind his head and his feet on the desk.

He could not face speaking to his mother again today and hearing how she had as good as given up on life.

Well, he would deal with all that tomorrow, for what Luka had to say would be better said face to face.

Leave him.

It wouldn't be the first time he had said it to his mother, but he hoped it would be the last.

Always he had hoped that his father would die first, if only to afford his mother some peace.

He glanced at the time and saw that it was approaching seven.

The meeting with Garcia was now scheduled for ten.

Luka got up and put on his jacket and then headed out of the office.

Cecelia didn't look up; instead she carried on tapping away on her computer, pretending she hadn't noticed him.

'Truce,' Luka said, and he saw her shoulders drop a little as her tense lips relaxed in a small smile.

'Truce,' Cecelia said, and she looked up at him.

'Let's go and get dinner.'

Her heart dropped.

Not that she showed it.

Cecelia wanted this day to be over.

More than anything she loathed going to dinner with him.

Or rather she loved going to dinner with him.

Luka was incredibly good company.

But that only made it all so much worse.

CHAPTER THREE

'I'LL JUST GO and freshen up,' Cecelia said and reached for her bag.

'Sure.'

He was lounging on her desk again and she had to step over his long legs to get past.

In the luxurious bathrooms of Kargas Holdings, Cecelia stared in the mirror and told herself that in four weeks this slow torture would be over.

She retied her hair and topped up her lipstick and, unable to help herself, checked her phone to see if her aunt—or anyone—had messaged her for her birthday.

No.

As disappointing as it was about her aunt and uncle, the real truth was that Cecelia could think of nothing nicer than going out for dinner with Luka on her birthday.

Except this wasn't a date—she was going out with her boss for a work dinner and Cecelia knew she would have to spend the next couple of hours constantly reminding herself of that fact.

When she came out, Luka was standing, waiting, and she felt his eyes on her as she retrieved her little bolero and put it on.

God, but he loathed it.

It was the colour of mustard and he'd far prefer to see her pale flesh. He would love to tell her just that, but with Cecelia he was constantly on his best behaviour.

'Ready?' he checked, and she nodded.

'Ready.'

His driver delivered them to a gorgeous Greek restaurant on the river that had recently opened.

'Time to check out the competition,' Luka said as they were led to a beautifully set table, but Luka refused it.

'We'll eat outside,' he said.

They were soon seated at a beautiful spot overlooking the river.

'The music would drive me crazy in there,' Luka told her, though the real reason was that they had the air-conditioning cranked up and he wanted her to be rid of that cardigan.

What the hell was wrong with him, Luka thought, that he would sit outside just for the thrill of seeing her upper arms.

Her arms!

'Here's perfect,' Cecelia said as she took her seat. 'There's a lovely breeze from the river.'

'Of course there is,' Luka said, but she didn't understand his wry smile.

It certainly wasn't the first time they had eaten together, although it wasn't often that they did. When they travelled, Cecelia had taken to having her breakfast sent to her hotel room as she could not bear to see him breakfasting with whomever he was seeing at the time.

Often, when away, she and Luka had lunch together but generally there were guests or clients involved.

As for dinner?

She had no idea, neither did she want to know what

Luka did by night and so, when away, and the working day had ended, she generally opted for room service.

Now she looked through the menu but could not concentrate for she was certain he would again try to dissuade her from leaving.

He didn't, though, and instead he selected the wine.

'What would you like?'

'Not for me.' Cecelia said.

'Of course not.' He rolled his eyes. Heaven forbid she relax in his company, but he asked for sparkling water.

She gave her order to the waiter, which, despite its fancy wording, was basically a tomato salad.

Luka ordered *bourdeto*.

She had seen it on the menu and read that it was made with scorpion.

Apt, for there would be a sting in his tail and she could feel it.

Oh, the surroundings were beautiful and the conversation polite but she could feel her own tension as she awaited attack. For Luka did not give in easily, that much she knew.

Life was a chessboard to him and every move was planned.

Now that his mother was ill, he had very good reasons to want an efficient PA, one capable of steering the helm while he was away.

Yes, she was braced, if not for attack then for the silk of his persuasion. But she must not relent, not now that she had finally had the courage to hand in her notice.

'A taste of home,' he said as their dishes were served.

'Will it be nice to be there?' Cecelia asked. 'Aside from the difficult news, I mean.'

Luka just shrugged.

'Will you be staying with your family?' she asked.

She wasn't probing, she told herself, for there were arrangements to be made that would undoubtedly fall to her.

'The resort is huge. They have a villa there but on the other side to mine.'

'What's it like in Xanero?'

'The island is stunning.'

'It's still a family business?' Cecelia checked.

'Yes.' It wasn't an outright lie but there was so much he left unsaid.

'Your father's still the chef there?'

Luka didn't answer straight away.

The truth was, his father had never been the chef there. Well, once, for the briefest of times.

It was all part of an elaborate charade that Luka went along with, only so that his mother could hold her head up in town.

'He's semi-retired,' Luka said, and that wasn't really a lie—Theo Kargas had spent his adult life semi-retired. Still, rather than talk about home he moved the subject to the upcoming weeks. Not everything had been cancelled. Luka would be working online and there was a trip to Athens he would keep. It was doable yet it was complex as Luka was booked out weeks and months ahead of time, so there was never much room for manoeuvre.

'I'll tell Garcia that the trip to New York will have to wait.'

'He won't like it.'

'Good,' Luka said. 'You know what they say about treating them mean to keep them keen. He needs me far more than I need him, yet he has started to forget that! Still, perhaps we can go when I return.'

'Of course.' Cecelia nodded. 'When you know more

how things are at home I'll schedule it again. Hopefully by then your new PA will be on board and he or she can go along too.'

He didn't like the sound of that.

Luka looked over to where she sat, sipping on sparkling water with that mustard-coloured cardigan covering cream shoulders, and *still* he wondered what made her tick.

Cecelia intrigued him.

She was as cold as ice and so buttoned up and formal that, even though he knew she'd been engaged, he privately wondered if she was a virgin, for he simply could not imagine her in bed.

But on occasion he found himself imagining it anyway!

'What happened to Gordon?' Luka suddenly asked.

Her silence was a pointed one.

'Come on,' he said, 'you're leaving—I can ask now.'

'I like to keep my private life private,' Cecelia said, stabbing an olive with her fork.

'I know you do,' Luka said. 'Come on, what happened?'

Cecelia hesitated.

Certainly she would not be telling Luka that at inappropriate times images of him had kept popping into her head! And neither would she tell him that she had thought herself content until he'd appeared in her life.

Instead, she told him a far safer version. 'I decided that my aunt and uncle's version of the perfect man for me didn't fit mine.'

'Your aunt and uncle?' he checked, recalling that Cecelia's aunt was her next of kin on her résumé.

'I was raised by them after my mother died.'

'How old were you then?'

'Eight,' Cecelia said through taut lips, for she was terribly uncomfortable with the subject, but Luka seemed very intent on finding things out tonight.

'What about your father?'

She gave a slight shake of her head, which told him nothing other than the subject was out of bounds.

Not just with Luka.

She had never told anyone about the time she had come face to face with him.

He had dark hair and had worn a wedding ring.

That was all Cecelia knew. That and the fact he had shouted at her mother. When the money had run out, Harriet had called him to tell him he had a child, but it hadn't produced the result her mother had obviously hoped for.

There had been no joyful greeting. His eyes had been furious when they had met hers, and Harriet had quickly sent her daughter to her room.

A lot of shouting had ensued and Cecelia had found out that her mother had once been given a considerable sum of money for... Cecelia had frowned when she heard a word that a seven-year-old Cecelia didn't understand.

Termination.

Soon after, to her terrible distress, she found out what her father had meant.

'I don't want to talk about my father,' she said to Luka.

'Fine.' He shrugged and then gave that wicked smile. 'Tell me more about your fiancé, then.'

'Ex,' she pointed out.

'That's right.'

At the time, the only reason he had guessed her engagement was over had been the lack of a ring and the absence of his calls. There had been no tears from Cecelia or days off and no impact on her efficiency that he'd been able to see.

'Was it you who ended it?'

Cecelia gave a terse nod.

'How did he take it?'

'Luka!' she warned.

'I'm just curious. I've never been with anyone long enough to be engaged. I can't imagine getting that close to someone.' His eyes narrowed a little as he looked at her, still trying, as he had been since the day they had met, to gauge her. 'Was there someone else involved? Is that why you ended it?'

'Of course not,' she bristled.

'Did you live together?'

'I really don't want to discuss my private life,' Cecelia said. '*You* don't.'

'Yes, I do.'

'No, Luka, you don't. I might deal with your exes but I know nothing about you—'

'That's not true.'

'How long has your mother been ill?'

His jaw gritted and Cecelia gave a little smirk as she took a sip of her water.

'Fair enough.' He watched as she put down her glass and told her a truth. 'I'm going to miss *not* getting to know you, though.'

She would miss him far more than he knew.

'Is there anything I can do to dissuade you from leaving?' he asked.

She looked up at his voice for his tone had surprised her. She had expected sulky, or manipulative, or for more money to be waved in front of her.

Instead he *asked* if there was anything he could do to keep her.

'No.' Cecelia said, and then she cleared her throat, for the word had come out huskily. 'Luka, I will be here for another month and I will find the best replacement that I can. I'll train her myself. It really has been an amazing year but I'm ready for a new challenge.'

'So I'm no longer a challenge?'

'Of course you are,' Cecelia said.

He was actually a constant challenge to her senses—recklessness crept in whenever he was near, which Cecelia had to fight constantly just to keep it in check.

'How was the *bourdeto*?' Cecelia asked as his plate was removed unfinished.

Luka shrugged.

He had far more on his mind than food.

'What if I promise to stop calling you Cece?' he suggested. 'It takes twenty-one days to form a habit.'

'It actually takes sixty-six days,' Cecelia corrected. 'So there isn't time for that. But thanks for offering.' And then she smiled, something Cecelia so rarely did.

Rather, she rarely smiled *properly*, but now, as she did so, Luka watched as she checked herself midway and it dimmed.

For Luka, the fading of her smile felt like summer was ending.

It was, of course.

In a few weeks' time summer would be gone.

Of course it would come around again, but this summer, *this* one, would never return.

'Was Gordon upset when you finished with him?' Luka asked. 'And before you tell me that it's private, I know it is.'

'So why ask now?'

'Because you're the best PA I've ever had, and I didn't want to push you into leaving by getting too personal, but now that you've already resigned I don't have to behave.'

'Yes, you do,' Cecelia said, and though her voice remained even there was a flurry of nerves low in her stomach as to what her boldness today had unleashed.

So she answered the question.

'Yes, he was upset, although, to be honest, I think he was more embarrassed than upset.'

'No, I imagine he was very upset,' Luka said in his deep, low voice, and met her eyes. Suddenly the cool breeze from the river felt like a warm one.

At times, Luka would disregard her professional boundaries and flirt with her.

Like now.

That little hint of his silken charm carried from his lips and sent a slow shiver the length of Cecelia's spine.

'I'd better get back to the office,' Cecelia said, 'and set up for your meeting.'

But he would prefer to linger.

The changing world was waiting and it was nice to be here by the river.

With her.

'Garcia can wait,' Luka said.

'One day he might get tired of waiting.'

'I doubt it,' Luka said. 'Right now he wants to wrap up the purchase.'

'I thought you wanted a hotel in New York City.'

'I do,' Luka said, 'but at a price of my choosing. Anyway, we need to talk about your replacement.'

'I've informed the agency you generally use,' Cecelia said, and Luka frowned.

'You weren't referred via them?'

'No.' Cecelia shook her head.

'Ah, that's right, you were working for Justin. How did you end up with him?'

'Via the agency,' Cecelia said, and she itched to get back and away from his gaze but Luka wasn't letting her go just yet.

'How did you become a PA?'

More questions, Cecelia thought, but this wasn't such a personal one and so she was a little freer in her response. 'I never intended to be. When I finished school I had wanted to travel,' she told him, 'or go to university, but...' Cecelia hesitated. 'My uncle had a friend who needed a nanny in France. I spoke French—well, a little—and he said that way I'd get to travel and work at the same time.'

'The trust fund ran out, you mean.'

'Sorry?' Cecelia blinked.

'They would have received money to raise you, but once you turned eighteen—'

'No,' Cecelia interrupted. 'It wasn't like that at all.' She shook her head. 'They were very good to take me in.'

'Did they have children?'

'No,' Cecelia said, and she swallowed because she believed they had very much been childless by choice.

Luka's comments needled for she had always felt rather in the way with her aunt and uncle, not that she'd admit it to him. 'My uncle had a contact who needed a nanny.'

'Really, Cece! You? A nanny?'

He could not imagine the very crisp and proper Cecelia working with children and he actually smiled at the very thought, parting those gorgeous lips to show his pearly white teeth.

Gosh, he had such a nice mouth.

'I hated it,' Cecelia admitted. 'I lasted four weeks before I gave notice, but then the mother, a television producer, asked if I could work for her instead. I guess it all started from there.'

'Do you still see your aunt and uncle?'

'Of course,' Cecelia said confidently, although inside she wavered for it had always been her making the effort rather than them.

They hadn't so much as sent a text for her birthday.

Perhaps a card would have arrived in the mail when she got home.

Or there would be flowers on her doorstep.

Yet she knew there wouldn't be.

Her birthday had passed by unnoticed again and it hurt.

She would not let Luka see it, of course, but his comment about the trust-fund money drying up had perturbed her.

'Do you want dessert?' he asked, knowing the answer.

'No, thank you.'

'Tough,' Luka said. 'You're getting one.'

She went to ask what he meant but at that moment the background music wafting out of the restaurant changed to a very familiar tune and she turned as she saw a waiter with a slice of cake and atop it a candle.

The tune was 'Happy Birthday'!

And it was being played for her.

'Luka…'

Cecelia was embarrassed.

Pleased.

And utterly caught by surprise.

No one remembered her birthday.

Ever.

As a child, it had fallen in the school holidays and her mother had only liked grown-up parties, certainly not the type Cecelia had dreamed of. And after she had died, Cecelia hadn't readily made friends. In fact, at boarding school she had been endlessly teased and bullied.

At eighteen, her aunt and uncle had given up on the perfunctory birthday card and last-minute present, which had always, *always* been something she needed rather than something she might want.

This was the first time that she'd truly been spoiled on her birthday.

There were two spoons and the cake was completely delectable—vanilla sponge drizzled in thick lemon syrup that was both tart and refreshing.

And she was sharing dessert on her birthday with him.

Luka Kargas.

Cecelia was almost scared to look up for she was worried there might be tears in her eyes.

'Here,' Luka said, 'is the other reason I came into the office today.'

Now Cecelia did look up as he went into his jacket and pulled out a gorgeous parcel and slid it across the table.

It was a long box wrapped in deep red velvet and tied with ribbon that had a little gold charm attached to it.

And she frowned because Cecelia recognised the packaging.

On one overseas trip, she had enjoyed staring into the window of a lavish boutique in the foyer of a Florence hotel where they had been staying. Whenever she'd been waiting for Luka, she had indulged herself with the joy of admiring the beautiful jewellery.

She pulled back the bow, but first she had a question for she didn't quite believe what Luka had said. 'You didn't really come in just because it's my birthday?'

'Of course I did. I always try to do the right thing on my PA's birthday.'

Luka knew full well that for Cecelia he had done more than just the right thing. Usually it was flowers and perfume, or a voucher for a spa hotel, but a few weeks ago, on a business trip, he had stepped out of the elevator and Cecelia's back had been to him. He had looked to where her gaze had been focused and spied the sparkling window display of the hotel boutique.

The next morning she had been looking again.

And the next.

It had sat in his bureau at home for weeks now.

Last night, just after he had fired off the text to say that he wouldn't be in, he had remembered her birthday.

Luka had been partying hard, trying to forget the news that had come in about his mother, trying to extend the weekend into a long one, just to delay the return home.

And then he had remembered the box inside his bureau.

'Oh!' She gave a gasp of recognition when she saw the necklace. 'How on earth…?' It was thick and lavish, coiled with rubies, or glass, she wasn't sure—Cecelia hadn't even asked the price at the time, for in either case it would have been way out of her league; she had simply adored it, that was all. 'Luka, it's far too much.'

'It can double up as your leaving gift,' Luka brooded. 'Do you want to put it on?'

'No,' she said too quickly, 'I'll wait till I'm home.'

She wouldn't be able to manage the clasp and she

would burst into flames at the touch of his hands if he so much as brushed the sensitive skin of her neck.

The breeze from the river wasn't helping at all now. The tiny cardigan felt like a thick shawl around her shoulders and she simply didn't know how to react.

'How did you even know it was my birthday?' Cecelia asked, because she hadn't mentioned it and certainly she hadn't made a note of it in his diary.

'I make it my business to know.' He could see she was shaken and her reaction surprised him. He had thought she'd be more than used to a fuss being made but she actually seemed stunned, even close to tears. 'I fired a PA once, about ten years ago,' he explained as a waiter put down two small glasses, a bottle of ouzo and a carafe of iced water on the table between them.

'No, thank you,' Cecelia said as he went to pour one for her. 'You were saying.'

Luka went ahead and added iced water to the ouzo and she watched as the clear liquid turned white.

How she would love to try it, but she had to keep her guard up, for it was becomingly increasingly difficult to remember that this was work.

He did this for all his PAs, Cecelia reminded herself, and forced herself to listen rather than daydream as he told her just why he had made such a nice fuss.

'As I was firing her she started to cry.'

'Tears don't usually trouble you,' Cecelia said, thinking of the many tears women had shed over him.

'They don't,' Luka said, 'but as she was clearing out her things she said that it was her worst birthday ever. She was a terrible PA and deserved to be fired, but I didn't set out to ruin her birthday.'

'You really felt bad?' Cecelia checked, pleased that he did have a conscience after all.

'A bit,' he agreed. 'Since then I have tried to keep track. Normally I would have taken you for lunch. In fact, that was what I had planned to do but when it came to it I was sulking too much to do so...'

She smiled again and back came summer.

'I thought, given it's your birthday, that you would have plans tonight. That's why I checked what time you had to leave by.'

'No, no plans.'

It was her best birthday ever.

Luka couldn't know that, of course, but even Gordon hadn't made much of a fuss.

They'd gone for dinner.

But there had been no candles and no cake.

Gordon had bought her a cloying perfume Cecelia hadn't liked.

It wasn't so much the lavishness of the gift Luka had given her that made it the best, more the thought behind it.

How he had seen her looking at the necklace.

That he had noticed...

Yes, she was right to leave.

Because of this.

Because of those moments when he put her world to rights and she was utterly and completely crazy about him.

She had grown up with the dour warning that she did not want to end up like her mother and that men like Luka could only lead her down a dangerous path.

Yet, to her shame, it beckoned her at times.

Times like tonight.

When the easiest thing in the world would be to thank him with a kiss.

She knew where it would lead, though, for that was exactly where she wanted it to lead.

And Luka wouldn't be hard to convince!

He was easy.

That much she knew.

He was, though, at least with her, the perfect gentleman.

Well, not perfect, and not always a gentleman, but from the beginning Luka had, in the main, accepted her boundaries and there had been no overt flirting.

Occasionally he would slip, but he'd quickly rein it in. He wasn't a sleaze and played only where welcome. More than that, though, his world worked far better with Cecelia in it. He recognised talent and certainly she was brilliant at her job. Luka knew full well that he would lose the best PA he'd ever had if he chased that perpetual want.

And there was want in him.

Yet he knew his own track record, and Luka had never lasted with anyone for more than a month.

But look where behaving had got him, Luka thought.

He'd lost her anyway.

He decided now was the time to find out more about her.

'How did your mother die?' Luka asked, though he had already guessed her response—*That's personal, Luka*, or, *That's not your concern.*

She was about to deliver a response just like that, but then she remembered she was leaving.

Perfection was no longer required now that she had resigned.

And so she told him the truth, or at least the little she knew of it.

'I believe she took too much cocaine.'

CHAPTER FOUR

OH, CECELIA!

Luka hadn't expected to find out much at all, let alone that her mother had died from a cocaine overdose.

He thought of her, so prim and controlled, and had assumed her upbringing had caused that. Well, he concluded, it *had*, but not in the way he had imagined.

Still, he said nothing, because he didn't want to say the wrong thing, and he desperately wanted to hear more.

Cecelia liked his patient silence. There wasn't so much as a flicker of reaction that she could read in his expression as she revealed the dark truth, and Cecelia inwardly thanked him for that. 'She was at a party, I've been told.'

'Was it a one-off—?' he started to ask, but Cecelia cut in.

'No, it was a regular occurrence. My mother loved to party, she lived a very debauched life.'

'And you lived with her?'

'I did.' Cecelia nodded.

'What was that like?'

She wanted warm memories of her early childhood.

Cecelia wanted to say that in spite of everything there had been so many amazing times and that despite her mother's ways she'd been loved.

Yet she could not, and so she described what it had been like to live with her mother. 'Unsafe.'

Yes, he understood her a little better now.

He thought of her neat desk and tidy drawers and her utter reluctance to unbend and have fun, but now he watched as she reached for her purse and stood.

'We had better get back,' Cecelia told him, deciding that she had said far too much.

'No, sit,' Luka said, but she shook her head.

'I don't have time to sit by the river and reminisce,' Cecelia said. 'And neither do you. You have a meeting with Garcia at ten.'

'I've already said he can wait.'

Well, she wouldn't.

Cecelia walked off swiftly, embarrassed and unsure why she had told him about her mother when usually she did all she could to conceal that side of her past.

Usually she loathed people's reactions to it—their shocked expressions and the recriminations. She felt like crying as she remembered her so-called friends' reactions at boarding school when they had stumbled on the salacious news articles and the endless dissection of her mother's death.

Schooldays had certainly not been the best times of Cecelia's life.

They had read out every embarrassing detail to each other with relish as she had lain in her bed in the dorm, night after night. And then had come the endless questions.

Was it a party or an orgy your mother was at?' Lucy, the ringleader had asked. *'And what do they mean by "compromising position"?'*

It hadn't been much better during term breaks. Cecelia's pace quickened as she thought of her aunt and uncle. They had rarely mentioned her mother and when they had they'd spoken in disapproving tones.

The deeper truth was that home had been no better, because actually her aunt and uncle had rarely spoken to her at all.

As for Gordon—well, with him, her mother had been *she who must not be named*, just a sordid part of Cecelia's past that was best forgotten.

Yet Luka had wanted to know more about it.

'Wait,' he called, and though she did not slow down he soon caught up with her. 'Why walk off when we're talking?'

'Because there's work to do, because…' *You're work.*

Constantly she had to remind herself of that fact.

Four more weeks of this felt too long, but then Cecelia reminded herself that he would be away for the next two.

She would be mad to get involved with him.

Mad.

She wasn't flattering herself to believe she could have him.

Cecelia also knew Luka well enough to know it would only be for a night, or a couple of weeks at best.

Cecelia knew, absolutely, how it would end—indifference, then avoidance—for she had seen it all too many times, and the trouble was that she did not know how she would recover.

She had never felt such *violent* emotions about someone before.

Luka Kargas was her one weakness and that would never do.

And so, after their gorgeous riverside dinner, they took the elevator back up in silence. Back in the office, she went to set up for the meeting that had been rescheduled and delayed over and over again. She made sure his notes were on his desk and she tried to ignore the rich scent of him as she chatted online with Stacey, who was Mr Garcia's PA.

'He's going to be another half-hour,' Stacey said, and Cecelia inwardly groaned for she just wanted this day to be over with. 'Are you able—?' Her voice cut off and the screen went black, and only then did Cecelia register that Luka had deliberately turned the computer off.

'What on earth are you doing?' she asked.

'I don't like to be kept waiting.'

'But you were the one who cancelled this morning's meeting.'

'So…' Luka shrugged '…tomorrow you can say that we lost the connection. I can't sit through a meeting about figures now.'

'Fine,' Cecelia snapped.

This bloody meeting had been moved and delayed so many times that she wondered how anyone did business with him.

Yet she knew the answer.

Luka was brilliant.

And they would wait.

'I want to talk to you,' Luka said.

'Is it about work?' Cecelia asked.

'No.'

'Then there's nothing to discuss. I'll go and pack for you,' Cecelia said. 'And then I'll be off.'

She headed to his suite.

Usually it took five minutes to pack for him as she had it down pat, but he wasn't going away for business and his wardrobe here consisted mainly of suits, shirts and ties.

She stood in his suite looking at his wardrobe for a moment as if more choices might appear, and then headed out.

He was sitting on her desk, as he had been this morning, only she chose not to sit down this time.

'I don't know what to pack,' she admitted. 'Are you staying here tonight?'

Luka nodded.

'Then I can go to your apartment and select a more casual wardrobe. I'll bring your luggage in with me in the morning.'

'Sure.'

She picked up her bag and gave him a tight smile. 'Thank you for dinner and cake and my gorgeous present.'

'You're most welcome.'

His dark eyes met hers and she wondered if she should give him a kiss on the cheek to thank him, just as she would anyone else who had given her such a nice night and gift.

Only he was not anyone.

But tonight of all nights, her hard-won control slipped and she leant in and gave him a light kiss on the cheek.

She merely brushed the skin of his cheek with her lips, and she even held her breath to lessen the impact the gesture would have on her senses. She would taste him later; in the elevator she would run her tongue over her lips and recall the warmth of his skin on her mouth.

And she would recall too the ache in her breast at the mere graze against his shirt.

She pulled back and her bag bit into her shoulder as she ached to drop it to the floor and give in to her craving for this man.

Luka did not want to get this wrong.

He read women with ease, and his kiss was so rarely refused—yet with her he could not be certain.

She had chastised him with her eyes on so many occasions, he could almost feel the sting of the slap she would deliver if he put so much as a finger wrong.

It would be worth it, Luka decided.

'I'll see you tomorrow,' Cecelia said, her voice a touch high as she willed her legs to move and take her from danger.

Yet, and yet… 'But if you need anything before that…'

She had said the same words a hundred times before— or was it a thousand times?—but they sounded different tonight.

His response was different tonight too. 'I need to be with you.'

No slap was delivered, she just stared back. And right when she thought she might finally know his kiss, instead his hands came to her arms.

'Aren't you going to try it on?'

She thought again of those slender dark fingers in her hair and his mouth near her cheek as he did the clasp, only this time, instead of refusing, she nodded.

'Let me help,' Luka said. He took her bag from her shoulder and retrieved the present and then dropped the bag to the floor.

He slowly prised open the box and as she watched his long finger run over the stones and she felt as if he was stroking her on the inside.

Luka could hear the trip in her breathing and felt the charge in the air; he breathed in the scent of seduction. For that was what she did, Luka concluded—without so much as a word or a move, she seduced.

'Turn around,' Luka said, and he moved from lounging against her desk.

Cecelia did so.

At his simple command she turned and faced the wall.

She had known how this evening would end, how this year would end.

And they ended tonight, she was suddenly rather certain of that.

But it didn't matter now.

She was leaving.

Cecelia went to lift the long ponytail she had retied many times today, but he pushed her hand down. 'I've got this,' Luka said.

She could barely breathe as she felt his hands come around her throat and the brush of his fingers against the pulse in her neck. He was tall and, she was certain, hard behind her, and she ached to lean back into him.

She felt the coolness of the necklace fall between her breasts as he put it on and the brush of his fingers as he did up the clasp. But then, instead of turning her around to admire the necklace, his fingers moved to the tiny bolero. She both heard and felt his voice. 'I hate this,' he said, and his words reverberated deep within her as he pushed the fabric down over her shoulders.

Luka would not rush this, for he had waited a long time and so first he removed the little bolero that he had loathed on sight.

One arm was freed, and then the other, and as the garment fell silently to the floor, she felt it dust her calf.

She shivered as he ran fingers along the bare flesh of her arms, something he had wanted to do all night.

'Luka...' His name from her lips was so loaded with lust that he did not take it as a reproach. Instead, he lifted her hair and the spine that had teased him this morning was now his to explore.

She felt his lips on the back of her neck as soft as the kiss she had delivered to his cheek and the message was the same, for it felt like a promise.

Every notch to her spine that was exposed by her dress was rewarded with a graze of his mouth, and then there was the ache of no contact for a moment.

Followed by delicious relief.

'I want to see this necklace on you as it should be seen,' he said. She felt his hands on her neck as he undid the tie of her halter neck and she bit her lip as he undid her flesh-coloured strapless bra.

Her breasts felt heavy and there was a yearning for his touch there, but instead he freed her hair and arranged it over her shoulders. For a second, just a second, his fingers grazed her breasts.

He felt her hard nipples, and now it was his breathing that was jagged for the longing to see her was intense. But their first kiss would be a naked one, Luka decided.

Cecelia could barely stand. She heard a noise and glanced to the side, seeing Luka toss his jacket over a chair. She turned back to face the wall, not sure whether she could bear to watch him undress.

And then she heard him strip off his shirt and she almost folded over at the thought of his naked chest behind her.

Her thighs were trembling and she would have no choice but to ask to sit soon, but then came his hands on her shoulders and another command. 'Turn around.'

Now she faced him and he looked at her usually pale face all flushed as if she'd already come. But instead of reproach in her green eyes there was the beckoning of an aurora as they glittered with the promise of what was to come.

'It's looks beautiful.'

The necklace fell between her breasts yet, as fine as it was, it garnered only a glance because he had found perfection elsewhere. He experienced a fierce desire to taste her there and to explore with his fingers, though they had not yet so much as kissed.

His lips were warm as they brushed over hers. Her breasts got the tease of his naked skin as their bodies came together, then his arms pulled her in as she moaned at the contact. He tasted of anise and all things forbidden and delicious.

And then he kissed her hard and she kissed him back hungrily, for she had craved him for close to a year. Her hands slipped through the arms that held her and came up behind his head to pull him closer.

He had expected reticence, that her tongue would require his coaxing, yet instead together they fuelled urgent desire. The woman who rarely blushed, who was always so cool and distant now burnt at his touch. He had imagined a slow seduction perhaps, and then he laughed in his head that he had thought her a virgin for the woman in his arms was wanton and wild.

He pressed against her hips and her grip tightened in his hair.

Tiny nips and wet, hot kisses were shared as Luka pressed her to the wall. She was grateful for the support it gave as her legs were trembling.

Luka pressed into her and moved her hands from his head and down past his flat stomach to the hard heat that was pressed into her.

He pulled back and their foreheads met as they watched her free him.

And, because it was Luka, of course he had protection to hand. But before he was lost to latex, Cecelia held him for a moment, as she had so long wanted to—stroking his thick, hard length as beads of silver moistened her palm.

She licked her lips and he moaned a low curse, for he wanted to carry her now to his suite. Luka wanted the rest of Cecelia's clothes to be gone, but his want was more immediate now. He pushed her hand away and sheathed himself with rapid, practised ease and then got back to her mouth.

He was so tall that even with Cecelia in high espadrilles she was no match for him.

Their teeth clashed and suddenly too much was not enough. He pushed up the dress and his hands roughly roamed her inner thighs and felt her hot and wet as he tore at her knickers and then crouched enough to sear into her.

He was rougher than she had ever known yet there was liquid silk to ease his path.

Cecelia had never been more frantic and as he lifted her legs she wrapped them around him. He was strong enough with his grip to allow her to hold his face and kiss him back hard.

It was the roughest and most delicious coupling.

For they matched.

His hands held her buttocks and his fingers dug in so deep that they would surely leave a bruise, yet she ground onto him. And far from reticence, it was Cecelia coaxing him to come. 'Luka!' She could not focus on kissing, and she tore her mouth away. He could feel the tease of intimate muscles and he thrust in hard and then swelled to the tight grip of her orgasm and her sensual sob called him to deliver deep.

Luka did, shuddering his release deep into her to the last twitches of hers.

And that part had her dizzy. The moan of him carried

without breath to her ears, and the sensual slide of their hot, damp bodies as they slowly brought themselves back from the far reaches of the divine space they had been in together. Kissing again, with languorous relish as the world faded in.

He lowered her down and she could feel the thump, thump of his heart against the flutter of hers. Cecelia rested her head on his shoulder and she was herself for the first time.

And herself was more reckless than she had ever dared to be.

'Come on.' He was tidying up, picking up discarded clothes, ready to be headed for his suite and to bed, to resume proceedings, this time at a more leisurely pace.

But she would not be waking up there, Cecelia decided.

One taste of heaven was more than enough and she had always sworn to leave before he dictated terms.

'I need to get home.'

She picked up her bra, but since it would be almost impossible to do it up she pushed it into her bag.

'Cece...' he said, and she didn't correct him, but she did pick up her shredded knickers and added them to her bag, and then with rather unsteady hands did up her halter neck.

'I really do need to get home, Luka.'

'You're not just running off.'

'I'm not running,' she corrected. 'I just want to go home.'

Her voice was incredibly composed. He looked at the necklace, heavy between gently curving breasts and the gorgeous flush of her climax.

But aside from throwing her over his shoulder, or

dragging her, it would seem that he couldn't stop her from leaving. She had made up her mind.

Usually it would be perfect.

A good orgasm, and then the absence of conversation—except there was more to her that he wanted to explore, and he was rather sure that there was more to come for *them*.

But she was checking herself in a small mirror compact, as she often did before she headed out.

'Thanks for an amazing night,' Cecelia said, and then, just as she had done previously, she leant forward and gave him a kiss on the cheek, as if the past half an hour had not taken place.

'Don't go home yet,' Luka said.

'I want to, though.'

And he couldn't really argue with that.

He watched as she walked to the elevator and pressed the button.

Cecelia stepped in and pressed for the lobby, unable to stop herself leaning against the cool mirrors, not really surprised by what had taken place.

She had wanted him so badly for months.

A man in a suit got in at the fourteenth floor and another at the seventh.

Cecelia nodded and smiled and then stared ahead as they inched down to the ground floor where she stepped out and walked across the foyer.

The cleaners had their buffers out and were polishing the marble floors.

Cecelia said goodnight to the doorman and stepped out into the night, but there was no cool breeze to greet her.

It was a sultry London night, but as she headed for the underground station she heard her name—'Ms Andrews?'

She turned around and saw that it was Luka's driver.

'Mr Kargas said you worked too late to take the underground.'

And of all the experiences of this night, this was the part she both hated and loved the most.

Loved that she was being taken care of by Luka, that he had thought to see her safely home.

Hated because by his very nature it was a mere temporary, tantalising glimpse of his world.

CHAPTER FIVE

CECELIA WAS TEMPTED to call in sick, but then that would suggest she regretted last night, which she didn't.

Instead, she regretted how she felt this morning, because rather than getting up to her alarm and facing the very early start to her day, Cecelia had brought a coffee to bed and sat in it looking at the necklace that Luka had given her.

Cecelia did not want to be one of those women who dared to hope that with her things might be different.

She just had to get through this morning and then she would have a bit of a reprieve in the next two weeks, and then hopefully by the time he came back from Xanero, normal services could be resumed.

For the first time, she hadn't put out her clothes the night before but Cecelia forgave herself that lapse.

She dressed in the navy suit that she should have worn yesterday and after checking her appearance left the flat. It was too early even for Mrs Dawson to be up and about as she left and took the Tube, not to the office but to Luka's apartment, to which she had keys.

The trouble with being a PA, especially to someone as successful as Luka, was that for the term of your contract you had access to their life in a way few did.

And, Cecelia had learned, if you happened to be crazy about the boss, it was a form of slow torture.

The doorman knew her and greeted her with a smile. She headed up in the elevator and then rang the bell and waited a moment before letting herself in.

Once, thinking he was still overseas, she had let herself in unannounced, without ringing the bell, and had found Luka in bed.

Neither alone nor sleeping.

Yes, working for Luka really was torture.

Cecelia walked in through the entrance hallway, but instead of heading to his bedroom she went through to the lounge and looked out over the view of Hyde Park, wondering how he would behave with her this morning in the office.

Would he carry on like it hadn't even happened, or would he expect her to be available to him as she served out her notice?

She gave a little shake of her head to clear such thoughts and wheeled the case she had brought with her towards the main bedroom.

Damn!

He was in bed, though thankfully this time alone.

And asleep.

It wasn't unusual to have to tiptoe around him, only this morning it was made more difficult, knowing she could have awoken next to him.

As quietly as she could, Cecelia opened up a wardrobe and, as the light inside came on, Cecelia heard him stir.

'Hey,' Luka said, his voice thick and sleepy.

'I'm just sorting out your luggage for your trip.'

And then he must have recalled what they had done the previous night because he asked, 'Why did you leave so abruptly?'

'Because I wanted to get home,' Cecelia said, and then she turned and gave him a small smile and did her best to keep it light. 'And I also wanted some sleep.'

'Yes, well, you wouldn't have got that had you stayed.' He put his hands behind his head and watched her pulling out a couple of casual shirts and adding them to the case.

'Will you be swimming when you're there?' she asked.

'What do you think, Cece?' he said.

It really had been a stupid question, given where he was headed, but it had been more to change the subject than to find out the answer.

'I think you should call me by my proper name,' she added, ignoring his question. Of course he would be swimming.

'It's not a holiday camp.' He grinned from the bed. 'The villas all have their own private pools,' Luka said as she headed into his en suite bathroom, then he let out a fond laugh of recall. 'Though there used to be just one main one. I used to work it.'

'Work it?' Cecelia laughed and called out from the en suite where she was collecting his cologne and things. 'Were you a cabana boy?'

'Yes.'

'Really?' She came to the door smiling, her hands full of toiletries. 'I was actually joking.'

'It's true, though. I used to head down there after school or during the holidays. It wasn't as luxurious then as it is now. There was a different owner then— Geo.'

'What was he like?'

'Lazy and a gambler,' Luka said, and he looked at her standing in the doorway and thought of all she had told him last night.

And all she had not.

There was a lot he hadn't told her either. He thought of her little jab yesterday about not everything being about money. She thought he'd had it all handed to him on a plate.

Everyone did.

He would have two weeks solid of it now; his father swanning around as if he had rebuilt the stunning complex from scratch, and—one thing that really annoyed Luka—complaining about the food when he feasted at the restaurant. Theo would sit there loudly stating that he made it better himself, when in truth Theo Kargas could not make his own coffee, let alone run a high-end kitchen.

Luka rather guessed that the uptight Cecelia might not be a forgiving audience for the story of his beginnings, and not the first person he would choose to share it with.

Luka wasn't used to sharing anything.

In business and in private he chose to take rather than to give.

Yet she had told him so much last night and the guilt of his past gnawed at his gut like a cancer—not that he would ever admit it.

'I would pick up the towels and get drinks and things. Then, when I finished school I got a job in Reception.'

Cecelia zipped up his toiletry bag and put it in his case and was just about to ask him about footwear when he said something that made her frown.

'Of course, I still *worked* the pool but it was in my own time and it wasn't towels that I was picking up.'

She looked up and met his eyes. 'Meaning?'

'Because I worked in Reception, I knew who the

richest women were because they had private access
to the beach and the ocean view.'

'I'm not with you…'

'I think you are, Cece.'

She added a belt to his case and did not look at him
but he could see two pink spots on her cheek.

In fact, she was embarrassed, wondering if it was
because of the fact that sex was constantly on her mind
around Luka that she was misinterpreting things.

'I made a lot of money, and I saved all of it. I made
enough that when Geo lost a small fortune and was
desperate for cash, I put in an offer for the restaurant
and it was accepted.'

'You bought the restaurant?'

'Yes,' Luka said. 'I bought it and gave my father a
share, so he might finally work in his own restaurant,
as he had always said he wanted to do. Growing up, we
had no money and he said there were no jobs but there
were jobs. Pot-washing jobs but, still, it was work. He
got really angry…' Luka didn't add that he'd got the
worst beating of his life that night. 'My mother said he
was a chef and that washing pots was beneath him. So,
when I had the money, I bought him a share in a restaurant, one with the Kargas name on the door.'

'But how on earth did a pool boy get the money to
buy a restaurant?'

'It wasn't the establishment it is now,' Luka pointed
out.

'But even so! Are you saying you were a gigolo?'

'If you choose to call it that then, yes, I was,' Luka
said, expecting her to snap his case closed and walk
away.

Yet she didn't.

'But how?' Cecelia asked. 'I mean, how does it work?'

Luka shrugged. 'A smile, a nod. Often they would buy me a drink.'

'I thought it would be the other way around.'

'No.'

'And did you name a price?'

'Of course not,' Luka said. 'That would be in poor taste.'

'But how?' she asked, intensely curious. 'I mean, I just can't imagine…'

'What?' he said. 'You can't imagine naming your wants?'

'No!' Cecelia admitted. 'I can't.'

'Perhaps you should try it before you knock it!'

'No, thank you,' she said primly. 'And I can't imagine giving the cabana boy a wink and a nod.'

Luka smiled. 'The first time it happened was a surprise. I got chatting to one of the guests. She was a widow. I didn't really know her but she asked me to join her for dinner. I said no, Geo would not like me dining with the guests. She said we would dine in her suite then. And so I went up and we ate and then we…' He smiled. 'I'm sure you can guess the rest.'

'But I can't,' Cecelia said, for she wanted to know more, and in her curiosity she found herself sitting down on the bed. 'How old was she?'

'A good bit older than I was then. In her thirties, I think,' Luka said. 'She was my first.' He looked at her. 'Who was yours?'

'I don't have to answer that.'

'If you want to know more you do.'

'Gordon.'

He wrinkled his nose and Luka was surprised as something that felt like it should be called jealousy surged in his chest.

Which was ridiculous when he was telling her about his own depraved past.

'Well, my first was actually stunning—a divorcée. She was there with friends but had her own villa. I was there every night until morning and I thought I had found the keys to heaven. The morning she left she came into Reception and when Geo wasn't looking she gave me an envelope. I thought it was a letter. When I opened it there was a whole load of cash. Until that point I had thought it was a romance.'

'Were you hurt when she paid you?'

'Hell no,' he said. 'To tell the truth I was already starting to get restless.'

Cecelia suppressed an eye-roll and refrained from saying that perhaps it was an indicator of things to come, as Luka spoke on.

'I was trying to work out how to break it off but had decided to do so after her holiday. I was the naïve one back then.'

Cecelia gave a wry smile at that. 'I doubt you were ever naïve. And after she'd gone there was another?'

'Of course, although it wasn't always cash. Sometimes they would take me shopping for a watch or such like. Once a car...'

'A car?'

She started to laugh. An embarrassed laugh, but she was also very curious. 'Luka!'

'What?' He shrugged. 'I was always careful and it wasn't all sex.'

'What else?'

'Romance. Dinner. Shopping. But mainly talking.'

'You mean, saying what they wanted to hear?'

'Yep.'

'Did you care for them?'

'Some I did,' Luka said. 'Mostly it was work.' He met her eyes. 'They didn't all care for me, Cece. They paid for the full Luka Kargas treatment.'

For a few years the pool had been his playground and the pickings had always been rich.

'Anyway,' he said, 'once I had bought the restaurant I hired a decent chef and changed the décor.'

'What about your father?'

Luka didn't answer directly.

It felt disloyal to his mother to admit that his father hadn't so much as lifted a saucepan.

'The restaurant started to do well and was too busy for one chef. Though it didn't do *too* well—I made sure of that.'

'Why?'

'Because I knew it wouldn't be long until Geo blew things again and would be forced to sell. When that happened I had planned to be in a good enough position to put in an offer on the resort. With help, of course...'

'Financial help?' Cecelia checked.

'No, one of the women I was seeing helped me get my papers in order to go to the bank.' He didn't add that the woman had also warned him not to bring his father into the hotel side of things.

It was advice for which he would be grateful for ever.

'How old were you by then?'

'Twenty-two. Once the resort was safely mine I hired the best chef I could find and things really started to happen. As the guests came in I started to buy up the houses and land around it. Out of all the hotels I own, it is still the jewel in my crown. From humble beginnings it's magnificent now.'

She looked at him. He mesmerised her, he truly did.

And she was nervous too, for the more she knew him, the more she wanted him.

'Is your father still your business partner?'

'Not fully.' He shook his head. 'The hotels are mine, the restaurants belong to us both.' And then, a touch unguarded, he admitted a little more. 'I should never have gone into business with him.'

'I agree about not going into business with family,' Cecelia said, because she had seen such things go wrong in her work before. 'And, Luka, I also think it's a really bad idea getting involved with an employer.' It was Cecelia who brought it back to them. 'I'm not saying that I regret last night, but it should never have happened. I take my career very seriously.'

'I know you do, but you're leaving anyway.'

'Yes,' she agreed. 'But I still don't think it's right and I don't want Bridgette or anyone knowing that something once happened between us.'

'Once?' he checked, and he took her hand to move it to the sheet beneath which he was hardening, but she resisted and her palm came to rest on his flat stomach.

There was no solace there for his skin was warm and she could feel the silk hair that led from his navel to paradise and she ached to move her hand lower.

So much had changed since yesterday.

Not just that she was leaving.

And not just that they had slept together.

He was creeping further into her heart.

'Luka, I really think we should just draw a neat line under what happened and when you come back from Xanero we'll go back to how we were.'

She was trying so hard to hold onto her heart, while at the same time sitting on his bed and looking into his eyes.

He pulled her head towards him, and she let him, and they shared a lingering kiss. He was leaving this morning, Cecelia told herself.

Order would soon be returned.

Just not yet.

Their tongues explored each other and their mouths were hungry for sensations.

He kissed down her neck and then moved the collar of her linen jacket and kissed the shoulders that had been revealed to him only yesterday, tracing her clavicle with his tongue until her neck arched.

'Don't leave a bruise...' she said, but he ignored her, biting into her flesh and sucking as his hand pushed between her thighs, which were pressed together.

'Come to bed,' Luka said.

And without hesitation she nodded.

Cecelia stood and his eyes were on her as she undressed. He watched as the navy jacket came off and he just stared as she removed her top to reveal the purple mark on her shoulder.

She slipped off her skirt and sandals and then straightened up and removed her bra. She could see he was hard beneath the sheet, and, in response to the command from her hungry eyes, he kicked it off.

He loved that he did not have to persuade her—that he did not have to slowly remove her bra and kiss her while sliding down her knickers.

Instead, she took care of that.

For this was no accident.

Her delicately shaped curls, which he had not had time to appreciate last night, had a coppery tinge that he stared at as she removed her bra. For the first time in years he was hungry to taste a woman, and reached for her to join him in bed.

'After this morning…' she warned, but he hushed her with his mouth. 'I mean it, Luka,' Cecelia said, pulling hers away.

'Sure,' he agreed, 'so this morning we make the most of it.'

Instead of kissing her, he knelt and lowered his head to her breast.

His tongue swirled around her nipple while his mouth closed and created a delicious vacuum. He sucked hard and Cecelia felt herself clench down below.

'Luka…'

'Nice?' he asked, removing his mouth and blowing on her erect nipple. Cecelia didn't know how to answer.

It was beyond nice, it was bliss, yet his moves were so practised and sure. She closed her eyes and then his mouth moved down her stomach.

'Am I getting the full Luka Kargas treatment?' she asked.

There was a moment of arrested silence while he paused, his mouth hovering over her stomach. What she didn't know was that in Luka's world the tables had turned many years ago. He no longer went down on women.

His start had been sex and Luka had long ago perfected his routine.

But now that his wealth exceeded theirs…

Well, he paid for *their* favours.

Not directly, of course.

With jewels and exotic weekends.

Now *they* went down on *him* instead of the other way around.

But not this morning.

It had been years since…

Years since *her* pleasure had mattered.

This morning it did.

'No,' he responded to her question. 'You're getting me.'

He kissed her stomach, not lightly but as deeply and intently as if it were her mouth, and Cecelia found her breath held in her throat as his hand slid between her closed legs. 'Open them.'

She did, just a little, and she lay there, determined almost not to enjoy it. To remind herself that this was his skill.

His thumb was intent and his fingers were inside her but Cecelia's throat was tight as he teased and stroked and rubbed, for she brought up her knees in an involuntary movement.

Women had paid him for this, she told herself as his tongue set to work alongside his thumb.

There was a moan building but she held onto it, yet he read it, for he moved between her legs to increase the intensity.

Luka heard her low moan and forgot his practised moves of old for this was new.

He heard her gasps, and finally learned the scent and taste of Cecelia on his tongue.

Her thighs were shaking as he probed deeply, and her hand pressed on his head, pushing him away. He knew she resisted pleasure.

So he upped the intensity again.

'Luka…' she sobbed, because it was too intense. His tongue was penetrating and he growled—and knew the moment she felt it. She wanted to come, but knew she would come so deeply that she was terrified to let herself go.

'Come, Cece,' he said, his voice rumbling through her. It was a command, an order her body could not ignore. Her back arched and her orgasm shot through her like lightning and earthed to his mouth.

He coaxed every flicker from her so that she was flushed and near crying when her body came down.

Never had it tasted this good. This was not like the work he used to do. This was different.

He slid up her body, Cecelia pulling him those final inches. They drank from each other in a desperate kiss that was both deep and heady. Luka came up on his arms but she pulled his head back down to claim a deeper kiss.

It was nothing like either of them had known before.

He was practised to the core and she was so new to passion, yet it was fire that they made together. She did not want him to be this good.

'That *wasn't* work,' he told her. 'That was bliss.'

And so was this.

He was there at her entrance and nudging a little way in. 'Come with me,' he said to the shell of her ear. 'To Xanero…'

Luka did not want to go and now had been presented with a way to make it more bearable.

She liked the thought of fourteen nights of this. But she held back.

'No,' she said, and he pulled out. 'I mean, no to Xanero…'

But yes to this.

Her eyes were closed as he slid in deep, all the way in. If she could have examined her thoughts she feared she would rediscover her self-control, and the part of her that knew this was wrong.

And so did Luka.

But they were past caring.

The feel of him unsheathed and stretching her was sublime.

And for Luka too, for she was slippery yet tight. He drove in deep and she let out a moan that he wanted to turn into a scream.

He reached for her leg and wrapped her calf around his thigh, pushing into her again. She was more open than she had ever been.

He thrust slowly and could feel the intimate welcoming grip of her.

Her nails dug into his buttocks and she moved with him until they were lost to each other and the moment.

'Luka…' She could barely breathe, yet at her plea he took her harder and faster, making her dizzy. She could feel her climax building and this time she welcomed it.

He angled himself and took her deeper and then he tipped into rapid, rhythmic thrusts from which there was no return. It was her scream that brought him back to consciousness.

It was her first scream in bed, Luka knew as his stomach lifted and he pulsed into her, shouting his release.

Her cry came from a place she had never known, and her orgasm was so intense that for a moment she felt possessed. As if her body had been taken over by someone else, by a woman who knew how to be free.

Yet as she gloried in the sensation, his weight atop her reminded her starkly that soon she would have to dig her way out of the ashes from the fire he had brought to her heart.

CHAPTER SIX

'COME WITH ME to Xanero.'

As the mist was clearing he said it again. His weight pressed down on her even as he still rested inside her. If there was ever a weak moment this was it and Cecelia knew she was about to say yes when Luka spoke.

'Not to the resort or anything,' he added, pushing up onto his forearms. 'Or my mother would think we were serious or something. You could stay on the yacht.'

Cecelia slid out from under him and rolled to her side. He did the same.

She had almost said yes.

In a delicious weak moment she had almost succumbed, and she failed to keep the bitter edge from her tone when she responded to his invitation. 'You mean, come to Xanero as your plaything.'

'I'd work you by day...' He smiled, completely unfazed as he toyed with her breast, still throbbing from his previous attention, for this was the life he led. 'And then make up for it by night.'

'So while you're on the island I'd be cooped up—'

'Hardly cooped up. It's not a tin boat with a gas stove....'

'I have seen your yacht, Luka.'

Well, she had seen pictures of it and had seen some

of the accounts for it. It was a luxury resort in itself, and of course she knew all about the wild parties that were held there.

And now she was being invited into the playboy's bed.

Oh, the dewy mist of his lovemaking was most certainly starting to clear for suddenly Cecelia pulled herself away and sat up.

And it was then that realisation kicked in. 'Luka, we didn't use anything…'

In a life spent not making mistakes, Cecelia had just made a huge one and there was no excuse.

For either of them.

'Are you on the Pill?'

'Yes, I'm on the Pill,' she snapped as she tried to remember if she'd taken it last night, because it hadn't just been putting out her clothes for the morning that had fallen by the wayside. But surely if she went home now and took it, then she'd be fine.

But pregnancy wasn't the only thing on her mind.

'It's not just that, though.' Cecelia turned and looked over to where he lay and saw that his expression was equally grim.

He'd just told her he'd once been a gigolo—she could not believe she had been so careless.

'Cecelia, you don't have to worry about anything there,' Luka said as he moved to reassure her. 'I *always* use protection.'

'Well, clearly you don't!'

It was as much her fault as his, Cecelia knew that, and her angry tone was aimed more towards herself.

'You'll be fine,' he said, which might have sounded dismissive, but neither did he want to admit just how impossibly rare this lapse was.

She gave a terse nod and headed for the shower while Luka lay there, his hands behind his head, trying to fathom what had just taken place.

This morning he'd forgotten the rules. This morning he'd been so wrapped in the feel of her, the feel of *them*, that he'd forgotten the care he usually took.

He had complete control in the bedroom, for though he was wild he was not reckless.

Yet this morning he had been.

Not only had he invited her to come to Xanero with him—at least he had quickly reacted and told Cece that she would only be on the yacht—but for a moment he had glimpsed it. His dream, showing off the first Kargas restaurant and the now stunning resort which was by far his proudest achievement to date.

And he had told her how his ascent to the top had started.

Luka wasn't particularly close to anyone.

He kept work and family neatly separated, and certainly he had never invited an employee, albeit one who had resigned, to join him there.

The yacht was for escape, for parties and fun. It had never been used as a couples' retreat.

She came out of the shower and dressed quickly. He was relieved that she seemed as keen to leave as he now wanted her gone, for she had messed with his head.

'I'd better take your case in to the office,' Cecelia said.

'Please.' He nodded. 'I'll be in later.'

No, he wasn't a perfect gentleman, for he did not tell her to leave the case and that he would take it.

And neither would his driver magically appear.

She could take the underground.

Cecelia had said herself that she wanted to draw a neat line and get back to being his PA.

That suited him just fine.

Last night had been amazing.

So had this morning, and yet now he was left feeling deeply unsettled.

Luka chose not to get close to anyone, but this morning he had.

Xanero really was hell in paradise.

For Luka, the first week there had been a protracted nightmare—his mother seemed resigned to her fate and his father continued to lord it over the restaurant and resort.

And he had found out that his father was bullying the staff.

Bastard!

While Luka disliked how his father had rewritten history to suit the image of himself he wanted to believe, Luka could live with it if it made life easier on his mother.

But bullying would not happen in one of Luka's establishments, and for all the lies and wealth that shaped his mother's life, she was finding it no easier that he could see.

Luka had taken the yacht out over the weekend, but the pop of champagne corks and the sound of music skimming over the Mediterranean had soon grated and he had cleared everyone off except the crew as he mulled things over. Now, back on Xanero, and midway through the second week, on the Wednesday morning his decisions were made and he was ready to execute them.

He walked through the alfresco area of the restaurant where diners were enjoying the morning sun and through to the cool darkness of the main restaurant.

Theo Kargas was at the bar, speaking with the bar manager, and Luka could feel the young man's tension from across the room.

'Hey,' he said to his father. 'We need to talk.'

'About?' Theo asked, even as he crammed white-bait, crisped to perfection, into his mouth. He was utterly relaxed, for any angry words from his son always took place out of earshot of the staff.

Yes, Luka's door was always closed.

Not so today.

'I want to discuss your appalling treatment of my staff and your inexcusable conduct towards my mother.'

Theo almost choked, but then attempted a recovery. '*Your* staff? We are partners. I gave you—'

'You gave me nothing,' Luka said, and got right in his father's face. 'You actually believe your own lies. Now, as I said, we need to talk…' He gestured to a table, for he too would prefer privacy for this but the fact he had first addressed the issues in front of the bar manager had been deliberate.

Theo *would* listen, or Luka *would* act.

'I bought this restaurant,' Luka said, 'from the money I made picking up rich woman…'

'Luka,' his father warned, for a waiter was setting up the table and could hear what was being said.

'What?' Luka shrugged. 'I'm not ashamed of it.'

Well, perhaps he was a bit, but having told Cecelia the real truth about his start he felt more reconciled with it.

So he told his father a truth that had consistently been ignored. 'I gave you an opportunity to work, and you spurned it. I have put up with it for years for my mother's sake. No more. I am hiring a new manager, who shall report directly to me. One more episode of your foul temper used on my staff and I shall take you through the courts to extricate you from our agreement and the restaurant's name shall be changed to Luka Kargas.'

'It would kill your mother.'

'She's already dying,' Luka pointed out, and then he looked right at his father. 'Actually, she isn't, because I am moving her to London for her treatments and I am going to ensure that she rests and is taken care of between them.'

'You can't just swan in here and dictate—'

'Oh, but I can,' Luka said. 'I own the complex, and I have a half-share in the restaurant, and,' he added, 'I can destroy you if I so choose. You should be pleading with your wife to seek treatment, because if it wasn't for her you'd be seeing your days out in a shack on the hills and, believe me, Theo, you don't want to test me on that.'

'I'm your father!' Theo reared and stood and leant across the table and grabbed Luka's shirt.

'More's the pity,' Luka said. 'And I strongly suggest that you get your hands off me. I'm not ten years old any more, or a skinny teenager up against a brute. I could floor you and I am more than willing to do it.'

Sensibly, his father removed his hand, for it was clear Luka meant every word. But he was not finished yet. 'You have no idea the ruthless bastard I can be. I could crush you and your so-called empire in the palm of my hand,' Luka said. 'And I will say it again, just so we're clear—the *only* reason I've held back where the resort is concerned is for the sake of my mother.'

It was Luka who stood up and walked off back towards his villa.

He'd have loved to have hit his bully of a father,

but what good could come from that? So instead he stripped off and dived into the pool, pounding out several lengths before hauling himself from the water a touch breathless.

And then he messaged Cecelia.

We need to talk.

His message came up on her computer and Cecelia tensed, because though they had spoken about work both online and on the phone on many occasions, this sounded rather personal.

She replied quickly.

I'm about to call someone in for an interview.

So?

Of course he didn't mean that they needed to speak about what had taken place between them, Cecelia scolded herself for her less-than-professional reply. If Luka Kargas wanted to speak to his PA it didn't matter if she'd been about to call someone in.

'I have to speak with Mr Kargas,' Cecelia said to the interviewee. 'I'll be back when I can.'

Cecelia didn't apologise for keeping Sabine waiting, for the potential PA might as well get a glimpse of what she would be in for.

A moment later his face appeared on her screen and Cecelia got more than a glimpse.

His chest was naked and her view was of a dark mahogany nipple surrounded by a swirl of black hair. But then he angled the screen better and she saw that his hair was wet and he was squinting from the bright sun.

'What can I do for you?' Cecelia asked.

Her voice was cool, her demeanour brisk and she was determined that they were back to business.

'What are you doing?' he asked.

'Working.' She frowned. 'Marco has a few things he needs to run by you but apart from that things are ticking along.'

She was wearing a grey dress with a sheer grey silky cardigan, because perish the thought that she might show too much skin. Her hair was neat and pulled back and yet now he knew another side to her he couldn't help but see her buttoned-up appearance for what it was. A defence strategy.

'I want you to fly here,' Luka said. 'I want you here tonight.'

Cecelia stared back at him. 'For work?'

'No.'

She liked it that he was direct.

In fact, Cecelia liked it that he had basically asked her to get on a plane for sex. But what happened when he got bored? She reminded herself of all the reasons she had refused his original offer.

He would wake up one morning and instead of kisses she would sense his restlessness.

His slight disdain.

Oh, she had seen it on too many occasions not to know what was in store for her.

At least here in London she was but a taxi ride away from salvaging her pride when he told her they were through.

But in Xanero?

Did she book her own flight home?

Or would they suffer it through until she left his employ less than three weeks from now?

'If it isn't for work, then I shan't be joining you.'

'Fine,' Luka snapped. 'In that case, I need you to go and view some apartments for me.'

'Sure.'

'And I want you to interview some private nurses. Make sure they speak Greek.'

Cecelia took down the details.

It was now all very businesslike. Surly, but businesslike. Yet she ached to know more about his mother, though she resisted asking for details that were not with the remit of a professional relationship.

They had spent one night together, and she knew from his reputation that that didn't give her the keys to his private life.

'How are the interviews for your replacement going?' Luka asked.

'I'm getting there,' Cecelia said. 'I'm on the second round, so I should have a shortlist of three for you to choose from.'

'Any stand-outs?'

Cecelia hesitated.

Luka was a demanding boss but she almost had to shake the stars from potential employees' eyes to ensure they understood what the job entailed.

But one had stood out.

Sabine.

She had an incredible work history and was bright and engaging. The only trouble was that Cecelia didn't like her.

'There's one,' Cecelia said. 'Sabine. I'm just about to interview her again and give her a tour but...'

'But what?'

'I don't know,' Cecelia admitted.

'Try telling me.'

'I don't like her.' Cecelia shrugged. 'But, then, she's not for me to like. I'll see how this interview goes. She speaks Greek, which might be a help with your mother, and...'

'My mother will be coming to London for treatment, not for little get-togethers with my PA.'

He turned off the computer and closed it up.

Luka really did not want her to leave.

And yet it was perhaps for the best because despite strong words about PAs not getting involved with his family, he had told Cecelia some things he had never told anyone. And he had her interviewing nurses and looking for apartments.

He trusted her, and Luka was more comfortable trusting no one.

With that awkward conversation over, Cecelia got on with the second-round interviews.

Cecelia was self-aware enough to know that it was probably for private reasons that she couldn't take to Sabine. The young woman was gorgeous, with piercing blue eyes and straight black hair cut in a jagged, edgy style. She made Cecelia feel terribly drab.

'Luka will probably call you Sab, or Sabby...' Cecelia said in an offhand comment as she showed her around. 'It drives me crazy.'

'He can call me what he likes as long as he pays me.'

Cecelia held in a breath.

Sabine was arrogant and overly confident perhaps, but she really was the perfect match for Luka.

She could almost hear the banter between them.

'This is his suite,' Cecelia explained as she opened the door. 'It's serviced daily but I tend to check it as it sometimes needs an extra service. Not currently, though, he's still in Greece.'

'So I read!' Sabine said.

Cecelia had been doing her level best not to read about him, but once the interviews were wrapped up she found that she could not resist.

The headlines were all in the same vein: *Xanero Magnate Returns.*

It would seem that the weekend had been spent out on his yacht and she knew full well what went on on board.

She clicked on the article and there were the glossy beauties that always surrounded him and the sun hanging low in a fiery sky.

Luka didn't even wait for nightfall to get a party started.

It wasn't just the resumption of his sex life that concerned her, though—oh, but it did, *desperately* it did—but also what had happened that morning between them.

Cecelia could not believe she'd had unprotected sex. Though she kept willing herself calm, yesterday she had caved and made an appointment with her GP.

At the conclusion of the interview today Cecelia was heading there.

'Well, thank you for coming in,' Cecelia said as she walked Sabine to the elevator. 'You can expect to hear from me by the end of the week.'

'I'll look forward to it.' Sabine smiled and the women shook hands.

Cecelia really didn't like her, but it would seem she was the only one to feel so.

'She seems really nice,' Bridgette commented as Cecelia walked back from the elevator.

Yes, it was probably for rather personal reasons that

she didn't like her, Cecelia guessed, and decided that she would be putting Sabine forward.

Luka could make the final call.

'I'm going out for a couple of hours,' she told Bridgette. 'I won't have my phone on.'

'What should I say if Luka calls because he can't get hold of you?' Bridgette checked, because his PA was always supposed to be available.

'Tell him I'm…' She didn't know what to say. 'Tell him I'm taking a long lunch.'

Lunch didn't come into it.

Instead, she took the underground until she was practically home and spent the next hour sitting in the waiting room at her GP's surgery.

Cecelia was rarely there and finally, when her name was called, she rather hoped she would be in and out in a few minutes with her mind eased.

Dr Heale introduced herself and Cecelia told her the reason she was there.

'It's probably nothing,' Cecelia started. 'In fact, I'm sure I'm wasting your time…'

'Why don't you let me be the judge of that?'

Very well.

Why was discussing sex always so awkward for her? The shame came from her aunt and uncle, Cecelia knew. They spoke in whispers and were still mortified by the salacious circumstances in which her mother had died.

Cecelia did her best to push all that aside and to speak in a matter-of-fact tone. 'I had unprotected sex last week.'

'When?'

'On Monday night,' Cecelia said. 'Or rather on the Tuesday morning.'

'You're on the Pill?' Dr Heale checked, reading through her notes.

'Yes,' Cecelia said, 'though I usually take my Pill at night…'

'And you didn't?'

'No.'

'Well, you've left it too late for the morning-after pill.'

She hadn't really thought about it the morning after, but now Dr Heale was telling her that she'd had a window of a week.

That window was closed to her now.

'But it's probably fine?' Cecelia pushed, only Dr Heale wasn't exactly rushing to put her at ease; in fact, she was reading Cecelia's notes.

'Are you still with your fiancé?' she asked.

Cecelia remembered the last time she had been there, carefully going on the Pill before she and Gordon did anything.

There had certainly been no up-against-the-wall sex with him!

'Er, no.'

'Do you have a new partner?'

'Not exactly,' Cecelia croaked. 'It was a one-off, well…'

'That's fine,' Dr Heale said. 'But with a casual encounter it is, of course, more important that you're careful.'

She was right, except there was nothing casual about Cecelia's feelings for Luka.

And there was that sting of shame again—not that Dr Heale turned a hair. If anything, she was very practical.

'Perhaps, while you're here, we should run a sexual health check,' she suggested.

It looked like Cecelia would not be in and out in a

couple of minutes; in fact, she returned from lunch a full hour late.

'Luka's been calling the office,' Bridgette warned. 'And he's not best pleased that your mobile's turned off.'

He certainly had been calling, Cecelia thought when she turned it back on. She had barely sat down before he called again.

'How was the dentist?' he asked, and there was an edge to Luka's voice for he was quite sure where she had been.

'Excuse me?' Cecelia flared.

'You're the one making up excuses. Were you off visiting your new office? Or perhaps having lunch with your new boss—whoever that may be?'

'No,' Cecelia calmly responded. 'I had an appointment. Now, what can I do for you?'

You can get here, Luka wanted to answer.

He had never had to chase or pursue, and the one woman who could have made him feel better had distanced herself from him.

'How did the second-round interviews go?'

'Very well. I have a shortlist of three for you to interview.'

'Bring them in early next week.'

'So you'll be back on Monday?' Cecelia checked.

But Luka had already rung off.

CHAPTER SEVEN

CECELIA KNEW HE was back the very second she stepped out of the elevator.

That tangy citrus scent of him had never really left the place but it was stronger today.

There was a knot of tight nerves in her stomach and she had no idea how to play this. She sensed he had come out of his office as she hung up her jacket, and this was confirmed when she heard him speak.

'Hi.'

His voice was low and deep and, though expected, she still had to fight not to jump. Instead she turned around at his greeting.

He looked amazing, and even if he had gone home to deal with a difficult situation it was clear there had been time spent in the sun.

'Hi, Luka.'

'How are things?'

'Great. But Mr Garcia is insisting that you speak with him today.'

'Tell him I can fit him in tomorrow.'

'Very well,' Cecelia said as she held in a sigh. 'And you have the applicants for my replacement coming in between two and four.'

'Good.'

He'd hoped she might reconsider, given what had taken place, but deep down he knew she wouldn't have.

Cecelia was professional, and even Luka, who in the past had happily slept with his PA, knew that a line had been crossed and that it would be impossible to go back to the way they had been.

For once he did not want to talk about work.

Neither did he want to hit the computer.

After a hellish two weeks at home, quite simply he wanted to take her to bed.

Instead, there was a lot to do.

The head of his legal team was in and out of his office all morning, and Marco, head of accounting, was there too. From what she could glean, Luka was looking to sever business ties with his father.

As his mother battled cancer!

Luka's ruthlessness made her shiver.

It was approaching one o'clock when Cecelia told him that an apartment she had seen would be available for him to view this evening.

'I shan't be going ahead with that.'

'Oh.'

He had asked his mother to come to London and concentrate on surviving but the answer had been no.

She had at least agreed to have treatments in Athens, on the condition she could return home after each course.

Luka rather guessed they were his father's conditions but his efforts to persuade her otherwise had fallen on deaf ears.

At least she wasn't simply giving up now, but Luka knew that he had to do more.

He had spent the morning testing the legal waters

with his team, but it would be long and protracted to have his father forcibly removed as joint owner.

And he did not want the extra stress on his mother.

In fact, Luka, who dreaded going home, even for the occasional weekend, was starting to realise that Xanero might soon have to act as his base, at least for a while.

'You said one of the applicants spoke Greek?' Luka checked.

'Yes, Sabine.'

'And she is okay with extensive travel?'

'Yes.' Cecelia nodded. 'But, Luka, I really think Kelly, the first applicant, is more suitable.'

'Does she speak Greek?'

'No,' Cecelia said, 'but then neither do I.'

'There's a lot of things you don't do,' Luka said, and from the curl of his mouth and the charge in the air, the meaning was explicitly clear.

'Don't!' Cecelia warned. She had been wondering how they would play this and if the past would be politely ignored—well, clearly not.

And Cecelia was furious.

'I'm the best bloody PA you have ever had and don't you dare forget it. Just because I won't hop on a plane to Xanero for a shag…' Her face was on fire as he stared right back and gave her a black smile, so she upped it. 'Or get down on my knees and blow you under the desk…' She knew he was hard and she was wet too, but, hell, he had brought it to work, and she wasn't going to back down now. 'It doesn't mean I'm not brilliant at my work. Don't forget that, Luka.'

He was saved from a smart answer when her phone rang and Cecelia glanced at it to see who was calling.

'Go ahead,' Luka said, but Cecelia shook her head.

'It's fine.'

She would not be taking a call from her doctor in front of Luka, especially given the nature of the tests last week! Instead she excused herself, returned to the privacy of her desk and called the surgery.

'This is Cecelia Andrews,' she said to the receptionist. 'A message was left, asking me to call.'

'One moment, please.'

It was closer to two moments and they were possibly the longest of her life.

'The doctor would like to see you to go over your test results.'

'I'm actually at work and it's terribly hard to get away. If I could speak with the doctor...'

'We have a policy that we don't give results over the phone. I have a vacancy next Monday at two fifteen.'

'Monday!' Cecelia yelped. There was no way she could wait.

'Actually, there's just been a cancellation for today at one thirty. If you can get here by then, it's yours.'

'I shall,' Cecelia said, and did her best to remember her manners as the world imploded on her. 'And thank you.'

Luka came out then with work on his mind. 'If you could call the Athens team now...'

'It's my lunch break,' Cecelia cut in, and Luka blinked.

'Well, get something sent up and eat at your desk. I need this sorted.'

'Luka,' she said, 'I'm entitled to a lunch break, and I'm taking it.'

She was panicking now, remembering his salacious past and what that could mean for her.

She headed to the bathroom and when she returned

he saw that she had redone her hair and refreshed her make-up.

'Good luck,' he said as she walked out.

'Excuse me?' She turned around, wondering if he had guessed where she was going.

'With your new boss.' His voice was tart. 'I assume that's where you're headed.'

Cecelia said nothing.

'Just make sure you're back on time. I believe you're *entitled* to an hour.'

She hated this.

Cecelia absolutely hated this. She should never have got involved with her boss and now everything had changed.

Bristling, Cecelia took the elevator down and with no time to lose she raced for the underground and made it just in time for her appointment, where they asked her to give another urine sample.

And then she sat for the longest half-hour of her life, thumbing blindly through magazines.

Until suddenly her eye was caught by a shot of Luka, pelvis to pelvis with some beauty and dancing the night away in Barcelona. Admittedly, it was an old magazine, though it was not the type of thing she needed to see right now.

'Cecelia Andrews?'

She put down the magazine and stood up, deciding she would kill him with her bare hands if he'd given her anything.

It was the same doctor she had seen the previous week and Cecelia sat as Dr Heale went through her notes.

'I've had a look through your results and I thought it better that I see you face to face.'

Cecelia felt her heart plummet.

'All the health checks came back clear. However, I asked you to repeat the urine specimen as your BHCG came back as elevated.'

'What does that mean?' Cecelia asked, her mind swinging from one horror to another.

'It's very early days,' the doctor said, 'but the second test confirms that you are pregnant.'

'The other tests…?' Cecelia asked for she could not take it in.

'They're all clear.'

'But I'm on the Pill—' Cecelia started, but then the high horse she had been sitting on while blaming Luka for any misfortune that might come to bear on her shifted.

This predicament really was down to her.

She had missed a pill, and at the very least should have looked into the morning-after pill while there was still time for it to be effective.

A baby was the very last thing Cecelia wanted.

She would be a single mother.

Just like her mum.

And she would be single, that much she could guarantee.

'I'm only just, though…' Cecelia vainly attempted, unsure what she was even saying. 'Two weeks.'

'Four weeks,' the doctor clarified. 'Your levels are spot on. It's calculated from the first day of your last period.'

Cecelia screwed her eyes closed. A little over two weeks ago they hadn't even kissed.

Yet now she was being told that she was four weeks pregnant.

By Luka Kargas who was, by any account, the biggest rake known.

'I don't know what to do,' Cecelia admitted. 'I honestly don't know how I feel.'

'Of course you don't,' Dr Heale said. 'Why don't you make an appointment with me for next week and by then the news will have had time to sink in a bit.'

Cecelia did just that and then she made her way out of the clinic. She stood on the busy London street full of people who were carrying on with their day, oblivious to the bombshell that had dropped on her world.

She wiped her cheeks with her hand and only then did Cecelia realise she was crying.

It was as if all her emotions were in full flight, for there were tears and her heart was hammering in her chest, yet Cecelia was barely aware of them.

'Numb.'

She said it out loud just to hear her own voice and to clarify that it was how she felt.

Numb.

She could hear her phone ringing but it did not even enter her head to answer it. Instead she walked and walked through London streets, carrying her bag in her hand rather than in its usual position over her shoulder.

A baby?

It had not been in her plans—at least, not her current plans.

Even when she and Gordon had spoken about one day having children it had been a sort of dim and distant thing in the far-away future, and even then she hadn't really been able to picture it.

Her career was the most important thing in her life. It was the only thing she really had, but how the hell was she going to be able to carry on with it with a baby?

Luka would carry on.

A baby wouldn't affect *his* career.

The numbness was fading and the sting of sensation was coming back as she briefly envisaged Luka's reaction if she told him the news.

And the aftermath.

She had worked with him for almost a year and knew the bastard he could be. As recently as this morning he'd had his legal and accounting teams working out how to screw over his own father.

She could not stand to think of the meeting that would take place about her if he found out about the baby!

Cecelia walked into a bar and ordered a glass of water. She sat on a stool but the world would not stop spinning.

She started a new job in a couple of weeks' time.

It was only a six-month contract, though.

Which would take her up to seven months pregnant.

Really, she could not have planned it better, except she had not planned on being pregnant at all.

Her phone was ringing again and, unthinking, she answered it.

'Where the hell are you?' Luka demanded. 'Bridgette's gone home with a migraine and I'm playing receptionist to my potential PAs!'

'You'll have to manage without me,' Cecelia said, for there was no way she could go back to work this afternoon and face him. Even keeping her voice remotely normal was taking a supreme effort.

He heard the chink of glasses and a burst of laughter in the background and the effort behind her words. He could picture her with her new boss, all cosy on some sofa in a club. 'You still have two weeks left to serve your notice, Cecelia. I suggest that you get back here now.'

'And I just told you that I can't.'

She was not being defiant, there was just absolutely no way she could make it into work.

He rang off and Cecelia sat watching a woman wheeling in her baby in a pram, wrestling with the glass doors.

It was not her world.

Meanwhile, Luka sat and stared at his phone.

It was not a world he was used to either and, as Luka quickly found out, rejection was certainly not his forte.

He did not kill her with kindness.

Cecelia arrived at work the following morning and nodded to the doorman.

She made her way up in the elevator and again saw that she had beaten Bridgette to it.

Yet she was not the first here.

Or the second.

Her desk had been moved. And it was not arranged the way she usually left it.

There was a laptop on it that wasn't hers and when she went behind it there was a bag on the floor that felt like finding the wrong shoes by the bed.

She had spent the night fighting not just whether or not to tell him but, if she did, how.

He had, she realised, removed the opportunity to do so.

'Cecelia.'

She turned to the low, familiar sound of his voice and the clipped tones at Luka's unfamiliar correct usage of her name.

'I have hired your replacement.'

'So I see.'

'There is no need for you to stay on.'

'What about…?' Her mind darted to the million and one things she needed to pass on. 'There's the Athens—'

'Sorted,' Luka interrupted. 'Of course, you shall be paid while *not* serving your notice.'

'And this is because I didn't return from lunch?'

'No, this is because of your attitude.'

'Am I back at school?' Cecelia flared.

'Did you have an attitude problem then?' Luka smoothly responded.

No, she hadn't had an attitude problem at school.

She'd been diligent and hard-working and had toed the line, determined that her life would be different from her mother's.

And neither had she had an attitude at home, for she'd been trying so hard not to get in her aunt and uncle's way.

Her attitude only changed when she was with him.

Luka brought out both the best and the worst in her.

And he was the worst.

She knew that, and it was proved when Sabine came out.

She had the grace to offer a somewhat awkward smile in Cecelia's direction.

Her black hair was a little messy, like she had a case of bedhead… It appeared they had worked through the night.

Or otherwise.

Cecelia didn't trust Luka enough not to consider *otherwise*.

And Cecelia knew then the answer to the problem she had wrestled with since the doctor had delivered the baby bombshell to her.

No way would she tell him.

She did not want her child subjected to the life he led.

Cecelia knew from experience the damage that could cause.

And if he could snuff her out of his life overnight, if he could so calmly watch as Sabine handed her a package with all her things and escorted her out, then he could easily do the same to his child.

CHAPTER EIGHT

THE DECISION ABOUT whether to tell him was not, of course, as clear cut as that.

For the first couple of months a generous dash of anger fired Cecelia's spirit, for she certainly hadn't deserved that.

How dared he have Sabine walk her out of the office? How dared he question her attitude, when he was the most arrogant person on earth?

Her anger, combined with a healthy dose of denial as to the truth of her predicament, got Cecelia through the first trimester of her pregnancy.

Cecelia did consider a termination, but in the end could not see herself going through with it.

Her father had wanted her mother to abort her, and she was also rather certain that Luka would suggest the same.

So she hid the news from the world and worked hard in her new job.

As long as she didn't show, she could work hard and pretend that nothing had changed.

At first she enjoyed the life where sixteen or more hours of her day were not devoted to Luka's exhausting schedule, and eight hours of night time were not spent rejecting the hunger of her body for him.

Except she lied, for now she had experienced him, it was not fantasy that peppered her thoughts and dreams but intoxicating memories.

Unlike Luka, her new diplomat boss was so stunningly politically correct that he made no mention of her expanding waistline. But as Christmas approached, Cecelia formally told him that she would not be renewing her contract at the end of her term.

Cecelia had always been sensible with money and had some savings, but she was starting to glimpse how impossible it would be to combine her regular work with motherhood.

Anxiety about the future woke Cecelia up in the middle of the night, and of course there were times that she considered telling Luka.

But not like this, Cecelia thought as she nervously headed to her aunt and uncle's house to tell them the news. Not when her heart was fluttering in fear and she was constantly on the edge of tears.

On the Tube she checked her hair and make-up and could see the anxiety in her own eyes in the mirror as she tried to fathom how they would take it.

'Cecelia.' Her aunt frowned when she opened the front door to her niece. 'You didn't call to say you were dropping by.'

Should she have to? Cecelia thought, but as usual said nothing.

And neither did she remove her coat.

She sat in the drawing room as tea was served and felt as uncomfortable as she had on the day she had first arrived here.

It was a very austere house and Cecelia could remember sitting on this very seat as her grandfather had spoken with his son about boarding school for her.

'How's work?' her aunt asked.

'It's going well.' Cecelia nodded. 'The hours are much better than in my previous job. However, I've told him that I shan't be renewing my contract.'

'Have you found something else?' her aunt asked.

Cecelia took a sip of tea and then replaced the cup in the saucer and made herself say it. 'No, I shan't be working for a few months because I've found out that I'm expecting.' When her aunt said nothing, Cecelia made things a touch clearer. 'A baby.'

'I wasn't aware you'd been dating since the break-up.'

'Gordon and I finished more than a year ago,' Cecelia attempted, but she felt her face flush, because what had happened that night with Luka couldn't even be described as a date, let alone a relationship.

They weren't a couple.

Quite simply, it had been the most impulsive night of her life.

And as for the morning...

Cecelia forced herself not to dwell on that. Right now she had to get through telling her aunt.

'My contract expires a couple of months before the baby is due and I can afford to take a few months off.'

'So what does the father have to say on the matter?'

'I haven't told him,' Cecelia admitted. 'Yet.'

Deep down Cecelia knew she had to tell Luka, but for now she was trying to get used to the idea herself. Certainly she did not want to be teary and hysterical when she told him the news, which was frankly how she felt most of the time.

Not that Cecelia showed it. As always, she appeared outwardly calm.

Yes, it might be a difficult conversation to have with her aunt but Cecelia hoped that she would soon come round.

And then hope died.

She watched as her aunt added another spoon of sugar to her tea and stirred, and then placed the spoon on the saucer.

The silence had been a long one and Cecelia did not attempt to fill it. Instead, she stayed quiet to allow her aunt to process the news. When she did, her eyes met Cecelia's.

'The apple doesn't fall far from the tree, does it? Well, I raised your mother's mistake,' she said. 'You need to know Cecelia that I shan't be doing it again for you.'

Cecelia felt a shiver run the length of her spine as she met her aunt's eyes, and in that moment the past twenty years or so made a little more sense.

She had never felt welcome here and now she knew why.

A mistake.

That was what her aunt had just called her.

Deep down, Cecelia had known it, for she had done all that she could not to make any trouble for her aunt and uncle and not to live up to her mother's reputation.

It would seem in her aunt's eyes she just had.

'I should go,' Cecelia said, polite to the very end. 'Please, give my love to my uncle.'

Instead of going home, Cecelia headed for her old workplace and sat in a café nearby, looking up at the towering high-rise that housed Kargas Holdings and wondering what to do.

A mistake.

Over and over it played in her mind.

They were the same words her father had used the one time she had seen him.

She tried to fathom Luka's reaction—she pictured his beautiful features marred by anger, and she imagined them locked in a bitter row, and right there in the café Cecelia started to cry.

She simply wasn't ready to reveal the pregnancy to him, Cecelia decided, if she was breaking down just imagining it.

No, she would tell Luka about the pregnancy when she felt calmer and when she could do it without being reduced to tears.

In the end, it was an uneventful but terribly lonely pregnancy.

Her six months working for the diplomat were soon up, and of course her contract was not renewed.

She was barely speaking to her aunt and uncle, and the few friends she had were somewhat aghast that she had gone ahead with the pregnancy.

Worse, though, she missed *him*.

Luka.

Not as the father of the baby she carried.

More, Cecelia missed the many different colours he had once added to her day.

She could feel the kicks of her baby, only it wasn't just duty that had her call Luka, it was the ache to hear his voice.

His private number must have been changed, for an automated voice told her to check the number and try again.

So she called the front desk and braced herself to speak with Bridgette or Sabine and to ask to be put through to Luka.

Instead it was an unfamiliar female voice she met with.

'I'm sorry, Mr Kargas isn't taking any unscheduled calls.'

'I used to work for him,' Cecelia explained. 'I was his PA and I—'

'As I said, Mr Kargas isn't taking any unscheduled calls.'

The voice was as brusque and efficient as Cecelia herself had once been when dealing with yet another slightly desperate female on the line.

'I have to speak with him,' Cecelia said. 'Can you let him know that I called?'

'Of course,' came the terse response. 'Can you spell your first name, please…'

He did not return the call.

It really was a terribly lonely time.

And now that Cecelia did not have work to occupy her, she caved under her broken heart for the first time.

She should have walked away at the outset.

Or she should never have turned to the huskiness of his voice that night.

Yet, even heavily pregnant, just the thought of the frantic sex that had taken place hit so low in her belly that she almost sank to her knees at the memory she could never erase.

But it hadn't even been that.

No, it was the morning after she would correct if she could.

She would peel away from his kiss and reach for a condom.

She would turn from his embrace and do things more sensibly.

Yet she could not see how, for she had been lost, *they* had been lost, and so deep into each other that even with the benefit of hindsight she could not play it another way, for she wanted him even now.

Spring came, and three weeks from her due date Cecelia tried to call him one more time.

'Mr Kargas isn't taking any unscheduled calls.'

'You sound like a broken record,' Cecelia snapped, and ended the call as she realised her pride had waned. Labour kind of did that to you, and perhaps mid-contraction wasn't the best time to tell him that she was having his child.

So she called for a taxi instead.

'Good luck, my dear,' Mrs Dawson called as Cecelia headed out.

'Thank you.'

Oh, it was lonely indeed.

And painful.

Cecelia wanted her old life back.

The ordered one.

The one she'd had prior to meeting Luka Kargas.

She did not want to be a mother, and certainly not a single one, so she sobbed through the pain and rued her mistakes.

But then, at ten minutes past six on a spring morning, for the second time in her life, Cecelia fell in love.

The first time had been with Luka.

There had never been anyone else in her life she had felt that way about, no one who came close.

But second-time love was the absolute shock of her life, for as she pulled the infant from her stomach into her arms, the world, in an instant, was put to right.

She had a daughter.

A tiny daughter who was very pink with a shock of dark hair and her cry was lusty and loud.

Oh!

Cecelia had told herself during the pregnancy that even if she felt little now, love would one day grow.

Her baby would never feel as unloved as her mother had been, even if she had to fake it for a while.

Yet there was never a love less fake, for Cecelia utterly adored her baby girl on sight.

'Have you thought of names?' the midwife asked as Cecelia gazed at her child.

'I liked Emily,' Cecelia said.

That had been before she had met her, though.

That was before she had locked eyes with a tiny, dark-haired, dark-eyed girl.

Her secret.

A secret she must one day reveal, Cecelia knew that.

But not yet.

She did not want the beauty of this tiny life marred just yet, she did not want the rows and accusations that would surely follow such a revelation.

The DNA tests, the lawyers, the disdain.

Cecelia could envisage it.

And that was at best.

She had nothing in her past to predict otherwise, and so she was in no rush to reveal to the billionaire playboy that she had birthed his child.

And she knew now her daughter's name.

It was, Cecelia knew, absolutely the perfect name for her and as she first said it she kissed her baby's soft cheek.

'Pandora.'

CHAPTER NINE

SUMMER HAD RETURNED.

Luka had by far preferred the previous one.

But it was good to be home.

Yes, he thought of London as such.

Xanero was beautiful, and of course family was there, but it was London that was his true home.

Luka glanced up from the letter he was reading and looked out through tinted windows as his driver inched the car along the busy street.

He had been in London on occasion, but it been a hellish year on the private front, and the city had not been his base.

Amber, his ultra-efficient PA, had handed him a pile of personal correspondence and he wanted it dealt with before he turned his mind to work.

There was a pile of sympathy cards and letters that spoke of a hard-working family man that Luka did not recognise as his father.

'How was the funeral?' Amber asked.

'It went well,' Luka nodded.

Yesterday his father had been buried.

This time last year he had thought it would be his mother's funeral he would attend first, yet after months of intensive treatment and care, Sophie Kargas was doing well.

Luka had flown with her to Athens and after each treatment he would check them into the luxurious hotel he had there. Sophie had enjoyed the Princess Suite and had been treated exactly as that for the first time in her life.

'You could have this every day,' Luka had said. 'Say the word and I will take care of you and you will never have to deal with him.'

'I shall never do that, Luka,' his mother would reply.

Yet she was so much happier and lighter without him, and her decision to stay was something he would never quite understand.

And then, after each treatment, when her strength had returned they would go back to Xanero, where the new manager that Luka had hired would report directly to him.

Theo had reluctantly behaved, for he had been given no choice but to do so.

Luka had, quite literally, bought his mother a year of peace to focus on getting well.

There had been little peace for Luka, though—spending more time in Xanero had meant he'd been forced to face his demons.

No, he was not particularly proud of his start and he was tired too of the life he led.

And he regretted how he and Cece had parted.

Her decision to leave had been something he had not understood, in much the same way as his mother's decision to stay, and so he had hastened it. He had made sure she would not work out her notice and had her removed from his life in his usual style.

Yet he still thought about her each day.

And just when he had decided it was time to return to London, just when his life could get back on track and he was considering looking her up, completely out of the blue his father had died.

The funeral had been hell for Luka.

He had delivered the eulogy, and for his mother's sake he had spoken of the family man, his humble beginnings and the restaurant Theo had started. It had been a further rewriting of the past.

It was over with now.

'Is there anything—?' Amber started to ask.

But Luka cut in. 'Everything has been taken care of.'

His family life remained out of bounds to his PA.

Sabine had proved to be a nightmare.

He should have paid more attention when Cecelia had said there was something about her that she didn't like.

He had arrogantly assumed it was that Sabine was beautiful and had perhaps hoped that his hiring her would rouse a response in Cecelia.

Instead, his new PA had been the jealous one.

Sabine could not accept that he did not flirt and had no real interest in her, and when he had found her going through his private emails, he had fired her on the spot.

Amber had taken her place and, while she didn't speak Greek, he had no complaints. She was diligent and efficient and had no interest in sleeping her way to the top.

Yes, while there was nothing to complain about on the work front, he missed Cecelia.

In every way.

And never more so than this week.

He had arranged the funeral, dealt with the legalities and the only calls he had made to Amber had been regarding work.

His own mood even he could not begin to gauge.

There was a sense of relief tempered by unexpected grief.

He had no fond memories of his father, so it didn't really make sense, but there was a hollow feeling that resided within him now and an ache of sadness that he had not anticipated.

Yes, it had been a difficult year, though not on paper.

The talks with Garcia had become more productive and there was now a hotel and restaurant in Manhattan and another soon to open in Singapore. A lot of his time had been spent divided between Athens, where his mother had had her treatments, and Xanero, where she had recuperated in between.

The luxurious complex was large enough that he certainly had no need to temper his ways—after all, his family were hardly living over the fence.

He had tempered them, though.

Because he *still* wanted Cece.

Unable to face yet another sympathy card, he got back to staring out of the window.

And then Luka decided that it really had been too long, because he thought for a moment that a woman walking down the street might be her.

On too many occasions in the past year Luka had thought that he'd seen Cece.

Confidently he had once tapped a woman on the shoulder in a bar, and had then found himself staring into the wrong face.

But now, as he craned his neck for a better look, there was something about this woman's posture that held Luka's attention.

'Slow down,' he told his driver, because he no longer trusted himself to be certain when it came to her.

She looked slimmer, and the usually immaculate blonde hair that she wore tied back was more strawberry blonde and fell in untidy curls around her shoulders.

The uncertainty was short-lived, because he suddenly remembered the morning she had undressed for him and he had found out she was a redhead after all.

It really was her.

She wore a navy shift dress and flat sandals.

And it was not a designer handbag that was strapped to her shoulder.

From the way she held the sling, her burden seemed far more precious than that.

And then he saw her look down and smile and realised that she was holding a baby.

No!

He hauled himself back from the appalling assumption that the baby might be his and reminded himself that she had been a nanny once.

But she had told him how much she had hated it and had said she would never be a nanny again.

The baby was hers, Luka knew it, from the way she smiled down and caressed its head.

'No.'

He said it out loud this time and Amber looked up. 'Is everything okay?'

Luka didn't answer her, his mind was moving too fast.

It had been a year since he'd been with Cecelia.

Not quite to the day, although it would be soon.

And he remembered the very date of their parting.

Even the time.

It had been just after nine when she had left the building.

In fact, he recalled so many details.

Because life had got crazy since then, he told himself.

And life had just got a whole lot more complicated now.

'Pull over,' he instructed the driver. 'In fact, turn around.'

His driver did not point out that this busy street was not the place to execute a U-turn, and instead he complied.

Luka could feel the thump of his heart in his chest as he searched the pavement for another sight of her but she was nowhere to be seen.

His face remained impassive but his eyes scanned the crowd until he caught sight of her again and instructed his driver to pull over.

Safe from view behind tinted windows, he watched Cecelia.

She was certainly a touch slimmer than he remembered and, from what little he knew about pregnancy, if the baby was hers, shouldn't it be otherwise?

Luka took out his phone and the number he had considered calling far too many times was dialled now.

He watched as Cecelia reached for her phone.

'Hello?'

She would not know it was him, Luka realised, for after he had fired Sabine he'd had no choice but to change all his numbers.

'Cecelia.'

At the sound of his voice the world stopped.

The traffic, the noise, the shoppers on the busy street all faded to nothing at the sound of her name on his lips.

She knew instantly it was him, yet she did not reveal that. Instead, Cecelia played for time. 'Who's this?' she asked, and ran a nervous hand through her hair.

'Luka.'

'Oh.'

'Have I caught you at a bad time?'

'No, no, I'm just…' And he watched as she held the baby tighter to her, 'I'm actually on my lunch break.'

'Well, I need to speak with you. I was wondering if you could call by the office. There are a few issues we need to discuss.'

'Luka, I haven't worked for you in a year.'

'It's just a couple of accounting queries. Nothing serious but my accountant needs to verify a few things…' He wasn't even lying, because if indeed this was his baby there were certainly some things that needed to be discussed!

He was suddenly surprised that he hadn't already been fleeced.

'Can you come in?'

'I told you, I'm working.'

'After work,' Luka said. 'It won't take long. I'll have Marco stay back.'

'It's not terribly convenient.'

'Life isn't, is it?' he said, and ended the call.

She couldn't breathe.

In the middle of a packed London street she was as panicked as she had been on the day she had found out she was pregnant.

More so, for she hadn't loved her baby then.

He couldn't know about Pandora, Cecelia told herself.

No.

It must be work related.

Some document she hadn't signed or some expense that hadn't gone through.

After all, just last week she'd had to go into the diplomat's office and tie up a few loose ends.

Then, though, she had taken in Pandora.

She could hardly do the same with Luka.

Cecelia looked down at her tiny baby. The world was closing in and she knew she had to tell him.

Calmly.

She did not want Pandora to be exposed to any negative reaction, even if she was far too young to understand.

And for the very same reason, she would not be calling her aunt!

She arrived home all flustered, and of course Mrs Dawson wanted to stop for a chat.

'My daughter's just found out she's having twins!' Mrs Dawson said.

'How many grandchildren will that make?' Cecelia asked.

'Eight!' Mrs Dawson beamed. 'How's Pandora?'

'Wonderful,' Cecelia said, and watched as the old lady made Pandora smile.

'She's such a happy baby,' Mrs Dawson said. 'I never hear a peep.'

'Mrs Dawson…'

Cecelia loathed asking for help or being an imposition but she simply didn't know what else to do and Mrs Dawson had offered on several occasions.

'Could I ask you to look after Pandora for a couple of hours this afternoon?'

'I'd love to!'

'I'll pay you, of course.'

'You certainly won't. It will be my absolute pleasure.'

Why, oh, why could her aunt not have said that?

* * *

Cecelia dressed as if for an interview.

The navy suit was put on again for her visit to Kargas Holdings.

And even though she would only be gone for a couple of hours and Pandora had just been fed, she made up two bottles just in case. And her blanket and loads of nappies as well as Cecelia's phone number...

She was terribly nervous at the thought of leaving her, but Mrs Dawson was so friendly and seemed thrilled to have been asked.

'I really shan't be long,' Cecelia said. 'I just have to pop into work and I'll come straight back.'

'Pandora will be fine.'

And Pandora would be fine, Cecelia knew as she took the Tube.

But would *she* be?

Cecelia couldn't fathom what Luka's reaction might be, and she actually felt a little sick as she came out of the escalators and the building loomed up.

Cecelia could remember sitting in the café opposite and willing herself to go in and tell him.

She had no choice now.

The doorman smiled and then frowned and instead of waving her through she was told to go to Reception.

There a call was made and she stood with pink cheeks, feeling like one of his exes.

Which she was.

Sort of.

Finally, she received a visitor's pass and the code for the elevator.

Cecelia's hand was shaking as she punched in the numbers.

The air-conditioner should have been blissful, but

instead she could feel the sheen of perspiration on her face. She rubbed her palms on her skirt, just in case he decided to shake her hand.

As the elevator doors opened there was no Bridgette to greet her; instead, it was an unfamiliar woman who sat at Cecelia's old desk.

'I'll just let Luka know you're here,' she said. 'Perhaps you'd like to take a seat.'

'Actually, I think I'm seeing Marco. If you could let him know that I'm here...' She would get work out of the way and then she would speak with Luka, Cecelia decided.

'Marco?' She shook her head. 'He isn't in today.'

And then Cecelia heard Luka. 'I'll deal with this.'

For the first time in a year she felt his presence and she prickled all over at the sound of his voice.

Her head wanted to spin to face him but she resisted and instead slowly turned to him.

'Cecelia,' he greeted her.

'Luka.'

She had forgotten the absolute impact of him.

The year that had passed had dimmed him in a way she had not expected. His ruthlessness and playboy ways had been somewhat tempered by the memories of them in bed.

And he did not look in the least pleased to see her.

'Come through,' he said.

'But I thought I was seeing Marco.'

'I'm sure you soon will be,' Luka said as he led her through to his office. 'Please, take a seat.'

Cecelia was very glad to, for her legs felt as if they were made of rubber, and not just because she was nervous—yes, she had forgotten the absolute impact of him.

He looked incredible.

Gleaming was the word that came to mind.

His raven hair was worn shorter than she ever remembered it being and it accentuated his sharp features. He was tanned, and although there had never been an ounce of spare flesh on him he now looked leaner.

Meaner, Cecelia thought, and her heart kicked into a gallop, though she did her level best not to show it.

Yes, being away from him for a year had certainly tempered Luka in her mind, for now she was back she remembered her despair at his reckless ways; the constant stream of women; his wealth and the power that came with that.

And he was her baby's father.

There had never been a doubt as to that, of course, but only now, back in his world, did it truly hit home.

He had essentially fired her on the last occasion she had been here. He had had her marched out of his life over the smallest slight.

Cecelia thought of his legal team and the constant battles they waged, for he would step over anyone to get a property he wanted.

And he was Pandora's father!

Cecelia did her best to meet Luka's eyes, which seemed no longer a velvet brown but as black as night as they appraised her. There was no hint of a smile on his mouth.

'Where are you working?' Luka asked.

'At the same place that I left here for,' Cecelia answered.

'You never did say where.'

'Didn't I?'

Oh, let the games begin, Luka thought.

He was turned on and enjoying the silent fight.

He watched her pink tongue run a nervous path along her lips. He looked at her cool green eyes and he fought not to walk right around that desk and shake the news from her.

He was certain the baby was his.

Why?

Because there had been no one else since that night.

Nearly a whole damn year—and not for the lack of options or opportunity.

And if he hadn't screwed his way out of the problem, then he was certain that neither had she.

Whatever had happened that night, or rather that morning, had taken a lot to get over.

He still hadn't.

And now he knew why—this morning he had found out he was a father.

But he had only found out by chance.

'How have you been, Cecelia?' he asked.

'You mean since I was marched out of the office?'

'Please,' he dismissed, 'you exaggerate.'

'How did Sabine work out?' Cecelia asked, remembering again the humiliation of that morning.

'She didn't,' he said. 'In fact, I *did* have *her* marched out of the office and I considered taking a restraining order out against her at one point.'

'Well, if you will insist on mixing business…' Cecelia started, but then she faltered. She just could not stand the thought of him with Sabine enough to pursue her line. 'Where's Bridgette?'

'She's on annual leave.'

Well, at least that sounded nice and normal.

'So what is it that you want to see me about?' Cecelia asked.

'There were a couple of expense forms that were flagged and Marco needed—'

'Could he not have emailed?'

'I guess,' Luka said, 'but I wanted to see you myself.'

She could not tell him now, Cecelia knew, for she simply couldn't make herself say it. She could barely look him in the eye, let alone tell him news that would turn his world upside down. Or maybe it wouldn't.

She needed to think this through properly, because Luka didn't play nice, she well knew it.

Luka Kargas had an entire legal team that worked on his behalf and if he decided she was the enemy then God help her.

Cecelia knew she must leave and go and get some proper advice and then she would tell him. 'Well, if you can have Marco email me when he's next in…' She picked up her bag. 'Anything else?'

'I'm not sure,' Luka said. 'Why don't we go and get dinner and catch up?'

'I don't think so.'

'A drink perhaps?'

'No.'

'It's been almost a year,' Luka said.

'How sweet that you remembered.' She gave a tight smile. 'You must celebrate a lot of one-night-stand anniversaries.' It looked like she could not do this without it descending into a row. 'Luka…' She stood. 'I'm going to go.'

The door looked a very long way off when Cecelia turned to face it. She had no idea the game he was playing but, whatever it was, she wanted out.

No way could she watch the anger flare in his features, for already the air was thick with tension.

But a tension she could not define.

Sex, with a dash of…

Cecelia didn't know what and she would not be staying to find out.

Her hand was on the handle of the door when he called to her.

'Have you forgotten something?' Luka asked.

Foolishly, she patted her bag. 'No.'

'I meant,' he said in a voice that was like a dagger wrapped in velvet, 'did you forget to tell me about my baby?'

The caress of his voice and then the knife to her back.

Her back was to him, but if there had been any doubt Luka knew now for certain that the baby was his, for her shoulders stiffened, followed by the slight buckle of her knees before she righted herself, although she still did not turn around.

'Sit down, Cecelia,' Luka said.

She did not follow orders any more.

Instead she stood there, trying to fathom how he knew. And, given that he did, Luka's reaction was the antithesis of anything she had expected. Cecelia had been sure that when she told him, the majority of any ensuing discussions would be convincing him that Pandora was his.

She was unprepared for this. Her reactions when around Luka were always extreme for he turned her from ordered to chaotic, and so, instead of turning around and calmly facing him, Cecelia wrenched open the door.

'Don't you dare walk off,' Luka warned in an ominous voice.

Except that was exactly what Cecelia did.

The was no one at her old desk and no one at Reception as she swiftly made her way through the vast space.

There was just the gleam of furniture and the scent of flowers in the air as she headed speedily for the lift.

She desperately wanted distance between them. She pressed the button for the lift, yet no light came on to indicate that it was on its way.

Cecelia pressed it again.

No, the lifts weren't out, she quickly realised, Luka must have changed the code! Usually it was altered to stop ex-lovers making their way up to him, never to prevent them from getting out!

Well, she'd take the fire escape, Cecelia decided, and turned angrily in time to see Luka calmly walking towards her.

'Come and sit down, Cecelia, and we will talk.'

'I'll take the stairs.'

'You can try.' Luka shrugged.

Cecelia knew he'd have no scruples about going after her and hauling her straight back.

'You can't keep me here, Luka,' she shouted. 'You had me come to the office under false pretences and you have no right—'

Oh, she knew she had said the wrong thing for even Cecelia stopped in mid-sentence as he walked towards her.

'Don't you dare speak to me about *rights* when you have denied me mine,' Luka warned, and he came so close that she shrank back against the cool wall of the elevator. 'Now you are to get back to my office so we can talk.'

'Luka…' she attempted. 'I was going to tell you.'

'I don't want to hear your lies and excuses,' he said. 'I don't care what you *might* have been going to do. I want to know about my child.'

'But I have to get back to her.'

She watched his jaw grit and the angry purse of his beautiful mouth as she realised that he had only just found out that their baby was a girl.

And Cecelia knew in that instant that she would never be forgiven for keeping Pandora from him.

'Luka, I know we have to talk and I understand that you're angry but I really can't do this now.'

'When then?' he demanded. 'On her eighteenth birthday? Or perhaps when your money has run out and you want to claim your meal ticket?'

'Luka, please.'

He watched as the ordered Cecelia put her hands to her ears.

'I can't row now.'

She was muddled, caught, confused.

And it wasn't just that he already knew.

The impact of being close to him again was an utter assault to her senses.

For the best part of a year she had fought not to think of him. Now that she faced him, worst of all, she was the liar and the guilty party.

'It's my first time away from her.'

A pathetic excuse perhaps, only it was the truth and it was killing her.

'Is she with your aunt?'

'God, no!' The words shot out and then she looked up at him. 'She's with my neighbour. Luka, I know we need to talk, I accept that, but it's not going to be wrapped up in an hour.'

'You clearly don't get it, Cecelia. Whatever the location, whatever the time, I shall be meeting my daughter tonight. You have denied me my rights for long enough.'

Cecelia had seen him like this before, though it had been in the workplace, and she knew Luka well enough to know that arguing would be futile. But aside from that, he was completely right—she had denied him his rights long enough.

'We can go to your home,' Luka said, 'or we can speak here or at mine, and then you take me to meet her or have her brought to me. But before you decide, know this, Cecelia. If you refuse to take me to my daughter, then the next contact we have shall be via a lawyer. I don't currently employ an expert in family law, but my team is already looking into it. Mess up again and the best shall be retained.' He saw her already pale skin go even paler but he felt no guilt. None at all. And he told her why. 'You started this, Cecelia.'

'Do you blame me?'

'Yes,' Luka swiftly answered. 'I blame you completely.'

CHAPTER TEN

CECELIA CHOSE HOME.

The drive to her flat had been a silent one. She had tried to speak once, to tell him his daughter's name, but he had told her to save it.

'If I want to know anything, I will ask.'

Right now, Luka had enough to process. He had a child. A girl.

He had been a father for three months and not known.

He could not deal with even one more piece of information that had been kept from him or he might just lose it.

Things would be at his pace from this point on and if Cecelia could take her time then so could he!

'I thought you said we needed to talk,' Cecelia pushed, wanting as much as possible out of the way before they got home.

'Well, I've changed my mind,' Luka said. 'It's too late for all that.'

Luka actually felt ill at the thought that anything could have happened to his daughter and he wouldn't have known.

He looked over at Cecelia, who sat opposite him, and he thought of the secret she had kept from him and that only by chance had he found out.

White hot was the rage that seared through Luka and he was doing his level best to contain it.

'We're here,' Cecelia said as his driver pulled up close to the main door to her flat. But as the driver came round and opened the door, Luka didn't immediately get out.

Luka, who could face anything, was for the first time nervous at the prospect of what lay ahead, for in a moment he would meet his daughter for the first time.

'Aren't you coming in?' Cecelia asked.

'Of course I am.' Luka shot Cecelia a look of contempt. 'I'm hardly going to meet her in the street.'

She could feel his loathing as he entered her small flat. She hadn't noticed how messy it was when she had headed out.

Cecelia noticed now.

The ordered world she had once inhabited, one where she put out her clothes for the next morning the night before, had long since gone. The tiny bundle that she had birthed meant that she lurched from one feed to the next and grabbed a quick shower and a scrape of her comb through her hair in the short bursts when Pandora slept.

Cecelia did not attempt a rapid tidy.

Instead, she glanced at the magazines on the coffee table to distract her anxious thoughts. There were some colic drops too and a couple of mugs, and some baby blankets strewn across the sofa—the aftermath of a difficult night.

It had been a difficult, yet wonderful three months.

She was permanently exhausted and lonely too. She was barely speaking with her aunt and uncle and she was not exactly inundated with friends. The few Cecelia had were either single or child-free by choice. There had been cards, flowers and visits when Pandora had first

been born, but, understandably they did not want their
Sunday brunches pierced by a baby's cries and Cecelia
didn't have space in her brain for decent conversation.

She was a mother.

A new one.

Yet she had a three-month head start on Luka.

'Would you like…?' Cecelia started but Luka wasn't
here for a chat and neither would he be taking a seat.

'Could you fetch my daughter, please?'

'Of course.'

Mrs Dawson was nosy enough that she would have
seen the expensive car pull up and know that Cecelia
had a guest, and so she didn't invite her in for a chat.

'She was as good as gold,' Mrs Dawson said, as she
handed Pandora over. 'Fell asleep in my arms.'

'Thank you so much.'

'And she's just been fed,' Mrs Dawson said as she
collected up her things.

Pandora was wrapped in a soft lilac blanket and Cecelia held her close and inhaled the delicious baby scent.
Oh, yes, her tiny world was changing and Cecelia did
not want to let her go. Having thanked Mrs Dawson,
she headed across the hall but Pandora picked up on her
tension and started to cry.

Good, Cecelia thought, even as she moved to hush
her. *Let him see how it really is. Tell me off, write your
cheque and be gone.* For she could not deal with the
thought of handing Pandora over to him. And, no, she
did not want her daughter spending weekends and holidays with a father who partied just as hard as he worked.

As she stepped into the lounge he was there waiting, so tailored and exquisite and with angry black eyes.
She could not believe that Luka was really in her home.

He did not belong here.

Luka belonged in his office castle or creating merry hell aboard his yacht.

The expensive scent, the stunning suit all felt like too much to process right now.

Her child's father was a reckless playboy, and in her arms she held the consequence of their one night together.

She soothed Pandora as Luka stood watching but he made no move to come over. 'I really was going to tell you,' she told him.

'Then why didn't you when I called you earlier today?'

'I was standing in the street!'

He heard the urgent sincerity in her voice and for the first time today he knew she was telling the truth. Cecelia did not know he had been watching her when she had taken the call.

Still, the grain of honesty from her barely appeased him for it accounted only for a few seconds of the past year.

'Why didn't you say anything back in the office?' he asked as he gazed at the bundle she held in her arms. Really he could see only the blanket and he was playing for time, nervous now to meet her.

'I couldn't do it face to face.' Another truth, not that he believed her, Cecelia could see. 'I tried to call you a couple of times during the pregnancy. I couldn't get through.'

'You didn't try very hard.'

'No,' she admitted.

'Why?'

That she couldn't really answer but she tried. 'I was scared of your reaction. I thought you'd tell me to get rid of her, or say that I'd tried to trap you by getting pregnant...'

'I was there that morning, Cecelia. I do know how babies are made and that it takes two.'

It was the closest she had come to a smile since facing him again, but Luka did not see it. He had no interest in the past right now, for in that second the small blanket slipped a little and he saw a shock of dark hair and a pale cheek and suddenly he forgot how to breathe. There in his chest it felt as if an iron fist had sunk in.

He walked over and Cecelia felt him enter her space—only it had nothing to do with her, simply the infant she held in her arms.

She watched one, long, olive finger come and tenderly stroke the little baby's cheek. 'Can I hold her?'

'She's a bit unsettled...'

'I was only asking, to be polite,' Luka said, and now he no longer asked—he told her instead in a voice that was calm but the words hit like sleet. *'Give my baby to me.'*

She handed Pandora to him and he took her into his arms, more skilfully than she had predicted—because, of course, she had imagined how her baby would look in his arms. She watched him cradle his daughter and carefully take a seat on the couch as his eyes never left Pandora's face.

'What name did *you* choose for her?' he asked, and Cecelia heard the scold in his tone.

He would change it if he did not like it, Luka decided.

How dared she take such an important choice from him?

There were tears at the back of her nose and throat and she had to swallow before she could respond. 'Pandora.'

But he would not be changing it, for the second he heard the name Luka loved it.

It meant 'all gifts', which indeed she was, and it was Greek and…

He let out a soft, yet not quite mirthless laugh. He had decided a caustic response was his to make, yet none came, for the name was completely perfect as for the first time Pandora opened her eyes to look at him.

They were navy and surrounded by spiky black lashes and she simply stared up at her father and met his gaze.

Luka pushed back the pale blanket to reveal more dark hair and he looked at her pretty rosebud mouth. For the first time in his life he felt the threat of tears.

Luka had never held a baby, let alone thought he might father one.

Now he held a daughter he had only found out existed today. His free hand held hers, looking at the slender fingers and tiny nails. Then he traced her eyebrows and imprinted her beauty on his mind—her little mouth and the soft pink of her skin—and when she stared back at him with sleepy navy eyes Pandora gave him a smile.

Her eyelashes seemed too heavy and he watched as she closed her eyes in sleep and he simply breathed in the baby scent of her and the miracle of her existence.

And had her mother got her way, Luka would never have known she was here.

Any tenderness left his eyes as he looked up at Cecelia. 'Pandora indeed,' Luka said. 'However, your secret is out now.'

'I really was going to tell you—'

'Save it.'

'Honestly Luka, when I first found out—'

'Save it,' he said again. 'I won't have this moment marred by your lies and I won't have this discussion in front of our child.' Then he looked down at Pandora. 'Perhaps it is time to put her down.'

He stood and Cecelia nodded and held out her arms to take Pandora but Luka did not simply hand her over. 'I can take her to the nursery.'

'Nursery!' She let out a wry laugh. 'Luka, it's a one-bedroomed flat, not a penthouse apartment.'

While true, there was a small study that could be turned into a nursery in the future, but for now Pandora had been sleeping in with her. Cecelia could not bear the thought of her daughter waking up and crying in the dark alone.

Luka handed over Pandora but Cecelia would not, or could not, meet his eyes. She just held her daughter close to her and headed for the bedroom.

She knew he was furious.

Cecelia was furious with herself.

She should have told him at the very least in his office but she had panicked.

Now she had no one to blame but herself for the situation she found herself in.

Cecelia put Pandora down. Unlike last night, when she had protested every time she had been lowered to the mattress, now Pandora made not a sound.

She stared at her for a moment, aware that Luka stood in the doorway, watching them.

He wanted to know his daughter's routines and things like how to put a tiny baby to sleep. All of this was completely alien to him.

He saw that Cecelia covered her with a blanket and then kissed her fingers and placed them on the baby's head before turning to leave the bedroom.

'I don't want to argue...' Cecelia said as she walked past him.

They moved into the hallway and she awaited the interrogation, but instead it seemed he was about to leave.

'You're going?' Cecelia checked, not really believing that was it, but he was heading for the front door.

'Yes, it has been a long day,' Luka said. 'I just returned from Greece this morning.'

He had been on his way back from the airport when he had seen her.

It felt like a lifetime ago.

'I was there for my father's funeral.'

It was as if the carpet beneath her feet had turned into a flying one, for she felt the jolt of the ground and the world tip off kilter.

She had known she would never be forgiven by Luka, but what he had just revealed told her that it was a certain fact now.

His father had died without knowing he had a granddaughter.

'I'm sorry,' Cecelia attempted.

'Oh, no, you're not,' Luka said. 'How could you be when you did not know him?'

She looked into his eyes, which were not entirely unreadable for she could see the loathing there.

'When do you want to see her again?' Cecelia attempted.

'Tomorrow,' Luka responded crisply. 'A car will be here for you at nine in the morning.'

'A car?' Cecelia checked. 'Am I to bring her to you or?'

'I am taking Pandora to Xanero tomorrow. Naturally, I would like my mother to meet her granddaughter.'

'Luka, no…' She reached and caught his arm but he shook her hand off as if he could not bear the slightest touch from her. 'She's not ready to travel.'

'Why ever not?' he demanded.

'She doesn't have a passport.'

'I have a contact at the embassy and an urgent one can be arranged on our way to the airport.'

'No! She's not ready.'

'Pandora is three months old and shall be travelling on my private jet accompanied by her mother. I don't see any issue.'

'I might have plans tomorrow,' Cecelia attempted.

To no avail.

'Then cancel them.'

'Luka, I'm not trying to keep you from her. You can see Pandora tomorrow, of course you can, but you can't just walk in here and tell me that tomorrow I have to leave for Greece...'

'Are you quite sure about that?' Luka checked. 'Because the way I see it, tomorrow you can either get on a plane and head to a luxurious resort for a week...'

'A week?' Cecelia gulped.

He nodded. 'There you shall be catered for and beautifully looked after. Once there, the best nannies will be available to assist as I get to know my daughter and her grandmother meets her.' He frowned as if bemused by Cecelia. 'I thought you would jump at the chance.'

'No!'

'So you would rather spend the next few days in court? When the outcome will be the same—Pandora will be coming to Xanero, my lawyers will see to that.'

She felt sick.

It was like David and Goliath, except she wasn't the good guy here and the courts might well agree.

She would be portrayed as the bitch who had kept him from his child, up against the might of Luka Kargas.

She had lost already, Cecelia knew as she watched

him walk down the small garden path, brushing against weeds and neglected overgrown bushes because for the past months gardening had been the furthest thing from her mind.

'I'll see you tomorrow!' he called. 'Be ready.'

And even if Luka was in no mood to speak, even if she had no right to an answer, Cecelia did have a question.

'How did you know?' she called out to the dark and watched him halt. She was not asking how he had known about the baby; she was asking how he had been so certain that Pandora was his.

'How did I know?' Luka checked exactly what she was asking as he turned around. 'Are you going to try and drag things out with a DNA test to keep her from me even longer?'

'Of course not. But most men would demand one. I'm just asking why you're so certain…' Her voice trailed off as he walked back toward her, and then he came and stood closer to her than he had all evening.

So close that she could feel his breath on her cheek as he answered the question.

'I know, Cecelia, because when your legs were wrapped tight around me…' She was dizzy from lack of oxygen and she could feel his breath warm her cheek as he painted a vivid picture. 'When I screwed you slow and deep and came inside you,' he continued and her neck was rigid and her eyes screwed closed as he taunted her with the vision of them, 'you may recall that I was unsheathed.'

'Luka…' She begged with a single word that he stop. He did not.

'And given how long it took to get inside you, I doubt you went from my bed straight to someone else's. And,' he continued, 'given your abhorrence that we did not use protection, I would guess that lapse was as rare for you as it was for me.'

His voice was a taunt, both sensual and cruel as he took her back to that night. 'That is how I know,' he said, and then the thick, rich voice stopped and he pulled back and looked at her face, flushed in the porch light, confusion darting in her eyes.

He confused her, he excited her and made her want to sink to her knees and run, all at the same time.

But then he made things abundantly clear.

'We were so hot, Cecelia, and we could have been good, but you chose to walk away. You left. And then you denied me the knowledge of my child and I hate you for that.' And then, when she'd already got the dark message, he gave it a second coat and painted it black. 'I absolutely hate you.'

'No mixed messages, then?' She somehow managed a quip but there was nothing that could lighten this moment.

'Not one. Let me make things very clear. I am not taking you to Greece to get to know you better, or to see if there is any chance for us, because there isn't. I want no further part of you. The fact is, you are my daughter's mother and she is too young to be apart from you. That won't be the case in the near future.'

'How near?'

Fear licked the sides of her heart.

'I don't know.' He shrugged. 'I know nothing about babies, save what I have found out today. But I learn fast,' he said, 'and I will employ only the best so very soon, during my access times, Pandora and I will do just fine without you.'

'Luka, please…' She could not stand the thought of

being away from Pandora and she was spinning at the thought of taking her daughter to Greece, but Luka was done.

'I'm going, Cecelia,' Luka said. 'I have nothing left to say to you.'

That wasn't quite true, for he had one question.

'Did you know you were pregnant when you left?' Luka asked.

'I had an idea...'

'The truth, Cecelia.'

And she ached now for the days when he had been less on guard and had called her Cece, even though it had grated so much at the time.

And now it was time to be honest and admit she had known she was pregnant when she had left. 'Yes.'

'But,' Luka pointed out, 'given we hadn't slept together then, your resignation had nothing to do with the pregnancy.'

That was another part that stung, Luka thought as his driver opened the door to his car—she'd been leaving already.

CHAPTER ELEVEN

Silence was cruel.

Where once there would have been conversation…
where once he had annoyed her by shortening her
name…now that delicious voice was no longer aimed
at her.

As promised, a car arrived at nine but, rather than
Luka, it was his latest PA who got out. She introduced
herself as Amber and gave Cecelia a very efficient
smile when she raised a question and assured her that
of course there was a baby seat in the car.

The driver dealt with her bags but Luka barely
looked up when she strapped in Pandora.

He was wearing khaki linen pants and a black T-
shirt—more casually dressed than she had ever seen
him—yet he certainly cut a dash. He was wearing
shades and looked very sullen, and only when Pandora was safely strapped in did he acknowledge them.

Cecelia got a brief nod.

For Pandora, he took off his shades and she got the
benefit of his full smile, a kiss on the forehead and the
warmth of his voice.

Cecelia watched as Pandora smiled and cooed up at
him and seemed to know him already.

He looked tired, Cecelia noted.

Beautiful, but very tired and she thought of the past few days he must have had, with his father dying and finding out that he had a daughter. Yet he turned on the smiles for Pandora. She had never thought this side to Luka existed, but then again she too had fallen in love with Pandora at first sight.

As they were driven to the embassy, the incredibly efficient Amber addressed Cecelia.

'The accommodation has all been arranged but anything that you or Pandora need, please just make me aware.'

Cecelia gave a curt nod.

That used to be her world, Cecelia thought—taking care of Luka's ex-lovers and all the ensuing dramas their trysts had created.

Admittedly, she hadn't been in Amber's situation, sorting out the sudden news that her boss had a baby, but Amber was handling the situation as if it happened every day.

Oh, please let him not have slept with her, Cecelia thought as Amber carried on with her questions. 'The chef has asked if there are any food issues or allergies?'

'No.' Cecelia shook her head, then tried to soften her terse response. 'I can eat anything…'

But that wasn't what Amber had been asking—'I meant are there any allergies or issues with Pandora?'

She glanced over at Luka, who was staring out of the window. She saw the ghost of a smile on his lips as she was put in her place.

This wasn't about the mother!

'Pandora drinks formula,' Cecelia tartly responded. 'I hardly need a gourmet chef to prepare her bottles.'

'Well, I do,' Luka said, and turned to look right at

her. 'So, please answer the questions correctly. From this day forward I need to know such things.'

Cecelia briefly closed her eyes. 'No,' she answered. 'Pandora has no allergies that I know of.'

'Good,' he said, and then got back to looking out of the window.

The embassy was efficient.

The flight was, for Cecelia, an emotional hell.

There was seemingly no strained atmosphere on his part, for he simply carried on as if she were not there.

His jet was luxurious and Cecelia knew it well, though it felt very different today. Instead of joining Luka at the table for a meal and talking work, once Pandora had been fed and settled, her meal was served in an area to the rear of the lounge.

The food was no doubt sublime, but Cecelia, who had earlier said she'd eat anything, just pushed it around her plate. She felt awkward as she dined alone while Luka and Amber sat at the table and went through the sudden changes to his schedule.

That used to be me, Cecelia thought.

Her old life seemed a very long way off right now. So much was different, but how she felt about Luka remained.

All she had put on hold by leaving, all she had attempted to erase by distance, had come flooding back.

Quite simply, Luka Kargas was as devastatingly stunning to Cecelia as he had been the day they had met.

Motherhood had changed an awful lot of things, but it seemed it hadn't changed that one thing in the slightest.

With the meals cleared away, Cecelia dozed, one ear trained to listen out for Pandora.

Amber was busy on the computer and, though tired, Luka knew he was too wired to sleep.

He walked over to the bassinet and looked at the daughter he had met just yesterday.

Pandora was perfection.

Her tiny nails were trim and neat as her fingers closed around his. And she wore a little white cotton baby suit dotted with daisies.

And then he looked over at her mother and this time his face did not harden.

Cecelia wore a grey linen dress that was rather crumpled, and he noticed her once immaculate hair needed a cut. There were grey smudges beneath her eyes and even her lips were too pale.

It was as if all Cece's colour, all her energy had drained into Pandora and the anger in him dimmed a notch when he thought of all she must have been through.

And then she must have felt him watching her, for Cecelia opened her eyes and met his.

'Why don't you go and lie down?' Luka suggested.

'Pandora's due to wake soon.'

'I'll be here.'

She felt dismissed as she was shown to a cabin, though it was utter bliss to lie down after a night spent frantically packing for Xanero.

A light touch to her arm jolted Cecelia awake. She got up from the bed and headed to the main cabin for the final descent into Xanero.

Thanks to rather too many searches on the Internet as she'd attempted to put together the mystery of him, Cecelia actually recognised the island from the air. She saw white Orthodox churches with their round domes, and the sprawling whitewashed buildings that gleamed against the backdrop of an azure Mediterranean.

They landed behind the sprawling complex and were driven in air-conditioned comfort to the villa that would be her home for the next week.

Luka got out and it was he who held Pandora as he pushed open a large cobalt-blue door and stood back as Cecelia stepped in.

It was stunning, with mosaic-tiled floors, huge couches and an endless view of the ocean, but she could not take it all in with Luka there.

'I'll be fine.'

'I want to check you have everything you need for Pandora.'

There was everything she could possibly need and a whole lot more should she possibly want it. She even had her own pool, Cecelia noticed as she looked out. Then she thought of Luka and his start in life and there was both jealousy and anger combined as she thought of him chatting up women.

Of course she said nothing, just remained quiet as he showed her around, until they came to what was clearly a nursery.

There was a room with white organza fluttering in the windows and a heavy dark wooden crib made up in white bedlinen. There was a little intercom on a table, and it was a long way off from the main suite.

'Pandora sleeps in with me.'

'I have had an identical room made up in my villa,' Luka said. 'The nanny suggested that it might help for her surroundings to be familiar when Pandora is with me.'

Yes, it made perfect sense, but she felt with her heart,

not her head. 'I would like her crib moved through to my room.'

'As you wish,' Luka said.

'And she's too young to be away from me overnight.'

'You're not breastfeeding,' he pointed out.

'Another black mark…'

'Oh, grow up,' he retorted.

'Luka, I don't want her waking up in the night and me not being there.' She was starting to panic, and that was something she did not want Luka to see, but she could remember waking up and calling out for her mother in the night and she would not put Pandora through the same. 'I am not having her apart from me.'

'You worry about a night spent away from your daughter, yet your silence sentenced me to three months without her. You denied me the chance to plan for her, or see my child when she was born…so don't start complaining about one night. Cecelia, it is time to get used to the fact that I am her father and I'm not going anywhere.'

He saw her throat tighten as she swallowed and caught her rapid blink and then watched as Cecelia sat down.

'Are you okay?'

'I'm just warm…'

He frowned because it was shady and cool in here and the journey had certainly been a comfortable one.

'I was up all night, packing, trying to make sure I had everything…'

'I told you that I would take care of all that.'

'Well, I'm not very used to…'

Cecelia stopped.

She was rather too used to having to take care of everything and could not quite get her head around the fact there was now someone else.

It both unsettled her and comforted her.

The decisions regarding Pandora felt so huge at times. Even giving up the breast for a bottle had been angst-ridden.

Never had she imagined that had Luka known about Pandora she might have been able to discuss it with him.

It wasn't the heat that had unsettled her, or exhaustion.

His words had hit like shrapnel buried deep and she sat there as he poured some iced water and then handed it to her.

Yet she could not think about how his words had effected her now.

'I guessed you wouldn't have time for shopping so Amber is sorting you out a wardrobe…'

'I can dress myself, Luka.'

'Well, there's not much call for navy suits here…'

It was a dig at her staid wardrobe.

'You don't know me out of work.'

'Oh, but I can guess.'

He was right.

Cecelia had sat on her bedroom floor with her suitcase last night and known that the truth was she had nothing to pack for a holiday.

Not really.

But then he surprised her.

'I apologise,' Luka said suddenly. 'That was uncalled-for. How you dress is your concern.'

It was a rather backhanded apology and she gave a small mirthless laugh.

'I've lost weight since last year,' Cecelia said. 'And finding a capsule wardrobe so I can swan off to Greece at a moment's notice hasn't exactly been high on my list of priorities.'

'Then it's lucky that it's being taken care of,' he said, and she nodded. 'Is there anything else you need?'

'No.'

'There is a spa and a salon. You don't need an appointment. I have told them to accommodate you whenever you so choose. And there is the restaurant and a table reserved solely for you for the duration of your stay. Naturally, if you would prefer to dine here, just say.'

Cecelia nodded.

'When she wakes up, if you call the number by the phone you will be put through to the nanny, who will come and fetch Pandora.'

'How can you have arranged a nanny so quickly? Luka, I'm not just handing her over to someone you've hired in a rush…'

'There are several nannies at this resort and, given the clientele, we hire only the best. The best of the best shall be caring for my daughter. Her name is Roula and she has worked here for more than five years and was once the private nanny to royalty. You didn't check with me before you left her with a neighbour, and I did not question that choice either. I assume you want the best for her. Please afford me the same courtesy and never again suggest that I don't have my daughter's interests at heart.'

He gave the sleeping Pandora a light kiss and handed her over before striding off. Cecelia sat there, holding her daughter, his words playing over and over in her head.

I'm not going anywhere.

They were words she had never expected to hear, and she was scared to believe them.

Fair enough, he was angry now about being kept in

the dark, but when that anger had faded, when Pandora was teething and screaming deep in the night…

Yes, it felt like shrapnel was making its way to the surface as she recalled the fear of waking up in a house with no one there.

Pushing open her mother's bedroom door and seeing the empty bed.

Creeping downstairs, ears straining for the sound of chatter and laughter and bracing herself to be scolded for disturbing the grown-ups.

But no one had been there.

She had never known when her mother would be back, and then one day she hadn't been. Cecelia held her daughter tight and swore she would never know the same.

Cecelia jumped as the sound of a soft bell reverberated through the villa.

At the door stood Amber and two porters, along with another woman who was sultry looking and wore a sarong.

'Luka said you wouldn't have time to pack,' Amber said as she breezed in with the porters, who carried a whole lot of designer bags. 'They won't be long…'

She was mildly grateful to Luka for the excuse he had given Amber.

'And this is Roula.' Amber introduced them. 'The nanny.'

Oh, my!

When Luka had said she'd been a nanny for royalty, somehow Cecelia had imagined a crisp white dress and big black rubber shoes.

Instead, the nanny was barefoot and stunning.

'Luka suggested that I come over and meet you,' Roula said. 'You can tell me your daughter's ways and anything I need to know and hopefully meeting me will make things easier on you.'

It would be easier if she wasn't so stunning.

Pandora woke up and smiled when Roula first met her and didn't cry when she was held.

'Sophie—Luka's mother—is so excited to meet her,' Roula said. 'After such a sad loss there is sunshine again.'

There was no more putting it off, and all too soon she watched as the gorgeous Roula headed off with her daughter.

And it hurt.

Not just that they were apart, more that there was a grandmother excited to meet Pandora, a family gathering taking place from which she was excluded.

After they had gone, she opened the huge dark wooden dresser to see what clothes had been chosen for her and glimpsed an array of terribly sexy one-piece swimming suits cut high in the leg with plunging backs.

She did not belong in this world.

There was a rose-gold bikini that Cecelia held for a moment, though could never imagine putting on, and she realised that there was colour now lining her wardrobe.

There was a rose-gold silk dress too, in the same fabric as the bikini, a sensual throw-on for when you dined by the pool, Cecelia guessed.

And there were fragrances and oils by the bath.

Heaven knew, she needed them.

Her habits had long since slipped by the wayside. First to go had been her routine foils and so now her hair was back to its original strawberry blonde, with some rather long dry ends.

And she had long since stopped straightening it.

So much for looking sleek and together when she faced him and told him about Pandora.

Instead he had found out on his own.

And now, here in Xanero, she faced his wrath.

CHAPTER TWELVE

PARADISE WAS LONELY without him.

She called for lunch and ate in the villa and then, after a doze, she put on the most modest of the swimming costumes, took a book outside and read by the pool.

The book didn't pull her in, though.

All too often Cecelia found herself looking up and thinking of Luka and his misspent youth.

And so she gave in, tied on a sarong and went for a walk along Luka's private beach.

The Mediterranean shimmered like an endless sapphire and the white sand was pristine, but there was no solace there either.

For Luka's yacht was moored in the distance and she thought of the morning he had invited her to join him.

As his plaything.

They were poles apart yet eternally joined by a daughter they clearly both loved.

She had thought she'd known hell before.

Working alongside him, while loving him had been torture.

But this was worse. It did not cease at the end of the working day and there would be no annual leave.

Instead, this was her future.

He was now a permanent part of her life.

So far, he hadn't put a foot wrong, but soon she would have to deal with the glamorous beauties and his tawdry social life.

Some time soon, Cecelia was sure of it, there would be his latest long-limbed beauty lying on the sun lounger, or splashing in the water beside him with *her* daughter.

And there was no escape from that.

Pandora would talk one day and no doubt she would hear about daddy's new friends.

So Cecelia returned to the poolside to brood and that was how he found her.

She was huddled under the shade as if the sun might bite and the pool and poolside were pristine from lack of use. She startled when she looked up and saw him.

He wore only bathers and carried Pandora with a muslin cloth over her. She was asleep against his chest.

And she wore only a nappy.

'Pandora should be covered in the sun…' Cecelia chastised.

'And she is,' Luka pointed out. 'She fell asleep on the walk over here. Shall I put her down?'

Cecelia nodded and held open the door to the villa. His hair was wet and she knew he'd been in the pool.

'You didn't have Pandora by the pool, did you?' Cecelia checked.

'Of course I did, but we were always in the shade and she loved the water.'

'You took her in!' There was horror in her voice as she followed him through the villa. 'Luka, she's far too young.'

'Pandora adored it.'

She was appalled—in fact, Cecelia was furious, but she held her tongue as he tenderly lowered his daughter.

Pandora was clearly exhausted.

She barely stirred as he lightly covered her with the muslin, and as Luka walked off he tried not to glance at the large bed, or Cecelia's rumpled dress flung over the chair.

And a pile of bikinis that she'd clearly tried on and discarded.

He kept having to remind himself how furious he was, yet this woman was a constant turn-on.

Out of her bedroom, he headed to the fridge and pulled out a bottle of wine and selected two glasses.

'This is my villa,' Cecelia pointed out, not liking his bold intrusion.

'Okay, you serve, then,' he said, and handed her the bottle and glasses. 'I'll be outside.'

God, he was arrogant, Cecelia thought, and spent five minutes trying to find a corkscrew before she worked out it was a screw top.

Her temper was still bubbling, and yet it was clear he was here to talk. Well, as long as he was prepared to listen too because there was no way he was taking Pandora in the pool again.

She walked outside but it wasn't the glare of the sun that had her momentarily close her eyes.

It was his beauty.

Practically naked, except for black trunks slung low on his hips, he lay on a lounger.

He had a restless energy to him that she recognised from a year of working alongside him, and she felt a flutter of nerves low in her stomach as she approached.

She poured him a glass of wine and sparkling water for herself and then she suppressed a smile at his *You serve, then* comment.

'Here,' she said, and handed him the glass. 'Luka, we need to talk about Pandora...'

'I know we do and it's the only reason I'm here,' he said, more to remind himself, for he was on slow boil for Cece—or Cecelia as he would remember to call her now.

'How was your mother with her?'

'They got on wonderfully. She's thrilled to have a granddaughter...' He kept trying to be angry, but the truth was, it felt as if there was less and less to be angry about. 'She is concerned for you, and all that you must have been through alone.'

'Oh.'

Luka was too.

But there was something else concerning him and it was something that urgently needed to be discussed.

'I've been speaking with my PR people in the UK and it would seem that there is a lot of press interest in me at the moment.'

Cecelia felt her heart sink.

'With my father's death and the new hotels...' He didn't bother to explain it all but Cecelia got the gist.

The press would love to get their hands on the billionaire playboy now a father.

He read her concern. 'It is secure here, that I can assure you. Nobody can get a photo while you are in the complex, I took care of that long ago. The only risky place is my yacht.'

'Well, I shan't be going there!' She gave a tight smile. 'But, even so, I can't be expected to stay behind the wall...'

'Firstly, it is hardly a prison complex. There are miles of walks and you have access to my private beach. You are hardly going to be confined to four walls. You can take Pandora for a walk in the village if you feel you want to get out. I doubt a mother and baby will raise much interest.'

'I mean, if she's seen with you. Oh, God!' She stood and looked out to sea as if a thousand cameras were trained on them.

'I've already told you that the hotel and grounds are secure and I won't be joining you on any strolls.'

She felt heat flood her cheeks as again he placed distance between them and she tried to quickly change tack. 'I meant in London.'

'For now, I shall see Pandora here.' He saw the small frown form between her eyes. 'You just said you don't want any photos taken.'

'But if you're going to be in her life, how can you avoid her while in London?'

'I'm not avoiding Pandora,' Luka said, and then he put things bluntly. 'I'm going to be avoiding her mother.'

'If you want to be in her life, then that's going to prove rather difficult.'

'Amber is going through my schedule and for now, one week a month I am arranging things so that I shall be working from here.'

'But you have a home in London and you can't ask me to upend my life!'

'Hold on right there. Had you done the right thing in the first place, we would have had time to organise things better. Had you bothered to tell me I was soon to be a father I might have been able to sort my schedule better. Had you—'

'I get it,' Cecelia said, and held up her hand to halt him.

'I don't think you do,' Luka said. 'I don't believe for a moment you were going to tell me. I cannot believe I could have gone through my entire life not knowing about Pandora. She's my *daughter*...' he said. She heard the throaty rasp in his voice and she knew then how badly it was hurting him.

'Luka, I thought you would tell me to take care of things.'

'You assumed an awful lot.'

'My father asked my mother to.'

'She told you that?'

'No, the one time I met him he was shouting at her, telling her that he'd given her money for a termination. I didn't know what it meant, of course, until I looked it up.'

'I would never have asked that.'

'What would you have said then?' she flared.

'I don't know...'

'Well, neither did I!' Cecelia said, and she fought to keep herself from shouting.

'But I would have taken care of you and I would have ensured the best of care for the birth. And I would have been there when she was born and held her. And who knows what would have happened between us, but you denied us any chance of finding that out.'

Yes, he was angry.

But, yes, he understood better.

'You should have trusted me enough to tell me.'

'Trusted you! With the reckless way you live your life and your disposable attitude to women?'

'They don't have an issue with it,' Luka said. 'Well, most don't. I deliberately choose women who know what they want and are more than happy to indulge in a good time.' He could see the burn on her cheeks and he turned the knife. 'Women who don't wake up with regret...'

'Women who paid you.'

'Do you know what, Cecelia, you used to be a turn-on but I'm sick of the constant disapproval in your eyes.'

But, oh, it wasn't disapproval in her eyes, it was jealousy and it was want—not that she told him that, and so Luka spoke on.

'You're so busy being the perfect parent and before that the perfect PA you don't even know how to have fun.'

'Yes, I do.'

'You haven't even been in the pool!'

'You don't get to dictate what I do with my time,' Cecelia snapped. 'And about the pool, I don't want Pandora in the water...'

'Roula is a trained swimming instructor and, given that Pandora's going to be spending a lot of time surrounded by water, it seems prudent to teach her to swim.'

'She's three months old!'

'And she swam straight to the top.'

'Are you telling me you threw her in?'

'Roula and I were in the water with her.'

She felt ill at the thought of Pandora in the water and sick too at the thought of him and Roula, sharing that time with her baby.

'I want Pandora back home,' Cecelia said. 'This is too much. Luka, I want her back in London.'

'Tough!' Luka said. 'One week a month you are going to be here, and you can mope around and check for photographers or you can live a little.'

She incensed him, she really did.

He thought of that body of hers that never saw the sun and he did the only thing he could think of in response. He threw her up over his shoulder and carried her to the pool.

'Luka!'

Cecelia was raging and furious, not that it stopped him. He just dropped her right into the deep end.

She flailed for a moment and then came up, and as she did, she heard another splash.

Luka.

He was there as she surfaced, spluttering and furious and swimming straight for the edge, but he caught her and held her at the waist as it was too deep to reach the bottom of the pool.

'How dare you!' she shouted.

'Have you never been thrown in the water before?'

'Of course not.'

'And do you know how to swim?'

'Of course I do.'

But it was nice, so nice to be in the water and facing him, nice to feel his hands strong on her waist and the sun beating on her shoulders.

Nice to know that her baby was doing things that she had never even dreamed of as a child and that she had a father who adored her.

And it was also scary to be under his spell again.

To know, from the ragged edge to his breathing, that he was turned on and to know from the warmth spreading through her that she was turned on too.

And to know that right now she could wrap her legs around him and be lost to Luka again.

But would it be *Bored on Monday so we might as well do it* sex for him? Cecelia pondered as she gazed into dark eyes.

Yes, she decided, because that was how he lived.

And so she disengaged from him and hauled herself from the water.

She was here as Pandora's mother.

That was all.

CHAPTER THIRTEEN

CECELIA WOKE EARLY.

Only not to the familiar cries of Pandora.

Silence really was cruel for she had been locked in a dream where Luka's kiss did not end and with an ache and heat low in her legs, and a body that throbbed for him.

She forced her eyes open and pulled herself out of bed and then went to check on Pandora.

She was asleep on her back with her little arms up above her head, as if cheering.

They had been here for almost a week and they were starting to get into a gentle routine.

The mornings were for her and Pandora alone, but around eleven Roula would come over and fetch her. Luka would take a long lunch break and spend time with her along with her *yia-yia*—her grandmother—who doted on her apparently.

Late afternoon, after her nap, Pandora would return to Cecelia.

And it was nice.

Cecelia was starting to relax into it and had, after her impromptu dip in the pool, started to swim each day and take regular walks along Luka's private beach.

It was a long stretch of cove that made for a perfect

walk, splashing through the breaking waves and breathing in the fresh sea air.

On her final full day in Xanero before she and Pandora flew home tomorrow, it wasn't by coincidence that Luka headed down to the beach to join her.

It still galled him that she had kept the news of the pregnancy from him, but he understood better why she had.

He wasn't exactly fatherhood material.

Or he hadn't been.

And he wasn't exactly a family man.

Yet he wanted to be.

He was still infatuated with Cecelia, and his desire for her had never gone, though he knew he must not rush things.

Even so, tomorrow she left for London. Three more weeks apart, and not just apart from his daughter.

He ached for Cecelia. He ached for the glimpse of the smile he sometimes prised from her reluctant lips, and for the way she sometimes made him laugh.

'Hey,' Luka said, and he saw that he had startled her.

'Where's Pandora?'

'Being spoiled,' he said. 'My mother wondered if you would like to join her for breakfast tomorrow, before we head off?'

'I've been here a week…'

'Cecelia, my mother would have had you over the first day if she'd had her own way. I have been the one keeping things separate…'

'Why?'

'Because that's what I always do,' Luka said, and then added, 'And because I was angry.'

They walked on.

'But I can't keep my worlds separate now,' Luka said.

'We have a daughter. My mother has a grandchild...' He looked at her. 'What about your aunt and uncle? Do they know about me?'

'No.' Cecelia shook her head. 'They would have had me straight over to a lawyer,' Cecelia said. 'And then they'd have gushed all over us both. You were right about them only taking me on to get to the money.'

She looked out to the cove and the glitter of his yacht but his wealth was not what beckoned her.

He saw where her gaze fell. 'Do you want to go over for lunch?' Luka asked.

'No, thank you.' It was hard enough just to walk alongside him and not break down. She wanted him so badly and was terrified she'd simply accept whatever occasional crumbs of affection he threw her way and so her response was tart. 'I thought the reason I was here was so you could spend time with your daughter.'

'Believe it or not, I actually have some work to do today—things were already piling up before my father died.'

'I'm sorry he never got to meet his granddaughter,' Cecelia said. 'I really do mean that. I feel terrible about it, in fact...'

'Don't.' Luka shook his head and then turned and looked at her 'Truth?'

'Please,' she said, and gave a pale smile. He really was a curious man, for he could so easily have held that over her. She was surprised to have her guilt so readily dismissed.

'I would not have insisted on a week of playing happy families had he been alive. I would never have exposed her to his toxic nature. Instead, I would have brought Pandora for lunch and that would have been it.'

'I thought the two of you were close.'

'That's what they wanted people to think.'

'Tell me…' Cecelia said, because she simply could not feign disinterest.

'Over dinner.' He nodded to the yacht. 'It's a nice place to talk and I'm not here by accident, Cecelia. My mother has asked if she can have Cecelia stay with her tonight.'

'Absolutely not.' Cecelia shook her head. 'I've given you as much time as you want with her but she is not spending the night away from me. There's no need for your mother to babysit.'

'But she would not be *babysitting*—she is family.' Luka closed his eyes in exasperation. 'She wants to have her granddaughter stay over and to boast to her friends. It's the Greek way.'

She could feel her panic building. It was irrational really, for she wanted Pandora to be surrounded by people who loved her, yet she could not bear the thought of her waking in the dark alone.

'Cecelia, do you really think I would leave Pandora with someone I did not absolutely trust?'

Of course not.

Cecelia knew that.

He had told her that.

And she knew that this was the future.

Time spent away from her daughter as Pandora spent time with people who loved her.

'Roula will be there too,' Luka said. 'Cecelia, I am sure most first-time mothers are anxious when they leave their baby for the first night, but that is co-parenting.'

'I know.'

She swallowed.

It sounded so odd to hear those words from him.

She had honestly thought he would have no interest in Pandora. Or, perhaps the odd visit. Cecelia had genuinely believed he would throw money at the situation.

Instead, Luka wanted to be a true parent. He wanted real time with his daughter and he wanted his family involved in her life.

He just didn't want *her*.

Only that wasn't entirely the case.

Luka turned so he was facing her and when she didn't do the same, he took her shoulders and moved her to face him.

'I want to take you to the yacht tonight because I think it's time that we speak about us.'

'Us?' An incredulous laugh shot from her lips. 'What us? You hate me, and I can't stand the way you live your life—'

'Yet we are parents together,' Luka interrupted. 'And for the record, I don't hate you, and I think you are referring to my former life.'

She assumed he meant prior to him finding out he was a parent.

For Luka, though, the anger was fading, and he was remembering how much he had missed Cecelia this past year.

And now the red mist of anger was clearing, he knew that what he felt for Cecelia had not changed.

Still, he was aware that he could be bullish and knew that to push her too fast would be wrong. She was as jumpy as a cat and a new mother too.

'Cecelia, before the world finds out we have a daughter, I think we should use that time to explore where we stand.'

'I'm not with you.'

'The desire is still there.'

He stated it as fact.

And it was.

Her nails were digging into her palms just from the effort of facing him calmly—the impact of Luka close up was as devastating now as it had been on the day they'd met.

'Perhaps, but sex isn't much to build a relationship on.'

'Why not?' Luka shrugged. 'We both enjoy it and it got us this far.'

She was about to say no but Luka would not be put off.

'Tonight we are going out on our first date.'

Second, she wanted to correct, for her birthday last year had been the most romantic night of her life.

CHAPTER FOURTEEN

THE SPA WAS gorgeous and perhaps more than a little overdue.

Instead of more foils, Cecelia had some length cut off, so that her strawberry blonde hair fell to just below her shoulders, and because it was shorter it coiled into waves.

'How about adding some more waves and wearing it down?' the hairdresser said, but Cecelia shook her head and asked for it to be straightened and put up.

There was an almost imperceptive tut from the hairdresser but she did as asked and smoothed it out and pinned it up.

Though her hair was redder than before, Cecelia felt a small sense of order returning to her world as she eyed her reflection, for she looked more like the Cecelia during her Kargas Holdings days.

Returning to the villa, she took for ever to choose what to wear—everything was too loose and to her mind too sensual.

It isn't work, though, she reminded herself as she found her hand linger upon the sheer rose-gold silk dress.

But it may well be work for Luka.

He adored Pandora, and she was terrified that he

might be merely attempting to do the right thing by his daughter. Cecelia doubted that even his best intentions could last.

She came upon the requisite little black dress and decided it was safer and closer to her usual fare. For a splash of colour she added a little sheer grey silk cardigan that she had packed herself—a throwback from her working days.

She looked at the birthday necklace and wondered if she should wear it, for it was absolutely her favourite thing.

Yet she did not want him to know that he meant everything to her. Luka had made a chance for them sound like a grim reality they ought to face.

Even as he came to her door, Cecelia was holding onto her heart.

Luka was immaculate in a suit and tie, and he had, did, and always would, take her breath away.

'You look very beautiful,' Luka duly said as she closed the door on the villa and they walked towards the speedboat that would take them out to his yacht.

Yet somehow it felt rather like heading to a formal work dinner than a romantic date. And Luka noted she was wearing another damned cardigan.

'How's Pandora?' Cecelia asked, for it felt like for ever since she had seen her. But if tonight didn't work then being apart from her daughter for prolonged stretches was something she would have to get used to.

Yes, there was an awful lot of pressure on this date.

'She is being spoiled by her *yia-yia* and also her great-aunt, my father's sister,' Luka said, and he took out his phone and showed her a photo he had taken just before he left.

If ever there was a baby who was doted on it was

Pandora. She had on a cerise dress and was a splash of gorgeousness between the two doting women dressed in black.

'My mother is so happy and relaxed. I cannot tell you the balm that our daughter is to her.'

As she boarded his stunning yacht, Cecelia couldn't help but think of all the wild debauched parties that had taken place here.

Tonight, though, there weren't the half-naked, sun-kissed and oiled bodies, or the pulse of music to dance to. And there was only one champagne cork that popped and no raucous laughter.

It wasn't so much his past that she loathed, more the certainty that he would tire of her and go back to it someday.

It was a gorgeous night, the sky as navy as Pandora's eyes and pierced with endless stars.

The deck was romantically lit and it was soft music that greeted her as they were led to a beautifully dressed table.

The waiter placed her napkin in her lap and Cecelia did her absolute best to relax.

They ate the best squid she had ever tasted—or *ka-lamari*, as the waiter called it—and she looked out at Xanero and saw the gorgeous buildings from her view on the water.

'It really is the most beautiful place,' Cecelia said.

'It has been both a blessing and a curse,' Luka said. 'It's a blessing now.'

'You mean now that your father's gone?' Cecelia tentatively asked, alluding to what he had said on the beach.

He nodded. 'My mother would say I should not speak ill of the dead, but there is nothing good that I can say about him. He was work-shy and a bully...'

'I thought you and he worked together in the restaurant, that he passed on all he knew.'

'He probably put in twelve hours tops in his entire lifetime,' Luka said. 'But my mother had always wanted a family business. I could have had him removed, but she pleaded with me not to. It was easier to stay away and run it from a distance.' He looked out across the water and then he told her something he could not explain, even to himself. 'And yet his death has rocked my world and I feel like I'm grieving.'

'I still grieve for my mother,' she admitted. 'Sometimes I think I miss what could have been.'

And then her eyes flicked away because, although they were talking about their parents, she was suddenly thinking of them and what *might* be, perhaps.

'I want you to love it here too,' Luka said, and she put down her fork. 'You've had a good week?' he asked.

'It's been better than I thought it would be.'

'There could be many more.'

'There's no could about it.' She looked at him and reminded herself who she was dealing with. 'Given that you've told me to be here one week a month or you'll see me in court.'

'I meant *this*, Cecelia. Us.' He saw her jaw tighten but he reached across the table and took her hand. It was as rigid as ever, her professional façade still in place. Yet as he toyed with her, she found her fingers intertwining with his and then he voiced her thoughts exactly.

'I'm going crazy, knowing you're here but not in my bed.'

He watched as her eyes screwed closed and assumed he had pushed too hard when in truth Cecelia was also fighting desire.

'We don't have to rush things,' he corrected, 'but maybe when you bring Pandora here, when there is no chance of us being seen, then away from prying eyes we can date, get to know each other, see how we work as a family...'

She felt like the only car in the showroom about to be taken on a reluctant test drive. 'And if we don't work?' she asked.

'Cecelia....'

'No, Luka, what you're basically proposing is that I be your mistress during the time Pandora and I are here in Xanero.'

'What I'm proposing is that we give us a try. I'm going to attempt to let go of the fact that you kept Pandora from me...'

'You're never going to forgive me for that, are you?'

'I don't know,' he admitted.

It killed her to hear that for it gave them such a lousy start and so she kicked back. 'Can you really blame me for not telling you?' Cecelia could no longer hold it in. 'Have you any idea the hell you put me through, dealing with all your cast-offs? I was crazy about you and you were into everyone but me!'

'And you didn't think to tell me?'

'You were my boss then!'

'Well, I'm not now.'

'No, but it's no better here, knowing what went on aboard this yacht and by the bloody pool...'

'Don't turn this around on me. You never gave me a single indication you were interested in me. In fact, you were engaged when I first hired you. I'm damned if I do and damned if I don't. You were the one in a serious relationship, remember?'

'And you were the one screwing around.' She flung

down her napkin and there was the scrape of her chair as she stood. 'I need to get back.'

'We need to speak.' Luka took her wrist.

'No, I want to get off…'

'Fine.'

He snapped his fingers to prepare the speedboat that would take them back to shore. 'Do you know something,' Luka said. 'I'm sick and tired of seeing the disproval in your eyes…'

'Well, someone has to be responsible,' she spat.

'And you elect yourself at every turn.'

'Because I'm scared that if I let go, then I might turn into my mother!' she shouted.

'Cecelia…' he was about to tell her that she was being ridiculous but then he looked at it from her side, the chaotic upbringing, the uncertainty, the abandonment. 'You will never be her. And I promise you this, the day you hit the cocaine, I shall put you over my knee…'

She almost laughed.

Almost.

But her throat was thick with tears.

'We're in this together,' Luka said. 'Did she leave you at night?'

'Many times.' Cecelia nodded. 'I would wake up and not know where she was. That's why I don't want Pandora—'

'The difference is,' Luka cut in, 'that, though it might not be her mother she wakes to, she will have family there, or a nanny who has been carefully chosen. Cecelia, there's a world of difference between having a night out and living the life your mother lived.' But Cecelia turned away and he shook his head for she would never see it from his point of view. 'We'll go and fetch her now.'

As the boat sped them to shore, Cecelia felt like an utter failure—back from a romantic night out before ten. As he helped her onto the pier she did not know how to explain it—she knew he was right, that Pandora was safe and loved, but it was about more than just that. 'Luka, you don't have to wake her. Leave her with your mother and Roula. I know she'll be fine.'

'Are you sure?'

Cecelia nodded.

'You're a wonderful mother, Cecelia.'

But as a lover she knew she had failed.

The night was over for them.

'Luka,' she tried to explain how she felt, 'I'm scared of us getting together and confusing her when we break up...'

'How about *if* we break up?' Luka asked. 'How about we don't ever break up? You're so bloody negative and contained.'

'Because the one time I lived a little, look what happened! The one time I made a mist—'

She stopped there because she didn't ever want to describe Pandora and what had happened as a mistake because she wasn't.

But Luka got there first. 'The one time you let your hair down and lived a little, to my mind, something rather beautiful happened.'

And then he looked down at her and he was angry, for she had refused on so many occasions to give them a chance.

'Cecelia, I'm not going to beg. You have to want it too.'

CHAPTER FIFTEEN

LUKA STRODE OFF.

She watched him walk angrily along the beach and she knew it was she who had messed up the night.

Yet the cheek of him!

On-call sex whenever she was here?

Or, a little voice to her heart said, could it serve as the start of being a real family?

Cecelia was terrified of loving him.

Yet she already did.

More, she was terrified of admitting to loving him and then losing him.

Of waking in the dark and it being *him* that was gone.

Or, worse, the cold pretence of normal, and pretending there was love, as her uncle and aunt had done.

Sex was all they had and when that novelty dimmed he would be back to his old life....

She walked along the white sandy beach, straying a little from the boundaries of the complex. This would be home for a while, she realised.

Not all the time, but for a year or so she would be here for a week every month.

And then not at all.

She was terrified to enjoy it and relax into it, knowing all the while that it would all soon be taken away from her.

He would always be there for Pandora, though.

She was starting to believe that things would be different for her daughter than they had been for her. That, despite her carelessness that one morning, she had chosen well for he was proving to be an amazing father—completely rearranging his world to accommodate his daughter.

'Live a little.'

She recalled his words as he had moved her little pottery jar and then she winced as she remembered her *No, thank you* response.

She remembered him throwing her into the pool and then joining her, his eyes imploring her to loosen up and be free.

He had been offering a chance for them, and rather than embrace that chance she was hiding from it. Rather than living the life she wanted to with him, she was running from it at every turn.

Yet Luka was right, the one time she had let her hair down and lived a little, something rather beautiful had happened.

She recalled his words. *'You have to want it too.'*

Oh, she did, she very much did, and she had to show him that somehow.

And so instead of heading back to the villa to spend the night feeling sorry for herself, Cecelia decided it was time to head out.

While she did head back to the villa it was only to change. She peeled off the cardigan and little black dress and instead of flesh-coloured knickers and a bra, she pulled on the rose-gold bikini.

For she might want a midnight swim!

She thought of Luka naked and wet and dripping water over her, as had been her fantasy for so long.

Over the bikini she pulled on the rose-gold dress that was so loose and flowing, and yet so sensual.

Her hair when she took it down was wavy and wild thanks to the salt spray of the ocean.

Her cheeks were flushed and her green eyes finally had their sparkle back after a week of doing nothing and actually sleeping.

Or did it have more to do with a week spent closer to him?

There could be many more weeks, if she had the courage to try....

A monthly tryst with Luka didn't sound so terrible now. They were like a little family, and being together in the pool once a month, rather than her lying lonely poolside on the other side of the complex, would be much better, wouldn't it?

Pandora would have the best mother, the best co-parents—and if Luka couldn't forgive her for not telling him about their baby that was his right.

She put on the necklace, the one he had given her and the one she would adore for ever, feeling the cold metal against her heated skin. Then Cecelia headed to the restaurant she had never so much as visited, preferring instead to hide away in the villa.

It was stunning and, yes, full of couples, but there at the bar was Luka, with his back to her.

'Your table is ready for you, Madam,' the greeter said, and she recalled it had been reserved for her all week.

The bar manager told Luka that Cecelia had arrived. He frowned, glanced over and saw that she was being seated—only it was not a Cecelia he recognised.

Well, perhaps the one he met at times in his dreams, for she looked amazing and relaxed and sexy too as she laughed at something the greeter said.

He looked over but she did not catch his eye. He was trying to work out what was going on when the bar manager spoke and placed in front of him a glass of the best champagne.

'Gia eséna kýrie, apó tin kyría.' For you, sir, from the lady.

And it was like in days of old, but so much better now. As he turned, Cecelia met his eyes and raised her own glass, adding a slight gesture of her head.

A gesture that invited Luka to join her.

She smiled a slow smile that was familiar from many years ago.

A flirt.

An offer.

Yes, Cecelia was a curious mix indeed, for never would he have envisaged this.

He walked over, his eyes never leaving her face. 'It's far too nice a night to drink champagne alone,' Luka said.

'I agree,' she said. 'Would you care to join me?'

'I would love to.'

He took a seat and looked over at a woman who had, from the day they had met, intrigued him. Never more so than now, and he slipped so easily back into the game. 'How long are you here for?'

'I fly back to London tomorrow,' she said. 'Although I believe it won't be the last time I'm here.'

'That's good to know,' Luka said. 'And are you here alone?'

'It's a little complicated, I don't really want to go into it.'

'That's fine.'

But this time it was not disapproval in her eyes, for it was like he was back staring into that aurora and he started to understand her some more. There was a wild side to Cecelia, one she had fought all her life to temper.

Not tonight.

She *could* be free around him.

'I have a daughter,' she said, 'but she's being taken care of tonight.'

'So you're on your own.'

'Yes,' Cecelia said. 'All night.'

'Poor you.' He gave her a smile, the one that had churned her heart since the day they'd met. 'I didn't catch your name.'

'Cece.'

He smiled that slow smile that made her stomach fold.

'I'm Luka. So, where are you staying.'

'At the Beach Side apartment.'

'Nice,' he said.

'Very.' She took a sip of champagne and then smirked. 'My ex is paying.'

'Even better,' he said, and then Luka laughed and it was the most delicious sound she had ever heard.

But then he met her eyes and his voice was serious. 'He must be a fool to have let you go.'

'Not really,' Cecelia said. 'I let him down.'

'I doubt it,' he said.

'Oh, but I did. I kept something very important from him.'

'Then he should have got over it, or perhaps he should have taken the time to work out why you did what you did.'

He saw a flash of tears and decided that there would be no tears now.

'I shouldn't really be seen drinking in the restaurant with a guest,' Luka said. He held her eyes and the tears dispersed like a chink in the mist.

'Then come back to mine.'

It was the bravest thing she had done and he was so deliciously casual in his response.

'Sure, though for the sake of discretion, you should leave first.'

She would never not want him, Cecelia knew as she stood to go, but he caught her wrist.

'Is there anything you'd like?' he asked. 'Anything at all?'

He was inviting her to name her wants.

This she did.

Cecelia bent over and whispered into his ear and then pulled back, wondering at his reaction and if he might laugh at her request, but he just nodded.

'No problem.'

She felt as if she was on a high as she arrived back at the villa.

A dizzy high and, yes, it might just be sex but she would take it if it afforded them a start.

She did not turn on the lights. Instead, she slipped off her clothes and lay on the bed. Her body felt as though it might burst into flames of desire as she lay there.

Waiting.

Not wondering as to their future, not berating herself with the impossibility of it all, just waiting for her night with him.

She heard the splash from the pool and closed her eyes as she listened to him move through the water and then she caught the slide of the villa doors.

And then, dripping wet, he leaned over her.

As per her request.

She felt the mattress indent as he knelt over her and relished the cold drops of water on her skin. 'I want you, Cece…' he told her. His mouth found hers and she closed her eyes to the bliss of his kiss. 'I've been crazy about you for so long.'

His voice was raw with want, and even if he was simply saying it for this night of fantasy, even if he simply knew how to pleasure women through years of practice, she didn't care just so long as this night he pleasured her.

His kiss tasted of salty ocean water and his body was cold and wet while hers burnt beneath him.

'There's been no one since you,' he told her. He broke the fantasy a little, yet she ached for it to be true and in response she gave in to his kiss.

His tongue was tender yet probing and she could feel his erection between her thighs. She yearned for him to enter her, yet he held back.

'I'm on the Pill,' she told him.

'That costs more, lady,' he teased. He made her laugh and he joined her, and then he stopped laughing and took her arms, which were wrapped around him, and held them above her head, so that she could not move, and could only look at him.

'I love you,' he told her, and she closed her eyes.

'Luka, don't.'

'Look at me,' he said, and she did.

'I love you.'

He was tired of holding back, tired of denying it.

'Please, please, don't just say it,' she begged. No matter how much she yearned to hear it, she could not stand that it might be a game and mere words delivered from silken lips by a man who knew what to say.

'But I do,' Luka said. He was starting to realise that Cece did need him to call the shots, and now he knew why and he went back to their conversation in the restaurant, when she had referred to him as her ex. 'Perhaps your ex should have understood that for you it's hard to believe someone might love you, when no one ever has before.'

He was so right, and so for a moment she allowed herself the bliss of believing he did as Luka took her deeply.

He moaned with relief as he slipped inside, and she gave in to bliss, to the dream that his love was hers and that the body that moved over and within her might be hers for ever.

Eyes open, she watched as he moved with her, each stroke of him inside bringing her nearer to a peak, and she gave in to his kiss and shattered to his bliss.

'Cece…' he groaned as he spilled inside her. There could be no place better than this.

In this still, dark place on a sultry night, she fell asleep in his arms and pretended this was love.

CHAPTER SIXTEEN

'I MEANT WHAT I said,' Luka told her.

She woke to his words and found he was spooned in behind her. His hand moved from her breast as he played with the stones of her necklace.

They were rubies, not glass, and way too much of a gift for a PA.

A mixed message indeed, even for him, for when it had finally arrived in his life, Luka had not recognised love either.

'Why couldn't you tell me how you felt, Cece?'

'Because so many woman have made fools of themselves over you and I didn't want to be another one of them.'

He could not argue with that.

'If it wasn't for Pandora,' Cecelia said, still facing away, 'there would be no us.'

'Had you been walking in the street that day alone, I would have called you. And,' Luka added, 'when my father died, it was you I wanted to reach out to. I told myself to wait. To get through the funeral and clear my head. I told myself I wasn't thinking straight, but I was lying because since that night with you things have never been clearer. There's been no one since you.'

She hadn't believed him when he'd told her that last

night. Cecelia had thought he was just saying the words she wanted to hear.

'I think I loved you back then but, hell, Cece, you made it hard to get close. All I can say was I loathed the thought of you being gone.'

She was starting to believe that there might be a chance for them, but her mind knew only how to doubt.

'Even if we try to make a go of it, one day you'll throw it back in my face that I kept Pandora from you…'

'Would the world end if I did?' Luka asked. He guessed that from the way life had treated her, or rather *people* had treated her, that, yes, it would seem that way to her.

He smiled that rare smile and she glimpsed a future, one where he tossed her flaw in her face and it did not end them.

'No.'

'And when—if—I do hurl it at you, perhaps you will remind me of the many women I bedded, and the flowers you ordered on my behalf, and what an ass I was…'

'Yes,' she said, torn between laughing and crying.

It was a love where perfection was not a prerequisite, one where you were allowed to mess up.

'Marry me, Cece.'

She sat up in bed and wasn't certain what she'd just heard. 'I thought we were going to take things slowly. I'll be back in a few weeks…'

'If you think I am letting you get on a plane this morning, then you don't know me at all.'

She turned and smiled.

It was the smile that felt like summer to him.

'Do you know what day it is?'

Cecelia shook her head.

'It's your birthday…'

But this year it wasn't candles and cake, or a necklace she was gifted with, but a ring.

'Were you going to ask me last night?' Cecelia gasped, as he slipped a huge diamond on her finger, faint with horror for her handling of things.

But she didn't know him completely yet, for Luka shook his head.

'No, it was always meant for this morning, because I don't want you ever to have another birthday that passed unnoticed.'

Sometimes she thought he just said the right thing, the things she wanted to hear. But this didn't feel like that. This felt real somehow.

'Come on, then!' He kicked off the sheet. 'We've a wedding to get to.'

'We can't just get married.' Cecelia laughed. 'We need approval, and what about guests and—?'

'I practically own the island,' Luka pointed out. 'I can do what I want, we can deal with the legalities later. I might just have to marry you again, but I want a wedding ring on your finger today and,' he added, 'it's never coming off.'

'But what about Pandora?'

'Where I come from, children don't generally attend their parents' wedding,' Luka said. 'Had you bothered to tell me you were pregnant we could have sorted it out and we'd have been married many months ago and Pandora wouldn't come from a broken home.'

He was throwing it all back in her face, yet she smiled.

'Luka, I don't have anything to wear.'

'Then I'll marry you in a sheet, but, Cece…' he took her arms and pinned her down, staring right into her eyes '…you have to want it too.'

'I do.'

'And you have to fight for us as well,' he said, and then halted, for she was the one who had fought for them last night. He thought of her, so shy and reserved, yet she had walked into the restaurant, and somehow forgiven his past. 'You're going to marry me now and then we're going to collect out daughter together. As a married couple, as her parents...'

Cecelia wore a silver sarong tied over one shoulder. Her hair was strawberry blonde and curly as she stood on the yacht and faced Luka.

He wore black dress pants and a fitted white shirt but no tie and he had not shaved.

It was informal, yet beautiful and impulsive too.

Yes, she might be a little more than just a visual replica of her mother, for the wanton side of her nature appeared at times. But though a sudden wedding aboard Luka Kargas's yacht might appear reckless to some, Cecelia knew that she stood before a man who was strong and who loved her.

And who would not let her fall.

The celebrant looked up at the sound of a helicopter buzzing overhead, and suggested that perhaps they move inside if they wanted to avoid being photographed.

'Sure,' Luka said, for he wanted to shield her, but as he went to take her hand and move below deck, she declined.

'It's fine.' Cecelia gave a little shake of her head. 'It will save us having to announce it.'

With him she was both brave and free.

'I love you,' he told her as he slid a wedding band on her finger. 'And if it takes the rest of my life to prove it to you, I will.'

'You already have,' Cecelia said, and then she looked into velvet brown eyes that were black when guarded. She knew him better than anyone else, and so she told him a truth. 'And I'm so proud to be your wife.'

She was.

Cecelia was proud not just of the man he was but the man he had been, for he had been strong in the face of an impossible start in life.

It meant everything to Luka to hear that.

The press got one shot—Luka Kargas on his yacht, kissing his bride, but by the time the paparazzi had got wind of the news and circled ahead, awaiting the pulse of music and wild celebrations, the happy couple had long since left.

They had somewhere else they wanted to be.

Cecelia walked up the path towards her mother-in-law's villa, feeling more than a little nervous, and saw Sophie sitting in a chair, holding Pandora. Beside them was a large silver box and a birthday and wedding breakfast awaiting.

The late-morning sun was high in the sky and there was peace in the air as they returned to their daughter… a family at last.

* * * * *

PRINCESS'S PREGNANCY SECRET

NATALIE ANDERSON

To my family, for your patience, belief,
bad-but-good puns and supreme fun…

We are such an awesome team,
and I am so very lucky.

CHAPTER ONE

DAMON GALE STALKED the perimeter of the crowded ball-room, dodging another cluster of smiling women whose feathered masks neither softened nor hid their hunger as they stared at him.

He shouldn't have discarded his mask so soon.

Turning his back on another wordless invitation, he sipped his champagne, wishing it contained a stronger li-quor. Women wanted more from him than he ever wanted from them. Always. While they agreed to a fling—fully informed of his limits—when it ended, recriminations and resentment came.

You're heartless.

He smiled cynically as the echo rang in his head. His last ex had thrown that old chestnut at him a few months ago. And, yes, he was. Heartless and happy with it.

And what did it matter? For tonight business, not plea-sure, beckoned. Tonight he was drawing a line beneath a decades-old disaster and tomorrow he'd walk away from this gilded paradise without a backwards glance. Just com-ing back had made old wounds hurt like fresh hits.

But for now he'd endured the outrageously opulent entrance, navigated his way up the marble staircase and walked through not one but five antechambers. Each room was larger and more ornate than the last, until finally he'd reached this gleaming monstrosity of a ballroom. The in-ternal balcony overlooking the vast room already brimmed with celebrities and socialites eager to display themselves and spy on others.

Palisades palace was designed to reflect the glory of the royal family and make the average commoner feel as inconsequential as possible. It was supposed to invoke awe and envy. Frankly all the paintings, tapestries and gilded carvings exhausted Damon's eyes. He itched to ditch his dinner jacket and hit one of the trail runs along the pristine coastline that he far preferred to this sumptuous palace, but he needed to stay and play nice for just a little while longer.

Gritting his teeth, he turned away from the lens of an official photographer. He had no desire to feature in anyone's social media feed or society blog. He'd been forced to attend too many of these sorts of occasions in years past, as the proof of the supposed strength of his parents' union and thus to maximise any political inroads they could make from their connections.

The bitterness of their falsity soured the champagne.

Fortunately *his* career wasn't dependent upon the interest and approval of the wealthy and powerful. Thanks to his augmented reality software company, he was as wealthy as any of the patrons in attendance at this palace tonight. But even so, he was here to make the old-school grace and favour system work for him just this once. Grimly he glanced over to where he'd left his half-sister only ten minutes ago. The investors he'd introduced her to were actively listening to her earnest, intelligent conversation, asking questions, clearly interested in what she was saying.

That introduction was all she'd agreed to accept from him. She'd refused his offer to fund her research himself and, while it irritated him, he didn't blame her. After all, they barely knew each other and neither of them wanted to dwell on the cancerous and numerous scars of their parents' infidelities. She had her pride and he respected her for it. But he'd been determined to try to help heal two decades of hurt and heartache caused by lies and deception, even in some small way, given his father's total lack of remorse. From the intensity of that discussion, it seemed his job was done.

Now Damon turned away from the crowds, seeking solace in solitude for a moment before he could escape completely.

Symmetrical marble columns lined the length of the room. On one side they bracketed doors to the internal courtyard currently lit by lights strung in the trees. But on the other side the columns stood like sentries guarding shadowy alcoves.

A wisp of blue caught his eye as he approached the nearest column and he veered nearer. A woman stood veiled in the recess, her attention tightly focused on a group of revellers a few feet away. Her hair was ten shades of blue, hung to her waist and was most definitely a wig. A feathery mask covered half her face like an intimate web of black lace. Her shoulders, cheekbones and lips sparkled in a swirling combination of blue and silver powder.

Damon paused, unable to ignore the way her long dress emphasised every millimetre of her lithe body, clinging to her luscious curves and long legs. Despite that sparkling powder, he could see the tan of her skin and it suggested she was more mermaid than waif. She definitely spent time in the sun and that toned body didn't come from sitting on a spread towel doing nothing.

She was fit—in all interpretations of the word—but it was her undeniable femininity that stole his breath. Her pointed chin and high cheekbones and perfectly pouted lips were pure prettiness and delicacy, while her bountiful breasts were barely contained in the too-tight bodice of her midnight-blue dress.

She hadn't noticed him as she stood still and alone, watching the crowd. So he watched her. Her mask didn't hide her emotions—while her intentions were not obvious, her anxiety was. Something about her stark isolation softened that hard knot tied fast in his chest and set a challenge at the same time.

He was seized by the desire to make her smile.

He was also seized by the urge to span his hands around her narrow waist and pull her close so he could feel the graceful combination of softness and strength that her figure promised.

He smiled ruefully as raw warmth coursed through his veins. Its unexpected ferocity was vastly better than the cold ash clogging his lungs when he'd first arrived. Perhaps there could be a moment of pleasure here after all, now his business was concluded and that personal debt paid.

He quietly strolled nearer. Her attention was still fixed on the people gathering in the glittering ballroom, but he focused on her. She hovered on the edge of the room, still in the shadow. Still almost invisible to everyone else.

Her breasts swelled as she inhaled deeply. He hesitated, waiting for her to move forward. But contrary to his expectation, she suddenly stepped back, her expression falling as she turned away.

Damon narrowed his gaze. He had his own reasons for avoiding occasions like this, but why would a beautiful young woman like her want to hide? She should have company.

His company.

He lifted a second glass from the tray of a passing waiter and stepped past the column into the alcove. She'd paused in her retreat to look over that vast room of bejewelled, beautiful people. The expression in her eyes was obvious, despite the mask and the make-up. Part longing, part loneliness, her isolation stirred him. He spoke before thinking better of it.

'Can't quite do it?'

She whirled to face him, her eyes widening. Damon paused, needing a moment to appreciate the layers of sequins and powder on her pretty features. She was so very blue. She registered the two glasses he was holding and darted a glance behind him. As she realised he was alone, her eyes widened more. He smiled at her obvious wariness.

'It's your first time?' he asked.

Her mouth opened in a small wordless gasp.

'At the palace,' he clarified, wryly amused while keenly aware of the fullness of her glittered lips. 'It can be overwhelming the first time.'

Fascinatingly a telltale colour ran up her neck and face, visible despite the artful swirls of powder dusting almost every inch of her exposed skin. She was *blushing* at the most innocuous of statements.

Well, almost innocuous.

His smile deepened as he imagined her response if he were to utter something a great deal more inappropriate. Her body captured his attention, and he couldn't resist stealing a glance lower.

Heat speared again, tightening his muscles. He dragged his gaze up and realised she'd caught his slip. Unabashed he smiled again, letting her know in that time-worn way of his interest. She met his open gaze, not stepping back. But still she said nothing.

Alone. Definitely unattached. And almost certainly on the inexperienced side.

Damon hadn't chased a woman in a long while. Offers from more than willing bedmates meant he was more hunted than hunter. He avoided their attempts to snare him for longer, bored with justifying his refusal to commit to a relationship. He had too much of what women wanted— money and power. And yes, physical stamina and experience. Women enjoyed those things too.

But the possibilities here were tempting—when she reacted so tantalisingly with so little provocation? Those too-blue eyes and that too-sombre pout were beguiling.

He'd barely expected to stay ten minutes, let alone find someone who'd rouse his playful side. But now his obligation to Kassie had been met, he had the urge to amuse himself.

'What's your name?' he asked.

Her pupils dilated as if she was surprised but, again, she said nothing.

'I think I'll call you "Blue",' he said leisurely.

Her chin lifted fractionally. 'Because of my hair?'

He had to stop his jaw from dropping at the sound of her husky tones. That sultriness was at complete odds with her innocent demeanour. She was as raspy as a kitten's tongue. The prospect of making her purr tightened his interest.

'Because of the longing in your eyes.' And because of the pout of her pretty mouth.

'What do you think I'm longing for?'

Now there was a question. One he chose not to answer, knowing his silence would speak for itself. He just looked at her—feeling the awareness between them snap.

'What should I call you?' she asked after a beat.

He lifted his eyebrows. 'You don't know who I am?'

Her lips parted as she shook her head. 'Should I?'

He studied her for a moment—there had been no flash of recognition in her eyes when he'd first spoken to her, and there was none now. How...*refreshing*. 'No,' he said. 'I'm no one of importance. No prince, that's for sure.'

Something flickered in her eyes then, but it was gone before he could pick it up.

'I'm visiting Palisades for a few days,' he drawled. 'And I'm single.'

Her lips parted. 'Why do I need to know that?'

That sultry voice pulled, setting off a small ache deep in his bones. He didn't much like aches. He preferred action.

'No reason.' He shrugged carelessly, but smiled.

Her lips twitched, then almost curved. Satisfaction seeped into his gut, followed hard by something far hotter. Pleasure. It pressed him closer.

'Why are you all alone in here?' He offered her the second glass of champagne.

She accepted it but took such a small sip he wasn't

sure that the liquid even hit her lips. A careful woman. Intriguing.

'Are you hiding?' he queried.

She licked her lips and glanced down at her dress before tugging at the strap that was straining to hold her curves.

Definitely nervous.

'You look beautiful,' he added. 'You don't need to worry about that.'

That wave of colour swept her cheeks again but she lifted her head. There was an assuredness in her gaze now that surprised him. 'I'm not worried about that.'

Oh? So she held a touch more confidence than had first appeared. Another shot of satisfaction rushed. His fingers itched with the urge to tug the wig from her head and find out what colour her hair really was. While this façade was beautiful, it was a fantasy he wanted to pierce so he could see the real treasure beneath.

'Then why aren't you out there?' he asked.

'Why aren't you?' Alert, she watched for his response.

'Sometimes attendance at these things is *necessary* rather than desired.'

'These "things"?' she mocked his tone.

'It depends who's here.'

'No doubt you desire these "things" more when there are plenty of pretty women.' She was breathless beneath that rasp.

But he knew she was enjoying this slight spar and parry. He'd play along.

'Naturally.' Damon coolly watched her over the rim of his glass as he sipped his drink, deliberately hiding his delight. 'I am merely a man, after all.' He shrugged helplessly.

Her gaze narrowed on him, twin sparks shooting from that impossible blue. 'You mean you're a boy who likes playing with toys. A doll here, a doll there...'

'Of course,' he followed her smoothly. 'Toying with dolls can be quite an amusing pastime. As can collecting them.'

'I'll bet.'

He leaned forward, deliberately intruding into intimate space to whisper conspiratorially, 'I never break my toys though,' he promised. 'I take very good care when I'm playing.'

'Oh?' Her gaze lanced straight through his veneer, striking at a weak spot he didn't know he had. 'If you say it, it must be true.'

Appreciating her little flash of spirit, he was instantly determined to take very great care…to torture her delightfully.

'And you?' he asked, though he already suspected the answer. 'Do you often attend nights like this?' Did she play with toys of her own?

She shrugged her shoulders in an echo of his.

He leaned closer again, rewarded as he heard the hitch in her breathing. 'Do you work at the hospital?'

Tonight's ball was the annual fundraiser and, while he knew huge amounts were raised, it was also the chance for hospital staff to be celebrated.

'I…do some stuff there.' Her lashes lowered.

Wasn't she just Ms Mysterious? 'So why aren't you with your friends?'

'I don't know them all that well.'

Perhaps she was a new recruit who'd won an invitation for this ball in the ballot they held for the hospital staff. Perhaps that was why she didn't have any friends with her. It wouldn't take long for her to find a few. Some surgeon would snap her up if he had any sense. Then it wouldn't be long before she lost that arousing ability to blush.

A spear of possessiveness shafted through him at the thought of some other guy pulling her close. Surprising him into taking another step nearer to her. Too near.

'Do you want to dance?' He gave up on subtlety altogether.

She glanced beyond him. 'No one is dancing yet.'

'We could start the trend.'

She quickly shook her head, leaning back into the shadows so his body hid her from those in the ballroom. Damon guessed she didn't want to stand out. Too late, to him she already did.

'Don't be intimidated by any of that lot.' He jerked his head towards the crowds. 'They might have the wealth but they don't always have the manners. Or the kindness.'

'You're saying you don't fit in either?' The scepticism in her gaze as she looked him over was unmissable.

He resisted the urge to preen in front of her like some damn peacock. Instead he offered a platitude. 'Does anyone truly fit in?'

Her gaze flashed up to his and held it a long moment. Her irises were such a vibrant blue he knew they had to be covered with contacts. The pretence of polite small talk fell away. The desire to reach for her—to strip her—almost overwhelmed him. Now *that* was inappropriate. He tensed, pushing back the base instinct. Damn, he wanted to touch her. Wanted her to touch him. That look in her eyes? Pure invitation. Except he had the feeling she was too inexperienced to even be aware of it.

But he couldn't stop the question spilling roughly from his lips. 'Are you going to do it?'

Eleni Nicolaides didn't know what or how to answer him. This man wasn't like anyone she'd met before.

Direct. Devastating. *Dangerous.*

'Are you going to do it, Blue?'

'Do what?' she whispered vaguely, distracted by the play of dark and light in his watchful expression. He was appallingly handsome in that tall, dark, sex-on-a-stick sort of way. The kind of obviously experienced playboy who'd never been allowed near her.

But at the same time there was more than that to him—something that struck a chord within her. A new—seductive—note that wasn't purely because of the physical magnetism of the man.

He captivated every one of her senses and all her interest. A lick of something new burned—yearning. She wanted him closer. She wanted to reach out and touch him. Her pulse throbbed, beating need about her body—to her dry, sensitive lips, to her tight, full breasts, to other parts too secret to speak of...

His jaw tightened. Eleni blinked at the fierce intensity that flashed in his eyes. Had he read her mind? Did he know just *what* she wanted to do right now?

'Join in,' he answered between gritted teeth.

She swallowed. Now her pulse thundered as she realised how close she'd come to making an almighty fool of herself. 'I shouldn't...'

'Why not?'

So many reasons flooded her head in a cacophony of panic.

Her disguise, her deceit, her *duty*.

'Blue?' he prompted. His smile was gentle enough but the expression in his eyes was too hot.

Men had looked at her with lust before, but those times the lust hadn't been for her but for her wealth, her title, her virtue. She'd never been on a date. She was totally untouched. And everyone knew. She'd read the crude conjecture and the jokes in the lowest of the online guttersnipes: *THE VIRGIN PRINCESS!!!*

All caps. Multiple exclamation marks.

That her 'purity' was so interesting and so important angered her. It wasn't as if it had been deliberate. It wasn't as if she'd saved herself for whichever prince would be chosen for her to marry. She'd simply been so sequestered there'd been zero chance to find even a friend, let alone a boyfriend.

And now it transpired that her Prince was to be Xander of the small European state of Santa Chiara. He certainly hadn't saved himself for her and she knew his fidelity after their marriage was not to be expected. Discretion was, but not that sort of intimate loyalty. Or love.

'Do you ever stop asking questions?' she asked, trying for cool and sophisticated for these last few moments of escape.

Wishing she could be as accepting as so many others who didn't doubt their arranged marriages. Because this was it. Tomorrow her engagement would be formally announced. A man she'd barely met and most certainly didn't like would become her fiancé. She felt frigid at the thought. But those archaic royal rules remained unchallenged and offered certainty. The Princess of Palisades could never marry a commoner. This disguise tonight was a lame leap for five minutes of total freedom. The only five minutes she'd have.

'Not if I'm curious about something.'

'And you're curious about—'

'You. Unbearably. Yes.'

Heat slammed into every cell. She couldn't hold his gaze but she couldn't look away either. His eyes were truly blue—not enhanced by contacts the way hers were—and hot. He seemed to see right through her mask, her carefully applied powder, her whole disguise. He saw the need she'd tried to hide from everyone.

She was out of place and yet this was her home—where she'd been born and raised and where her future was destined, dictated by duty.

'You have the chance to experience this…' he waved at the ballroom full of beautiful people '…yet you're hanging back in the shadows.'

He voiced her fantasy—reminding her of her stupid,

crazy plan. She'd arranged for a large selection of costumes to be delivered to the nurses' quarters at the hospital for tonight's masquerade. No one would know that one dress, one wig, and one mask were missing from that order. All done so she, cloistered, protected, precious Princess Eleni, could steal one night as an anonymous girl able to talk to people not as a princess, but as a nobody.

She could be no one.

And yet, when it had come to it, she'd swiftly realised her error. She'd watched those guests arrive. Clustered together, laughing squads of *friends*—the kind she'd never had. How could she walk into that room and start talking to any of them *without* her title as her armour? What had she to offer? How could she blend in when she hadn't any clue what to discuss other than superficial niceties? She'd ached with isolation, inwardly mocking her own self-piteous hurt, as she'd uselessly stared at all those other carefree, relaxed people having fun.

Privileged Princess Eleni had burned with jealousy.

Now she burned with something else, something just as shameful.

'I'm biding my time,' she prevaricated with a chuckle, drawing on years of practising polite conversation to cover her shaken, unruly emotions.

'You're wasting it.'

His bluntness shocked that smile from her lips. She met his narrowed gaze and knew he saw too much.

'You want a night out, you need to get out there and start circulating,' he advised.

Her customary serene demeanour snapped at his tone. 'Maybe that's not what I want.'

The atmosphere pulsed between them like an electrical charge faulting.

Heat suffused every inch of her skin. Now she truly was unable to hold his gaze. But as she looked down he reached out. The merest touch of fingers to her chin, nudging so she looked him in the eye again. She fought to quell the uncontrollable shiver that the simple touch generated.

'No?' Somehow he was even closer as he quietly pressed her. 'Then what do you want?'

That she couldn't answer. Not to herself. Not now. But he could see it anyway.

'Walk with me through the ballroom,' he said in a low voice. 'I dare you.'

His challenge roused a rare surge of rebellion within her. She who always did as she was bid—loyal, dutiful, serene. Princess Eleni never caused trouble. But *he* stirred trouble. Her spirit lifted; she was determined to show strength before him.

'I don't need you to dare me,' she breathed.

'Don't you?' He called her bluff.

Silent, she registered the gauntlet in his hard gaze. The glow of those blue eyes ignited her to mutinous action. She turned and strode to the edge of the alcove. Nerves thrummed, chilling her. What if she was recognised?

But this man hadn't recognised her and she knew her brother would be busy in the farthest corner of the room meeting select guests at this early stage in the evening. Everyone was preoccupied with their own friends and acquaintances. She *might* just get away with this after all.

'Coming?' She looked back and asked him, refusing—yet failing—to flush.

He took her hand and placed it in the crook of his elbow, saying nothing, but everything, with a sardonic look. The rock-hard heat of his biceps seeped through the fine material of his tailored suit and her fingers curled around it instinctively. He pressed his arm close to his side, trapping her hand.

He walked slowly, deliberately, the length of the colonnades. To her intense relief, he didn't stop to speak to anyone, instead he kept his attention on her, his gaze melting that cold block of nervousness lodged in her diaphragm.

It turned out she'd been wrong to worry about recognition. Because while people *were* looking, it was not at her.

'All these women are watching you,' she murmured as they drew near the final column. 'And they look surprised.'

A smile curled his sensual lips. 'I haven't been seen dating recently.'

'They think I'm your date?' she asked. 'Am I supposed to feel flattered?'

His laughter was low and appreciative. 'Don't deny it, you do.'

She pressed her lips together, refusing to smile. But the sound of his laugh wasn't just infectious, it seemed to reach right inside her and chase all that cold away with its warmth.

'There.' He drew her into the last alcove, a mirror of the first, and she was appallingly relieved to discover it too was empty at this early hour.

'Was that so awful?' he asked, not relinquishing her hand but walking with her to the very depths of the respite room and turning to face her.

Inwardly she was claiming it as a bittersweet victory. A date at last.

'Who are you?' She felt foolish that she didn't know when it was clear many others did. 'Why do they look at you?'

He cocked his head, his amusement gleaming. 'Why do *you* look at me?'

Eleni refused to answer. She was *not* going to pander to his already outsize ego.

His lazy smile widened. 'What do you see?'

That one she could answer. She smiled, relishing her release from 'polite princess response'.

'I see arrogance,' she answered boldly. 'A man who ﬁes convention and doesn't give a damn what anyone

e?'

She angled her head, mirroring his inquiring look. 'You don't wear a mask. You don't make the effort that's expected of everyone else.'

'And I don't do that—because why?' His attention narrowed—laser-like in its focus on her.

'Because you don't need to,' she guessed, seeing the appreciation flicker in his eyes. 'You don't want their approval. You're determined to show you don't need *anything* from them.'

His expression shuttered, but he didn't deny her assessment of him. Her heart quickened as he stepped closer.

'Do you know what I see?' Almost angrily he pointed to the mask covering most of her face. 'I see someone hiding more than just her features. I see a woman who wants more than what she thinks she should have.'

She stilled, bereft—of speech, of spirit. Because she did want more and yet she knew she was so spoilt and selfish to do so. She had *everything*, didn't she?

'So what happens at midnight?' That tantalising smile quirked his lips, drawing her attention to the sensuality that was such a potent force within him.

She struggled to remind herself she was no Cinderella. She was already the Princess, after all. 'Exactly what you think it will.'

'You'll leave and I'll never see you again.'

His words struck deep inside her—sinking like stones of regret.

'Precisely,' she replied with her perfectly practised princess politeness.

She shouldn't feel the slightest disappointment. This was merely a fleeting conversation in the shadows. Five minutes of dalliance that she could reminisce over a whole lot later. Like for the rest of her life.

'I don't believe in fairy tales,' he said roughly, his smile lost.

'Nor do I,' she whispered. She believed in duty. In family. In doing what was right. Which was why she was going to marry a man she didn't love and who didn't love her. Romance was for fairy tales and other people.

'You sure about that?' He edged closer still, solemn and intense. 'Then flip it. Don't do the expected. Don't disappear at midnight.' He dared her with that compelling whisper. 'Stay and do what you want. You have the mask to protect you. *Take* what you want.'

She stared up at him. He was roguishly handsome and he was only playing with her, wasn't he? But that was…okay. Intense temptation and a totally foreign sensation rippled through her. The trickle soon turned into a tsunami. From the deepest core of her soul, slipping along her veins to ignite every inch of her body.

Want.

Pure and undeniable.

Couldn't she have just a very little moment for herself? Couldn't she have just a very little of *him*?

He couldn't hide his deepening tension. It was in his eyes, in the single twitch of the muscle in his jaw as the curve of his smile flatlined. That infinitesimal *edge* sharpened. But he remained as motionless as the marble column behind him, hiding the ballroom from her view. Waiting, watching.

Take what you want.

That dare echoed in her mind, fuelling her desire.

She gazed into his eyes, losing herself in the molten steel. She parted her lips the merest fraction to draw in a desperate breath. But he moved the moment she did. Full predator—fast, powerful, inescapable—he pressed his mouth to meet hers.

Instinctively she closed her eyes, unable to focus on anything but the sensation of his warm lips teasing hers. Her breath caught as he stepped closer, his hands spanning her waist to draw her against him. She quivered on impact as she felt his hard strength, finally appreciating the sheer size of the man. Tall, strong, he radiated pure masculinity.

He took complete control, his tongue sliding along her lips, slipping past to stroke her. Never had she been kissed like this. Never had *she* kissed like this, but his commanding passion eviscerated any insecurity—and all thought. Lost to the sensation she simply leaned closer, letting him support her, pressing her into his iron heat.

Heavy, addictive power flowed from him to her as he kissed the very soul of her. His arms were like bars, drawing her against the solid expanse of his chest. A moan rose in the back of her throat and he tightened his hold more. She quivered at his defined strength—not just physical. It took mental strength to build a body like his, she knew that too.

Her legs weakened even as a curious energy surged through her. She needed him closer still. But his hand lifted to cup her jaw and he teased—pressing maddeningly light kisses on her lips instead of that explosive, carnal kiss of before. She moaned, in delight, in frustration.

At that raw, unbidden response, he gave her what she wanted. Uncontrolled passion. She clutched at him wildly as her knees gave out—swept away on a torrent of need that had somehow been unleashed. She didn't know how to assuage it, how to combat it. All she could do was cling— wordlessly, mindlessly begging for more. The intensity of his desire mirrored her own—she felt him brace, felt the burning of his skin beneath her fingertips as she touched his jaw, copying his delightful touch.

But now his hand stroked lower, pressing against her thigh. Breathless she slipped deeper, blindly seeking more. But she felt his hesitation. She gasped as he broke the kiss to look at her. Unthinking she arched closer, seeking to regain contact. But in the distance she heard a roaring. A clinking of—

Glasses. *Guests*.

Good grief, what was she *doing*?

Far too late those years of training, duty and responsibility kicked in. How could she have forgotten who and where she was? She could not throw everything away for one moment of *lust*.

But this lust was all-consuming. All she wanted was for him to touch her again—decisively, intimately, now.

Brutal shame burned from her bones to her skin. She had to get alone and under control. But as she twisted from his hold a long tearing sound shredded the unnatural silence between them. Time slowed as realisation seeped into her fried brain.

That too tight, too thin strap over her shoulder had ripped clear from the fabric it had been straining to support. And the result?

She didn't need to look to know; she could feel the exposure—the cooler air on her skin. Aghast, she sent him a panicked glance. Had he noticed?

Of course he'd noticed.

She froze, transfixed, as his gaze rested for a second longer on her bared breast before flicking back to her face. The fiery hunger in his eyes consumed her. She was alight with colour and heat, but it wasn't embarrassment.

Oh, heavens, no.

She tugged up the front of her dress and turned, blindly seeking escape.

But he drew her close again, bracketing her into the protective stance of his body. He walked, pressing her forward away from the crowd she'd foolishly forgotten was present. And she was so confused she just let him. Through a discreet archway, down a wide corridor to space and silence. He walked with her, until a door closed behind them.

The turn of the lock echoed loudly. Startled, she turned to see him jerkily stripping out of his dinner jacket with barely leashed violence. His white dress shirt strained across his broad shoulders. Somehow he seemed bigger, more aggressive, more sexual.

Appallingly desire flooded again, rooting her to the spot where she clutched her torn dress to her chest. She desperately tried to catch her breath but her body couldn't cope. Her lips felt full and sensitive and throbbed for the press of his. Her breasts felt tight and heavy and, buried deep within, she was molten hot and aching.

All she could do was stare as he stalked towards her.

All she could think was to surrender.

CHAPTER TWO

'SLIP THIS AROUND your shoulders and we can leave immediately.' He held the jacket out to her. 'No one will...' He trailed off as she stared at him uncomprehendingly.

He'd only been stripping in order to *clothe* her? To protect her from prying eyes rather than continue with...with...

Suddenly she was mortified. She'd thought that he'd been going to—

'*No.*' She finally got her voice box to work. 'No. That's impossible.'

Nervously she licked her lips. What was impossible was her own reaction. Her own *willingness*. Horrified, she stepped away from the temptation personified in front of her, backing up until she was almost against the wall on the far side of the room.

He stood still, his jacket gently swinging from his outstretched hand, and watched her move away from him. A slight frown furrowed his forehead. Then he shifted, easing his stance. He casually tossed the jacket onto the antique sofa that now stood between them.

His lips twisted with a smile as rueful as it was seductive. 'I'm not going to do anything.'

'I know,' she said quickly, trying and failing to offer a smile in return.

She wasn't afraid of him. She was afraid of herself. Her cheeks flamed and she knew a fierce blush had every inch of her skin aglow. Shamed, she clutched the material closer to her chest.

This had been such a mistake. More dangerous than she ever could have imagined. Her breathing quickened again. She was so mortified but so *sensitive*. She glanced at him again only to have him snare her gaze in his. He was watching her too intently. She realised that his breathing was quickened, like hers, and a faint sheen highlighted his sun-kissed skin.

'Are you okay?' he asked softly. 'I'm sorry.'

But he didn't look sorry. If anything that smile deepened.

But she also saw the intensity of the heat banked in his expression and something unfurled within her. Something that didn't help her resistance.

'It wasn't your fault,' she muttered. 'It's a cheap dress and it doesn't really fit that well.'

'Let me help you fix it,' he offered huskily. 'So you can get out of here.'

'I can make do.' She glanced at the locked door behind him. 'I'd better go.'

She knew there was another exit from the room, but it was locked by the security system. She couldn't use it without showing him she was intimate with the palace layout. He could never know that. Maybe she could drape the blue and purple hair of her wig over her shoulder to hide that tear.

'Trust me,' he invited gruffly. 'I'll fix your dress. Won't do anything else.'

That was the problem. She wanted him to do something. Do *everything* or *anything* he wanted. And that was just crazy because she couldn't set a lifetime of responsibility ablaze now. What made it worse was that he knew—why she'd moved to put not just space, but furniture between them.

'You can't get past them all with that strap the way it is now,' he muttered.

He was right. She couldn't get away from him either. Not yet.

So she stepped nearer, turning to present her shoulder with the torn strap. 'Thank you.'

Holding her breath, heart pounding, she fought to remain

still as he came within touching distance. The tips of his deft fingers brushed against her burning skin as he tried to tie the loose strap to the torn bodice. She felt it tighten, but then heard his sharp mutter of frustration as the strap loosened again.

She inhaled a jagged breath. 'Don't worry—'

'I'll get it this time,' he interrupted. 'Almost there.'

She waited, paralysed, as he bent to the task again, trying desperately to quell her responsive shiver to the heat of his breath on her skin but he noticed it anyway. His hands stilled for that minuscule moment before working again.

'There,' he promised in a lethal whisper. 'All fixed.'

But he was still there—too close, too tall, too everything. She stood with her eyes tight shut, totally aware of him.

'You're good to go.'

Good. She didn't feel like being good. And she didn't want to go.

She opened her eyes and saw what she'd already felt with every other sense. He was close enough to kiss.

She shook her head very slightly, not wanting to break this spell. 'It was a dumb idea. I shouldn't have come.'

She hadn't meant to tell him anything more but the secret simply fell from her lips.

'But you've gone to such trouble.' He traced one of the swirls of glitter she'd painted on her shoulder. His finger roved north, painting another that rose up her neck, near her frantically beating pulse, and rested there.

'You shouldn't miss out.' He didn't break eye contact as he neared, but he didn't close the half-inch between their mouths.

She had to miss out. That was her destiny—the rules set before she was even born. Yet his gaze mesmerised, making her want all kinds of impossible things. Beneath those thick lashes the intensity of his truly blue eyes burned through to her core.

'You'd better get back out there, Blue.' He suddenly broke the taut silence and dropped his hand. His voice roughened, almost as if he were angry.

'Why?' Why should she? When what she wanted was right here? Just one more kiss? Just once? Hot fury speared—the fierce emotion striking all sense from her. 'Maybe I can…' she muttered, gazing into his eyes.

'Can what?' he challenged, arching an eyebrow. 'What can you do…?'

She tilted her chin and reached up on tiptoe to brush her lips over his. Sensation shivered through her. This was right. This was *it*.

He stiffened, then took complete control. He gripped her waist and hauled her close, slamming her body into his. She felt the give of her stupid dress again. She didn't mind the half-laugh that heated her.

'You can do that,' he muttered, a heated tease as he kissed her with those torturous light kisses until she moaned in frustration. 'You can do that all you like.'

She did like. She liked it a *lot*.

Kisses. Nothing wrong with kisses. Her bodice fluttered down again, exposing her to him. Thank goodness. His hands took advantage, then his mouth. The drive for more overwhelmed her. Never had she felt so alive. Or so good.

She gasped when he lifted her, but she didn't resist, didn't complain. He strode a couple of paces to sit on the sofa, crushing her close then settling her astride his lap.

She shivered in delight as he kissed her again. She could die in these kisses. She met every one, mimicking, learning, becoming braver. Becoming unbearably aroused. Breathless, she lost all sense of time—could only succumb to the sensation as his hand swept down her body, down her legs. Slowly he drew up the hem of her dress. His fingertips stroked up her hot skin until he neared that most private part of her. She shivered and he lifted his head, looking deep into her eyes. She knew he was seeking permission.

She wriggled ever so slightly to let him have greater access because this felt too good to stop. Still watching her, he slid his hand higher.

'Kiss me again,' she whispered.

Something flared in his eyes. And kiss her he did, but not on her mouth. He bent lower, drawing her nipple into the hot cavern of his mouth while at the same time his fingertips erotically teased over the crotch of her panties.

Eleni gasped and writhed—seeking both respite from the torment, and more of it. No one had touched her so intimately. And, heaven have mercy, she liked it.

She caught a glimpse of the reflection in the mirror hanging on the opposite wall. She didn't recognise the woman with that man bending to her bared breasts. This was one stranger doing deliciously naughty things with another stranger—kissing and rubbing and touching and sliding. Beneath her, his hard length pressed against his suit pants. It fascinated her. The devilish ache to explore him more overtook her. She rocked against his hand, shivering with forbidden delight. She was so close to something, but she was cautious. He pulled back for a second and studied her expression. She clenched her jaw. She didn't want him to stop.

'Take what you want,' he urged softly. 'Whatever you want.'

'I...'

'Anything,' he muttered. 'As much or as little as you like.'

Because he wanted this too. She felt the tremble in his fingers and it gave her confidence. Somehow she knew he was as taken aback as she by this conflagration. She might not have the experience, but she had the intuition to understand this was physical passion at its strongest.

Her legs quivered but she let him slide the satin skirt of her dress higher. It glided all the way up to her waist, exposing her almost completely. Her legs were bared, her chest, only her middle was covered in a swathe of blue. She sighed helplessly as that hard ridge of him pressed where she was aching most.

She struggled to unfasten his shirt buttons; she wanted to see his skin. To feel it. He helped her, pulling the halves of his shirt apart. For a moment she just stared. She'd known he was strong, she'd felt that. But the definition of his tense muscles—the pecs, the abs—still took her by surprise. The light scattering of hair added to the perfection. He was the ultimate specimen of masculinity. She raised her gaze, meeting the fire in his, and understood the strength he was holding in check.

'Touch all you like,' he muttered, a guttural command.

She liked it *all*. Suddenly stupidly nervous, she pressed her palm over his chest—feeling the hardness and heat of him. But she could feel the thump of his heart too and some-how that grounded her. She read the desire in his eyes, in-tuitively understanding how leashed his passion was. That he, like she, wanted it *all*.

'Touch me,' she choked. Her command—and his reply—dislodged the last brick in the wall that had been dam-ming her desire inside. She did not want him to hold back with her.

He caressed her breasts with his hands, teasing her as she rocked on him, rubbing in the way the basic instinct of her body dictated—back and forth and around.

'So good,' she muttered, savouring the pressure of his mouth, the sweep of his hands, the hardness of him under her. 'So good.'

It was so foreign. So delicious. Feverish with desire, she arched. Pleasure beyond imagination engulfed her as faster they moved together. Kisses became ravenous. Hands swept hard over skin. Heat consumed her. She moaned, her head falling back as he touched her in places she'd never been touched. As he brought her sensuality to life.

She heard a tearing sound and realised it had been the

crotch of her panties. They'd not survived the strength of his grip. She glanced and saw he'd tossed the remnants of white silk and lace onto the wide seat. Now she could feel his hand touching her again so much more intimately.

'Oh.'

She dragged in a searing breath and gazed into his eyes.

'That's it, Blue,' he enticed her in that devilish whisper. 'Come on.'

She couldn't answer—not as his fingers circled, and slipped along the slick cleft of her sex, not as they teased that sensitive nub over and over and over. She bit her lip as that searing tension deep in her belly tightened. She rocked, her rhythm matching the pace of his fingers as they strummed over and around her. He kissed her, his tongue soothing the indent of her teeth on her lip, then stroking inside her mouth in an intimate exploration of her private space. Just as his finger probed within her too.

She tore her mouth from his and threw her head back, arching in agony as she gasped for breath. He fixed his mouth on her breast, drawing her nipple in deep. Pleasure shot from one sensitive point to another, rolling in violent waves across her body. She shuddered in exquisite agony, crying out as she was completely lost to this raw, writhing bliss.

When she opened her eyes she saw he was watching her, his hand gently stroking her thigh.

She breathed out, summoning calm and failing. Giddy, she gazed at him, stunned by the realisation that she'd just had an orgasm. She'd let him touch her and kiss her and he'd made the most amazing feelings flood through her. But the hunger had returned already and brought that special kind of anger with it.

That emptiness blossomed, bigger than before. There was more to this electricity between them. More that she'd missed. More that she wanted.

A chasm stretched before her. A choice. A line that, once

crossed, could never be reclaimed. But it was *her* choice. And suddenly she knew exactly how she wanted this one thing in her life to be. Within her control.

For this first time—for only this time—she wanted physical intimacy with a man who truly wanted her back. A man who wanted not her title, not her purity or connections. Just her—naked and no one special. This man knew nothing of who or what she was, but he wanted her. This was not love, no. But pure, basic, brilliant lust.

Just this once, she would be *wanted* for nothing but herself.

Almost angrily she shifted on him, pressing close again, kissing him. He kissed her back, as hard, as passionate. She moaned in his mouth. *Willing* him to take over. But he drew back, pressing his hand over hers, stopping her from sliding her palm down his chiselled chest to his belt.

'We're going to be in trouble in a second,' he groaned. 'Stop.'

She stared dazedly into his face as he eased her back along his thighs, almost crying at his rejection.

'I need to keep you safe,' he muttered as his hands worked quickly to release his zipper. 'One second. To be safe.'

She couldn't compute his comment because at that moment his erection sprang free. Never had she seen a man naked. Never had she *touched*. He reached into his trouser pocket and pulled out a small packet that he tore open with his teeth. Her mouth dried as she stared avidly.

Of course he was prepared. He was an incredibly handsome, virile man who knew exactly how to turn her on because *he* was experienced. He was used to this kind of anonymous tryst and he definitely knew how to make a woman feel good. And that was...*okay*.

As she tore her gaze away from the magnificence of him she caught sight of their reflections in that gleaming mirror again. The image of those two strangers—half naked and entwined—was the most erotic thing she'd ever seen in her life. Their pasts didn't matter. Nor did their futures. There was only this. Only them. Only now. She turned back to look at the overwhelming man she was sitting astride with such vulnerability—and with such desire.

Princess Eleni always did the right thing.

But she wasn't Princess Eleni tonight. She was no one and this was nothing.

'Easy, Blue.' He gently stroked her arm.

She realised her breathing was completely audible—rushed and short.

'Just whatever you want,' he muttered softly.

He wasn't just inviting her. He was giving her the choice, *all* the control. Yet his voice and his body both commanded and compelled her own and there was no choice.

This once. This *one* time. She wanted everything—all of him. She shimmied closer. The sight of his huge straining erection made her quiver and melt. She didn't know how to do this. She looked into his eyes and was lost in that intensity. And suddenly she understood.

She kissed him. Kissed him long and deep and softened in the delight. In the *rightness* of the sensation. She could feel him there beneath her. She rocked her hips, as she'd done before, feeling him slide through her feminine folds. His hands gripped her hips, holding her, helping her. She pressed down, right on that angle, every sense on high alert and anticipation. But her body resisted, unyielding.

She *wanted* this.

So she pushed down hard. Unexpectedly sharp pain pierced the heated fog of desire.

'Blue?' A burning statue beneath her; his breathing was ragged as he swore. 'I've—'

'I'm fine,' she pleaded, willing her body to welcome his.

'You're tight,' he said between gritted teeth.

'You're big.'

He filled her completely—beneath her, about her, within

her. The force and fire of his personality scalded her. Her breath shuddered as she was locked in his embrace, and in the intense heat of his gaze.

'Have I hurt you?' His question came clipped.

'No.' It wasn't regret that burned within her, but recognition. This was what she wanted. 'Kiss me.'

And he did. He kissed her into that pure state of bliss once more. Into heat and light and sparkling rainbows and all kinds of magic that were miraculous and new. Touching him ignited her and she moved restlessly, eager to feel him touching her again too. That fullness between her legs eased. Honeyed heat bloomed and she slid closer still to him. She sighed, unable to remain still any more. His arms tightened around her, clasping her to him as he kissed her back—exactly how she needed. *Yes.* This was so good, it had to be right. He shifted her, sliding her back, and then down hard on the thick column of his manhood.

He suddenly stood, taking her weight with no apparent difficulty. Startled, she instinctively wrapped her legs around his waist. He kissed her in approval and took those few paces to where that narrow table stretched along the wall. He stood at the short end and carefully placed her right on the edge of it, then slowly he eased her so she lay on her back on the cool wood. Her legs were wound around his waist, her hips tilted upwards as he braced over her, his shaft still driven to the hilt inside her. That mirror was right beside her now but she didn't turn her head to look again at those strangers; she couldn't. Her wicked rake claimed every ounce of her focus.

'This is madness,' he muttered. 'But I don't care.'

Nor did she. This moment was too perfect. Too precious. Too much to be denied.

His large hands cupped her, holding her as he pressed into her deeply, and then pulled back a fraction, only to push forward again. Again, then again, then again. Every time he seemed to drive deeper, claiming more and more of her.

And she gave it to him. She would give him everything, he made her feel so good. He gazed into her eyes and in his she saw the echo of her own emotions—wonder, pleasure, *need*.

She'd never been as close to another person in all her life. Not so passionately, nakedly close. Nor so vulnerable, or so safe. Never so free.

She kissed him in arousal, in madness, in gratitude. Trusting him implicitly. He'd already proven his desire to please her.

'Come again,' he coaxed in a passionate whisper. 'I want to feel you come.'

She wanted that too. She wanted exactly that.

He touched her just above the point where they were joined, teasing even as he filled her. She gasped as she felt the sensations inside gather once more in that unstoppable storm.

'You…please…' she begged incoherently as she feverishly clutched him, digging her fingernails into his flesh. She wanted him to feel the same ecstasy surging through her. She needed him on this ride *with* her. As she frantically arched to meet him she heard his groan. His hands gripped tighter, his expression tensed. She smiled in that final second. She wanted to laugh. She wanted to revel in it and she never, ever wanted it to end.

His face flushed as sensation swept the final vestige of control from his grasp. Pleasure stormed through her again, surging to the farthest reaches of her body. She sobbed in the onslaught of goodness and delight and his roar of satisfaction was the coda to her completeness.

Her eyes were closed. She could hear only the beating of her heart and his as they recovered. She was pinned by his weight and it was the best feeling on earth.

But then laughter rang out. Not hers. Nor his.

'What's in this room?'

Eleni snapped her head to stare at the door as someone on the other side tried the handle.

'Hello?'

More laughter reverberated through the wood.

Reality returned in a violent slam, evaporating the mist of delight. Suddenly she saw herself as she'd look to anyone who burst through that door—Princess Eleni of Palisades, ninety per cent naked, sprawled on a table with her legs around the waist of some stranger and his body ploughed deep into hers.

Sordid headlines smashed into her head: *shameless wanton...a one-night stand...the eve of her engagement...* There would be no mercy, no privacy—only scorn and shame. She had to get out of here. Aghast, she stared up at the handsome stranger she'd just ravished. What had she done?

Damon watched his masked lover's eyes widen in shock. Beneath the blue sparkled powder, her skin paled and her kiss-crushed lips parted in a silent gasp. This was more than embarrassment. This was fear. He was so stunned by her devastated expression he stepped back. She slipped down from the table and tugged at her crumpled clothing. Before he could speak someone knocked on the door again. More voices sounded out in the corridor.

Her pallor worsened.

'I'll get rid of them,' he assured her, hauling up his trousers so he could get to the door and deny anyone entrance to the room. He was determined to wipe that terror from her face.

He pressed a hand on the door. Even though he'd locked it, he couldn't be sure someone wouldn't be able to unlock it from the other side. He listened intently, hoping the revellers would pass and go exploring elsewhere. After a few moments the voices faded.

He turned back to see how she was doing, but she'd vanished. Shocked, he stared around the empty room, then stalked back to where she'd been standing seconds ago.

Only now did he register the other door tucked to the side of that large mirror. There were two entrances to this room and he'd been so caught up in her he'd not even noticed.

He tried the handle but it was locked. So how had she got through it? Keenly he searched and spotted a discreet security screen. Had she known the code to get out? She must have. Because in the space of two seconds, she'd fled.

Just who was she? Why so afraid of someone finding her? Foreboding filled him. He didn't trust women. He didn't trust anyone.

If only he'd peeled off that mask and seen her face properly. How could he have made such a reckless, risky decision?

Anger simmered, but voices sounded outside the other door again, forcing him to move. He glanced in the mirror at his passion-swept reflection. Frowning, he swiftly buttoned his shirt and fixed his trousers properly. Thank heavens he'd retained enough sense to use protection. But as he sorted himself out he realised something he'd missed in his haste to ensure that door was secure. The damn condom was torn. And more than that? It was marked with a trace of something that shouldn't have been there. He remembered when she'd first pushed down on him. When she'd inhaled sharply and tears had sprung to her eyes.

Uncertainty. *Pain.*

Grimly he fastened his belt. He'd been too lost to lust to absorb the implications of her reaction. Now his gut tensed as he struggled to believe the evidence. Had she given him her virginity? Had she truly never had another lover and yet let him, a total stranger, have her in a ten-minute tryst in a private powder room?

Impossible. But the stain of her purity was on his skin. His pulse thundered in his ears. *Why* would she have done something so wild? What was her motivation?

Hell, what had *he* been thinking? To have had sex with

a woman he'd barely met as fast and as furiously as possible? Almost in public?

But her expressive response had swept all sensible thought from his head. She'd *wanted* him and heaven knew he'd wanted her. He was appalled by his recklessness; his anger roared. But a twist of Machiavellian satisfaction brewed beneath, because he was going to have to find her. He was going to have to warn her about the condom. The instinct to hunt her pressed like the blade of a knife. She owed him answers.

Find her. Find her. Find her.

His pulse banged like a pagan's drum, marching him back to the busy ballroom. He even took to the balcony to scan the braying crowd, determined to find that blue hair and swan-like neck. But he knew it was futile. The midnight hour had struck and that sizzling Cinderella had run away, never wanting to be seen again.

Least of all by him.

CHAPTER THREE

'YOU LOOK PEAKY.'

Eleni forced a reassuring smile and faced her brother across the aisle in his jet.

'I have a bit of a headache but it's getting better,' she lied.

She felt rotten. Sleeplessness and guilt made her queasy.

'The next few weeks will be frantic. You'll need to stay in top form. They want the pretty Princess, not the pale one,' King Giorgos turned back to the tablet he'd been staring at for the duration of the flight.

'Yes.'

She glanced out of the small window. Crowds had gathered with flags and celebratory signs. She quickly dug into her bag to do a touch-up on her blush, thankful that the jet had landed them back on Palisades.

Giorgos had escorted her on a three-day celebration visit of Santa Chiara to meet again with Prince Xander and his family. Not so long ago she'd have inwardly grimaced at her brother's smothering protectiveness, but she'd been glad of his presence. It had meant she'd not been left alone with Prince Xander.

The Shy Princess captures the Playboy Prince...

Their engagement had captured the imaginations of both nations. Her schedule and the resulting media interest had been beyond intense these last few weeks. At least all the appearances had kept her too busy to think. But late at night when she was alone in her private suite?

That was when she processed everything, reassuring herself she was safe. She would never tell anyone and that man from the ball would never tell anyone. He didn't even know who she was. She didn't know his name either. Only his face. Only his body.

She shivered but forced another smile when her brother glanced at her again. 'I'm going to go to my hospital visit this morning,' she said brightly.

Giorgos frowned. 'You don't wish to rest?'

Always protective. And also, always frowning.

She shook her head.

It had been nothing more than a sordid physical trans-action. A ten-minute encounter between strangers. And surely, *please, please, please*, she would soon forget it. Be-cause right now the memories were too real. She relived every moment, every word, every touch. And the worst thing? She wanted it again, wanted more, wanted it so much she burned with it. And then she burned with shame. Tears stung at the enormity of her betrayal. She was now engaged to another man yet all she could think of was *him*, that ar-rogant, intense stranger at the ball.

Thankfully displays of physical affection weren't 'done' between royals so the few 'kisses for the camera' on her tour with Prince Xander had been brief—her coolness read by the media as shyness. In private her fiancé had seemed happy to give her the time and space to adjust.

It was Giorgos who had asked if she was going to be happy with Xander and who'd reassured her that her fi-ancé's 'playboy' status was more media speculation than solid truth. For a moment she was tempted to confess her dreadful affair, but then she saw the tiredness in the back of her brother's eyes. He worked so hard for his people.

And she couldn't bear to see his crushing disappoint-ment. She remembered how Giorgos had teased her with big-brother ruthlessness and laughter. But how he'd aged a decade overnight when their father died. Under the burden of all that responsibility he'd become serious, distant and more ruthless, without that humour. She understood he was wretchedly busy, but he'd tried his best for her—sending people to educate her, protect her, guide her. He just hadn't had the time himself. And she could not let him down.

He believed Xander to be the right fit for her—from a limited pool of options—and perhaps he was. So she'd make the best of it.

For Giorgos.

But the thought of her wedding night repulsed her. As crazy as it was, that brief conversation with that stranger at the ball had engendered far more trust in her than any of the discussions she'd had with polite, well-educated, aiming-to-please but ultimately careless Prince Xander. She simply didn't want him like that. She shivered again as that cold, sick feeling swept over her.

'I don't want to miss a visit,' she finally answered as she rose to disembark the jet.

She needed to do something slightly worthwhile because the guilt was eating her up. Her brother nodded and said nothing more. If anyone understood duty before all else, it was he.

An hour later, as she walked the corridor towards her favourite ward, that cold queasiness returned.

'Princess Eleni?' Kassie, the physiotherapist escorting her to the ward, stopped.

From a distance Eleni registered the woman was frowning and her voice sounded distanced too.

'Are you feeling okay?'

Damon Gale was barely existing in a state of perpetual anger. He hadn't left Palisades without trying to find and warn his mystery lover there might be consequences from their time together. He'd described her to his half-sister Kassie, but she'd not been able to identify the woman either. No one could. None of his subtle queries had given any answers. Where had she disappeared to so quickly? Heaven knew, when he found her he was giving her a piece of his mind. But at night she came to him in dream after dream.

He woke, hard, hungry and irritable as hell. There was so much more they should have done. But now she was hiding. Not least the truth about who she was. Why?

He loathed nothing more than lies.

So this morning, weeks since that damn ball, he'd once again flown back to Palisades. Now he waited for Kassie at the hospital in her tiny office, looking at the clever pen and ink drawings of the child patients pinned to the noticeboard.

He heard a footstep and a low, hurried whisper just outside the door.

'Ma'am, are you sure you're feeling all right?'

That was Kassie. Damon's muscles tensed.

'I'm just a bit…dizzy. Oh.' The woman groaned.

He froze, shocked at the second voice. He *knew* those raspy tones. She spoke in his dreams. Every. Damn. Night.

'Do you need a container?' Kassie asked delicately.

'I had a bug a few days ago but I thought I was over it or I'd never have visited today,' the woman muttered apologetically. 'I'm so sorry. I'd never want to put any of your patients at risk.'

'They're a hardy lot.' Now Kassie's smile was audible. 'I'm more concerned about you. Are you sure I can't get a doctor to check you over?'

'No, please. No fuss. I'll quickly go back to the palace. My driver is waiting.'

Palace? Damon was unable to move. Unable to speak. His woman had known the security code to get through that second door in the palace. Did she work there? But she'd said she worked at the hospital. That was why he was back here again.

'Maybe you should rest a moment,' Kassie urged softly.

'No. I need to go. I shouldn't have come.'

Damon stood. Those words exactly echoed ones he'd heard that night at the masked ball. Those exact tones in that exact, raspy voice. It was *her*.

He strode across the room and out into the corridor. But

his half-sister had her back to him and she was standing alone. Damon looked past her and saw no one—the corridor ended abruptly with a corner.

'Who was that?' he demanded harshly.

Kassie spun, startled. 'Damon?' She blinked at him. 'I didn't know you were coming back again so soon.'

'I have another meeting,' he clipped. 'Who were you talking to?'

'I'm not supposed to say because her visits are strictly private,' Kassie answered quietly. 'But she wasn't feeling well today and left early.'

'Whose visits?' What did she mean by 'private'?

'The Princess.'

Damon stared dumbfounded at his half-sister.

Princess Eleni of Palisades?

Wasn't she the younger sister of King Giorgos, a man known for his protectiveness and control over everything— his island nation, his emotions, his small *family*. Hadn't he been the guardian of the supposedly shy Princess for ever?

Now the covers of the newspapers at the airport flashed in his mind. He'd walked past them this morning but paid little attention because they'd all carried the same photo and same headline—

A Royal Engagement! The Perfect Prince for Our Princess!

But the Princess was not perfect. She'd fooled around with a total stranger only a few weeks ago. And now she was engaged. Had she been rebelling like some wilful teen? Or was there something more devious behind her shocking behaviour? And, heaven have mercy, how *old* was she?

'What do you think was wrong with her?' he asked Kassie uneasily. He needed to get alone and research more because an extremely bad feeling was building inside him.

'I'm not sure. She was pale and nau—'

'Where did she go?' he interrupted.

Kassie was staring at him. 'Back to the palace. She visits my ward every Friday. She never misses, no matter what.' Kassie ventured a small smile. 'She doesn't seem your type.'

He forced himself to answer idly, as if this didn't matter a jot. 'Do I have a type?'

Kassie's laugh held a nervous edge as she shook her head. 'Princess Eleni is very sweet and innocent.'

But that was where Kassie was wrong. Princess Eleni wasn't sweet or innocent at all. She was a liar and a cheat and he was going to tear her to shreds.

Thank God he finally knew where and how he could get to her. He just had to withstand waiting one more week.

CHAPTER FOUR

IN HER BATHROOM Eleni stared at her reflection. Her skin was leached of colour and she felt sick and tired all the time. Wretched nausea roiled in her stomach yet again, violent and irrepressible. She'd been avoiding mirrors since the ball. She couldn't see herself without seeing those two strangers entwined...

It had been over a month since that night. Now she gazed at her breasts and held in her agonised gasp. Was it her imagination or were they fuller than usual? That would be because her period was due, right? But finally she made herself face the fact she'd been trying desperately to forget. Her period was more than due. It was late.

Two weeks late.

She'd been busy. She'd been travelling. Her cycle could be screwed up by nerves, couldn't it?

Frigid fear slithered down her spine as bitter acid flooded her mouth again. Because a lone, truly terrifying reason for her recurring sickness gripped her.

Surely it was impossible. She'd seen him put on that condom. She couldn't possibly be pregnant. That foul acid burned its way up into her mouth. She closed her eyes as tears stung and then streamed down her face. She needed help and she needed it now.

But there was no help to be had. She had no true friends to trust. Her childhood companions had been carefully selected for their families' loyalty to the crown and swiftly excised from her life if they'd slightly transgressed. There were acquaintances but no real confidantes and now most were in continental Europe getting on with their careers.

Eleni had studied at home. It was 'safer'; it endorsed

their own, prestigious university; it was what Giorgos had wanted. She'd not argued, not wanting to cause him trouble.

She was terrified of troubling him now.

But she was going to have to. Shaking, she showered then dressed. She quickly typed an email to Giorgos's secretary requesting a meeting for this evening. Her brother was busy, but Prince Xander was arriving from Santa Chiara tonight for a week's holiday with her. They'd be travelling to the outer islands to spend more time together. She was dreading it. She had to speak to Giorgos first. She had to tell him the truth.

Still incredibly cold, she grabbed a jacket and stuffed a cap in the pocket while her maid, Bettina, phoned for her car.

It was far later than when she usually went to the hospital, but she was desperate to get away from her suite where her maid was lining up sample wedding dresses from the world's top designers. The only thing she could do while waiting to meet Giorgos was maintain some kind of schedule. Given she'd left her visit so abruptly last week, she couldn't miss this week as well. She'd control the nausea and control her life.

Once she got to the hospital she asked Tony, her security detail, to wait for her outside. But she didn't go into the ward, and instead walked along the corridor to the other side of the building. She tugged on the cap and headed out to the private hospital garden. She needed to steel herself for the polite questions from the patients she'd come to help entertain. But she'd been lying all day, every day for the last few weeks and it was taking its toll. Telling people over and over again how excited she was at the prospect of marrying Prince Xander was exhausting. And horrible. But the bigger the lie, the more believable it apparently was.

She leaned over the wrought-iron railing, looking down at the river. She was going to have to go back and front up to Giorgos. Her gut churned, but it wasn't the pregnancy hormones making her nauseous now. How did she admit this all to him?

I'm sorry. I'm so sorry.

Sorry wasn't going to be good enough. She dreaded sinking so low in his eyes. Never had she regretted anything as much as her recklessness that night at the ball.

A prickle of awareness pressed on her spine—intuition whispered she was no longer alone. Warily she turned away from the water.

'You okay?' The man stood only a couple of paces away. 'Or are you feeling a little blue?'

The bitterness in that soft-spoken query devastated her. It was *him*. Her blood rushed and the edges of her vision blackened as she shrank back. Something grasped her elbow tightly, the pain pulling her from the brink of darkness.

'It's okay, I'm not going to let you fall.'

He was there and he was too close, with his words in her ear and his strength in his grip and his heat magnetic.

Oh, no. No.

'I'm sorry.' Eleni ignored the sweat suddenly slithering down her spine and snapped herself together.

He released her the second she tugged her arm back, but he didn't step away. So he was close. Too close.

'I don't know what came over me.' She leaned against the railing, unable to stop the trembling of her legs or the jerkiness of her breathing.

'Yeah, you do.' He leaned against the wrought iron too, resting his hand on the rail between them. Not relaxed. *Ready to strike.*

Tall, dark and dangerous, he looked like some streetwise power player in his black trousers, black jersey, aviator sunglasses and unreadable expression.

'There's no point trying to hide any more, Eleni,' he

said. 'I know who you are and I know exactly what your problem is.'

She froze. 'I don't have a problem.'

'Yeah, you do. You and I created it together. Now we're going to resolve it. Together.'

All strength vanished from her legs. They'd *created* it? The full horror hit as she realised he *knew*.

'I'm sorry,' she repeated mechanically. 'I don't know who you are and I don't know what you're talking about.' She willed her strength back. 'If you'll forgive me, I need to go.'

'No.' He removed his sunglasses. 'I won't forgive you.'

Her heart stuttered at the emotion reflected in his intense blue eyes. Accusation. Betrayal. Anger...and something else.

Something she dared not try to define.

She clenched her fists and plunged them into the pockets of her jacket, fighting the paralysis. 'I have to leave.'

'Not this time. You're coming with me, Eleni. You know we need to talk.'

'I can't do that.' Why had she thought it wise not to tell her security detail where she was going?

'Yes, you can. Because if you don't...'

'What?' She drew in a sharp breath as a sense of fatality struck. 'What will you do?'

Of course it would come to an ultimatum. The determination had been on his face from the second she'd seen him. He was livid.

'You come with me now and we take the time to sort this out, or I tell the world you're pregnant from screwing a stranger at the palace ball.'

His tawdry description of what they'd done stabbed. It hadn't been a 'screw'. It had meant more than she could ever admit to anyone.

'No one would believe you,' she muttered.

'You're *that* good at lying?' He was beyond livid. 'You

want this scandal dragged through the press? That you're going to marry a man without telling him that you're pregnant, most probably by another?'

She flinched at his cruelly blunt words but she latched onto the realisation that he wasn't *sure* the baby was his.

'You want the whole world to know that you're not the perfect Princess after all?' he goaded her relentlessly. 'But a liar and a cheater?'

'I've never been the perfect Princess,' she snapped back, defensive and hurt and unable to stay calm a second longer.

'Come on.' The softness of his swift reply stunned her.

Her heart thundered. He'd echoed the forbidden words from weeks ago. Heat flared. So wrong.

'I can't,' she reminded him—and herself—through gritted teeth. 'My fiancé is arriving in Palisades tonight.'

'Really?' He glared at her. 'That cheating life is what you really want?' His frustration seeped through. 'That's why you're standing by the river looking like you're about to throw yourself in? You're lost, Eleni.'

'You don't know what I am.'

He knew nothing about her and she knew as little about him—not even his damn name.

Except that wasn't quite true. She knew more important things—his determination, his strength, his consideration.

And *her* guilt.

'The one thing I do know is that you're pregnant and the baby very well might be mine. You owe me a conversation at least.'

He wasn't going anywhere and he was perfectly capable of acting on his threat, she knew that about him too. She tried to regain her customary calm, and decided to bluff. 'So talk.'

'Somewhere private.' He glanced up at the multi-storeyed hospital building behind her. 'Where we can't be seen or overheard.'

That made sense but it was impossible. She shook her head.

'My car is just around the corner,' he said, unconcerned at her latest refusal.

Her heart thudded. She shouldn't go anywhere alone with any man and certainly not this one.

'I'll go straight to the media,' he promised coolly. 'And I have proof. I still have your underwear.'

She was aghast; her jaw dropped.

'You *wouldn't*,' she choked.

'I'm prepared to do whatever is necessary to get this sorted out,' he replied blandly, putting his sunglasses back on. 'I suggest you walk with me now.'

What choice did she have?

She hardly saw where she was going as she moved back through the hospital, then to the right instead of the left. Away from her guard. Hopefully Tony wouldn't notice for a few minutes yet—in all her life she'd never caused trouble for him.

She slid into the passenger seat of his car.

'Five minutes,' she said just as he closed the door for her.

He was still laughing, bitterly, as he got in, locked the doors and started the engine. 'You might want to put on your seat belt, because it's going to take a little longer than that this time, sweetheart.' He pulled out into the road. 'We have a lifetime to work out.'

'Where are you taking me?' She broke into a cold sweat.

'As I said, somewhere private. Somewhere where we won't be disturbed.'

'You can't take me away from here.' Frantically she twisted in her seat, terrified to see the hospital getting smaller as they moved away from it.

'I know how quickly you can move, Eleni. I'm not taking the risk of you running from me this time.'

Surprised, she turned to face him.

'Relax.' He sent her an ironic glance. 'I'm not going to hurt you, Princess. We just need to talk.'

Sure, she knew he wouldn't hurt her physically. But in other ways? She tried to clear her head. 'You have the better of me. I don't even know your name.'

'So you're finally curious enough to ask?' His hands tightened on the steering wheel. 'My name is Damon Gale. I'm the CEO of a tech company that specialises in augmented reality. I have another company that's working on robotics. Most women think I'm something of a catch.'

Damon. Crisp and masculine. It suited him.

'I'm not like most women.' She prickled at his arrogance. 'And a lot of men think I'm a catch.'

'You definitely took some catching,' he murmured, pulling into a car park and killing the engine. 'Yet here we are.'

Eleni looked out of the car window and saw he meant literally. He'd brought her to the marina. 'Why are we here?'

'I need the certainty that you won't do one of your disappearing acts, but we can't have this argument in the front seat of a car and…' He hesitated as he stared at her. 'We need space.'

Space? Eleni's heart thundered as she gazed into his eyes. Beneath her shock and fear something else stirred—awareness, recognition.

This is the one I had. This is the one I want.

Suddenly that forbidden passion pulsed through every fibre of her being.

Unbidden. Unwanted. Undeniable.

CHAPTER FIVE

HE'D KNOWN HER eyes weren't that unnaturally intense indigo they'd been at the ball, but the discovery of their true colour had stolen a breath that Damon still hadn't recovered. They were sea green—a myriad of bewitching shades—and he couldn't summon the strength to look away.

She lies.

He reminded himself. Again.

The alluring Princess Eleni Nicolaides had used him and he couldn't possibly be considering kissing her. He'd not been completely certain before but he was now—she was pregnant. To him.

Grimly he shoved himself out of the car and stalked around it to open her door. Impatiently he watched the emotions flicker across her too-expressive face—wariness, curiosity, decision—and beneath those? Desire.

His body tightened. More than anger, this was possessiveness. So off-base. Rigid with self-control, he took her arm, steeling himself not to respond to the electricity that surged between them. It took only a minute to guide her down the steps and along the wooden landing to his yacht. She stopped and stared at it.

'Eleni,' he prompted her curtly. 'We need to talk.'

'You have to take me back soon.' She twisted her hands together. 'They'll be wondering where I am.'

'They can wonder for a while yet,' he muttered.

He hustled her past the cabin and through to the lounge. The windows were tinted so no one on deck could see them, and his sparse crew were under strict instruction to stay out of sight and work quickly. He remained in front of the only exit to the room. He couldn't be careful enough with her.

'Take off the cap.' He could hardly push the words past the burr in his throat, but he needed to see her with no damn disguise.

She lifted the cap. Her hair wasn't long and blue, it was cut to a length just below her chin and was blonde—corn silk soft, all natural and, right now, tousled.

'How did you figure out who I was?' she asked in that damnably raspy voice.

He shook his head.

Once he'd realised who his mystery lover was, he'd been lame enough to look online. But she was more perfect in the flesh. Tall and slender, strong and feminine, with those curves that caused the most base reaction in him. Her complexion was flawless and her sweetheart-shaped face captivating. But her beauty was a façade that apparently masked a shockingly salacious soul. He was determined to get to the truth.

'You knew I was going to be at the hospital,' she said after he didn't reply to her first question. 'How?'

Her fingers trembled as she fidgeted with the cap, but he'd not brought her here to answer *her* questions.

'Were you going to tell him?' he asked.

He glared as she didn't answer. She was so good at avoiding everything important, wasn't she?

He felt the vibration beneath the deck as the engines fired up. About time. Icily satisfied, he silently kept watching. Now she'd be tested. Sure enough, as the yacht moved she strode to the window.

'Where are you taking me?' she asked, her volume rising.

'Somewhere private.' Somewhere isolated. Triumph rushed at the prospect of having her completely alone.

'This *is* private. We don't need to move to make it more so.' Panic filled her voice and turned wide eyes on him. 'This is abduction.'

'Is it?' he asked, uncaring. 'But you agreed to come with me.'

'I didn't realise you meant…' She paled. 'I can't just *leave.*'

He hardened his heart. 'Why not? You've done that before.'

This was the woman who'd had sex with him when she knew she was about to announce her engagement to another man. Who'd then run off without another word. And who was now pregnant and concealing it—apparently from everyone.

The betrayal burned like no other. He hated being *used.* His father had used him as cover for his long-term infidelities. His mother had used his entire existence to promote her political aspirations—hell, she'd even told him she never would have had him if it weren't for the possible benefit to her career. His father had not only agreed, he'd expected Damon to understand and become the same. A parasite—using anyone and anything to enhance success. He'd refused and he'd vowed that he'd never let anyone use him again.

But Eleni had.

Yet that look on her face now was torture—those shimmering eyes, the quiver of her full lips.

Desire tore through his self-control, forcing him closer to her. Furious, he locked it down, viciously clenching his fists and shoving them into his trouser pockets. It was this uncontrolled lust that had got him into this mess in the first place.

It was insane. Once more he reminded himself he knew nothing of importance about her other than her shocking ability to conceal information. But as he watched, she whitened further. Whitened to the point of—

'Eleni?' He rushed forward.

'Oh, hell.' She pressed her hand to her mouth.

Oh, hell was right. He reached for a decorative bowl just in time.

* * *

Oh, no. No.

Eleni groaned but the sickness couldn't be stopped. Of all the mortifying things to happen.

'Sit down before you fall down,' he muttered.

'I'm not used to being on the water,' she replied.

'If you're going to lie, at least try to make it believable. It's well known you love sailing, Princess. Your illness is caused by your pregnancy.'

She was too queasy to bother trying to contradict him. What was the point? 'I need fresh air.'

'You need to stay in here until we're away from the island.'

'You can't be serious.' Aghast, she stared up at him. 'You're going to cause an international incident.'

'Do you think so?' He stared at her grimly. 'I think the spectacle is only going to get even more insane when they find out I'm the father of your unborn child.'

She closed her eyes and groaned. 'At least let me use a bathroom.'

'Of course.'

He guided her to a small room. He opened a drawer and handed her a toothbrush, still in its packet. She took it, silently grateful as he left her in privacy.

But he was just outside the door when she opened it again a few minutes later.

She walked back into the lounge just as a uniformed crew member was leaving. The man didn't say a word, didn't meet her eyes. He simply melted from the room.

'Who was that?' she asked.

'Someone extremely discreet and very well paid.'

He'd left fresh water in a tall glass and a few crackers on a plate. She turned away; there was no way she could eat anything right now.

'You're naive if you think he won't sell your secrets.'

The man had recognised her. It was only a matter of time before people came to her rescue.

'I've been betrayed before, Eleni. I know how to make my business safe.'

Eleni looked at the hard edge of Damon's jaw and wondered who had betrayed him. 'Your business?'

'My baby.'

Her blood chilled. 'So you planned this.'

There'd been a crew ready and waiting on this boat and no doubt he paid them ridiculously well. He'd gone to huge trouble to get her away from the palace. Maybe she ought to feel scared, she barely knew him after all, but she didn't believe she was in danger. Rather, in that second, the craziest feeling bloomed in her chest.

Relief.

His eyes narrowed. 'You know this isn't about rescuing you.'

His words hit like bullets. She shrank, horrified that he'd seen her *selfishness*. Guilt brought defensiveness with it. 'I don't need rescuing.'

His smile mocked. 'No?'

Damon was more dangerous than she'd realised. She couldn't cope with her reaction to him. It was as if everything else in the world, everything that mattered, simply evaporated in his presence. His pull was too strong.

But then she remembered he wasn't certain she was pregnant to *him*. Perhaps her way out was to convince him he *wasn't* the father. Then he'd return her to Palisades. She'd go to Giorgos. She should have gone to Giorgos already.

'I *can't* stay here,' she pleaded.

'Give in, Eleni,' he replied indifferently. 'You already are. The question is, can you be honest?'

Not with him. Not now.

But she burned to prove that she didn't need 'rescuing'—not from her situation, or from herself. He strolled towards her but she wasn't fooled by the ease of his movement. He was furious. Well, that made two of them.

'How many other possibilities are there?' he asked too softly, his gaze penetrating.

'Excuse me?' She tensed as he came within touching distance.

'Who are the other men who might be the father of your child?' He watched her so intently she feared he could see every hidden thought, every contrary emotion.

'Can you even remember them all?' he challenged.

She flushed at his tone, lost for words.

'You have sex with me at a ball within five minutes of meeting me,' he murmured, continuing his hateful judgment. 'You didn't even know my name.'

'And you didn't know mine,' she flared. 'And we used protection. So there you go.'

'But *I* wasn't engaged to anyone else at the time.'

That one hurt because it was truth. 'Nor was I,' she mumbled weakly.

'Not "officially".' His eyes were so full of scorn that she winced. 'But you *knew*. You knew the announcement was about to be made. You owed him your loyalty and you cheated.'

Damon was right, but he didn't know the reality of the marriage she faced. He'd never understand the scrutiny and crazy constraints she endured in her privileged world.

At her silence now, pure danger flashed in his eyes. She backed away until the wall brought her to a stop. Her heart raced as he followed until he leaned right into her personal space.

'So, how many others?' he asked again, too softly.

She'd brazen it out. Disgust him so he'd take her back to Palisades in repulsion. 'At least four.'

'Liar.' Slowly he lifted his hand and brushed the backs of his fingers over the blush burning down her cheekbones. 'Why won't you just tell me the truth, Eleni?'

His whisper was so tempting.

She lifted her chin, refusing to let him seduce her again. And at the same time, refusing to run. 'I don't have to tell you anything.'

'What are you afraid of?' he taunted huskily. 'The world finding out your secret? That Princess Eleni The Pure likes dressing up in disguise and doing it fast and dirty with a succession of strangers? That she can't get enough?'

Anger ignited, but something else was lit within as well. That treacherous response. She *had* liked it fast and dirty. With him. She closed her eyes but he tilted her chin back up, holding it until she opened them again and looked right into the banked heat of his.

'Are you ashamed of what happened, Eleni?'

Tears stung but she blinked them back. Of *course* she was ashamed. She couldn't understand how it had happened. How she could have lost all control and all reason like that. And how could her body be so traitorous now—aching for him to take that half step nearer and touch her again?

The intensity deepened in his eyes. A matching colour mounted in his cheekbones.

Hormones. Chemicals. That crazy reaction that she still couldn't believe had happened was happening again.

'You like it,' he muttered. 'And you want it.'

'And I get it,' she spat, reckless and furious and desperate to push him away. 'From whomever, whenever I please.'

'Is that right?'

'Yes,' she slammed her answer in defiance.

He smiled. A wickedly seductive smile of utter disbelief.

'You'll never know.' She was pushed to scorn.

'You don't think?' He actually laughed.

'Maybe I'm pregnant with my fiancé's baby,' she snapped. Reminding him of her engagement might make him back off. She *needed* him to back off.

His smile vanished. 'I don't think so, Princess.'

She stilled at his expression.

'You haven't slept with him,' Damon said roughly. 'I was your first, Eleni. That night with me, you were a virgin.'

She gaped, floundering in total mortification as he threw the truth in her face.

How had he known? How? She pressed against the cool wall, hoping to stop shaking.

'Why lie so constantly?' he demanded, leaning closer, the heat of his body blasting. 'You still have nothing to say?'

How could she possibly explain? She couldn't answer even her own conscience.

'There is nothing wrong with liking sex,' he said roughly. 'But there is something wrong with lying and cheating to get it.'

She trembled again, appalled by how aroused she was. She could no longer look him in the eye; he saw too much. She wanted to hide from him. From herself. Since when was she this wanton animal who'd forgo all her scruples simply to get a physical fix?

'Eleni.'

She refused to look at him.

But she couldn't escape the sensations that the slightest of touches summoned. He brushed her cheek with a single finger, and then tucked a strand of her hair back behind her ear. She stood rigid, desperate not to reveal any reaction.

'Let's try this again, shall we?' He leaned so close.

She bit the inside of her cheek, hoping the pain would help keep her sane, but she could feel his heat radiating through her.

'No lying. No cheating,' he murmured. 'Just truth.'

The tip of his finger marauded back and forth over her lips; the small caress sent shock waves of sensuality to her most private depths.

Her pulse quickened, but his finger didn't. Slowly he teased. Such pleasure and such promise came from a touch so small, building until she could no longer hold still. He teased until she parted her lips with a shaky breath.

He swooped, pressing his mouth to hers, taking advantage to slide his tongue deep and taste until he tore a soft moan from her. So easily. He wound his arm around her waist and drew her close, holding her so he could kiss her. Again. Then again.

After all these sleepless nights he was with her—with all his heat and hardness. She quivered, then melted against him. Immediately he swept his hand down her side, urging her closer and she went—her body softening to accommodate the steel of his.

With his hands and with his lips, he marauded everywhere now. Kissing her mouth, her jaw, her neck, he slid his hand across her aching breasts, down her quivering stomach, until he hit the hem of her skirt. He pushed under and up. High, then higher still up her thigh. Demanding—and getting—acceptance, intimacy, willingness. So quickly. So intensely. She curled into his embrace, then arched taut as a bowstring as he teased her.

'Eleni…' he whispered between kisses and caresses. 'How many lovers have you had?'

Unable to contain her need, she thrust against that tormenting finger that was so close, that was stirring her in a way that she could no longer resist. On a desperate sigh she finally surrendered her not so secret truth. 'One.'

He rewarded her with more of that rubbing designed to drive her insane. She couldn't breathe. Closer, *so* close.

'And how many times have you had sex?'

She shook with aching desire. With the need for him to touch her again. Just once. One more touch was all she needed. 'One,' she muttered breathlessly.

Her answer seemed to anger him again. He held her fast and kissed her hard. Passionate and ruthless, his tongue plundered the cavern of her mouth. He was dominant and claiming and all she could do was yield to his passion.

But the fires within him stoked her own. She kissed him back furiously, hating him knowing how aroused she was. But there was no controlling her reaction. No stopping what she wanted. And she *wanted*. *Now*.

It was at that moment, of her total surrender, that he tore his mouth from hers.

'How many men have kissed you like that?' he rasped.

She panted, her nipples tight and straining against her suddenly too tight bra. *'One,'* she answered, pushed beyond her limits.

'And how many men have kissed you liked that, but *here*?' His fingers pushed past the silk scrap of material covering her, probing into her damp, hot sex.

She gasped at the delicious intrusion. Her limbs trembled as release hovered only a stroke or two away. She gazed into his gorgeously fiery eyes, quivering at the extreme intimacy connecting them.

'Answer me, Eleni.' He ground out a brutal whisper.

'None.' Her answer barely sounded.

She registered his sharp exhalation but then he kissed her again. Somehow she was in his embrace, his body between hers. Heaven help her, she went with him to that sofa. She let him. Wanted him. But as he pushed her skirt higher and slid lower so he was kneeling between her legs she realised where this was going. A lucid moment—she gasped and shifted.

'Don't try to hide. I'm going to kiss you. There won't be even an inch of you that I haven't tasted. Every intimacy is *mine*.'

His blunt, savage words stunned her. Blindly she realised that his control was as splintered as her own. That he too was pushed beyond reason. Pleasure surged and she couldn't resist or deny—not him. Not herself.

She groaned at his first kiss, shocked at how exposed she felt and embarrassed by just how much she ached for his touch. It was like being taken over by a part of herself she didn't know was there. That lustful, brazen part. She flung her arm over her face, hiding from him. From herself. But there was no hiding from the sensations he aroused and the delight and skill of his mouth on her. His tongue. There. Right there.

She moaned in unspeakable pleasure.

'Look at that,' he muttered arrogantly in the echo of her need. 'You like it.' His laugh was exultant. 'You like it a lot.'

His attention was relentless. She arched again, pressing her hands against her eyes but unable to hold back her scream as a torrent of ecstasy tore through her. She shuddered, sweet torture wracking her body.

Then she was silent, suspended in that moment where she waited for his next move. For him to rise above her, to press against her, to take her. She ached anew to feel him. She wanted him to push inside and take her completely.

But he didn't. He didn't move at all.

She lay frozen, her face still buried in her arm as the last vestiges of that bliss ebbed. And then shame flooded in. Bitter, galling shame.

She twisted, suddenly desperate to escape. But he grasped her hips hard, prevented her moving even an inch.

'Stop hiding,' he growled savagely. 'There are things we must discuss.'

'Discuss? You think you discuss anything?' She threw her arms wide and snarled at him. 'You dictate.' He *bulldozed*. 'And you…you…'

'Take action.' He finished her sentence for her, as breathless and angry as she. 'And I'll continue to do so. And first up, you're not going to marry Prince Xander of Santa Chiara. You're going to marry me.'

CHAPTER SIX

'I'M NOT MARRYING YOU,' Eleni snapped, furiously shoving him. 'I'm not marrying anyone.'

'Right.' He lazily leaned back on his heels and sent her a sardonic look. 'That's why the world is currently planning party snacks for the live stream of the royal wedding of the century.'

She was sick of his smug arrogance. Awkwardly she curled up her legs to get past him and angrily pulled her skirt down, too mortified to hunt for her knickers. 'I wasn't going to go through with it.'

'Really?' He stood in a single, smooth movement, mocking her with his athletic grace. 'What was the plan?'

She loathed how inept he made her feel. How easily he could make her lose all control. How much her appallingly stupid body still wanted his attention. 'You have no idea how impossible it is for me to get away.'

'As it happens, I do have some insight into the technical difficulties.' His gaze narrowed. Hardened. 'So you were going to go through with it.'

She'd never wanted to but she'd known it was what was expected. Since she'd suspected her pregnancy her desperation had grown. She glared at him from the centre of the room. 'I didn't know what to do.'

'Why not try talking to him?'

She rolled her eyes. He made it sound so easy.

'Giorgos wouldn't listen.'

'Giorgos?' Damon's eyebrows shot up. 'What about the man you were supposed to marry?'

Who? Oh. He meant Xander. As if she could talk to him—she barely knew him.

'I'm guessing you don't love him. Prince Xander, that is,' Damon added sarcastically.

She turned away from Damon. Her heart beat heavy and fast and she perched on the edge of a small chair—far, far away from that sofa. 'Obviously not or I wouldn't have… done what I did with you.'

'Then why marry him?'

'Because it is what has been expected for a long time.'

'So it's duty.'

'It would benefit our countries…'

'Because a royal wedding is somehow going to magically smooth away any serious issues your respective countries may be facing?' He laughed derisively. 'And you'll throw in some rainbows and unicorns to make it all prettier and perfect?'

'You don't understand the subtleties.'

'Clearly not,' he muttered dryly. 'And was my child meant to be the fruit of this fairy-tale unity?' he demanded. 'When in reality she or he will grow up lonely in a house devoid of warmth and love with parents absent in every sense.'

Eleni stared, taken aback by his vehemence. And his insight.

'I'll never let my child be used that way.' His eyes were hard. 'I know the unseen impact of a purely political union and I'll do whatever it takes to ensure my kid doesn't endure that kind of bleak upbringing.'

'I'm not going to marry him,' she said in a low voice. 'I know I can't.'

'But if you don't marry someone, your child will be labelled a bastard. We might live in modern times, but you're a *princess* and there are certain expectations. What kind of life will your child have without legitimacy? Will she be kept cloistered in the shadows, even more stifled than you were? Look how well that turned out for you.'

She flinched. He saw too much and he judged harshly.

But the horrible thing was, he was right. She had to think of a better way. She leapt to her feet and paced away from him, twisting her cold hands together. She didn't want to involve *him*—he twisted everything up too much.

'I need to call Giorgos,' she said. It must be almost two hours since she'd left Palisades and her brother would be irate already.

'I agree.'

She spun on the spot. 'You do?'

'Of course. It'll be better if you're completely honest with him. Do you think you can be—or are you going to need help with that again?'

She flushed, remembering just how Damon had dragged the intimate truth from her only minutes ago. Now his biting sarcasm hurt and she felt sick enough at the thought of confessing all to her brother.

'What, you expect me to cheerily tell him I'm here of my own free will?' She flared. 'That you didn't bundle me into a boat and set sail for the high seas before I could blink?'

'The choice was yours.'

'What choice did you give me?' she scoffed.

'To speak the truth, or give you time. I think it was a reasonable choice.'

'It was blackmail. Because you're a bully.'

'You've already admitted you didn't know what to do. You couldn't figure a way out. Here it is and you're happy about it. Don't dramatise me into your villain.'

Eleni rubbed her forehead. Damon's words struck a deep chord. She'd been refusing to admit to herself how glad she was he'd stolen her away. She'd been unable to think up an escape and he'd offered one. She wasn't as much mad with him, but mad with herself for needing it—and for layering on complications with her wretched desire for him. Her emotional overreactions had to end.

She'd been too scared to admit to Giorgos how badly

she'd screwed up. But if she wanted her brother to treat her as an adult, she had to act like one.

'Okay.' She blew out a breath and turned to look Damon in the eye. 'I'm not sorry you took me away. You're right. I needed this time to think things through. Thank you.'

'How very gracious, Princess,' Damon drawled. 'But don't be mistaken. Like I said, this isn't a rescue. I'm not doing you a favour. I'm claiming what's mine. And I'm protecting it.' He picked up a handset from a small side table and held it out to her. 'Phone your brother.'

Eleni's hands were slick with sweat as she tapped the private number onto the screen.

'Giorgos, it's me.' She turned away from Damon as her brother answered his private line immediately.

'Eleni. Where are you?' Giorgos demanded instant answers. 'Come back to the palace now. Do you have any idea of the trouble you've caused?'

'I'm not coming back yet, Giorgos. I need time to think.'

'Think? About what?' Her brother dismissed her claim. 'Your fiancé is already here. Or had you forgotten that you're about to go on tour with him?'

'I can't do it, Giorgos.'

'Can't do what?' Giorgos asked impatiently.

Eleni closed her eyes and summoned all her courage. 'I'm pregnant,' she said flatly. 'Prince Xander isn't the father.'

Silence.

Seven long seconds of appalled silence.

'Who?' Giorgos finally asked in a deadly whisper. *'Who?'*

'It doesn't matter—'

'I'll kill him. I'll bloody— Tell me his name.'

'No.'

'Tell me his name, Eleni. I'll have him—'

'Call off the hounds, Giorgos.' She interrupted her brother for the first time in her life. 'Or I swear I'll never return.' Her heart broke as she threatened him. 'I will disappear.'

Her guilt mounted. Her horror at doing this to the brother she loved. But she pushed forward.

'It doesn't matter who it was. He didn't seduce me. I was a fully willing participant.' She screwed her eyes tight shut, mortified at revealing this intimacy to her brother, but knowing the way he'd assume she'd been taken advantage of because he still thought of her as an innocent, helpless kid. She needed to *own* this. 'I made the mistake, Giorgos. And I need to fix it. Tell Xander I'm sick. Tell him I ran away. Tell him anything you like. But I'm not coming back. Not yet. Not 'til I've sorted it out.'

'Are you with the bastard now?' Giorgos asked impatiently.

'I'm not marrying him either,' Eleni said.

She didn't catch Giorgos's muttered imprecation.

'This child is mine. Pure Nicolaides.' She finally felt a segment of peace settle in place inside.

This was what she should have done at the beginning. She had to make amends now—to all the people she'd involved. 'And please don't blame Tony for losing track of me. It wasn't his fault.'

'Your protection officer has no idea where you've gone. He's clearly incompetent. He has been dismissed.'

'But it's not his fault.' Eleni's voice rose. Tony had been with Eleni for years. He had a wife and two children. He needed the work. 'I told him—'

'Lies,' Giorgos snapped. 'But it *is* his fault that he lost track of you. His employment is not your concern.'

'But—'

'You should have thought through the consequences of your actions, Eleni. There are ramifications for *all* the people of Palisades. And Santa Chiara.'

Twin tears slid out from her closed eyes. She would make it up to Tony somehow. Another atonement to be made.

'How do I stop a scandal here, Eleni?' Giorgos asked.

She cringed. Was that what mattered most—the reputation of the royal family? But she knew that was unfair to Giorgos. He was trying to protect *her*. It was what he'd always done. Too much.

'I'm so sorry,' she said dully. 'I take full responsibility. I will be in touch when I can.'

She ended the call before her brother could berate her any more. She turned and saw Damon casually leaning against the back of the sofa as if he were watching a mildly entertaining movie.

'Did you have to listen in?' Angered, she wiped the tears away. 'You know they'll have traced the call.'

'And they'll find it leads to some isolated shack in Estonia.' He shrugged. 'I work in the tech industry, Eleni. They won't find us in the next few days, I promise you that. We're hidden and we're safe.'

'What, this is some superhero space boat that can engage stealth mode?' She shook her head. 'They'll be checking the coastline.'

'And we're already miles away from it and your brother knows you're not under duress. You've shocked him, Eleni. I'm sure he'll wait to hear from you. The last thing he'll want now is the publicity from mounting a full-scale search and rescue operation.'

She'd shocked Giorgos. Once he'd got past that, the disappointment would zoom in. She was glad she wasn't there to see it.

'There's one option we haven't talked about,' Damon said expressionlessly. 'It is early enough in the pregnancy for termination to be—'

'No,' she interrupted him vehemently.

She had such privilege. She had money. This child could be well cared for.

And it was *hers*.

That was the thing. For the first time in her life she had

something that was truly, utterly her own. Her responsibility. Her concern. Hers to love and protect. No one was taking it away from her. There was a way out of this if she was strong enough to stand up to her brother's—and her nation's—disappointment. And she was determined to be.

'I'm not marrying Prince Xander,' she said fiercely. 'I'm not marrying you. I'm not marrying anyone. But I *am* having this baby.' She pulled herself together—*finally* feeling strong. 'I have the means and the wherewithal to provide for my baby on my own. And that is what I will do.'

'Do you?' Damon looked sceptical. 'What if Giorgos cuts you off completely? How will you fend for yourself then?'

'He wouldn't do that.' Her brother would be beyond disappointed, but he wouldn't abandon her. She should have trusted him more, sooner.

'Even so, what price will you pay for one moment of recklessness?' Damon badgered. 'The rest of your life in disgrace.'

'I could step away from the spotlight and live in one of the remote villages.' She would ask for nothing from the public purse.

It was the personal price that pained her. She'd let her brother down in both public and private senses. But she would not let this baby down. She'd made her first stand, and now she had to follow through and not let Damon block her way either.

'So that's your escape neatly done,' he noted softly. 'But what price will my *child* pay if you do that?'

She flushed, unsettled by his cool sarcasm. He made it sound as if she was thinking only of herself, not her baby. But she wasn't. She'd understood what he'd said about a child growing up with all that expectation and wasn't this a way of removing that?

But he clearly considered that she'd been stifled and cloistered and, yes, spoilt. He thought her behaviour with him at the ball a direct consequence of that. Maybe he was right. That flush deepened. She loathed this man.

'I'm not marrying you,' she repeated. She *couldn't*.

The absolute last thing Damon Gale wanted to do was marry—her or anyone—but damn if her rejection didn't just irritate the hell out of him. What, was his billionaire bank balance not good enough for her spoilt royal self?

He'd sworn never to engage in even a 'serious' relationship. But the worst of all possible options was a 'politically expedient' wedding. Yet now he was insulted because, while she'd agreed to a political marriage once already, she was adamantly refusing his offer. Why? Because he wasn't a *prince*?

'I'll never let you use my baby for your political machinations.' He glared at her.

All she did was stick her chin in the air and glare back.

His body burned and he paced away from her. That damned sexual ache refused to ease. Heaven only knew why he wanted this woman. But it had been like this since the moment he'd first seen her at that ball. To his immense satisfaction, he'd had her—there and then. He'd immediately wanted more, but then she'd fled.

Now he'd finally found her again, yet within moments of getting her alone on his boat he'd totally lost control and done exactly what he'd promised himself he wouldn't. He'd touched her. Instead of verbally tearing her to shreds, he'd pressed his mouth to her until she'd warmed like wax in his hands. Pliable and willing and ultimately so wanton and gorgeous. It had taken every speck of self-control to not claim her completely there on the sofa.

He knew he could use this mutual lust to get the acquiescence to his proposal he needed, but he wanted more than her gasping surrender. He wanted her to accept that he was *right*. Poor little princess was going to have to marry a mere man. A man she wanted in spite of herself, apparently.

'What were you thinking at that ball?' He couldn't understand why she'd taken such a massive risk. Was it just lust for her too or had there been more to it? Had she been trying to sabotage that engagement? But to throw away her virginity?

'Clearly I wasn't. What were *you* thinking?'

He leaned back against the wall. He'd been thinking how beautiful she was. How something vulnerable in her had pulled him to her.

'I tried to find you because I realised the condom had torn, but you'd vanished from the ball like a—' He broke off. 'I was on a flight the next day. I came back several times, but couldn't find any information about you. I asked—'

'You asked?'

'Everyone I knew. No one had seen you there. You never went back into the ballroom.' He shook his head and asked again. 'Why did you do it?'

Her shoulders lifted in a helpless shrug.

He hesitated but in the end was unable to stop the words coming out. 'Did you even think of trying to get in touch with me?'

Her beautiful face paled. 'I didn't know your name. I wasn't about to run a search on all the guys who'd been at that ball. I couldn't risk anyone suspecting me. How could I tell anyone?'

'How hard would it have been to go through that guest list?' he asked irritably. 'To identify men between a certain age? To look at security footage? You could easily have found out who I was, Eleni. You just didn't want to.' And that annoyed him so much more than it should.

'If I'd tried to do that, people would have asked *why*.'

'And you didn't want them to do that, because you'd already made a promise to another man.' He ran his hand through his hair in frustration. 'I've seen those "official" photos. They weren't taken the day after you slept with me. They were taken before, weren't they?'

She couldn't look him in the eye. 'Yes.'

Damon's blood pressure roared. 'Yet you never slept with him.'

'You're going there again?'

'But you kissed him?' He pressed on, relentless in his need to make his point.

'You can watch it on the news footage.'

He had already. Chaste, passionless kisses. She'd looked nothing like the siren who had writhed in *his* arms and pulled him closer, begging him with her body. The Princess that Damon had kissed was hot and wanton.

'The only time you kiss him is when there are cameras rolling?' He moved forward, unable to resist going nearer to her. 'You don't kiss him the way you kiss me.'

She flung her head up at that. 'Are you jealous?'

So jealous his guts burned right now. 'He doesn't want you,' he said bluntly.

Something raw flashed across her face. 'What makes you say that?'

He stopped his progress across the room and shoved his fists into his trouser pockets. 'If he wanted you the way he ought to, then he'd have moved heaven and earth to find you already. But he hasn't found you. He hasn't fought at all.'

That engagement was a political farce, so he had no reason to feel bad about cutting in and claiming what was already his. They'd sacrifice a year of their lives in sticking it out in a sham of a marriage until the baby was born. That was the only solution. Lust faded and there sure as hell was no such thing as for ever. Princess Eleni here was just going to get over her snobbishness and accept her marriage, and her divorce. And that he was no prince of a man.

* * *

Eleni inwardly flinched at that kicker. Because there it was—the cold, unvarnished truth.

Her fiancé didn't want her. Her brother found her an irritant. She had no worthwhile job. And now that her 'purity' was sullied, she'd no longer be desired as a prince's wife anyway. 'I guess my value's plummeted now I'm no longer a virgin,' she quipped sarcastically.

'Your value?' Damon's eyes blazed. 'He shouldn't give a damn about your virginity.'

His anger surprised her. 'In the way you don't?'

A different expression cut across his face. 'Oh, I care about that,' he argued in a slow, lethal whisper.

'It was none of your business,' she said haughtily.

'You don't think?' He laughed bitterly. 'That's where you're so wrong. And who you sleep with is now my business too.'

'I'm. Not. Marrying. You.' She utterly refused.

'It won't be for ever, Eleni,' he assured her dispassionately. 'We can divorce easily enough in time, without destroying the union of two entire nations,' he added pointedly. 'I will retain custody of our child. You will go back to being a princess.'

'Pardon?' The air was sucked from her lungs.

'I'll raise our child alone, without the pressure of public life.'

'*What?*' She stared at him, horrified to read the utterly cool seriousness on his face. 'But I'm this child's mother. A child needs her mother.' If anyone knew that, she did.

There was a thick silence.

His expression shuttered. 'A child needs parents who want her. Who love her. And if they're together, they need to be in love with each other.' His words dropped like heavy stones into a still pond. 'While we want each other, we don't—and won't—love each other. This isn't some fairy-tale romance, Eleni. This is real. And we have a real problem to deal with. As adults.'

Not a fairy tale.

She knew theirs was a connection forged by nothing but lust and hormones. But now? What he'd just said came as a greater shock than any the day had brought so far.

He wanted to take her baby from her.

'You've had a long day. You must need something to eat.' He changed the subject easily, as if he hadn't just shaken her whole foundation.

'I couldn't…' She was too shocked to contemplate something so banal as food.

'Suit yourself.' He shrugged carelessly. 'You obviously need sleep to get your head together. But starting tomorrow we'll look at ensuring your diet is appropriate.'

Appropriate? What, he thought he was going to dictate every aspect of her life now?

'How lovely of you to care,' she said acidly.

'I care about my child.' He turned his back on her. 'I'll show you to your quarters.'

Silently she followed him along the gleaming corridor of the large yacht that was still steaming full-speed away from Palisades.

He stopped almost at the end. 'You're in here,' he said briefly, gesturing through the doorway. 'I'm in the cabin next door, if you decide you do need something.'

She didn't move into the room immediately; she was too busy trying to read him. Beyond the too-handsome features, there was intense determination.

A fatalistic feeling sank into her bones. There was no escaping, no getting away from what he wanted. And he didn't actually want *her*—only her baby.

But earlier she'd felt his hardness, his heat, she'd heard his breathlessness as he'd kissed her into ecstasy. Surely he'd wanted her? But he hadn't taken her. And he could have, they both knew that.

All of which merely proved that it had been just sex for him, while she'd thought it had been somehow special...

Strain tightened his features. 'I'm not going to kiss you goodnight,' he muttered. 'I'm too tired to be able to stop it from escalating.'

As if she'd been waiting for him to kiss her? Outraged, she snarled. 'You don't think I could stop it?'

'Maybe you could,' he said doubtfully. 'But I'm not willing to take the risk.'

She stepped into the cabin and slammed the door right in his face.

Not a fairy tale.

No. This was nothing less than a nightmare. She glanced angrily at the large, smooth bed. As if she were ever going to sleep.

CHAPTER SEVEN

'ELENI.'

The whisper slipped over her skin like a warm, gentle breeze. Smiling, she snuggled deeper into the cosy cocoon.

'Eleni.'

She snapped her eyes open. Damon was leaning over her, his face only a breath from hers.

'Oh…hey… What are you doing in here?' she asked softly.

'Making sure you're okay,' he answered, equally softly.

'Why wouldn't I be?' She'd been buried deep in the best sleep she'd had in weeks.

His smile appeared—the magnetic one that had melted all her defences that night at the ball. The one she hadn't seen since. 'Well, I was wondering if you were *ever* going to wake up.'

Why would he think she wouldn't? Had he been trying to rouse her for hours already? His smile diverted her sleepy thoughts onto a different track—had he been about to try waking her with a *kiss*?

Blood quickening, she clutched the sheet to her chest and tried to sit up.

'Easy.' He held her down with a hand on her shoulder. 'Not so fast.' He sat on the edge of her bed and pointed to the bedside table. 'I brought food and water. You must be hungry now.'

The dry crackers on the plate brought her fully awake with a sharp bump. This was no fairy tale. Damon had no thought of romance, only practicality—preventing her morning sickness from surfacing.

'Thank you.' She pulled herself together, determined

to be polite and battle him with calm rationality. No more emotional outbursts that only he drew from her. All she needed now was for him to leave.

But clearly he didn't hear her unspoken plea, because he watched her expectantly. With an expressive sigh she lifted the glass of water.

'You normally sleep this late?' Damon asked.

'What time is it?'

'Almost eleven.'

She nearly spat out the mouthful of water she'd just sipped.

That amused grin flashed across his face again. 'I take it you don't usually sleep in.'

Of course not. Never in all her life.

'Has anyone been in contact?' she asked, trying to distract herself from how infuriatingly gorgeous he looked in that old tee and jeans combo.

'You're asking if they've tracked you down?' He shook his head. 'Radio silence.'

She didn't quite know how to feel about that. 'Perhaps they're planning a rescue raid and are about to break in and arrest you,' she muttered acidly. 'Any second now.'

'You came willingly.' That evil amusement lit his eyes. 'More than once.'

Uncontrollable heat washed through her, threatening an emotional outburst. Eleni levered up onto her elbow and glanced about for her robe. It wasn't there. Of course. None of her wardrobe was. The clothes she'd worn yesterday were on the floor where she'd left them. She blushed, imagining the reprimand.

Lazy, spoilt princess.

Awareness prickled. She snuck a look at him from beneath her lashes.

'Got a problem, Princess?' The slightest of jeers, low and a little rough and enough to fling her over the edge.

'Yes,' she said provocatively. 'I don't have anything fresh to wear.'

His eyes widened and for the briefest of seconds his raw reaction to her was exposed. He wanted her still. She was too thrilled by the realisation to stop.

'Hadn't thought of that in all your evil planning, had you?' she purred.

But his expression blanked. 'Maybe I felt clothes weren't going to be necessary.'

'Oh, please.'

But he'd turned that desire back on her, teasing her when she'd wanted to test him.

'You love the idea.' He leaned closer, his whispered words having that warm, magnetic effect on her most private parts. 'And as we're going to be married, there's no need to be shy.'

Her reaction to his proximity was appalling but all she wanted now was to know he was as shattered as she.

'We're *not* going to be married.' She summoned all her courage and threw back the sheet, meeting his bluff with a fierce one of her own. 'But you want me to spend the day naked?'

As he stared, she fought every instinct to curl her legs up and throw her arms around her knees. Instead she stayed still, utterly naked on the soft white linen.

His gaze travelled the length of her body—lingering on those places too private to mention. She gritted her teeth so she wouldn't squirm. But as his focus trained on her breasts, she felt the reaction—the full, tight feeling as her nipples budded and that warmth surged low within. He looked for a long, long time—and then looked lower, rendering Eleni immobile in the burning ferocity of his attention. Her skin reddened as if she'd been whipped and the slightest of goosebumps lifted. It took everything she had not to curl her toes and die of frustration.

Finally, just when she'd felt she was about to explode,

he moved. Wordlessly he pulled his tee shirt over his head and held it out to her.

Desire flooded impossibly hotter still as she stared at his bared chest. Her senses ravenously appreciated his warm tan, the ridged muscles, that light scattering of hair arrowing down to—

'Put it on,' he snapped.

She snatched it from him. But if she'd doubted whether he wanted her as much as she wanted him, she now knew.

Just sex.

She forced herself to remember that this was just sex to him. But a trickle of power flowed through her veins.

He didn't move back as she got out of the bed—he just sat there, too close, his head about level with her breasts. So she stood in front of him—refusing to be intimidated.

The tee skimmed midway down her thighs and swamped her with a sense of intimacy as his scent and warmth enveloped her. Stupidly she felt as if she were more exposed than when she'd had nothing on. Her gaze collided with his—locked, and held fast in the hot blue intensity. She wanted him to touch her again. She wanted more of that pleasure he'd pulled so easily from her last night. She was almost mad with the need for it.

'Stop looking at me like that, Princess,' he said shortly.

The rejection stung. 'Don't call me Princess.'

'Why not?' he challenged almost angrily. 'It's who you are.'

'It's not all I am,' she answered defiantly. 'I don't want that to be all I am.'

She just wanted to be Eleni. She didn't want the reminder of who she *ought* to be all the time and of her failure to do her duty.

Hormones. It had to be the hormones. Here she was facing the biggest mess of her life, rupturing the royal connection of two nations, but all she wanted was for Damon to haul her close and kiss her again. She made herself walk to the door.

'Take me back to Palisades,' she said calmly, trying to sound in control.

'So now that you've used me to hide from your brother's wrath, you want to use your brother to protect you from me.'

She turned back and saw the bitterness of Damon's smile. 'That's not—'

'No?' He shook his head in disbelief. 'Sorry, Eleni, I'm not a servant who you can order around and who'll fulfil your every whim.'

'No?' she echoed at him angrily. His opinion inflamed her. She stalked back to where he still sat braced on the edge of her bed, his fists curled into the linen. 'But that's what you said I could do. You said I could take what I wanted from you.'

'That's what you really want, isn't it?' he asked roughly, reaching out to grab her waist and hold her in front of him. 'You want me to make you feel good again.'

She wanted it so much—because she wanted it *gone*. But she knew what he wanted too. He might not like her much, but he still wanted her.

'Actually,' Eleni corrected him coolly, 'now I'm offering that to you. Take what you want from me.'

If he did that, she was sure she'd be rid of this wretched, all-encompassing desire. It was too intense—she couldn't *think* for wanting him.

His mouth tightened as he stared up at her, insolence in his expression. 'Look at Princess Sophisticated,' he jeered through gritted teeth. 'What do you think you're doing? Trying to soften me up with sex?'

She froze at the anger now darkening his eyes. 'I just don't think this needs to be that complicated.'

'This couldn't be *more* complicated. And sex only makes

things worse.' He laughed unkindly. 'I'll have you again, don't you worry about that. But only once we've reached an agreement.'

He'd laughed that night too. When she'd had the most intense experience of her life, he'd *chuckled*. Her bold pretence fell, leaving angry vulnerability in its wake.

'You can seduce me until I scream,' she said furiously. 'But you can't make me say yes to *marrying* you.'

He stood, slamming her body against his as he did.

She gasped at the intense wave of longing that flooded her. But it roused her rage with it.

'You'll never get my total surrender.' She glared up at him, even as tremors racked her traitorous body as he pressed her against his rock-hard heat.

'And I don't want it,' he growled back, rolling his hips against hers in a demonstration of pure, sensual power. 'Lust passes.'

She hoped to heaven he was right. But his smug superiority galled her. 'You just have to know it all, don't you?'

But she didn't need another overprotective male trying to control every aspect of her life.

His gaze narrowed. 'I only want what's best for my baby.' He released her and stalked to the door, turning to hit her with his parting shot. 'We will marry. The baby will be born legitimately. And ultimately my child will live a safe, free life. With me.'

He slammed the door, leaving her recoiling at his cold-hearted plan. Shame slithered at her lame attempt to seduce him, suffocating the remnants of the heat he'd stirred too easily. He was too strong, too clinical when she'd been confused with desire. She was such a fool.

But that he truly planned to take her child horrified her. She had to fight him on that. She had to win.

Eleni snatched up her skirt. She marched out to the lounge to confront Damon again, only to catch sight of the large screen revealed on the wall. The sound was muted, but she recognised the image. Stunned, she stepped forward to look more closely.

Bunches and bunches of flowers and cards from well-wishers were placed at the gates of Palisades palace. The camera zoomed in on one of the bunches and she read the 'get well soon' message written—to *her*. Giorgos had taken her idea literally and told the world she was too unwell to embark on her tour with Prince Xander.

'There are so many.' She sank onto the nearest sofa.

'Why are you so surprised?' Damon walked forward and sat in the chair at an angle to her sofa, his voice cool. 'You're their perfect Princess.'

She rubbed her forehead. She was an absolute fraud and all those people were being kind when she didn't deserve it.

'It's not a total lie. You *don't* feel well,' he added gruffly.

'I've made a mess of everything.'

'So marry me. We'll live together away from Palisades until the baby is born.'

And then he was going to take her child from her.

Suddenly she broke; tears stung her eyes even as she laughed hopelessly. 'The stupid thing is, I don't even know for sure that I am pregnant.'

'Pardon?'

Of course she was pregnant. She knew it. She was late and there were all those other signs—morning sickness, tender breasts...

'Eleni?' Damon prompted sharply.

She sighed. 'I haven't done a test.'

He gazed at her, astounded. 'How can you not have done a test?'

'How could I?' She exploded, leaping back to her feet because she couldn't contain her frustration a second longer. 'How would I get a test without everyone finding out?' She paced, railing at the confines of the luxurious room and of the life she was bound by. 'I don't even do my own personal shopping—how can I when I don't even carry my own damn *money*?' She'd never shopped alone in all her life. She registered the dumbfounded amazement on Damon's face.

'I don't have any income,' she explained furiously. 'If I want anything I just ask someone and it arrives. Is that someone now you?' She gestured wildly at him. 'I don't have a money card, Damon. Or any cash. I've never needed it. I know that makes me spoilt. But it also makes me helpless.' It was beyond humiliating to be so dependent. 'It makes me useless.'

She flopped back down on the sofa and buried her face in her hands, mortified at the sting of fresh tears. So much for controlling her emotional outbursts.

'All this effort you've gone to, to steal me away might be based on one massive mistake.' She laughed bitterly at the irony. Wouldn't that just serve him right?

Damon hunched down in front of her, his hands on her knees. 'Eleni.'

His voice was too soft. Too calm.

'What?' She peered at him.

He studied her, his expression uncharacteristically solemn. 'Even if you're not pregnant, could you really marry him now?'

'Because I've spent the night on board a boat with another man and no chaperone?' She glared at him, hating that old-school reasoning and the expectation that she'd stay 'pure'—when no prince, no man, ever had to.

But Damon shook his head. 'Because you don't love him. You don't even want him.' He cocked his head, a vestige of that charming smile tweaking his lips. 'At least you want me.'

She closed her eyes. She *hated* him. And she hated how much she wanted him.

There was nothing but silence from Damon. She realised he'd left the room but a moment later he returned, a small rectangular box in his hand.

'You always have pregnancy tests on board?' Humiliation washed over her at her ineptitude.

'No. But as I suspected you were pregnant, I thought it might be useful.' So easily he'd done what she was unable to.

She snatched the box from his outstretched hand. 'I'll be back in a minute.'

CHAPTER EIGHT

DAMON GAZED DOWN at the distressed woman who'd word-lessly waved a small plastic stick at him as she returned to his sofa. The positive proof hit him—she truly had no clue. Her one escape plan had simply been to *hide* and now she was lost. Her lies yesterday had been those of an inexperienced, overly sheltered girl trying to brazen her way out of a dire situation.

He grimaced—was he actually feeling sorry for her now? Fool.

She could be confident when she wanted and had strength when she needed it. She was *spoilt*, that was her problem. Utterly used to getting her own way and never having to wait. He gritted his teeth as he remembered the way she'd flung back her bed coverings and taunted him. So brazen. So innocent. So damned gorgeous he was still struggling to catch his breath.

But she was going to have to wait for that now. And so was he.

Never had he understood how his father could have completely betrayed his mother. Why he'd risked everything he'd worked so hard to achieve. But now Damon understood all too well what could cloud a man's reason and make him forget his responsibilities and priorities.

Shameless lust. The age-old tale of desire.

He was not making the mistakes of his father. He was not abandoning his child to illegitimacy. But nor would he remain in a loveless marriage for years on end.

'You need to marry me, to protect the baby.' He tried to stay calm, but her repeated refusals were galling.

He'd never allow his child to be used for political manoeuvring. His baby would be raised in a safe environment with him. Their divorce would be better than being trapped in a home where the parents tolerated each other only for 'the look of it'.

Eleni paled.

'You know that, away from the palace, my child can have a normal life.' He tried to speak reasonably. 'Not hounded by press or burdened by duty.'

He saw her mouth tremble. He'd known this was how he'd get to her. She'd told him earlier—she didn't want to be *only* a princess.

'*I* can give this child everything,' she argued.

'Really? Can you give her complete freedom? With me, she can be free to do whatever she wants. Study whatever, live wherever. No pressure to perform.'

'And your life isn't in the public eye?' she queried sharply. 'Don't you billionaires get picked for "most eligible" lists in magazines?'

'When you're not a prince and therefore not public property, privacy can be paid for.'

'But this child will be a prince—or princess,' she pointed out, her voice roughening. 'And you can't deny this child his or her birthright.'

'The child can decide whether to take on a royal role when it's old enough.'

Eleni laughed at him. 'You think it's something you can just *choose*?'

'Why not?' Damon challenged her.

She shook her head. 'Giorgos would never allow it.'

'I don't give a damn what Giorgos wants.'

'But I do. Since our father died, he's been brother, father and mother to me and all the while he has that huge job. The hours he works—you have no idea...' She trailed off, pain shadowing her eyes.

Damon remembered when the King had died just over a

decade ago. His father had returned to Palisades for the funeral and taken an extra week to visit his long-term lover—Kassie's mother. Grimly Damon shoved that bitter memory aside. But he couldn't recall much about the Queen at all. He frowned at Eleni. 'Where's your mother?'

Eleni looked shocked. Then she drew in a deep breath. 'She died twenty minutes after giving birth to me.' Despite that steadying breath, her voice shook. 'So I know what it's like not to have a mother. And I know what it's like to have your parent too busy to be around to listen… I want to be there for my child. And I will be. In all the ways she or he needs. *Always*.'

Damon stared at her fixedly, ignoring her passion and focusing on the salient information. Her mother had died in childbirth.

He pulled out his phone. 'You need to see a doctor.'

Eleni gaped at him, then visibly collected herself. 'I'm not sure if you know how this works, Damon, but the baby isn't due for *months*.'

So what? She needed the best care possible from this moment on.

'Just because my mother died in childbirth, doesn't mean that I might have trouble,' she added stiffly.

'You need a basic check-up at the very least.'

'Because you don't trust me to take care of myself?'

Blood pounding in his ears, he ignored her petulance. Quickly he scrolled through his contacts to find his physician and tapped out a text asking him to find the best obstetrician he knew. Sure, women gave birth round the world almost every minute, but not always in full health and Eleni's news had caught him by surprise.

'I don't need cotton-wool treatment.' Her tone sharpened.

'I don't intend to give it to you,' he muttered, feeling better for having started the search. 'But I'm not going to ignore your condition either.'

'It's just pregnancy, not an *illness*,' she rasped. 'And I am sensible enough to ensure I get the best treatment when I get back to shore. Trust me, I don't want to die. But you can't make me see someone I don't want to see, nor stop me from doing the things I like.'

Looking at her was always a mistake—especially when she was passionate and vitality flowed from her glowing skin. Had people stopped her doing the things she'd liked in the past? He couldn't resist a tease. 'And what do you like?'

She glared at him, picking up the heavy innuendo he'd intended. 'Not that.'

He laughed even as a wave of protectiveness surged. 'Did you know some women have a heightened libido when pregnant?'

'I'm not one of those women.'

Her prim reply was undermined by the quickening of her breath. It spurred him to tease her more. 'No, you have the appetite of a nymphomaniac all the time.'

'I do not.'

'Yeah, you do.' He laughed again at her outraged expression. But that sensual blush had spread over her skin and sparks lit up her green-blue eyes.

There was no denying the chemistry between them. But he'd not realised just how inexperienced she was in all areas of life—not just the bedroom. Not to have access to cash? To have any normal kind of freedom?

Yes, she was spoilt, but she was unspoilt in other ways. She'd been too sheltered for her own good. And finally he could understand why. She was the precious baby who'd lost her mother far too soon. Raised by her bereft, too-busy father, and then a brother too young and too burdened to know how to care for a young girl and let her grow. All they'd wanted to do was protect her.

It was a sentiment Damon was starting to understand too well.

And now guilt crept in. He regretted the horrible scenario he'd painted—threatening to take her child from her. What kind of cold-hearted jerk was he?

But he'd been angered by her constant refusals and he'd lashed out, instinctively striking where it would hurt most. He drew in a calming breath. He'd win her acceptance with care, not cruelty.

'So it was the three of you, until your father died?' he asked, wanting to understand her background more.

'My father was a very busy man,' Eleni answered softly. 'He was the King—he had a lot to occupy his time. So for a long while it was Giorgos and me. He's a bit older, but he was always fun.' Her expression warmed briefly. 'When Father died, Giorgos took over.'

'Giorgos was young for that.'

'He is very highly regarded,' she said loyally.

'You're close.'

Her gaze slid from his. 'He has a big job to do. Back then he knew some of the courtiers didn't think he was old enough to handle the responsibility—'

'So he worked twice as hard to prove them wrong.' Damon smiled at her surprised look. 'It's understandable.'

She gazed out of the window. 'He's not stopped working since.'

And she was left lonely in her little turret in the palace. Damon saw how easily it had happened. She was loyal and sweet but also trapped and stifled.

'I'm supposed to marry a royal,' she said quietly. 'It's tradition. I know you think it's stupid, but it's how it's always been. I wanted to do the right thing for Giorgos.'

'Well, I'm not a prince and I never will be.' Damon took a seat. 'But won't it be easier to divorce me, a commoner, than cause conflict with two countries if you divorce your Prince?'

Her lips tightened. 'I'm not supposed to get divorced,' she said quietly. 'That's not part of the fairy tale.'

'Times change. Even royals live in the real world, Eleni. And they get divorced.'

She looked anywhere but at him. 'I barely know you.'

'Do you know Prince Xander?' Damon asked bluntly.

The shake of her head was almost imperceptible.

'Then what's the difference between marrying him and marrying me?' His muscles pulled tighter and tighter still in the face of her silence. The urge to go to her, to kiss her into acquiescence, made him ache. Despite her denial earlier he knew he could do it. All he'd have to do was kiss her and she'd be breathless and begging and he needed to get away from her before he did exactly that. He wanted to hear her say yes to him without that. 'Am I an ogre?'

'You want to take my child from me.'

'And you tried to deny the child was mine. I figure that makes us even.' He stood, unable to remain in the same room as her without succumbing to reckless action. 'Take your time to think about your options, Eleni. I'm in no rush to go anywhere.'

Why didn't she want to marry Damon? Eleni couldn't answer that honestly—not to him when she could barely admit the truth to herself. She'd never wanted anyone the way she wanted him. Her marriage to Xander would have been a loveless union. But safe compared to the tempestuous gamut of emotions Damon roused in her. She was terrified of what might happen to her heart if she stayed with him for long.

She scoffed at her inner dramatics. She needed to grow up and get a grip on her sexual frustration. Because that was all this was, right? Her first case of raw lust.

She turned off the large computer screen and foraged in the bookcase lining one of the walls, her thoughts circling around and around until her stomach rumbled and she realised how ravenous she was.

Quietly she left the room and found her way to a sleek

galley kitchen. No one was in there, thank goodness, because she was starving. She located the pantry, pouncing on an open box of cereal.

'You okay?'

'Oh.' She swallowed hastily as she turned. 'You caught me.'

He had been swimming, probably in the pool on deck. Eleni stared, fascinated by the droplets of water slowly snaking down his bronzed chest until they were finally caught in the towel he'd slung low around his hips.

'Not yet.' He walked forward. 'What are you doing that is so awful?'

Staring at your bare chest.

'I shouldn't have helped myself,' she mumbled. 'Eating straight from the packet.'

'That's not awful. That's survival instinct.' He reached into the box she was holding and helped himself to a couple of the cereal clusters. 'Don't you go into the kitchen at the palace?'

She shook her head, forcing herself to swallow.

'You just ask one of the servants?'

'What do you expect?' She bristled. 'I live in a palace and that comes with privileges.'

'But what if you wanted to just make a sandwich?'

'Then someone makes it for me.'

'You never wanted to make your own sandwich?'

'It's not my place to.' She refused to rise to his baiting. 'I'm not going to take someone's job from them.'

He looked at her as she snaffled another cereal snack. 'What would you have done if being a princess wasn't your place?'

'I studied languages and art history.' She shrugged. 'I'd probably teach.'

'But what would you have done if you could have chosen anything?'

Eleni sighed. 'My brother loves me very much but he is

very busy and most of my education was left to an older
advisor who had ancient ideas about the role of a princess.'

'You're there to be decorative.'

'And quiet and serene—'

'Serene?' He laughed. 'You're a screamer.'

She sent him a filthy look.

'So?' He teased, but pressed the point. 'What would
you have done?'

'I wanted to be a vet.' But she'd known it was impossible. The hours of study too intense when she had public
duties to perform as well.

'A vet?' He looked taken aback.

'I like dogs.' She shrugged.

'You have dogs?'

'I had a gorgeous spaniel when I was younger.'

'So why not vet school? Did you not have the grades?'

'Of course I had the grades.' She gritted her teeth and
turned away because she knew where he was going with
this, so she didn't tell him she'd wanted to do Fine Arts
first. Again she'd been denied—too frivolous. She was a
princess and she had to remain demure and humble. But
was hers really such an awful life to bestow upon a child?
Yes, there were restrictions, but there was also such privilege. Couldn't she make it different?

'You know I can offer our child a level of freedom that
you can't,' Damon said. 'Isn't that what you want, your
child not to have to "perform" the way you've had to all
your life?'

'I want the best for my child in every way,' Eleni said
calmly. And she knew exactly what she had to do for her
child now. Nothing was ever going to be the same. She
sucked in one last deep breath. 'They're all going to figure
out that I was pregnant when we married.'

He stilled; his gaze glittered. 'Either we lie and say
the baby was born prematurely, or we say nothing at all.'
He cleared his throat. 'The second option gets my vote.

There will always be whispers and Internet conspiracy theories but we rise above it with a dignified silence and carry on.'

She nodded. 'I understand what you're saying about giving our child freedom, but I'm its mother and I won't walk away from it. Ever.' She braced and pushed forward. 'If you're serious about doing what's best for our child, then you won't ask me to.'

He carefully leaned against the bench. 'So you'll marry me.'

'If we work out a plan. For after.' When their marriage ended, it needed to be smooth. 'I think there are precedents in other countries for a child not to take a royal title,' she said bravely. Giorgos would have a fit but she would have to try to make him understand. 'We can keep him or her out of the limelight and work out some kind of shared custody arrangement.'

Her heart tore at the thought, but her child had the right to be loved by both its parents.

'Then we'll work it out.' Damon looked out of the window.

'So now you've got what you wanted,' Eleni said.

He looked back at her. His blue eyes had darkened almost to black. 'And what's that?'

'Me. Saying yes.' She watched, surprised to see his tension was even more visible than before. 'What, you're not satisfied?'

'No.'

'Then what do you want?'

He took the two steps to bring himself smack bang in front of her. 'I want my tee shirt back.'

Desire uncoiled low and strong in her belly. 'But I'm not wearing anything underneath it.'

'Good.' His blunt expression of want felled her.

'Are you wearing anything under the skirt?' he asked roughly, gripping the hem of the tee.

She could barely shake her head. 'I thought you said this would only complicate things.'

'Now we're in agreement on the big issues, we can handle a little complication.'

He tugged the tee shirt up. She lifted her arms and in a second it was gone. She was bared to his gaze, his touch, his tongue.

She gasped as he swooped. There was no denying this. He desired her body. Fine. She desired his. Reason dissolved under sensual persuasion. He pressed the small of her back—holding her still, keeping her close, until he growled something unintelligible and picked her up to sit her on the edge of the bench. He pushed her knees apart so he could stand between them. Elation soared through Eleni.

This was what she wanted.

His kiss was nothing less than ravaging. She moaned as he plundered, his tongue seeking, tasting, taking everything and she did more than let him. She gave—straining closer. She wound her arms around his neck, arching and aching. His hands swept down her body, igniting sensation, sparking that deeper yearning. He slid his warm palm under her skirt. She trembled as he neared where she was wet and ready. His kiss became more rapacious still as he touched her so intimately, and her moan melted in his mouth. He lifted away only to tease her more—kissing the column of her neck, down to her collarbones and then to the aching, full breasts pointing hard for his attention.

But the nagging feeling inside wouldn't ease—resistance to this hedonism. It had been wrong before; it was still wrong now. She closed her eyes, turning her face to the side as heat blistered her from the inside out.

'Don't hide.' He nudged her chin. 'Let me see you.'

'I can't,' she muttered, desperately turning her face away.

He pulled back completely, forcing her to look into his eyes. 'You're not cheating. Your engagement is broken now.'

She was ashamed that he knew her desire for him had

overruled her duty and her loyalty. Her engagement to Xander had been a loveless arrangement, but Damon was right. She was an appalling person.

'This is nothing much more than what happened yesterday.' Damon tempted her again.

Wrong. It was so much more. If she let him in again, she wasn't sure she could cope. The passion was all-consuming, addictive and all she could think about at a time when she should be concerned with her family. With her duty. But she couldn't think clearly when she was within five hundred paces of this man.

And she doubted him. He'd wanted to find her after the ball only because he'd known there was a risk of pregnancy, not because he'd wanted more time with her. He was only taking advantage of the situation now—certainly it wasn't that he liked her.

But he'd *wanted* her when he *hadn't* known who she was. He wasn't going for the 'perfect Princess' that night, he'd wanted just *her*. There was something still seductive about that.

Damon was studying her too intently. It was as if he could strip back all her defences and see into her poor, inexperienced soul.

'Why didn't you tell me you were a virgin?' he asked softly.

There was no point holding back the truth now. 'Because you would have stopped.'

He expelled a harsh breath and framed her face with surprisingly gentle hands. 'You could have said you were inexperienced.'

'I was pretending I wasn't,' she muttered, mortified. The mask, the costume had combined to make her feel confident. He'd made her feel sexy and invincible. Unstoppable. 'I had a persona that night…now I don't.'

'Are you sure it was a persona?' Damon challenged. 'Or

was it the true you?' He skimmed the tips of his fingers down her neck until she shivered.

Was she that person? That woman who took such risks—and found such pleasure?

You want more than what you think you should have.

'There is nothing wrong with liking this, Eleni.' He tempted her to the point of madness.

'But I like it too much.' She confessed that last secret on the merest thread of a breath. 'It's not *me*. It scares me.'

That was why she'd resisted his proposal initially. The intensity of her desire for him terrified her.

His expression tightened. 'I scare you?'

'Not you. Me,' she muttered. 'I never behave like this. Like *that*.' She was appalled at how she'd behaved that night and since. All those outbursts? The waves of emotion? 'You were right. I lied. I cheated. I'm every bit that awful, spoilt person you said I was.'

Damon shifted away from her.

Eleni watched, suddenly chilled at the loss of contact. Her body yearned for the closeness of his again. But he'd switched it off. How could he do that so easily?

Hurt and alarm hit. She shouldn't have spoken so rashly. She shouldn't have stopped him because at least she could've been rid of the frustration that now cut deeper than ever.

'You need to be at peace before this happens again,' Damon said quietly—too damn in control. 'Then you won't need to hide. Then you can truly let go.'

She watched, amazed and horrified as he walked to the doorway. How, exactly, was she supposed to find peace when he was making the decision for her? When he was leaving her this...*needy*.

'I hate you,' she called. One last emotional outburst.

'I'm sure.' Damon glanced back with a smile. 'I'd never dream that you could love me.'

CHAPTER NINE

'I'M NOT WAITING for Giorgos to hunt me down like some fugitive. I want to go to him.' Eleni braced for Damon's response as she sat opposite him at the table the next morning.

She wasn't letting him make all the decisions any more. After the most desultory dinner, she'd spent the night mentally practising her confrontations with both Damon and Giorgos and it was time to put both plans into reality.

Damon arched a sardonic eyebrow. 'Good morning, fire-breathing warrior woman, who are you and what have you done with my meek fiancée?'

'I need to see him,' she insisted.

Damon's answering smile was uncomfortably wicked. 'The yacht turned around last night. We'll be back at Palisades in less than an hour. I've just let him know I have you.'

Eleni stared as his words knocked the wind from her sails.

'Well.' It was going to happen so much sooner than she'd expected. She puffed out a deep breath but it didn't settle her speeding heart. 'We might want to let him know I'm safe on board, otherwise he might try to blow up your boat.'

Damon chuckled. 'I thought Palisades was a peace-loving nation.'

It was, but when Damon's yacht entered the marina, Eleni's nerves tightened unbearably. Never before had she defied Giorgos's wishes and now the weight of his inevitable disappointment was crushing.

'I should handle him by myself,' she said to Damon

as she counted the number of soldiers waiting on the pier ready to escort her. It was a heavy-handed display of her brother's authority. 'I should have done that in the first place.'

Damon turned his back on the waiting men with an arrogant lift to his chin. Apparently he was unfazed by the latent aggression waiting for them. 'I'll stay silent if that's what you wish, but I will be beside you.'

Because he didn't trust her?

Except there was something in Damon's eyes. Something more than protectiveness and more than possessiveness. She turned away, not trusting her own vision. Because the last thing she deserved was tenderness.

The military men wordlessly ushered them into a car and drove them straight to the palace. The gleaming building felt silent, as if everyone were collectively holding their breath—waiting for Giorgos's explosion. For the first time in her life Eleni felt like a stranger in her own home. The only person not tiptoeing on eggshells was Damon. He casually strolled the endless corridors as if he hadn't a care in the world.

They weren't taken to either her private suite or to Giorgos's. Instead her brother's assistant led them to a formal room usually reserved for meetings with visiting Heads of State. Chilled, Eleni paused in the doorway. Giorgos grimly waited in full King mode—white dress uniform, jacket laden with medals and insignia, boots polished to mirror-like sheen. All that was missing was his crown.

'I've cancelled an engagement at the last minute. Again.' Giorgos fixed a steely stare on Damon.

But her brother's barely disguised loathing apparently bounced off as Damon blandly stared right back.

'You took advantage of an innocent,' Giorgos accused shortly. 'You seduced her.'

Was she invisible? Straightening her shoulders, Eleni stepped forward.

'Maybe I seduced him.' She clenched her fists to hide how badly her hands were shaking, but she was determined to take control of this conversation. *She* was having the input here, not Damon.

Her brother finally bothered to look at her, but as he faced her he became like a marble sculpture. Expressionless and unreadable.

'Damon and I will be married as soon as possible,' she said, determined to state her case before he tore her to shreds.

Giorgos continued to look unmoved. 'Last time we spoke you insisted you were not marrying either Prince Xander or Mr Gale.'

'I was upset,' she conceded coolly. 'But this is the best course of action, Giorgos.'

'He is not a prince. He has no title whatsoever.'

Of course her brother knew Damon's background already—he'd have had his investigators on it from the moment he'd gotten the message this morning. From Giorgos's frown, Damon's success mattered little to him. 'You know the expectations—'

'Change the law, create a new custom.' For the second time in her life Eleni dared to interrupt her brother. 'You're King. You have the power.'

'And should I abuse power trusted to me, for personal gain?'

'Is it personal gain, or would you simply be granting the same right that any other citizen in Palisades already has?' Why couldn't she have the right to choose for herself?

Giorgos's eyes narrowed. 'So I simply ignore centuries of custom and duty? I abandon all levels of diplomacy and the expectations of our important neighbours and alliances?'

'My personal life shouldn't be used for political manoeuvring.'

'So you got yourself pregnant instead of simply making that argument?'

She recoiled in shock and her anger unleashed. 'Of course I didn't. But would you be listening to me if I *wasn't* pregnant?'

Giorgos sent Damon the iciest look she'd ever seen. 'You know about our mother?'

'Yes. I will ensure Eleni receives care from the best specialists.'

Giorgos shook his head. 'Our doctor is ready to give her a check-up now.'

Eleni gaped. Did her brother think she was somehow incapacitated?

Damon answered before she could. 'I don't think that's necessary—'

'It is entirely necessary. She must be—'

'Stop trying to overrule each other.' Eleni interrupted Giorgos again, her heart and head pounding. 'My medical decisions will be made by *me*.'

'Dr Vecolli is already here,' Giorgos insisted.

'I'm not seeing Dr Vecolli.'

'He's been our family physician for twenty years.'

'Which is exactly *why* I'm not seeing him. He's like a grandfather to me. I would like to see a female doctor.' She glared as Giorgos frowned at her. 'What, do you think no woman can be a doctor, or is it just me you thought so incapable I couldn't even be trusted with animals?'

'I once wanted to be an airplane pilot.' Giorgos dripped cold sarcasm. 'But you *know* we cannot hold down a full-time job while fulfilling royal duty. It is impossible.'

'*Why?*' she challenged. 'Couldn't I be useful other than cutting ribbons and awarding prizes?'

'You're going to have your hands full with your baby, or had you forgotten that?'

Eleni flared anew at Giorgos's patronising tone. 'So while plenty of other mothers work, I can only be a brood

mare? Do you think I'm that incompetent?' She was outraged—and *hurt*.

'I don't think you're—' Her brother broke off and ran a
hand through his hair.

'Why are we so enslaved by the past?' she asked him
emotionally. 'Just because things have always been done
a certain way, doesn't mean they always have to continue
in that same way.' And she was more capable than he believed her to be—wasn't she?

Giorgos was silent for a long moment. Then he sighed
softly. 'Then how do you plan to manage this?'

'By marrying Damon. I'll have the baby and then…'
She drew in a steadying breath. 'Beyond that, I don't really know. But I don't want all those limitations on me any
more. They're untenable.'

She braced for his response. She couldn't yet tell him
her marriage had an end date already. One let-down at a
time was enough.

Giorgos's expression revealed more now. But he didn't
need to worry; this wedding wouldn't end the world.

'It could be leaked that Eleni was corralled into the wedding with Prince Xander.' Damon broke the tense silence.
'She was too afraid to stand up to you and the Prince. Public sympathy will be on her side if it is cast as a forbidden
love story.'

She didn't deserve public sympathy.

'She fell in love with me during her secret hospital visits.' Damon embroidered the possible story. 'But you refused your consent for her to have a relationship with a
commoner. She was so distraught she really did get sick.
Only then did you realise how serious she was.'

Eleni winced at the scenario he'd painted. Did everyone
need to know she'd been unable to stand up for herself?
More importantly, it didn't do her brother justice.

'Do we need to make Giorgos sound such a bully?' She
frowned.

Giorgos's eyes widened with an arrested expression.

'Prince Xander is still the injured party,' Damon continued after a beat. 'But it can be spun that they'd not spent much time together. Therefore her defection won't make him appear any less attractive.'

Eleni smothered her startled laugh. Damon was light years more attractive than Xander.

For a long moment Giorgos studied the painting hanging on the wall opposite him. With every passing second Eleni's heart sank—recriminations and rejection were inevitable.

'You might have met your match, Eleni.' Giorgos slowly turned to her, the wryest of smiles in his eyes. 'He won't curl round your little finger.'

'The way you do?' Eleni dared to breathe back.

'You will be married in the private chapel today.' Giorgos's steely seriousness returned. 'I will release a public proclamation together with a few photographs. You will not make a public appearance. Rather you will go away for at least a month.'

'Away?' Eleni was stunned at the speed of his agreement.

'You need to get your personal situation stable while this fluff is spread in the press.' Giorgos's sarcasm edged back. 'You'll go to France. I have a safe house there.'

'But the safest house of all is this one,' Eleni argued. She was not letting her brother banish her. Not when she had to get to grips with a husband she barely knew and to whom she could hardly control her reaction. Staying home would give her the space and privacy to deal with Damon.

'Remaining in Palisades would give Damon a chance to learn palace protocol and understand the expectations for our...*future*.' She glanced at Damon, fudging just how short their future together was going to be.

Damon shrugged but his eyes were sharp. 'I'm happy to hang here for a while if that's what you wish, Eleni.'

'I am scheduled to spend a few weeks at the Summer House,' Giorgos said stiffly. 'So that would work.' He turned icily to Damon. 'But understand that I will be watching you, even from there. I don't trust you.'

'Fair enough,' Damon answered equally coolly. 'If I were you, I wouldn't either.' He smiled as if he hadn't a care in the world. 'I'll not take a title, by the way. I'll remain Damon Gale.'

'While I'll remain Princess Eleni Nicolaides,' Eleni answered instantly.

'And the child will be Prince or Princess Nicolaides-Gale—we get it,' Giorgos snapped. 'Let's just get everything formalised and documented before it leaks. I expect you at the chapel in an hour. Both of you looking the part.'

Her brother stalked towards the door, his posture emanating *uptight King*.

'I'll send someone to the yacht to fetch a suit,' Damon drawled once Giorgos had left. 'I guess you'd better go magic up a wedding dress.'

She stared at her fiancé and clapped a hand over her mouth in horror.

'Don't worry.' Damon's satisfied smile turned distinctly wicked. 'You can wear as little as you like—I will not say no. That busty blue number you wore at the ball would be nice—'

Flushing hotly, Eleni swiftly walked out on him, desperately needing a moment alone to process everything. But her maid hovered at the door to her suite, the woman's expression alert with unmistakable excitement.

'Oh, Bettina. I'm sorry I've been away.' Eleni quickly pasted on a smile. 'And I'm not back for long.'

Bettina nodded eagerly. 'I have done the best I can in the last half hour. I've hung the samples so you can choose. There are nine altogether—from New York, Paris, and one from Milan.'

'Samples?' Eleni repeated, confused.

'The wedding dresses.'

Nine wedding dresses? Eleni gaped. If that wasn't being spoilt, she didn't know what was.

'Would you like to try them on?'

Eleni saw the sparkle in her maid's eyes and realised the fiction that Eleni was marrying her long-secret love had already spread. She drew in a deep breath and made her smile bigger. 'Absolutely.'

But her smile became a wide 'oh' as Bettina wheeled out the garment rack she'd hung the gowns on. And then Eleni surrendered to vain delight—at the very least she could look good on her wedding day.

The sixth option was the winner; she knew as soon as she stepped into it. It was exactly what she'd choose for *herself*—not as something befitting 'Princess Eleni'. The sleek dress with its svelte lines and delicate embroidery was subtle but sexy and she loved it.

As Eleni walked away from her maid, her suite and her life as she knew it, butterflies skittered around her stomach, but she determinedly kept her smile on her face.

She couldn't let the fairy-tale image fall apart just yet.

Giorgos stood waiting for her at the entrance to the private chapel. Her smile—and her footsteps—faltered as she saw his frown deepening. But this might be her only chance to speak to him privately.

'I'm sorry I let you down,' she said when she was close enough for only him to hear.

'You haven't.' Her brother held out a small posy of roses for her.

Tears sprang to her eyes as she took the pretty bouquet from him. 'Thank you,' she whispered.

He nodded, stiffly. 'Do you love him?' Giorgos suddenly asked.

The direct question stole her breath. For the first time that she could recall, her brother looked awkward—almost unsure—as he gazed hard at a spot on the floor just ahead of them.

She couldn't be anything but honest. 'I don't know.'

That frown furrowed his brow again. 'Make it work, Eleni.'

Then he held out his arm, that glimpse of uncertainty gone. She nodded, unable to speak given the lump in her throat, and placed her hand in the crook of his elbow.

As Giorgos escorted her into the chapel, Eleni caught sight of Damon standing at the altar. He was dressed in a stunningly tailored suit. He seemed taller, broader; his eyes were very blue. He claimed the attention of every one of her senses. Every thought. Her pulse raced, her limbs trembled. She tried to remember to breathe. She couldn't possibly be *excited*, could she? This was only part of the plan to secure her child's legitimacy and freedom. This was only for her baby.

But those butterflies danced a complicated reel.

It's just a contract. It's only for the next year. It doesn't mean anything...

But reciting her vows to Damon in the family chapel heightened her sense of reverence. Here—in front of her brother, in front of him, in this sanctuary and symbol of all things past and future—she had to promise to love him.

He's the father of my child.

She could love him only for that, couldn't she? It wasn't a lie.

But a whisper of foreboding swept down her spine and she shivered just as Damon turned towards her. She met his gaze, almost frozen by the enormity of their actions.

But Damon wasn't frozen. He had that slightly wicked expression in his eyes as he reached to pull her close.

The kiss sealing their wedding contract should have been businesslike, but he lingered a fraction too long. That heat coursed through her veins. She closed her eyes and in that instant was lost. Her bones ached and the instinct to lean into him overwhelmed her. Only at the exact moment of her surrender, he suddenly pulled away. She caught a glimpse of wildness in his eyes but then her lifetime of training took over. She turned and walked with him out of the chapel and into the formal throne room. There she dutifully posed for endless photos with Giorgos on one side of her, Damon on the other. She smiled and smiled and smiled. Perfectly Princess Eleni.

Her brother took her hand and bowed. 'You make a beautiful bride, Eleni.'

Because all that mattered was how she looked and how this arrangement looked to the world? But Giorgos's expression softened and he suddenly gave her a quick hug.

'Take care of yourself.' With the briefest of glances at Damon, her brother left.

A little dazed, Eleni gazed after him. It had been years since he'd hugged her. Her nerves lightened. The worst was over, right? Now she could move forward.

'Eleni.'

She turned.

Damon stood too close, too handsome, his expression too knowing. That little respite from inner tension was over as she realised the first night of her marriage lay ahead. The beginning of the end of the thing neither of them had wanted in the first place.

'We should take a couple of photos somewhere less formal,' Damon suggested.

Eleni shook her head as his glance around the ornate room revealed his less than impressed opinion.

'There's nowhere "less formal" anywhere in this palace,' she informed him with perverse pleasure.

'What about outside?' Damon eyed up the French doors that no one had opened in Eleni's life.

'That's locked,' she said.

Damon turned the handle and the door opened silently and easily on the hinge.

Of course it did.

He sent her a triumphant smile that did even more annoying things to her insides.

'You're the most irritating creature alive,' she grumbled.

'I know,' he commiserated drolly. 'But you still want me.'

'What are you doing?' she whispered, stalking outside to get away from him as much as anything.

'This is your palace, Eleni. You're allowed to run around in it, right?' He was still too close.

'You're...'

'What?' he challenged, arrogance in his eyes as he wrapped his arm around her waist, stopping her flight and drawing her close. 'What am I?'

Not good for her health.

Eleni half laughed, half groaned as she gave into temptation and leaned against him. But she refused to answer.

Damon retaliated physically. Magically. Reigniting those embers settled so slightly beneath her skin. The kiss banished the last butterflies and a bonfire burned, engulfing her body in a delicious torture of desire. This time he held nothing back, pulling her close enough for her to feel just how she affected him. Desire flared, compounded by the awareness that, this time, there was nothing to stop them.

Click. Click, click, click.

She put her hands on his broad chest and pushed, remembering too late there was a freaking photographer following them.

'I'm the Princess,' she muttered, mainly to remind herself.

But Damon kept her close with one arm around her waist and a light grip on her jaw. 'I didn't marry "the Princess".'

'Yes, you did.' There was no separating who she was

from what she was. She had to accept that and now he did too.

The photographer looked disappointed when Damon sent him away. As he left, thudding blades whirred overhead and she glanced up to see her brother's helicopter swiftly heading north.

'So now we're alone,' Damon said softly. 'And not a second too soon.'

She suppressed the shiver at the determination in his tone and gazed at the rings on her finger to avoid looking at him. He'd surprised her in the chapel, sliding an engagement ring on her finger as well as a wedding band.

'You don't like them?' he asked, inexorably escorting her towards that open French door.

On the contrary, she loved them, but she was wary of showing it. She couldn't quite make out his mood. Was he angry as well as aroused? 'How did you pick them so quickly?'

A grim smile briefly curved his mouth. 'I had just a little longer to prepare for our wedding than you did.'

Even so, his organisational skills were impressive. 'It's a sapphire?'

He shook his head. 'A blue diamond for my blue bride.'

Her heart knocked. The stone's colour was the exact shade of the dress she'd worn that fateful night.

'You still look blue.' He cocked his head curiously. 'Why? You have the support of your brother. Everything that mattered has been resolved. So why so sad?'

Because this wasn't going to last. Because for all the foolishness in the garden, this was as much of a charade as her wedding to Xander would have been. Because she was a romantic fool. Part of her had wanted real love on her wedding day.

You can't be a child any more, Eleni. You're having a child.

Unable to answer his demanding tone, she walked

through the palace towards her private apartment. There wasn't a servant or soldier to be seen, as if by some silent decree they knew to stay out of sight. And it was a good thing too. She'd seen the banked heat in Damon's eyes. She knew he wasn't about to show her any mercy.

Her pulse skittered, speeding up the nearer she got to her rooms. At the foot of the staircase he reached out and took her hand.

She tried to hide the quickening of her breath but she knew he could feel the slamming pulse at her wrist and she could see the tension tightening his features too.

He wanted and he would have. Because she wanted too. And maybe this 'want' would have to do. Maybe they could make this work. With the reluctant acceptance of her brother, with the physical attraction binding them, with the baby…maybe this could work *indefinitely*.

She paused at the top of the staircase, drawing in a deeper breath to try to steady her anticipation. Damon released her hand, only to swing her into his arms.

'What are you doing?' she whisper-shrieked, clutching his shoulders as he suddenly strode down the last corridor to her apartment. 'You're not carrying me over my own threshold?'

'Indulge me.'

Excitement rippled down her spine, feathering goosebumps across her skin at his intensity. 'I didn't think you'd be one for wedding traditions.' Her throat felt raspy as she tried to tease.

His grip on her tightened for a nanosecond, and then eased again.

'I was never getting married,' he said carelessly as he kicked the door shut behind them. 'But seeing as that vow has been torn up, I might as well make the most of it.'

She looked into his face as he set her down, wishing she could read his mind. 'Why didn't you want to marry?'

He hesitated for a split second. 'It's not in our nature to be with one person all our lives.'

Our nature, or just *his*? His warning stabbed deep, bursting the warm bubble of desire.

'You don't believe in monogamy?' she clarified, his harsh reality cooling her completely.

'No. I don't.'

So he would cheat on her.

He caught her shoulders, preventing her from walking away from him. 'I think it traps people into a perceived perfection that can't be maintained,' he said quietly, forcing her to meet his gaze. 'No one is infallible, Eleni. Certainly not me. Definitely not you.'

'I can control myself.' Rebellious anger scorched her skin. 'And I intend to keep the vows we just made.'

He smiled. 'Of course you do. And so do I. Until the time when we dissolve the deal. It is just a contract, Eleni. Nothing more.'

Her deeply ingrained sense of tradition and honour railed against that declaration. She'd stood in that chapel and she'd meant those vows. But for Damon, this was nothing more than a business proposition. So why had he carried her only a minute ago?

'But it is a contract with particular benefits,' he added.

'And you intend to make the most of those benefits?' She wasn't buying it.

'As much as you do. Or are you going to try to deny yourself because I've annoyed you?' His smile was all disbelief.

'I'm going to deny *you*.' This might be her wedding night but it made no difference. She wasn't sleeping with him now.

'I've made you angry.' His eyebrows lifted. 'You're very young, sweetheart.'

'No. You're very cynical.' She shoved his chest, but he only took two paces back from her. 'And I'm *not* a child.

Just because I haven't slept with half the world, doesn't mean I'm more stupid than you. Sex doesn't make you smarter. If anything it makes you more dense.'

'Come here, Eleni.'

What, he was going to ignore her argument and simply demand her submission just because he knew she found him sexy?

'Get over yourself.'

'You're saying no?' he asked, his early anger giving way to arrogant amusement. 'Because you're the one used to giving orders?'

'No, that's my brother,' she answered in annoyance. 'I'm the one used to standing in the corner doing what she's told.'

'Then why aren't you doing as you're told now?' He stood with his legs wide like some implacable pirate captain. 'Come here.'

The entrance vestibule of her apartment wasn't huge but it might as well have been the Grand Canyon between them.

'You come over here,' she dared, ignoring the pull of his attraction. 'I'm tired of being told what to do. I'm doing the telling this time.'

His eyes widened fractionally. For a long moment he regarded her silently. She could see the storm brewing in him and braced. Him walking closer was what she wanted. And what she didn't want.

'I'm not yours to boss around or *control*,' she said, touching her tongue to her suddenly dry lips but determinedly maintaining her bravado regardless. 'I'm going to do what's necessary. And *only* what is necessary.'

He took those two paces to invade her personal space again and swept his hand from her waist to her hip. 'This is necessary, Eleni.'

She turned her head away, her heart pounding. 'Not any more.'

'Because you're mad with me.' His lips brushed her cheek. 'Because I've ruined your belief in fairy tales?

There's only the real world, Eleni. With real complications and real mess.'

'And temporary desires,' she ended the lecture for him.

'That's right.'

'And you're feeling a temporary desire now?' she asked.

'Definitely.'

'Too bad.' She clamped her mouth shut.

He laughed again. 'You say you don't play games.' He gifted her the lightest of kisses. 'Say yes to me again, Eleni,' he coaxed, teasing too-gentle hands up and down her spine. 'Say yes.'

She glared at him for as long as she could but she already knew she'd lost. 'You're not fair.'

'Life isn't fair. I thought you knew that already.' He moved closer still, forcing her to step backwards until she was pressed hard between him and the wall. 'Say yes.'

She could hold out but it would only be for a little while. She wanted him too much. She had from the second she'd seen him that night. And it was just sex, right? Nothing to take too seriously. She might as well get something she wanted from this 'contract'.

'Yes.' It was always going to be yes.

His smile was triumphant but she swore she saw tenderness there too. Except it couldn't be that—he'd just told her this was only temporary. He brushed a loose tendril of hair back from her face.

'Don't pet me like I'm a good dog,' she snapped.

He laughed. 'Definitely not a dog. But very good. And very worth petting.' He put hands on her shoulders and applied firm pressure. 'Turn around.'

She met his gaze and sucked in a breath at the fire in his eyes. Wordlessly she let him turn her, surrendering this once.

'This dress is beautiful,' he said softly. 'But not as beautiful as the woman inside it.'

Eleni bowed her head, resting her forehead on the cool

wall. He undid the first button and pressed his lips to the tiny patch of bared skin. His fingers traced, then teased down to the next button. In only a heartbeat Eleni was lost in the eroticism—of not seeing him, but of feeling him expose her to his gaze, to his touch, to his tongue again, inch by slow inch.

Desire unfurled from low in her belly. Her body cared not for the complications and confusion of her heart and mind. Her body cared only for his touch, only for the completion he could bring her.

He teased too much. Too slow. Until she was trembling and breathless.

When her dress slithered to the floor in a rush he put firm hands on her waist and spun her to face him again. She'd worn no bra beneath the gown, so she was left with lacy panties, stockings, kitten heels and nothing else. His gaze was hot and suddenly she was galvanised, reaching out to push him to recklessness again. She wanted him as breathless, as naked—she needed to feel his skin against hers.

But she couldn't undo his buttons. She was too desperate for release from the tension that soared with every second she spent with him. His choked laugh was strained and he took over, swiftly discarding the remainder of his clothes until they lay in a tumble at their feet. For a second she just stared at him. And he at her.

Before she could think, let alone speak, he pulled her close again, as if he couldn't stand to be parted from her for a second longer. He devoured her—with his gaze, then his fingers, then his mouth. He kissed every exposed inch. Somehow they were on the floor and he was braced above her—heavy and strong and dominant. She gasped breathlessly, aching for him. But just at that moment, he lifted slightly away and she almost screamed in protest.

'What?' she snapped at him. Why was he stopping *now*? His smile was both smug and twisted. 'I've had numerous lovers, Eleni, but you're the first one to run away afterwards.'

'Did I hurt your ego?' She half hoped so; that'd be pay-back for what he was doing to her now.

'You frustrated me. You still do.' A seriousness stole into his features. 'You know I don't want to hurt you.'

She understood frustration now. 'I'm not afraid.'

And he wasn't going to hurt her—he'd made it very clear that this was only this. Only lust. Only temporary.

'No?' He held fast above her. *So close.* 'You're not going to run away again?'

'Not while I'm this naked.' She sighed, surrendering to his seriousness. 'I can handle you.'

'Then no more hiding either,' he ordered, cupping her cheek. 'In this, hold nothing back.'

She was lost in the blue of his intense eyes. He wanted it all his way—acceptance that this was only sex. But at the same time he wanted everything from her. It wasn't fair. But it was life. And it was just them again.

'Okay.' She breathed. A wave of pleasure rolled over her as she accepted his terms. This total intimacy was fi-nally okay.

Less than a second later he drove deep into her body. She cried out as he claimed her with that one powerful thrust. Trembling, she wrapped her arms around his mus-cular body. Maybe she couldn't handle him. She couldn't cope with how completely he took her, or how exquisitely he now tortured her by just holding still—his invasion total.

'Easy...' he muttered.

There was no easy. 'Please,' she begged, trying to rock her hips beneath him to rouse him into action. 'Please.'

She needed him to move—to take her hard and fast and break the terrible tension gripping her. Because this was too, too good and she was going insane with the de-sire for release.

'Damn it, Eleni.' He growled and rose on his hands, grinding impossibly deeper.

Passion washed over her. It felt so good she all but lost her mind in the fire that burned out of control so quickly. She was like dry tinder. With one spark the inferno licked to the bone. But suddenly, blessedly, he flared too. Ferociously he rode her. She moaned with every panting short breath until they bucked in unison. Waves of ecstasy radiated through each cell in her body with every one of his forceful thrusts. Fierce and fast she arched, taut and tight around him.

'Eleni.'

She loved the way he ground her name through his clenched teeth. Over and over he stroked her. She clenched her fists as the shuddering rush of pleasure started. Gasping for breath, she revelled in the floods of release as he shouted and thrust hard that one last time, pressing her flat against the wooden floor.

Her emotions surged as the waves of her orgasm ebbed. It was shocking how good he made her feel. How *shattered*. She didn't think she could possibly find the energy to stand, let alone smile. And she wanted to smile. More than that, she wanted him again. Already. She struggled to catch her breath before it quickened, but there was no reining in the rapacious desire that he'd unleashed within her. Only then she felt him moving—away.

Damon winced. Every muscle felt feeble. He'd meant to go more gently and ensure she was with him every step of the way. Hell, he'd meant to make her come first and more than once. But she'd provoked him, and he'd wanted her too much, until he'd taken her like this on the floor—unstoppable and unrestrained and so damn quick all over again.

He rolled onto his side to see more of her lithe, passion-slick, sated body. And this time she turned her head to look back at him. Letting him see her. Her green-blue eyes were luminous. His mouth dried as he read the craving within them. For all his teasing, he understood how much she wanted this. As much as he did. Something shifted inside—a warning that this was far too intense. But it was too late.

If he was any kind of a good guy he'd have wed her and then left her right alone, because, as he'd told her, sleeping together again would lead to complication and she was so inexperienced he didn't want to mess with her emotions. But he wasn't a good guy.

Not a prince, remember?

Fortunately he'd recovered from the whim to carry her into the apartment. That action had turned her soft skin pink, so he'd had to remind her of the reality of their situation. His words had snuffed the starry-eyed look from her face. Now all that remained was the flush of raw desire. Because that was all this was. Romance wasn't real. Love didn't last.

So, better him to be doing this with her than some other jerk, right? At least he was the one she wanted.

He was determined to please her. The sound of her sighs and the fierce heat of her hold were his ultimate reward. The intensity of their chemistry both angered and enthralled him. Now his exhausted body roared with renewed energy. He scooped her into his arms and stood. He'd ached to have her this close. To have her unable to say no to him, wanting and welcoming him—and only him.

He walked through the ornate lounge room, going on instinct to find her bedroom—a surprisingly simply decorated room. He was just so glad to see the bed. He placed her in the centre of it, gritting back the primal growl of victory. His skin tightened as his muscles bunched. Now they'd solved the problem of their immediate future, they could thrash this attraction that burned between them. An understanding of pleasure was the one thing he could give her. The enjoyment of what their bodies were built for, with no shame, no reticence and no regret. Just passion and play.

Satisfaction oozed as he started to tease that wild response from her again. He loved finally having her on the bed with all the time in the world to explore her properly. Her cheeks flushed, her eyes gleamed—dazed, passionate, willing.

He'd had her. He'd have her again. But something ached—something that was missing despite the almost intolerable ecstasy of the last orgasm they'd shared.

'Eleni.' He uttered a plea he hadn't meant to let free.

He'd coerced her into this marriage, but while she'd finally agreed—and accepted that it was only a contract—somehow he wasn't appeased. Not yet. Not even when he made her writhe uncontrollably. Not when she moaned again or when her hands sought to hurry him. Because he refused to be hurried. Not this time. He was slow and deliberate and determined to touch and taste and tease every last inch of her. But even when he'd done that, the nagging gap still irked.

Finally he allowed himself to invade her body with his own again. Helplessly groaning at the unbearable bliss, he locked into place. The driving need to get closer consumed him. He craved her heated softness and tight strength.

'Eleni.' He strained to stay in control.

'Yes.' Her sweet answer rasped over his desire-whipped skin and he drove deeper into her fire. Every muscle tensed as he fought the urge to give in already.

Too soon. It was too soon.

'Damon.' She tracked teasing fingers down his chest until he caught her hand and held it close and she whispered again. Sheer lust vocalised. 'Damon.'

His heart pounded. That was what he wanted. His name on her lips. Her eyes on his. Her body drinking his in. Her whole focus only on him. She arched, willing and

sultry, and suddenly her enchanting smile was broken
by her release.

'Damon!'

His name. *Screamed.*

A torrent of triumphant energy sluiced through every
cell as the last vestige of his self-control snapped. He could
no longer hold back, growling his passion as he furiously
pounded his way closer. To her. To bliss. His world blackened as rapture hit and satisfaction thundered.

He had won.

CHAPTER TEN

DAMON QUIETLY PACED about the lounge in Eleni's apartment within the palace. His bags had been delivered before the ceremony yesterday and he drew out his tablet now.

The number of emails in his inbox was insane even for him and it wasn't yet eight in the morning. He clicked the first few open and grimaced at the capital letters screaming *CONGRATULATIONS!* at him.

Rattled, he flicked on the television, muting the volume so he couldn't hear the over-excited, high-pitched squeals of the presenters as they gushed about the surprise nuptials of Princess Eleni. A ticker ran along the bottom of the screen repeating the amazing news that she'd married a commoner—one Mr Damon Gale.

The piece they then played was about him. His business interests got a brief mention while his personal ones were explored in depth and all but invented. They focused on his upbringing, his family, his illegitimate half-sister...

He winced when he saw the media crews camped outside Kassie's small apartment in the village. But the horror show worsened in a heartbeat as his father flashed on the screen. Damon automatically iced his emotions—the response had taken him years to perfect. But the sensation of impending doom increased and he flicked on the audio to hear his father in action. Apparently John Gale was 'thrilled' that Eleni and his son Damon's relationship was finally public. His father didn't use her title as he talked, implying intimacy—as if he'd ever met her? But he wasn't afraid of using anyone to push himself further up the slippery pole of success; Damon knew that all too well.

He could hear his father's avaricious glee at the coup his son had scored.

'You must be very proud of Damon,' one reporter yelled.

His father visibly puffed up. 'Damon is brilliant. He inherited his mother's brains.'

Damon gritted his teeth. His father's false praise poked a wound that should have long healed. His parents were anything but normal. Narcissistic and concerned only with image, neither had hearts. Truth be told, nor did he. That was his genetic inheritance. No capacity for love. No capacity for shame. All his parents had was ambition. He had that too.

But he'd learned to define his own success. To make it alone, be the one in control, be the boss. His parents had been uninterested and absent at best, and abusive at worst, and they'd taught him well. Yeah, now he had the burning ambition not to need them or *anyone*.

'What about your daughter, Kasiani?' Another reporter jostled to the front. 'Is she also a friend of Princess Eleni's?'

His father didn't bat an eyelid at the mention of the daughter he hadn't seen in years and the reference to the women that he'd abandoned entirely—not just emotionally, but financially as well. Damon had actually been jealous of Kassie until he'd learned his father was truly fickle and incapable of any kind of decent emotion.

'I really can't comment further on Eleni's personal relationships.' He didn't need to comment further when the smug satisfaction was written all over his face.

Damon watched as his father walked past the reporter. But as the cameraman swung the camera to keep filming, Damon realised just where the interview had taken place—outside the terminal at Palisades airport.

Which meant his father was here. Now.

Damon muted the sound on the screen and strode from

Eleni's private apartment. He needed to speak to the palace secretary immediately.

'Mr Gale.'

Damon stopped mid-stride down the hallway as Giorgos's private secretary called to him.

'It's your father,' the secretary added.

'Please take me to him,' Damon said quietly.

John Gale had been shown to one of the smaller meeting rooms very near the entrance of the palace. Damon's appreciation of Giorgos's secretary increased and he nodded at the man as he stood back respectfully.

Drawing in a breath, Damon closed the door and faced the father he hadn't seen in five years. Not much had changed. Perhaps he had a little more grey in his hair, a few lines around his eyes, but he still wore that surface-only smile, neat suit and non-stick demeanour.

Damon didn't take a seat, didn't offer one to his father. 'Why are you here?'

'I wanted to congratulate you in person.'

The bare nerve of the man was galling.

'You're very quick off the mark. I haven't been married twenty-four hours yet.'

His father's smile stayed crocodile wide. 'I never thought you had it in you.'

'Had what in me?'

'To marry so…happily.'

'Happily?' Damon queried. 'You mean like you and Mother?'

'Your mother and I have a very successful arrangement.'

Yeah. An arrangement that was bloodless and only about making the most of their assets. 'And that's what you think this is?'

'Are you saying you're in love with her?' His father laughed. 'I'm sure you love the power and opportunity that come with her beautiful body.'

Revulsion triggered rage but Damon breathed deeply,

settling his pulse. He wasn't going to bite. His father wasn't worth it. But he couldn't help declaring the obvious. 'I'm not like you.'

His father frowned. 'Meaning?'

'You have at least one other child that you have done nothing for. You abuse people, then abandon them.'

His father's expression narrowed.

'How many others are there?' Damon asked bluntly.

'That was one mistake.'

Mistake?

'I saw you with her,' Damon said softly, knowing he'd regret the revelation but unable to resist asking.

'Who?'

'Kassie's mother.' Damon had followed him once, here in Palisades—the opulent island of personal betrayal had taken Damon on a swift bleak journey to adulthood and understanding. He'd seen his father kiss that woman with such passion. Damon had actually thought his father was truly in love. That he was truly capable of it and it was just that he didn't feel it for either Damon or his mother. 'Why didn't you leave us and stay with her?' He'd never understood it.

An appalled expression carved deeper lines in his father's face. 'I would never leave your mother.'

'Not because you love her,' Damon said. 'But because her connections were too important to your career. It was your arrangement.'

Because he was that calculating. That ruthlessly ambitious. That incapable of real love.

'Your mother and I make a good team. We understand each other.'

By turning blind eyes to infidelities and focusing on their careers. They'd used his funds and her family name. Connections and money made for progress in political circles. They'd had Damon only to cement the image of the 'perfect career couple'. Not because he'd actually been wanted, as his mother had told him every time he'd disappointed her. And that had been often.

'So you abandoned your lover and your daughter and refused to help when they were struggling because of the risk to your stupid career and supposedly perfect marriage.' Damon was disgusted.

'I offered her money but she was too proud to accept it. That was her choice.'

'You knew she suffered and you didn't go back.'

'What more could I have done, Damon?' his father asked. 'Was it my fault she chose to remain in that squalid little cottage?'

Damon understood it now—he'd realised the horrific truth when he'd learned how that woman had suffered for so long, so alone. His father had never loved Kassie's mother. He'd wanted her, used her and walked away when he'd had enough. When she'd refused his money his conscience was cleared and he'd considered himself absolved.

No guilt. No shame. No heart.

'It'll look strange if you don't invite us both here soon,' his father said, his callousness towards Kassie and her mother apparently forgotten already. 'Your mother would like to stay as a guest.'

'I'm never inviting either of you here,' Damon said shortly. 'How can you act as if we're close when we haven't seen each other in years?' Bitterness burned up his throat. He wanted the taint of the man nowhere near Eleni.

'We've all been busy.'

His father hadn't realised he'd been avoiding him? 'No. We have no relationship. You're not using this. You're not using me.'

'You can't get away from your blood, Damon.' John Gale laughed. 'You're my son. Just because we're more alike than you want to admit, doesn't mean it isn't so. You can't get away from who you are.'

He'd never wanted to be like either of his parents. They

were why he'd never wanted a serious relationship, let alone to marry. Why he'd wanted to build his company—his success—on his own terms. In isolation and not dependent on manipulated relationships.

'I might not be able to deny my blood, but I can deny you access to my wife and to our home,' Damon said coldly. 'You're not welcome here. You'll never be welcome here. I suggest you leave right now, before I have the soldiers throw you out.'

'Your wife's soldiers.'

'Yes.' Damon refused to let his father get a rise out of him. 'Don't come back. Don't contact me again. And don't dare try to contact Eleni directly.'

'Or?'

'Or I'll let the world know just *what* you are.' He'd strike where his father cared the most—his reputation, his image.

John's eyes narrowed.

'It will be much better for you to return to New York and whatever project it is you're about to launch,' Damon said lazily. 'And no more gleeful interviews mentioning Eleni and me. You're showing your lack of class.'

That blow landed and Damon watched as his father's complexion turned ruddy. After that, John didn't stick around and Damon slowly wound his way back up to Eleni's apartment. He'd done the right thing getting him out of the palace as quickly as possible. But his father's slimy insincerity stuck.

He didn't want it getting to Eleni. As soon as the baby was born he'd begin the separation process because she'd be so much better off without him. But he'd still be the Princess's ex-husband, the father of her child. Another prince or princess.

Too late he realised her life was now intrinsically tied to his. His gut tightened as he mulled the possible configurations of their futures and the fact that she would always be part of his world. In the cold light of day he realised he'd not 'won' anything at all.

Nor had she.

But he'd meant what he'd told her. Relationships never lasted. Not for anyone. And certainly not him. Never him. He refused.

He paused for a moment outside her apartment door to draw in a breath. Then he let himself in. It was too much to hope she was still in bed. She was dressed in a simple tee shirt and skirt and his wayward body tightened at the sight of her lithe legs.

'Where have you been?' she asked, sending him a sleepy smile, but her sea-green eyes were too searching for him to cope with.

'I have a company to run,' Damon said sharply, picking up his tablet and staring at it. Hard. 'I've neglected it long enough while tracking you down.'

Silence filled the room, tightening the invisible string connecting his eyes to her body and in the end he could no longer resist the tug.

A limpid look was trained on him. 'Perhaps you should have slept a little longer.'

He couldn't help but smile at that most princess-polite sass.

She wandered over to the window, affording him an even better view of her legs and the curve of her body. She had no idea of her sensuality.

'So what have you been working on that's caused your mood to…deteriorate?'

'It's not important.'

'It wouldn't have anything to do with your father, would it?'

He froze. 'Your palace spies have reported in already?'

'No spies. I saw a replay of the interview with him at the airport.' She turned to face him. 'Is he here?'

'He's already left.'

'You didn't want me to meet him?'

'No.' He didn't want to explain why. But he saw the wounded flash in her eyes. 'He's not a nice man.'

Her lips twisted. 'You don't need to protect me.'

'Yes, I do.' He huffed out a breath and glared at his tablet again, gripping it as if it were his life-support system.

His marriage to Eleni could be nothing like his parents' one. For one thing, it wasn't about to last. It wasn't about his career and never would be. It was about protecting his child. It was about protecting Eleni.

'Are you sure it's me you're protecting?' she asked quietly.

He glanced across at her. 'Meaning?'

'Your father…and you.' She looked uncomfortable. 'You're not close…'

'No.' Damon couldn't help but smile faintly. Definitely not close. 'I haven't had contact with him in almost five years.'

'None at all?'

He shook his head.

'He cheated on your mother.' She still looked super awkward. 'Kassie at the hospital…'

'Is my unacknowledged half-sister. Yes.'

'But you're in touch with her.'

'Yes.' He sighed and put the tablet down on the low table. 'My father isn't. My mother pretends she doesn't exist. Kassie is too proud to push for what she's owed.' He leaned back on the edge of the sofa, folding his arms across his chest. He'd had to find out what had happened. 'I once saw him with her mother,' Damon said. 'Years ago when we lived here in Palisades.'

'That must have been hard to see.'

Damon frowned at the floor. 'I couldn't understand why he didn't leave us for them when it was so obvious…'

'Did you ever ask him?'

About five minutes ago and his father had confirmed

what Damon had learned in later years. 'His career was too important. It was always too important to both my parents. The only reason they had me was to tick that box on their CV—happily married with one son…'

'But they must be proud of you.'

He laughed bitterly. 'Proud of a teenager who wasted his time making lame computer games?' He shook his head.

'But now you have a hugely successful company. More than one. How can they not be—?' She broke off and her expression softened. 'You shouldn't have had to "achieve" to get the support any child deserves.'

'I got more than my half-sister did,' he muttered shortly. 'He wouldn't even support them financially. Her mother died a long, slow, painful death. Kassie has been struggling since.'

'Is that why you got in touch with her?'

He nodded. 'But she wouldn't let me help her.' He rolled his shoulders. It still knotted him that Kassie had refused almost everything he'd offered. 'I can understand it.'

Sadness lent a sheen to Eleni's eyes. 'And your parents are still together.'

'Still achieving. Still silently seething with bitterness and unhappiness. Still a successful marriage. Sure thing.'

'He cheated more than once?'

'I expect so,' he sighed.

'So.' Eleni brushed her hair back from her face. 'That's why you made it clear our marriage is only to provide legitimacy for our baby. Why you think no relationship lasts.'

'As I said, a child shouldn't be raised in the household with unhappily married parents.' Unloving parents. 'We married for the birth certificate, then we do what's right. I didn't want this baby to be a tool for some political purpose. Not paraded as the future Prince or Princess or whatever. And I won't abandon it either.'

'I understand,' she said softly. 'I don't want that either.'

She bit her lip and looked down at the table between them. 'I'm sorry your parents...'

He held up a hand. 'It's okay. We all have our burdens, right?' She'd lost both her parents. She had expectations on her that were far beyond the normal person's. He shouldn't have judged her as harshly as he had.

'Damon?'

He glanced up at that roughened note in her voice.

Storms had gathered in her sea-green eyes. 'This baby was unexpected, unplanned...' she pressed a hand to her flat belly as she gazed across at him '...but I promise you I'll love it. I already do. I'll do whatever it takes to protect and care for it.'

'I know.' He believed her because she already was. He'd seen her stand up to her brother—knew that had been a first for her. And she was trying here, now, with him.

But somehow it made that discomfort within him worse. He wasn't like her. He didn't understand how she could love the child already. The truth was he didn't know how to love. He had no idea how to be a husband. He sure as hell had no idea how to be a father. When he'd first suspected she might be pregnant his initial instinct had been not to abandon his child. He was not doing what his father had done to Kassie.

But he had no idea how even these next few months were going to work. The tightness in his chest didn't ease. Disappointment flowed and then ebbed. Leaving him with that *void*. He ached for a real escape.

'Is that the photo Giorgos approved for release?' Eleni's voice rose in surprise.

He glanced at the muted screen still showing the number one news item of the world.

'Yes.' He cleared his throat. 'There's another with him in it as well, but this is the one the media have run with.'

'I can't believe he chose that one. It's...'

'What?'

'Informal.'

Damon knew why the King had chosen that particular picture. Eleni looked stunning with her skin glowing, her hair and dress beautiful...but it was that luminosity in her expression that was striking. While Damon was looking at her with undeniable desire, she was laughing up at him—sparkling, warm, delighted. This image, snapped in that moment in the garden, would sell the 'truth' of this fairy tale.

This image stole his breath.

But now another picture of him flashed on the screen—him at an event with another woman. Then another. Inwardly he winced. It seemed anyone who'd dated him in the past wanted their five minutes of fame now and had opened their photo albums to show off their one or two snaps.

'Wow, lots of models, huh?' Eleni muttered, her rasp more apparent. 'That's very billionaire tech entrepreneur of you.'

'It wasn't a deliberate strategy.' He stepped nearer to her, needing to touch her skin. 'They just happened to be at the parties.'

She subjected him to a long, silent scrutiny. 'You know my history. I don't know yours at all.'

'You mean lovers?' He grinned in an effort to shake off the prickling sensation her piercing greenish gaze caused. 'I've had a few. No real girlfriends. There's nothing and no one to trouble you.'

She didn't look convinced.

He shrugged. 'I'm busy with my work and I like to be good at it.'

The ugly fact was he was a hollow man—as success obsessed as his shallow parents. Just less visible about it. He liked to think he had a smidge more integrity than they did—by refusing to use other people to get to where he wanted to be. Utter independence was what he craved.

'Do you know I've got at least twenty new work offers

today purely because of my involvement with you?' he said a little roughly.

She lifted her eyebrows. 'And that isn't good?'

'*I* haven't earned these opportunities, Eleni.'

'Perhaps you could take advantage of them to enable other people to progress as well. To create jobs and other contracts—'

Her naive positivity hit a raw nerve. '*I* built my company from scratch.'

'And you don't want your association with me compromising your success story?' Her cheeks pinked. 'At least you had the choice to forge your own path. I'm one of the most privileged people on the planet and, while I am grateful for that, I'm also bound by the rules that come with it. I couldn't do what I want.'

And it seemed she still couldn't. He grabbed his tablet again and showed her the endless list of invitations and formal appearances the palace official had sent him. 'Is this amount normal?' he asked. 'Which would you usually decline?'

Her eyebrows shot up. 'None.'

None? He paused. 'There are too many requests here.'

Were they were trying to schedule her every waking moment? Damon wasn't having it.

'You don't say no.' The shock on her face said it all.

She really was a total pawn in the palace machine. Well, he wasn't letting them take advantage of Eleni, or her child, or him. Not any more.

'I'm okay with saying no,' he said.

'Well, I don't like to be perceived as lazy.' Her lips tightened. 'Or spoilt.'

And that was why Princess Eleni had always done as she was told—wore what was expected, said what was polite, did what was her duty. She'd obediently played her princess role perfectly for years.

Except when it had come to him. That night with him

she'd done what she *wanted*. She'd taken. And since then? She'd argued. She'd stood up for herself. She'd been everything but obedient when it came to him…

He didn't want that changing because she felt some misguided sense of obligation now she was married to him. Hell, she was likely to want to play the part of the 'perfect wife' but he wasn't letting it happen. For the first time in her life, he wanted Eleni Nicolaides to experience some true freedom.

'Why did you want to stay in Palisades rather than go to Giorgos's safe house in France?' he asked roughly.

She looked down. 'This probably sounds crazy, but it's actually more private here.'

'You're *happy* to be trapped inside the palace walls?'

She shrugged her shoulders. 'It's what I'm used to. I can show you how it works.'

He didn't need to know how it worked. He had a headache from all the gilded decorations already. 'I know somewhere even more private.' He rubbed his shoulder. 'I think we should go there.'

'You don't understand—'

'Yeah, I do. I know about the paparazzi and the press and the cell phones in every member of the public's hands. But my island is safe. It's secure. It's private.'

She stilled. 'Your island?'

She really hadn't done any research on him, had she? That both tickled him, and put him out.

'You have your island, I have mine.' He sent her a sideways grin. 'I'll admit mine isn't as big, but good things come in small packages.'

The look in her eyes was decidedly not limpid now. 'Are you trying to convince me that size doesn't matter?' she teased in that gorgeously raspy voice. 'Of course, I have no basis for comparison, for all I know I might be missing out—'

'You're concerned you're missing out?' He rose to her

bait, happy to slip back into this tease and turn away from the too serious.

'You tell me.' She batted her eyelashes at him.

This was the woman from that night at the ball—that playful, slightly shy, deliciously fun woman.

'Hell, yeah, you're missing out.'

Her mouth fell open.

'Come with me and I'll show you.'

Her lips twisted as colour flowed into her cheeks.

'It's in the Caribbean,' he purred.

She closed her mouth. 'That is also very tech billionaire of you.'

'Yeah. It is. So let's go there. Today.' He stood, energy firing. For the first time since seeing that damn screen this morning he felt good.

'But Giorgos—'

'But Giorgos what? We can let him know where we've gone.' He paused, waiting to see if she'd defy her brother's orders.

A gleam lit in her eye. Damon suppressed his smug smirk—seemed his Princess had unleashed her latent rebellious streak. He liked it.

'How long does it take to get there?'

CHAPTER ELEVEN

ELENI SAT ACROSS from Damon in one of the large leather recliners in his private jet and tried not to stare at him. Her face heated as she recalled what he'd done to her, what he'd encouraged her to do to him. Last night had been the first time she'd ever shared a bed. The first time she'd slept in a man's arms. She couldn't even *remember* falling asleep, only a feeling of supreme relaxation as she'd lain entwined with him.

'It's a long flight. You should rest while you can.' That wicked glint ignited his smile as if he knew exactly what she was thinking about.

'I need rest?'

'For the days ahead, yes.'

'Empty promises...threats...' she muttered softly.

He leaned forward and placed his finger over her lips. 'Don't worry. I'll make good on every one. When we're alone.'

'I see no cabin crew.' She blinked at him.

'You want them to hear you?' His eyebrows arched. 'Because you're not going to be quiet.'

'I can be quiet.'

'Can you?' He studied her intently, not bothering to add anything more.

Heat deepened and spread, heating her from the inside out. Every, single cell. Realisation burned. She was never going to be quiet with him.

'You're...' She couldn't think of her own name, let alone a suitable adjective this second.

'Good.' Looking smug, he leaned back in his seat and pulled his tablet out. 'I'm very good.'

'Full of yourself,' she corrected.

She couldn't sit for hours with nothing to occupy her except sinful thoughts. She burrowed in her bag and fetched out the paper and small pencil tin that she always had stashed. Sketching soothed, like meditation. And she'd spent so many hours with a pencil in hand, it was calming.

He didn't seem to notice her occupation. She became so engrossed in her work she lost track of time. When she glanced up she discovered he'd closed his eyes. She wasn't surprised; he'd had as little sleep as she. And he'd been worryingly pale when he'd returned to her apartment this morning after that meeting with his father.

With that downwards tilt to his sensual lips now, she understood that he was vulnerable too and much more complex than she'd realised. He'd been hurt. His parents' infidelities, their lack of support and interest. Their falseness.

Yet he'd grown strong. Now she understood his fierce independence and the fury he'd felt when he'd thought she'd somehow betrayed him. He didn't trust and she didn't blame him. He only wanted his child to avoid the hurt he'd experienced.

She looked down at the sketch she'd done of him and cringed. She'd never want him to see this—too amateur. Too embarrassing. She folded the paper over and put it in the small bin just as the pilot announced they weren't far from landing. Damon opened his eyes and flashed her a smile.

'It's just a short hop by helicopter from here,' he said as the plane landed.

'That's what you say to everyone you bring here?'

He met her gaze. 'You already know I never brought any of my women here. This is my home.'

'Heaven forbid you'd let any of them get that close.'

'Wouldn't want them getting the wrong idea.'

'I'm glad I "trapped" you into marriage, then, now I get to kick about on your little island.'

Damon grinned at her. Yeah, he couldn't wait for her to kick about. But he held back as Eleni gathered her small bag and stepped ahead of him to exit the plane. He'd seen her discard the drawing she'd been working on and he was too curious to let it go. On his way out he swiftly scooped up the paper and pocketed it. Given she'd been secretive and clearly hadn't wanted him to see it, he was going to have to pick the moment to ask her about it.

The helicopter ride was smooth but wasn't quick enough. He ached to get there—to his home. His own private palace. His peace.

He breathed out as they finally landed and he strode to the open-topped Jeep that he'd ordered to be left waiting for their arrival.

'Let me take you on a tour.' He winked at her. 'You can see exactly what kind of prize husband you've claimed for yourself.'

'You're not the prize. I am,' Eleni answered sassily as she shook her hair loose in the warm sunshine. 'It really is your island?'

'It's the company compound,' he drawled. 'We futuristic tech companies must have amazing work places for our staff. It's part of the image.'

'I didn't think you were a slave to any society's required "image". You're the man who doesn't care what anyone thinks of him, right?'

Right. *Almost.*

Reluctant amusement rippled through him. He liked it when she sparked up.

She stared as the pristine coastline came into clear view. He heard her sharp intake of breath. Now as he drove they could see a few roofs of other dwellings amongst the verdant foliage. He knew it was beautiful, but he was glad she could see it too.

'They live here all year round?'

'No.' He laughed that she'd taken him so seriously. 'It really is just my island. It was a resort, now it's not. My people stay for stints if they need to complete a big project, or to recharge their batteries. Every employee has at least six weeks a year here. Families can come too, of course.' He parked up by the main beach. 'Energy-wise it's self-sufficient, thanks to all the solar-power generation, and we grow as many supplies as we can.'

'So it's paradise.'

'Yeah.' Pure, simple luxury. 'There's no paparazzi. No media. No nosey parkers watching your every move. It is completely private.'

She glanced up into the blindingly blue—clear—sky. 'No drones? No spy cams everywhere?'

'No helicopters. No long-range lenses. No nothing. Just peace and security,' he confirmed, but grimaced wryly. 'And half my staff…but they'll be busy and you can do whatever you want, whenever you want.'

'With whomever I want?' she asked. There was an extra huskiness to her tone that made him so hard.

'No.' He reached across and turned her chin so she faced him. 'Only with me.'

She mock-pouted, teasing in that playful way he adored—demanding retribution of the most erotic kind. But after only a kiss he reluctantly pulled away. He couldn't bring her here and hurry her into bed. He could be more civilised than that.

'Come on,' he said briskly, getting out of the Jeep and pointing to the meandering path through the lush trees. 'I'll show you around the complex.'

Then he'd take her to his house and have her all to himself at last.

Eleni didn't want to blink and miss a moment. His island was like a warm jewel, gleaming with the promise of heat and holiday and indefinable riches. And with that total privacy, it was the ultimate treasure. A feeling of relaxation slowly unfurled through her body, spreading warmth and joy and such anticipation she could hardly contain it.

'This is the "den"—our main office here.'

She followed him into the large building. It was a large open space filled with desks, computers and space for tinkering and was currently occupied by five guys all standing round a giant screen.

'Going from left to right, we have Olly, Harry, Blair, Jerome and Faisal,' Damon said to her in a low voice. 'You have that memorised already, right?'

She smiled because, yes, she had.

'Guys,' Damon called to them. 'I'd like you to meet Eleni.'

Not *Princess*. Not *my wife*. Just Eleni. That different kind of warmth flowed through her veins again.

The men turned and shouts erupted. But not for her. It was pleasure that their boss had returned. One of the guys stepped to the side of the swarm around Damon to greet her.

'Nice to meet you, Eleni.' Olly's accent placed him as Australian.

The other men nodded, smiled and positively pounced on Damon again.

'Look, D—I know you're not here for work, but can I just run a couple things past you?' Faisal asked.

Damon was already halfway across the room, his gaze narrowing at the gobbledegook on the screen. 'Of course.'

All the men perked up but Eleni saw Olly and Jerome exchange a look and a jerk of the head towards her. The next second Jerome walked over.

'Eleni…' Jerome cleared his throat. 'Welcome. You must…ah…'

'I'm really happy to be here.' She smiled to put him at

ease. Eleni could make conversation with anyone. 'What is it you guys are working on?'

He led her to the nearest table that was covered in an assortment of electronics components and plastic figurines. 'We're designing a new visuals prototype and we need his thoughts on the latest version.'

'Visuals prototype?'

To his credit, Jerome spent a good five minutes explaining the tech to her and answering her questions. But it was obvious he was eager to talk to Damon too and in the end she put him out of his misery. 'Go ask him whatever it is you need to. I'm fine,' she laughed.

'Are you sure?' Jerome looked anxiously between her and Damon.

'Of course.'

He hurried away to join the conference around the screen. Damon stood in the centre, listening intently then quietly offering his opinion. The Australian was making notes on a piece of paper while Harry asked another question prompting another concise answer. It was evident they valued his every word and had missed his input. Everyone in the vicinity was paying total attention—to him. Eleni gradually became aware she was staring at him too. And for once no one was staring at *her*.

Blushing, she turned away and stepped outside to take in some fresh air. Her muscles ached slightly and a gentle feeling of fatigue made her sleepy. She leaned against the tall tree just outside the building and looked across at the beautifully clear water.

Ten minutes later Damon walked back to where she waited in the shade.

'Sorry,' he muttered as he reached to take her hand. 'That took longer than I realised.'

'It's fine. I enjoyed looking around.'

Damon sent her a speculative look that turned increasingly wicked the longer he studied her. 'What have you been thinking about?' he asked. 'You've gone very pink.'

The heat in her cheeks burned. 'Don't tease.'

'Oh, I'll tease.' He tugged on her hand and pulled her closer to him. 'But first let me show you the rest.'

'I think rest is a good idea.' She wanted to be alone with his undivided attention on *her* again. And right now she didn't care if that made her spoiled.

'There's a restaurant room,' he said.

Of course there was. Right on the beach, with a bar and a woman who waved and smiled at Damon the second she saw him. Eleni's spine prickled.

'Rosa will cook anything you want, as long as you want fresh and delicious.' Damon waved at the relaxed, gorgeously tanned woman and kept walking past.

'This place is just beautiful.' Eleni glanced back at the restaurant.

'Rosa is married to Olly, the guy with—'

'The beard.' Eleni sighed, stupidly relieved. 'The Australian.'

Damon grinned as if he'd sensed her irrational jealous flare. 'They live here most of the year round.'

'Lucky them.' She walked across the sand with him. 'Do you live here most of the year too?'

'Meetings take me away, but I'm here when I can be.'

Eleni could understand why; if it were her choice she'd never leave. But his marriage to her was going to make that problematic for a while. She had duties in Palisades that she had to perform.

'Where next?' she asked. 'Your house?'

'Not yet. You haven't seen the playroom.'

'Playroom?' she asked, startled.

He laughed and gave her a playful swipe. 'Not *that* kind of playroom.' He cocked his head. 'But now I know you're curious…'

'Shut it and show me the room.' She marched across the sand, cheeks burning.

It was a boat shed and it was filled with every water-sport toy imaginable—from surfboards, to kayaks to in-flatables and jet skis. 'Okay, this is seriously cool.' She stepped forward to get a closer look.

'I knew you liked the water,' Damon said smugly. 'You swim, right?'

'Indoors at the palace,' she answered, checking out the kayaks stacked in racks up the wall. 'Giorgos had a resis-tance current feature installed so I can train each morn-ing in privacy.'

'You don't swim in the sea?'

'With everyone watching?' She stared at him as if he were crazy. 'Rating my swimsuits every morning?' She shook her head. 'And he'd never let me on a jet ski.'

'No?' Damon's eyes widened.

'Safety issues.' She shrugged and straightened. 'And again, too many photographers.'

'You like to avoid those.'

'Do you blame me?'

'No.' He leaned against the door frame and sent her a smouldering look. 'I'm really good on a jet ski,' he said ar-rogantly. 'You can come with me.'

She crossed her arms and sent what she hoped was a smouldering look right back at him. 'Can I drive?'

'Sure. I have no problem with that.'

'But what if I want to go fast?' She blinked at him in-nocently.

'I think I can keep up.' He lifted away from the door frame and strolled towards her.

'You think?' Her voice rose as he stepped close enough to pull her against him.

'I think it's time you saw my house,' he growled.

'It's beyond time,' she whispered.

He guided her across the sand and up a beautifully maintained path through the well-established trees to the gorgeous building at the end.

An infinity pool—the perfect length for laps—was the feature at the front. Comfortable, beautiful furniture was strategically placed to create space for relaxation, conversation and privacy. The house itself was wooden, with two storeys, and not monstrously huge but nor was it small. Damon didn't speak as he led her inside—he simply let her look around. It was luxurious, yes, but also cosy with a sense of true intimacy. She didn't know why that surprised her, but it did.

He still said nothing, but smiled as if he sensed her appreciation. She took his outstretched hand and he led her up the curling wooden staircase. She assumed it led to his bedroom. Her heart hammered. A delicious languorous anticipation seeped into her bones.

But while there were doors to other rooms on one side, the room he drew her to wasn't for sleeping. It stretched the length of the building. Unsurprisingly it was dominated by symmetrical windows overlooking the sand, sea and sky. A long table took up half the space. It was clearly his desk, given the neatly stacked piles of papers and the writing utensils gathered in a chipped mug. A long seat took up much of the remaining window space. A single armchair stood in front of the large fireplace that broke up the floor-to-ceiling bookshelves that covered the wall opposite the windows. Books were stacked on every shelf. Books that had clearly been read and weren't just there for the look of it. This was more than his workspace. It was his think space—his escape.

'I can see why you love it.' She stood in the middle of the room and gazed from the intriguing space inside to the natural beauty outside.

'Best view on the island.'

'The beauty is more than the view.' She noted the shades for the windows, the pale warmth of the walls, the art that he'd chosen to complement the space. 'The light is lovely,' she said softly. 'The colour. It must help you focus.'

'It's not a palace,' he said with a keen look.

'It's better than any palace.'

A small smile flitted about his mouth. 'So you like it?'

Intrigued that her opinion genuinely seemed to matter, she turned her back on the view to face him directly. 'Did you honestly think I wouldn't?' She wasn't that spoilt, was she?

'There's not a lot of gold leaf and crystal chandeliers.'

'Did you think I wasn't going to like it because there's no ballroom?' She felt slightly hurt. 'You don't need a ballroom—you have a beach.' She looked out across the water again. 'You're lucky to have a home, not a museum in which you live.'

She and Giorgos didn't own the palace, they were the guardians for the future of it, and for the people of Palisades. This small island was utterly Damon's and she had to admit she was a little jealous.

'You can stay here any time,' he said.

She sent him a crooked smile, rueful that he'd so clearly read her mind. She didn't want to think about the future yet. She just wanted to enjoy this freedom, in this moment. Enjoy him, while she had him.

'Thank you.' She faced him, determined to take the initiative, despite the mounting burn in her cheeks. 'So may I sit in the driver's seat?'

His focus on her sharpened. 'Meaning?'

Silently she just looked at him. He knew exactly what she meant already.

'Tell me,' he said softly—a combination of demand and dare. 'You can tell me anything.'

His easy invitation summoned that streak of boldness within her, just as it had that very first night. Something in him gave her the courage to claim what she wanted. The courage she got only with him. Only for him.

'I want to kiss you,' she muttered huskily and swallowed before continuing. 'The way you've kissed me.'

He stared at her so intently she wondered if he'd turned to stone.

'I dare you to let me,' she whispered.

'Is this what you've been thinking about?'

'All day,' she admitted with a slow nod.

His smile was as rueful—and as honest—as hers had been only moments earlier. He lifted his hands in a small gesture of surrender. 'That's why you drew this?' He held up a piece of paper.

She winced as she saw what he was holding. 'I put that in the rubbish.'

'Which was a shame.'

That he'd seen that drawing was the most embarrassing thing. Because it was him. Half nude. Heat flooded her. Mortifying, blistering heat.

'Why didn't you study Fine Arts?' he asked.

'It would have been arrogant to assume I had talent.' She hadn't been allowed.

'You do have talent.'

His words lit a different glow in her chest but she laughed it off. 'You're just flattered because I gave you abs.'

'I do have abs.'

'I don't usually draw…' She couldn't even admit it.

'Erotic pictures?' He laughed. 'What do you usually draw?'

'Dogs,' she said tartly.

'The pictures in Kassie's ward at the hospital are yours, right? You draw them for the children.'

He'd seen those? 'They're just doodles.' She shrugged it off.

'You're talented, Eleni.'

'You're very kind.' She bent her head.

He gripped her arms and made her look at him again.

'Don't go "polite princess" on me. Accept the compliment for what it is—honest.'

That fiery heat bloomed in her face again.

'Do you paint as well?'

'Sometimes, but mostly pen and ink drawings.'

'You're good, Eleni.'

'You promised me you were good,' she whispered.

A smile sparked in his eyes but he shook his head. 'You're trying to distract me.'

'Is it working?'

'You know it is. But why can't you take the compliment?'

Because it was too intimate. Too real. It meant too much. His opinion of her shouldn't matter as much as it did. But she didn't say any of that. She just shrugged.

'You have a lot to offer the world,' he said softly.

For a moment it was there again—that flicker of intensity that was different from the pure desire that pulled them together in the first place. This was something deeper. Something impossibly stronger. And she backed away from it.

'Stop with the flattery or I'll never leave,' she joked.

There was a moment of silence and she couldn't look at him.

'Where will you have me?' With those husky words he let her lead them back into that purely sensual tease. The easier, safer option.

'Here. Now.'

She walked, nudging him backwards. All the way to that comfortable armchair. She pushed his chest and he sat. She remained standing, looking down at him. He'd not had the chance to shave since their flight and the light stubble on his jaw lent him a roguish look. That curl to his lips was both arrogant and charming.

She leaned forward. 'Damon,' she breathed as she kissed him.

'Yes.' He held very still beneath her ministrations.

'You're irresistible.' She sent him a laughing look.

He chuckled. 'I'm glad you think so.' He tensed as she slowly undid his buttons. 'What a relief.'

'You don't seem very relieved.'

'I'm trying to stay in control.'

'Why would you want to do that?'

'I don't want to scare you.'

She laughed. 'You're no ogre.'

'I don't want you to stop,' he whispered.

'Why would I? I want you to lose control. You make me lose control all the time.'

'Eleni...'

'It's only fair,' she muttered. Not teasing.

'Fair? You know that's not how it works.'

A frisson of awareness reverberated through her body. Delight. Desire. Danger. That intensity flickered again. But she moved closer. Took him deeper. Stroked him harder. Doing everything she'd secretly dreamed of doing. She'd show him *not fair*.

He groaned. 'Don't stop.'

Pleased, she kissed him again and then again. His hands swept down her sides, stirring her to the point where she couldn't concentrate any more. She drew back.

'Stop touching,' she growled at him. 'It's my turn.'

He half laughed. She squeezed. Hard.

'Mine,' she said seriously—and for more than just this 'turn'.

He met her gaze. The blue of his eyes deepened as that something passed between them. No matter that she tried to dance past it, it kept curling back—entwining around them.

He lifted a hand, threading his fingers through her hair to cup the nape of her neck. 'Mine.'

His echo was an affirmation, not an argument. He was hers to hold. Hers to have. And yes, she was his too.

For now. Only for now.

She closed her eyes and let herself go—taking exactly what she wanted, touching in the way she'd only dreamed and never before dared. She liked feeling his power beneath her. Liked his vulnerability like this—letting her pleasure him.

'Eleni.'

She felt his power and restraint and fought to topple it. He curled his hands around the armrests and she heard his breathing roughen. His muscles flexed and she tasted salt as sweat slicked his skin.

'Eleni.'

She tightened her grip, swirling her tongue, and simply willed for him to feel it the same way she did—that unspeakable bliss. 'Let me make you feel good.'

That was what he did for her.

Spent and satisfied physically, a different need surged fiercely through Damon. He didn't want her doing this out of gratitude or pity. He lifted her onto his lap and cupping her chin, stared hard into her eyes—heavy-lidded, sea-green storms of desire gazed back at him. Dazed, yet seemingly seeing right into his soul.

Pure instinct drove him. He kissed her, slipping his hand under her skirt, skating his fingers all the way to her secret treasure. His heart seized as he discovered how hot and wet she was and satisfaction drummed in his heart. She'd not gone down on him from a sense of obligation; she'd almost got off on it. The least he could do was help her get the rest of the way. This thing between them had them equally caught. Her need—her ache—was his. Just as his was hers. She moaned as he flicked his fingers and pushed her harder, faster. He kissed her again and again, almost angry in the pleasure and relief of discovering her extreme arousal. It took only a moment and then she was there, pleasure shuddering through her body.

She was inexperienced, yet lustful. Her shy but unashamed sensuality felled him—he wanted to make it better and better for her. But there was no bettering what was already sublime. No beating the chemistry that flared so brightly whenever they came into contact.

He held her in his arms and stood, carrying her down the stairs to the comfort of his bed. In this one thing, at least, he could meet every one of her needs.

Again, again, and again.

CHAPTER TWELVE

'I THINK YOU can go a little faster than that.' Damon double-checked her life vest and then dared her.

'It's even more fun than I imagined.' Eleni smiled at him from astride the jet ski.

He grinned at the double-meaning glint in her eye. With wild hair and without a speck of make-up his Princess was more luminous than ever. With each moment he spent with her, he grew more intrigued. But he forced a laugh past the lump in his throat. 'Because you like fast.'

'I must admit I do.'

'Then why not see if you can beat me.'

Her eyes flashed again and he relished the way she rose to his challenge. He liked seeing her this happy. The one thing he could do was give her more moments of freedom before she returned to full-time royal life and that damn goldfish bowl she lived in.

He got on the other jet ski. 'Come on, we'll go to the cove.'

Her laughter rang out as she took off before he was ready. Grinning, he revved his engine and set out to hunt her down.

Two hours later Eleni sat on the beach suffused with a deep sense of contentment. The place was paradise—and Damon in paradise? Heartbreaking. He talked, teased, laughed. But she liked him like this too—just sitting quietly alongside her, relaxed and simply enjoying the feel of the sun.

Now she understood why he'd been unable to trust her initially. Why he didn't want his child caught between parents knotted together unhappily. But now that she knew, things had changed. Her feelings for him were deepening, growing, causing confusion.

She sat forward as a shiver ran down her spine. She didn't like the cold streak of uncertainty; she'd bring forward warmth instead. She sent him a coy look. 'I think I should go back to the house and have an afternoon nap.'

'Ride with me this time. One of the guys will come get the other jet ski later.'

He sped back to the main beach while she unashamedly clung, loving the feel of the wind on her face and the spray of the sea, taking the chance to rest before what was to come. But when they walked up to the house, he diverted to the staircase, turning to her with a smile on his face.

Eleni stood on the threshold and stared at the new desk that had replaced the window seat in Damon's office. It was angled, an artist's desk. A cabinet stood beside it, together with a folded easel. Boxes of art supplies were neatly stacked on the top of the cabinet and instinctively she knew that were she to open the drawers, she would most likely find more. Paper, paint, pens, pencils, pastels, ink, brushes, canvas—so many art supplies and a desk and chair that were not for Damon to use. But for her.

Her heart raced. 'When did you arrange this?'

Why had he arranged this? She stared at the beautifully set out equipment and then looked at him.

That gorgeous smile curved his mouth but he just shrugged. 'I unleashed one of the graphic designers in an art store in the States. He got in last night and set it up while we were out just now.' His gaze narrowed on her. 'Would it have been better for you to choose the supplies yourself?'

'No. No, this is…amazing. It's so much better than what I use at home.'

He nodded slowly. 'You don't spend money on it because—'

'It's just a hobby,' she answered quickly.

'But it's more than a hobby to you.'

She was unbearably touched that he understood how much she loved it. 'It's not going to bother you that I'm working here?'

Damon's smile faded, leaving him looking sombre, and suddenly that intensity flared between them. That silent pull of something that tried to bind them closer. 'I'm not going to tease you with the obvious answer because this is actually too important.' He reached out and cupped her face. 'I don't want you to sit in the corner and be decorative and silent. I like your company. And not just...'

He let the sentence hang and his smile said it all.

Eleni stared up at him, her own smile tremulous. He'd put her in his space—placed her desk next to his and drawn her close to his side. He wanted her near him. Eleni had never had such a gift.

'Thank you,' she said softly. 'I like your company too.'

When she woke the next morning Damon had already risen. She showered and put on a loose summer dress. She took some toast and fruit from the breakfast tray and climbed the stairs to see him. He glanced up from the book he was reading. In his white tee, beige trousers and bare feet, he was too gorgeous.

Even more so when that roguish smile lit up his eyes. 'I thought you might sleep in.'

Heat burned in her cheeks as she remembered the little sleep they'd stolen through the night. But she was determined to tease him every bit as much as he teased her, so she adopted her most princessy tone.

'I might take a nap later. You may care to join me then.' She gestured at her desk. 'I thought I'd take a look at my new toys, if that's okay.'

He shut his book with a snap and sent her a stern look. 'You ruined it with that last bit. You don't need my permission. You're free to do whatever you want.' He reached for another book on his desk. 'I'm not your King, Eleni. Not your master.'

She knew that. 'I was just trying to be polite.'

'You don't need to try to be anything with me, Eleni. You can just be yourself.'

She was self-conscious to start with, too aware of how near he was and nervous of making too much noise as she removed plastic wrap and opened packets. She'd never really shared space like this with anyone.

'I'm messy,' she said, glancing at the bottles of ink she'd opened to test out. 'Sorry.'

'That's okay. I'm messy too.'

That was a lie; his desk was immaculate. But as the morning progressed, the piles beside him began to grow. He read more than she'd have thought possible. He sent emails in batches, took video calls over the Internet. His focus didn't surprise her, nor his ability to recall facts or tiny facets of design and interface.

Rosa appeared with another tray of food—fresh, beautifully prepared and presented. Eleni was used to immaculate service but this was different. This was more intimate, more relaxed, more friendly. Just like the island itself. He had such privacy and freedom here. It was the perfect holiday escape for her.

But it was his reality. His life. The space he'd secured for himself to think and create and build.

He connected or disconnected from the rest of the world as he pleased. No wonder he'd looked so uncomfortable at the thought of spending serious time in the palace. It wasn't that he couldn't handle it, it was just that he didn't want to. He had other things to think about—fascinating things, much more meaningful to him than gallery openings and charity visits.

And he had history back in Palisades—bitter family history that hurt. She understood that, for him, attendance at glittering events was only to promote the fallacy of his parents' marriage. He thought everything about those evenings was false. But he was wrong.

They did important work. They had value too. She just had to help him understand it.

Lost in thought, she opened the drawers of the cabinet and selected a sheet of paper. She needed this time out to figure out their future. To accept it.

As she settled into her exploration of pen nibs and ink and the tin of beautiful pencils, time snuck away. When light glinted on the glass of water beside her desk, she looked up from the picture she'd fallen into drawing. To her surprise, the sun was almost at its zenith and she knew both the sand and the water would be warm. Her whole body melted at the thought.

'I just need to get this message sent and I'll go with you.'

Startled, she glanced over and met Damon's knowing gaze. He smiled at her and then looked down to his tablet, his fingers skipping over the keyboard.

She sat back, relaxing as she appreciated how hard he worked. People counted on him and he delivered. No wonder he'd become as successful as he had. An outlier—fiercely intelligent, gifted, and hard-working. But he liked to do things his way—in his place, in his time.

'It's looking good.' Damon rose and studied her page.

She chuckled and shook her head.

He pointed at the faint lines she'd drawn in. 'You've had training.'

'Well, drawing classes were quite an acceptable occupation for a young princess.'

'Until you wanted to get serious about it?' Damon was too astute.

Even she'd understood that it was impossible—as had her art professor. She still saw him sometimes. 'I used my interest to become knowledgeable about the art and antique treasures in the palace.' She stood and stretched, keen to get out to the warm sunshine. 'I like to take the tours sometimes.'

'As the guide?' Damon's eyes widened.

She nodded, laughing at his expression.

'No wonder they're always booked out so far in advance—they're all hoping to get on one of your days.'

'I don't commit to an exact timetable,' she admitted.

'Because you don't want to become an exhibit yourself.'

No. Trust him to understand that. And she hadn't wanted to disappoint people. She turned to get past him and head out to the beach.

'I don't see why it has to be only a hobby,' he said, still studying the incomplete drawing. 'You could sell them. People would buy them.'

Eleni laughed again. 'They'd sell only for the signature. There'd be no honest appraisal from anyone. Some fawning critics couldn't be objective for fear of offending the royal family while others would damn me to mediocrity for daring to think I could do something with skill.'

'You're afraid of what they think.' He sent her that stern look again. 'You don't need to give a damn, Eleni. You could sell them for charity. Imagine what you could raise.'

'But I do give a damn and so I raise money anyway. But I don't want this tied to that. This is my escape.' Just as this island was his.

'Then do it anonymously. We could find a dealer.'

'Or I could just do them for myself.' She sent him the stern look back. 'For my own enjoyment.'

'They'd bring joy to other people too,' he said charmingly.

'Flatterer.' She mock slapped him as she walked away.

'I have no need to flatter you when I already own your panties,' he called after her.

She stopped and swivelled to send him a *death* stare that time. 'Oh, that is—'

He threw back his head and laughed. 'True. It's true.'

* * *

Playing in the sea with Eleni was too much fun. She was so beautiful, lithe and, as he'd suspected that very first moment he'd seen her, strong. Now, as he sat on the sand beside her and let the sun dry his skin, satisfaction pooled within him. The same feeling that had crept up on him while she'd been seated beside him upstairs all morning.

But it was the quiet moments like these that unsettled him the most—when he felt too content.

Moments like these became too precious. And moments didn't last. Nor did marriages.

He stood, needing some space for a second to get them back to that light teasing. He turned and tugged her to her feet. He only had to whisper a dare and they raced back to the house. Play came so easy with her now she was free.

'How do you ever force yourself off this island?' she asked, breathless as he caught her.

'Actually we're leaving in the morning,' Damon muttered.

'What?' Her shocked query made him turn her in his arms so he could see her eyes.

'It's only twenty minutes by helicopter to the next island,' Damon quickly explained. 'There aren't many shops but...' He strode to a small cabinet in the lounge and retrieved a small purse that he tossed to her. 'Here. You can go wild, practise counting out the right currency before you hit the big cities.'

She caught the bag neatly with one hand but wrinkled her pretty nose. 'I don't want your money.'

'Well, until you earn your own I think you're stuck with mine, because I'm your husband and apparently that makes me responsible.' He sent her a deliberately patronising smile. 'I can give you an allowance if you'd like.'

The nose-wrinkle morphed into a full-face frown.

Chuckling, he backed her up against the wall. 'If our

positions were reversed, you'd do the same for me,' he whispered.

'Don't be so sure.'

'Oh, I'm sure.' Laughing, he kissed her.

But her lips parted and she didn't just let him in, she pulled him closer, hooking her leg around his waist, her towel dropping in the process.

'If you keep this up I'll get you a credit card, so you don't even have to count.' He rolled his hips against her heat, giving into the irresistible desire she roused in him.

'Payment for services rendered?' she asked tartly. 'Finally you've figured out I married you for your money.'

'I knew it.' He failed to claw back some semblance of sanity from the ultimate temptation she personified.

'It certainly wasn't for your charm.' She glared at him.

'Then spend every cent.' He smiled, loving the sparks in her eyes. Those few shops mainly stocked bikinis. The thought made his mouth dry. 'Meanwhile...' he stepped back and unfastened his shorts '... I was thinking you might want me to model for you.'

'You're...' Her gaze dropped and her words faded.

'You're not concerned about people taking photos?'

He shook his head as their helicopter descended. 'The people here appreciate the privacy of their visitors.'

To be frank, the island was barely larger than Damon's. There were only a few shops along the waterfront and, when Eleni saw this, her expressive features were a picture of mock outrage. He laughed, enjoying his little joke.

'They sell bikinis.' He held up his hands in surrender. 'I thought you'd love it.'

'You're the biggest tease ever.' She growled at him with a glint in her eye. 'You're the one who wants me to get the bikinis.'

'Have you ever bought a bikini before? All by yourself?'

'Actually I have. Online.'

'In the privacy of the palace.'

'Of course.'

'Well, you can cruise the whole mall here.'

She rolled her eyes.

'If you don't want to shop for skimpy little swimsuits, why don't you spend some coin and buy me an ice cream?' He dared her.

'Because you don't deserve it.'

She flounced off to the bikini store and he lazily loitered outside, watching her through the wide open doors as she browsed the racks. In less than five seconds she lost that faux indignance and relaxed. As she chatted to the woman serving behind the counter she relaxed even more and that gorgeous vitality oozed from her skin. His gaze narrowed as it finally clicked—*interaction* with others was what gave her that luminescence. The ability she had to be able to talk to anyone, and to put them at ease, wasn't just learned skill from being 'the Princess', it was a core part of *who* she was. Warm, compassionate. Interested. Caring.

So much more than him.

Now she'd stopped to talk to another couple of customers and she was positively glowing. One of the women was balancing a wriggling toddler in her arms. Damon watched as Eleni turned to talk to the child, who immediately stopped wriggling and smiled, entranced—as if Eleni was some damn baby whisperer. Of course she was—she had that effect on everyone, big and small. They stopped what they were doing and smiled when she came near. Because she was like a beautiful, sparkling light.

She was going to be such a great mother, given her truly genuine, generous nature. He narrowed his gaze as his imagination caught him unawares—slipping him a vision of how she was going to look when cradling their child in her arms. Primitive possessiveness clenched in his gut, sending a totally foreign kind of heat throughout his veins.

His woman. His baby. His world.

He blinked, breathing hard, bringing himself back to here, now, on the beach. Her body had yet to reveal its fertile secret—while her breasts were slightly fuller, her belly had barely a curve. But their baby was safe within her womb.

Despite the summer sun, a chill swept across his skin and he cocked his head to study her closer. The baby was safe, wasn't it? And Eleni. She was slim but strong, right? But icy uncertainty dripped down his spine—slow at first, then in a rush as he suddenly realised what he'd been too full of lust and selfish haste to remember.

Eleni's mother had lost her life in childbirth.

Damon felt as if some invisible giant had wrapped a fist around his chest and was squeezing it, making his blood pound and his lungs too tight to draw breath.

How could he have forgotten that? How could he have dragged her here to this remote island without seeing that damn doctor back in Palisades? He'd promised her brother that she'd get the best care, yet he'd been in too much of a hurry to escape his own demons to put her first. To put his child first.

He'd been thinking only of himself. His wants. His needs. His father had done that to Kassie and her mother. Now Damon was as guilty regarding Eleni and their unborn child.

How could he have neglected to tend to something so fundamental? He'd been so smug when he'd texted his assistant to find an obstetrician that day on the boat. As if he'd thought of everything—all in control and capable.

But he wasn't either of those things. Turned out he was less than useless—to not even have a routine check done before flying for hours out to somewhere this isolated? What the hell kind of father did he think he was going to make anyway?

He'd failed before he'd even begun. Both his wife and child deserved better. He huffed out a strained breath. At least seeing the truth now cemented the perfection of his plan. They'd be better off apart from him. He'd always known that, hadn't he? Wasn't that why he'd insisted on his and Eleni's separation in the first place?

This whole marriage and kids and happy-ever-after was never going to be for him.

Except, just for this little while on his island, he'd let himself pretend.

That he could have it all with her. Be it all for her.

But he couldn't.

Bitterness welled, a surging ball of disappointment within himself. For himself.

'Are you okay?' Eleni gave him a searching look as she joined him to stroll along the beach.

'Fine.' He flashed a smile through a gritted jaw and kept strolling along the beach, staring down at the sand.

But he wasn't and wasn't it typical that she'd already sensed that? She was too compassionate. Too empathetic.

'Did you spend up large?' He made himself make that small talk.

'Every cent.' She held up a carrier bag and shook it, a twinkle in her eye that he couldn't bear to see right now.

'Then let's go back,' he said briskly.

He sensed her quick frown but she simply turned and quietly walked alongside him.

Of course she did; that was Eleni all over—doing what was asked of her, knowing her place, unquestioning when she sensed tension.

It was how she handled Giorgos, how she handled the public and palace demands on her. And, apparently, it was now how she handled him.

It was the last damn thing that he wanted. He wanted impetuous, spontaneous, emotional Eleni who liked nothing more than to challenge him. But what he wanted no longer mattered. Because she was vulnerable and he didn't have the skills that she was going to need long term. He'd just proven that to himself. The lust they shared wasn't ever going to be enough and the sooner they separated, the better.

He was such a damn disappointment to himself—let alone to anyone else.

'I'm going to the workshop for a while,' he said the second their helicopter landed.

'Sure.'

He turned his back on that hint of coolness in her voice. The tiniest thread of uncertainty. Of hurt. He had to walk away to stop hurting her more. That was the point.

The guys were heads down, but he waved them away when he walked into the room. He'd rebalance in here. Get stuck in another of the projects. But while he could take in the info his team had sent him, he couldn't make it stick. The future kept calling—her pregnancy, the baby. What he was never going to be able to do for them both.

'Which do you want to go with?' Olly ventured over to Damon, showing him three designs for a new logo.

'I need to think about it.' Damon lifted the sheet displaying the three options, his gaze narrowing as he registered the colours. He wanted to do more than think about it. He wanted to ask Eleni. She had a better eye than any of them.

'I had a call from one of those futurist foundations,' Olly said as Damon headed to the door. 'They'd like you to speak at next year's gala.'

More like they wanted him to bring his beautiful Princess wife. He did *not* want her used that way.

'Next year?' Damon asked idly, still staring down at the sheet.

'They're planning well ahead of time. Futurists,' Olly joked.

Time. Damon walked out of the den. In time, according to Damon's plan, he and Eleni would be sharing custody but living separately. They'd be on their way to divorce already. She wouldn't be curled next to him in bed, or sitting at a desk at his side any more. And their child would be a few months old. Their tiny baby with its tiny heart would still be so vulnerable. His chest tightened. He had no idea how to provide the required protection. How did he protect Eleni? How did he give either of them what they needed when he hardly knew what that was? When he'd never had it himself?

Eleni had changed so much in the few days she'd had of freedom. He realised now how much more she needed. How much more she deserved. She was loving and generous and kind. She deserved someone who could give all that back to her tenfold.

She was going to be a far better mother to their child than his mother had been to him. She was open; she was generous. She was loving.

What did *he* have to offer her? She had a workaholic brother and no one else close in her life. She needed a husband who could offer her a warm, loving family. All he could offer were sycophantic grandparents who'd leech everything they could from the connection—and offer nothing. No warmth. No love.

Damon had money, sure. But King Giorgos would never let his little sister suffer financial hardship. There was nothing else he really had to offer her—other than orgasms and the occasional cheesy line that made her laugh. He didn't know how to be a good father, or a good husband. She deserved more than that. She deserved the best.

And he had to help her find that somehow. He owed her that much at least, didn't he?

He walked to the house, missing her already, wanting her advice on the decision he couldn't quite make, just wanting to be near her again. He found her at her desk—her new favourite place—clad in a vibrant orange bikini that was bold and cheerful and sexy as hell. She wore a sheer white shirt over it that hung loose and revealed a gently tanned shoulder. Her hair wasn't brushed into smooth perfection but looked tousled and soft and there wasn't a scrap of make-up on her glowing skin.

She looked beautiful and relaxed; he'd never seen her look happier. She was thriving, from so little. She should have so much more. More than he could ever give her.

Her welcoming smile pained him in a way he'd never been pained before.

'You're busy.' He hesitated, staying at a distance, trying to resist that fierce, fierce pull.

She deserves better.

'It's okay.' She put down her pen and turned her full focus on him. 'What did you want?'

He'd forgotten already. But her gaze grazed the paper he was holding.

'I just...' he glanced down at the images he held '... wanted your opinion on this.'

'My opinion?' she echoed softly.

'You have an artist's eye.' He gruffly pushed the words past the block in his throat. 'I wanted to know which you think is better.'

Eleni blinked, pulling her scattered wits together. He walked in here looking all stormy and broody and sexy as hell and then wanted her opinion on something he was clinging to as if it were worth his very soul?

'Are you going to let me see it?' She smiled but he didn't smile back.

He put the page on her desk. She studied the three designs that had been printed on it. That he valued her input touched her and it took her a moment to focus on what he'd asked her to do. 'I think this one is cleaner. It stays in the mind more.' She pointed to the one on the left. 'Don't you think?'

'Yes,' he said, nodding brusquely. 'Thank you.'

A defiant, determined look crossed his face as he stepped back from her. She stilled, trying to read all the contrary emotions flickering in his expression. He always tried to contain such depth of feeling, but right now it was pouring from him and she could only stare, aching to understand what on earth was churning in his head.

'What?' His lips twisted in a wry, self-mocking smile. 'I don't know why you're staring at me when you're the one with ink on her nose.'

'Oh.' Embarrassed, she rubbed the side of her nose with her finger.

He half snorted, half groaned. 'Come here,' he ordered gruffly, tugging a clean tissue from the box on his desk.

She loved being this close to him. Loved the way he teased her as he cared for her. She held ultra-still so he could wipe the smear from her face. He was so close, so tender and she ached for that usual teasing. But his eyes were even more intensely blue and his expression grave. He focused on her in a way that no one else ever had. He saw beyond the superficial layers through to her needs beneath. Not just her needs. Her gifts. He saw *value* in her and he appreciated it. That mattered to her more than she could have ever imagined. Suddenly, thoughtlessly, she swayed, her need to be closer to him driving her body.

'Eleni?' He gripped her arms to steady her, concern deepening the blue of his eyes even more. 'You okay?'

All the feelings bloomed in the face of the irresistible temptation he embodied—the capricious risk he dared from her with a mere look. But beneath it was the steadfast core of certainty. He'd caught her. Just as he'd caught her and held her close that very first night. Somehow she knew he'd always catch her. He was there for her in a way no one had ever been before. That spontaneous tide of emotion only he stirred now swept from her heart, carrying with it those secret words until they slipped right out of her in a shaky whisper of truth that she breathed between them.

'I love you.'

CHAPTER THIRTEEN

'I'M NOT SORRY I said that,' she said shakily, determined to believe her own words.

Impulsive. Impetuous. Spontaneous. *Stupid.*

Because he stood rigid as rock, his fingers digging hard into her upper arms and his eyes wide. But his obvious shock somehow made her bold. She could have no regrets. Not about this. Not now. So she said it again—louder this time.

'I've fallen in love with you, Damon.'

It felt good to admit it. Terrifying, but good.

His expression still didn't change. Just as it hadn't in the last ten seconds. But then he released her so quickly she had to take a step back to maintain her balance.

'You only think you're in love with me because I was your first.' He finally spoke—harsh and blunt. And then he turned his back on her.

That was so out of left-field that she gaped as he walked away towards his desk. 'Give me some credit.' She was so stunned she stormed after him and yanked on his arm to make him face her again. 'Even just a little.'

But he shrugged her hand off.

'Eleni, look…' He paused and drew breath. 'You've never felt lust before. You haven't had the opportunity until now. I'm just the first guy you've met who got your rocks off. But lust doesn't equal love. It never does.'

'Actually I do know that.' She wasn't stupid. And she didn't understand why he was lashing out at her. She was utterly shocked.

'Do you, Eleni?' He looked icier than ever. 'You've got freedom here that you've never had in all your life. I think you're confused.'

'Because I've been able to hang out at the beach without worrying about any photographers in the bushes? You think that's made me think I'm in love with you?' She couldn't believe he was saying this. 'I might not have had a million lovers, but I know how to care. I do know how to love.'

'No, you know how to acquiesce,' he said scathingly. 'How to do as you're told while suffering underneath that beautiful, serene exterior. While not standing up for yourself.'

'I'm standing up for myself now.'

He shook his head 'You're confused.'

'And you're treating me like the child my brother sees me as. You don't think I'm capable of thinking for myself?' Was he truly belittling her feelings for him? He didn't believe her and that hurt. 'This is real.'

'No, it isn't.'

'Don't deny my truth.'

'Eleni.' He closed his eyes for a second but then he seemed to strengthen, broadening his stance. He opened his eyes and his stark expression made her step back.

'I have used you. I have treated you terribly. You can't and don't love me.' He drew in a harsh breath. 'And I'm sorry, but I don't love you.' He seemed to brace his feet a bit further apart. 'We are only together now because you're pregnant.'

His words wounded where she was most vulnerable. Because underneath she'd known this had never been about *her*. He never would have sought her out again if he hadn't been worried about the contraception mistake that night. He'd never wanted to see her again—not just for her.

'This has only ever been for the baby,' she said softly.

'Yes. For its legitimacy and protection.'

'Yet you were happy to sleep with me again.'

His gaze shifted. Lowered.

He'd been happy to string her along. 'And Princess Eleni was an easy conquest because she was so inexperienced and frustrated it took nothing to turn her on…is that how this has been?' She couldn't bear to look at him now, yet she couldn't look away either.

'Eleni—'

'Maybe I was inexperienced and maybe I was starving for attention—' She broke off as a horrible thought occurred to her. 'Have you been laughing at me this whole time?'

Suddenly her skin burned crimson at the recollection of her unbridled behaviour with him. So many times.

'Never laughing.' His skin was also burnished. 'And I'm not now. But you *are* mistaking lust for deeper affection.'

She didn't believe him. She couldn't.

'So you don't feel anything for me but lust?' When he sat with her on the beach and they talked of everything and nothing? When they laughed about stupid little things?

There was a thin plea in her voice that she wanted to swallow back but it was too late. Maybe he'd been trying to keep his distance and now she'd forced him into letting her down completely. 'You don't think we could have it all?'

'No one has it all, Eleni. That's a promise that doesn't exist.'

'No. That's your excuse not to even try. It works out for plenty of people. Maybe not your parents—' She broke off. 'Is this what you learnt from them? Not to even try?'

'Yes.' He was like stone. 'I'm not capable of this, Eleni. Not marriage. Not for ever. Certainly not love.'

'You don't mean that.'

'Don't I?' He laughed bitterly. 'How can you possibly think you're in love with me?' He stalked towards her. 'I seduced you—an innocent. I knew you were shy that night. I knew you weren't that experienced. Did I let that stop me from taking you in a ten-minute display of dominant sex? No. It made it even hotter. But I got you pregnant. Then I kidnapped you. I forced you into marrying me. Tell me, how is that any kind of basis for a long-term relationship?' His short bark of laughter was mirthless. 'It will *never* work.'

'It wasn't like that.'

'It was exactly like that.'

No, it hadn't been. He was painting himself as a villain like in one of the games he'd once designed.

'You don't care about me at all?' She couldn't stop herself from asking it.

'Enough to know you deserve better.'

'Better than what—you?' She stared at him. 'You're more sensitive than you like to admit. More caring. You're kind to your employees, you've been kind to *me*.' She tried to smile but couldn't because this was too important and because she could already see he wasn't listening. And he certainly wasn't believing her. 'You're thoughtful, creative. And you think I don't mean it.'

'You only think you mean it.'

Could he get any more insulting? She'd prove him wrong. She glared at him. 'I know you don't want any part of royal life. You don't value what I am. So I will relinquish my title.'

'What?' He looked stunned—and appalled.

'I'll tell Giorgos that I want to live as a commoner. We could live anywhere then. Here, even. Maybe I could get a normal job, not just cut ribbons and talk to people. I could do something useful.'

He laughed.

Eleni chilled and then burned hot. He'd thrown it back at her—her love. Her proof. He was treating her as everyone else in her life had—as if she were a decorative but ultimately pointless ornament with no depth, no real meaning. No real value. When for a while there, he'd made her think he felt otherwise. That he saw her differently—that he thought she had more to offer. He'd shown her such caring and consideration. Hadn't he meant that at all?

'Why won't you believe me?' she asked him, so hurt she couldn't hide. 'Are you too scared to believe me?'

He just stayed frozen. 'You don't mean it, Eleni.'

'Why is it so impossible to believe that I could love you?' She demanded his answer. Because she was certain this rejection came from fear. 'Or that I could want to give up everything to be with you?'

'So now you think there has to be something wrong with me because I don't want your love?' he asked cruelly. 'Maybe you suddenly want to give up your title because *you* don't like being a princess.'

'Poor me, right?' she said bitterly. 'I have to live in a castle and wear designer clothes and have all these things—'

'You're not materialistic,' he interrupted harshly. '*Things* aren't what you want. What you *want* is out.'

'No. What I want is *you*.'

He stared at her.

'I want you with me,' she carried on recklessly. 'At the palace. Not at the palace. I don't care. I just want you there wherever I am. I want to know I have you by my side.' She totally lost it. 'I don't care what companies you own or what tech you help create. I just want the man who makes me smile. Who laughs at the same things I do. The man who's passionate and who, usually, can think like no one else I've met.' She drew in a short breath. 'What I'm trying to do is put you first. Put you ahead of my brother. My family. My duties and obligations. Don't you get it? I want *you*.'

'I don't want that,' he said harshly. 'I don't want you like that.' His eyes blazed. 'I'm not in love with you, Eleni. Don't you understand that I'll *never* be in love with you? And you'll soon realise you're not in love with me.'

She sucked in a shocked breath as his total rejection hit like a physical blow.

Hadn't the first rejection been humiliation enough? No. She'd had to go on and argue. But the fact was he didn't want to love her. He never had.

All their time together had been nothing but a physical bonus while he put up with their marriage to make the baby legitimate. Eleni was simply a temporary side issue.

She'd mistaken his affection and amusement for a growing genuine attachment, but the support he offered her was probably the kind he'd give any of his cool employees.

'I have to leave,' Eleni said dully. There was no way she could stay here with him now.

'You're going to run away?' he asked coldly. 'Because that's always worked so well for you in the past.'

No. She wasn't going to run away. In that one thing he was right. Running away never worked.

'This child is a *Nicolaides*.' She drew herself up tall. 'She or he will be royalty. And until Giorgos finally has a family of his own, she or he will be next in line to the throne after me. It seems there's no getting away from that. So I'm going to return to Palisades.' She was suddenly certain. And determined. 'That is where I belong.'

He stood very still. 'You won't see out these few months?'

If she hadn't believed that he didn't love her before, she did now. He had no emotion at all—no understanding of just how cruel that question was.

'I've just laid myself bare for you, Damon,' she choked. 'And you don't accept it. You don't accept me. You don't believe in me.' Her heart tore as she accepted *his* truth. 'You want me, but you don't love me. That's okay, you don't have to.' But bitterness choked her. 'One day, though, you are going to feel about someone the way I feel about you. And then you'll know. Because no one is immune, Damon. You're human and we're all *built* to feel.'

She stared hard at him as she realised what she'd failed to see before—and she hit him with it now. 'But what you feel most of is fear. That's why you hide away on your island paradise. Controlling every one of your interactions, having those brief affairs when you go to some city every so often. Keeping yourself safe because you're a coward. I get that your parents were less than average. I get that they hurt you. But don't use them as your excuse to back out of anything remotely complicated emotionally.'

She drew in a desperately needed breath. 'You don't think what I do has value—that I deserve more? Well, you're right, but not in the way you think. I help people. It may not be much, it may appear superficial, but in my role as Princess of Palisades I can make people smile. And I do deserve more. As a *person*. How can you possibly think I could stay here with you like this but not get all I need from you?' It would destroy her slowly and utterly.

The irony was *he* was the one to have shown her what she could have. What she'd hoped to have with him.

'You can't give me what I need, but I can't settle for less,' she said. 'So no, I won't "see out these few months". I can't stay a second longer than I have to.' Even though it was just about going to kill her to leave.

Eleni might never be loved personally. But as a princess she was. And that would have to do.

CHAPTER FOURTEEN

DAMON PACED ALONG the beach, waiting for her to finish packing. She couldn't leave soon enough. He'd spoken the truth. She didn't 'love' him. She was in 'lust'—with him a little, but mostly with the freedom he'd provided for her. It wasn't *him personally*. It was the situation. Any other man and she'd feel the same about him. It was only fate that had made Damon the one.

He clenched his fists, because she offered such temptation. She made him want to believe in that impossible dream. In her.

But it was better to end it now. The pain in her eyes had been so unbearable he'd almost had to turn away. He hadn't meant to hurt her. But she was inexperienced and naive and he realised now their divorce might hurt her more if they didn't part now. He didn't want to lead her confused emotions on.

She didn't look at him as she climbed into the helicopter that would take her back to his jet, and then to Palisades.

'I'll have rooms set aside for you,' she said regally. 'You may visit at the weekends, so we maintain the illusion of a happy marriage until after the baby is born.'

He *'may'*? His brewing anger prickled at her tone. 'And after?'

'You may visit whenever you want. I won't stop you from seeing the baby.'

Even now she was generous. His anger mounted more, but he contained it. She would care for their child better than he ever could. He understood that now. Because his father had been right—they were alike. Damaged. Incapable and frankly undeserving of love.

He couldn't damage Eleni or his child any more than he already had.

* * *

The sun and the sand mocked him. His team were abnormally quiet and left him alone. He stood it for only two days before summoning the jet. He needed to get further away. San Francisco. London. Berlin. Paris.

He wanted her. He missed her. But he did not love her. He did not know how to love. It was easy to stay busy in cities—to arrange endless, pointless meetings that filled his head with fluff. But people asked about the Princess and he had to smile and pretend.

She was better off without him.

His head hurt. His body hurt. His chest—where his heart should be if he had one—that hurt too. But he didn't have a heart, right?

Yet all he could think about was Eleni. He spent every moment wondering what she was doing. Whether she was okay. If she was smiling that beautiful smile at all.

She'd given, not taken. She'd offered him the one thing that was truly her own—her heart. He knew she'd never done that before. She'd been at her most vulnerable. And he'd rejected her.

But he'd had to, for her. Because he didn't deserve her love. He had no idea how to become the man who did. If she was freed from the marriage to him, she might find some other man to treat her the way she deserved. That would be the right thing to do.

Hot, vicious, selfish anger consumed him at the thought of someone else holding her. Of someone else touching her. Of someone else making her smile.

He didn't want that. He *never* wanted that.

He clenched his fist, emotions boiling into a frenzy. He had no freaking idea how to manage this. And that was when he realised—so painfully—how much he didn't want to let her go. He *never* wanted to let her go.

He logged into his computer, searching for somewhere to go and sort himself out for good. Far from Palisades.

Far from his own island that was now too tainted with the memories of her presence. He had to escape everything and pull himself together. But as he scrolled through varying destinations, his emails landed in his inbox.

There was one from the palace secretary.

Damon paused. It would probably be another schedule of engagements that they wanted him to approve or something. Unable to resist, he clicked to the email and opened it. But it wasn't a list. It was a concise couple of sentences informing him that Princess Eleni had seen the obstetric specialist of her choosing who'd written a brief report, the contents of which had been inserted into the email. In one paragraph it explained that the baby was growing at a normal rate. That the condition that had taken Eleni's mother was not hereditary. That the pregnancy posed no abnormal risk to her. That everything was progressing as it ought for both mother and baby.

His breath and blood froze. There was an image file attached to the email. Dazed, Damon opened it on auto. A mass of grey appeared. He looked at the arrow and markers pointing out a particular blob set in a darker patch in the middle of the picture. It was an ultrasound scan. It was his baby.

He tried to breathe but he just stared at that tiny, little treasure in the centre of his screen. It was there. It was real. It was happening. Heat swept through him in a burning drive to claim what was—

Mine.

Both hands clenched into fists.

Eleni.

The thought of her consumed him—her strength, her decisions, her role in all this. She was well. She was strong. She was safe. He ached to reach for her, ached to see her smile as she saw this picture—he just knew she'd smile at this picture. And the realisation rocked him.

Ours.

They had made this beautiful child *together*. That night she'd come with him and he'd claimed her and somehow in that insanely wonderful moment they'd created this miracle. It never should have happened—but it had. And Eleni was taking it on. She was doing her bit and she was doing it so damn well. And if he wanted to be part of that, *he* was the one who had to shape up. Seeing this now, reading Eleni's results, he realised just how much he wanted in and he burned with acidic shame. He'd missed so much already. He wished like hell he'd been there with her when she'd seen this doctor and when she'd had this scan. He should have been holding her hand for every damn second.

He bent his head, squeezing his eyes shut so he could no longer see the image on that screen. But the truth snuck in and stabbed him anyway. The fact was he had a heart. He really, truly had a heart and it hurt like hell. Because it was no longer his.

Eleni had it. It was all hers. He had to tell her. He had to apologise. He had to get her back. Groaning, he closed the picture file and read the doctor's report again. And again. Sucking in the reassurance that Eleni was healthy. Strong. Safe.

She'd asked if he was scared of love and at the time he'd refused to answer. He'd been utterly unable to. But now he faced the stark facts. He was terrified. Like a freaking deer in the headlights he'd simply frozen.

Frozen her out.

Where she'd been brave, proudly standing up to him, he'd been unable to admit, even to himself, how much he wanted her in his life. And when she'd unconditionally offered him everything she had, he couldn't believe her. No one had ever offered him that before.

Eleni had been right. He was a coward. He hid because it was easier. But in truth he was no better than his parents—putting all emotion aside for work. But she'd got under his skin and he'd been unable to resist—he'd taken everything she'd offered. He'd even convinced himself he was doing her a favour. He'd encouraged her to blossom and let all that sweet enthusiasm and hot passion out. He'd thought she'd needed freedom away from the palace. Freedom to take what she wanted—to ask for what she wanted.

And she had.

Eleni had offered him her love. And she'd asked for his in return.

But he'd rejected her. The worst thing he could have done was not take her seriously. Only he'd done even worse. He'd scoffed at her.

That hot streak of possessiveness surged through his veins as he clicked open that ultrasound image again. But he sucked in a steadying breath. He didn't get to be possessive, not without earning her forgiveness first. Not without begging to make everything better. And how did he get to her now she was back in that damn prison of a palace?

CHAPTER FIFTEEN

'ARE YOU SURE you're feeling up to this, ma'am?' Bettina asked Eleni carefully.

'That's what blusher is for, right?' Eleni answered wryly. 'And I still have quite the tan on my arms.' She forced a smile for her maid. 'I'm fine to go. It'll be fun. But thank you.'

She needed to fill in her day. She needed to feel *something*.

She'd been buried in the palace for almost a fortnight, hoping she'd hear from him. But she hadn't. She couldn't face drawing, couldn't face the pool. She'd tried reading. But her mind still wandered to him. She hated how much she ached for him.

He doesn't deserve me.

She tried to remind herself, but it didn't lessen the hurt. Hopefully this gallery visit would take her mind off him even for a few minutes. The fact that it was a children's tour was even better because children asked questions fearlessly—with no thought to privacy or palace protocol. It would be a good test. She'd have to hold herself together when they mentioned his name. And they would ask. They'd want to see her engagement and wedding rings. They'd want to see her smiling.

They expected a blushing, beyond happy bride.

Giorgos had sounded harried when he'd phoned, which was unlike him. And for whatever reason that he hadn't had time to explain, he was still residing at the Summer House and he'd asked if she'd attend the small gallery opening on his behalf. Of course she'd agreed. She'd been going insane staying inside. She needed to build a busy and fulfilling life. Then she could and would cope with the break in her heart.

But she'd appreciated the concern in Giorgos's voice. Just as she appreciated Bettina's quiet care. And her bodyguard's constant, silent presence.

She smiled as Tony opened the car door for her. 'It's nice to have you back.'

'Thank you, ma'am.'

'I promise not to disappear on you today,' she teased lightly, determined not to hide from the past.

'I understand, ma'am.' Tony's impassive expression cracked and he smiled at her. 'You won't be out of my sight for a second.'

'I understand and I do appreciate it.'

It was a beautiful late summer morning but she'd added a light jacket to complement the floaty-style floral dress she'd worn to hide her figure and deflect any conjecture and commentary. That suspicion would be raised soon enough. But preferably not today.

Twenty minutes later she stepped out of the car at the discreet side entrance of the new art space. She took a moment to accept a posy of flowers from a sweet young girl. But as she turned to enter the gallery she froze, her heart seizing. She blinked and moved as Tony guided her forward. But she glanced back as something caught her eye. For a second she'd thought she'd seen a masculine figure standing on the far side of the road—tall, broad, more handsome than Adonis...

Wishful, impossible thinking.

Because there was no man there now.

Releasing a measured breath, she walked with the small group of children through the new wing of the gallery, focusing her mind to discuss the paintings with them. But despite the easing of her morning sickness over the past few days, maintaining her spark during the visit drained her more than she'd thought it would. She was relieved when she saw Tony give her the usual signal before turning slightly to mutter into his mobile phone.

Damon had half expected soldiers to swoop on him and frogmarch him straight to the city dungeons, but the coast was clear and the path to the car easy. It was unlocked and he took the driver's seat, waiting for the signal. Anticipation surged as his phone rang. He could hardly remain still.

Finally the passenger door opened. He heard her polite thanks.

He started the engine. As soon as she'd got into the car and the door closed behind her, he pulled away from the kerb.

'Tony?' Eleni leaned forward in her seat.

'Damon,' he corrected, a vicious pleasure shooting through his body at just hearing her voice again.

He glanced up and looked in the rear-view mirror and almost lost control of the car in the process. She was so beautiful. But that soft colour slowly leeched from her skin as she met his gaze in the mirror and realised it truly was him. If he'd suffered before, he really felt it then. He'd killed her joy. The make-up stood out starkly against her whitened face. She'd had to paint on her customary vitality—her luminescence stolen. By him.

Her eyes were suddenly swimming in tears but she blinked them back. The effort she was expending to stay in control was immense. He hated seeing her this wretched. But at the same time, her distress gave him hope. His presence moved her. She hadn't forgotten him. Hadn't got over him.

He didn't deserve her.

'Why are you here?' She demanded his answer in the frostiest tones he'd ever heard from her.

All he wanted was to enfold her in his arms but he couldn't. She was furious with him and she had every right to be. He had to talk to her. Ask for forgiveness. Then ask for everything.

When he'd already rejected her.

He gripped the steering wheel more tightly as anxiety sharpened his muscles and he tried to remember where the hell he was going. Because this was going to be even harder than he'd imagined. And he'd imagined the worst.

'I'm kidnapping you.' He ground the words out, holding back all the others scrambling in his throat. He needed to get them somewhere that they could talk in private.

He glanced back at the rear-view mirror. Her emotion had morphed into cold, hard rage.

'I'm not doing this to Tony again,' she snapped, turning to look out of the window behind her to see if any cars were behind them. 'He'll be following. He doesn't deserve—'

'Tony knows you're with me,' he said quickly. 'So does Giorgos.'

She flicked her head back, her eyes flashing. 'So you planned this with everyone but me?'

He didn't want to answer more. He was only making it worse. Damn, it turned out he was good at that.

'This is *not* okay, Damon,' she said coldly.

'None of this is okay,' he growled, swerving around the nearest corner. 'And I can't wait—' He broke off and parked on one of the narrow cobbled streets.

'Can't wait for what?' she asked haughtily.

Eleni waited for his answer, trying to remain in control, but underneath her calm demeanour her heart was pounding and it was almost impossible to stop distress overtaking her sensibility. Damon was here. Not only that, he'd colluded with her brother and her bodyguard and she couldn't bear to think about *why*.

It mattered too much. *He* mattered too much.

But it was too late. He'd made his choice. He'd let her go. He'd let her *down*.

She refused to believe in the hope fluttering pathetically in her heart. This was too soon. She hadn't grown a strong enough scab over her wounds to meet him yet.

'Eleni.'

She closed her eyes. He couldn't *do* this to her.

One look. One word. That was all it took for her to want to fall into his arms again. She refused to be that weak. She couldn't let him have that power over her.

'Take me back to the palace,' she ordered.

He killed the engine. She watched, frozen, as he got out of the car and swiftly opened the rear passenger door. But before she could move he'd slid into the back seat with her and locked the doors again.

'Give me ten minutes,' he said, removing his aviator sunglasses and gazing intently at her. 'If you wish to return to the palace afterwards, then I'll take you there. I just want ten minutes. Can you give me that?'

She wanted to give him so much more already. But she couldn't. She'd been a fool for him already; she wasn't making that mistake again. 'What more is there to say, Damon? We want different things.'

'There's plenty more to say,' he argued shortly.

'Too late. You had your chance.' She glanced behind her, hoping Tony was less than a block away. But there was no car. No people.

'Ten minutes,' he pushed. 'I'm not letting you go until you listen to me.' He was silent for a moment. *'Please.'*

At that urgent whisper she turned back to face him. Starved of his company for days, she couldn't help drinking in his appearance now. He was studying her with that old intensity. Always he'd made her feel as if she were the only thing in the world that mattered.

Not fair. Not true. Not for him.

'Five minutes,' she answered flatly.

Only five. Because tendrils of hope were unfurling, reaching out, beginning to bind her back to him. That weak part of her wanted him to take her in his arms and kiss her. Then she might believe he was actually here. That he'd come back for her. But at the same time she knew that if he touched her, she'd be lost.

His smile was small and fleeting and disappeared the second he opened his mouth again. 'I'm so sorry, Eleni.'

Her heart stopped. Her breath died. She didn't know if she could take this. Not if he wasn't here to give her everything.

'Words said too easily,' she whispered.

'That night at the ball—'

'No,' she interrupted him furiously. 'We're not going back there. You're not doing this.'

'Yes, we are. It's where it all began, Eleni. We can't forget what's happened. We can't ignore—'

'You already have,' she argued. 'You already denied—'

'I lied,' he snapped back. 'Listen to me now. Please. That night was the most extreme case of lust I've ever felt,' he confessed angrily. 'And for you too. You know how powerful it was. How it *is*. You never would have let just any man touch you that way, Eleni. You never would have let just any man *inside*.'

She sucked in a shocked breath.

'I know I didn't want to admit it,' he said. 'But what's between us is something *much* more than that.' He gazed at her so intently, the blue of his eyes so brilliant it almost blinded her.

But she shook her head. Not for him, it wasn't.

'For me too,' he declared, rejecting her doubts. 'It was and is, Eleni. I've denied it for too long.' He bent closer, forcing her to look him right in those intense eyes. 'You were flirtatious, you were shy...so hot and so sweet.'

She winced. She couldn't bear for him to revisit her inexperience. Her naiveté. He'd thought she had nothing more than a teenage *crush* on him. He'd felt sorry for her.

'I belittled you when you told me your feelings,' he said.

'I didn't believe you. I couldn't…and I'm so sorry I did that to you.' Somehow he was sitting closer, his voice lower. His gently spoken words hit her roughly. 'I never should have let you go.'

'Why shouldn't you have?' She succumbed to the hurt of these last intolerably lonely days. 'You miss having my adoration? My body? My naive protestations of love?' She was so mortified. The imbalance was so severe. It was so unfair.

'Not naive.' He shook his head. 'Not you. *I'm* the ignorant one. I didn't know what love was, Eleni. I've never had someone give me what you've given me. And like the idiot I am, I didn't know how to handle it.' His gaze dropped. 'I don't know how to handle you or how I feel about you. It is so…' He trailed off and dragged in a breath. 'It's huge.' He pressed his fist to his chest. 'I was overwhelmed and I threw it away like it was a bomb you'd tossed at me.' His voice dropped to a whisper again. 'But the fact is, you'd already detonated my world. You took everything I thought I knew and turned it on its head. I thought I had it all together. The career. The occasional woman. The easy stroll through life. No complications. Every success was mine… but you made me *feel*.'

'Feel what?' she asked coldly, twisting her fingers together in her lap, stopping herself from edging anywhere nearer to him. She needed to hear him say so much more. She still couldn't let herself *trust*—

'Need,' he said rawly. 'Need to be with someone—to have you to talk to, to laugh with, to show everything, to hold, to just keep me company…to love…' He trailed off.

'So this is about *your* need?' She sent him a sharp look.

A harsh breath whistled out between his clenched teeth. 'I don't know how to be the kind of father that this baby deserves,' he gritted. 'I don't know how to be the kind of husband that you deserve. I have had awful examples of both and for a long time I believed…' Words failed him again.

Eleni didn't speak. She couldn't believe and it was becoming too hard to listen.

'I never imagined this would happen to me. And for it to be *you*?' He visibly paled. 'You deserve so much more than what I can give you.'

She shook her head, her rage surging. 'That's a cop-out, Damon.'

'You're a princess—'

'That's *irrelevant*,' she snapped.

'I don't mean your lineage. I mean in here.' He pressed his fist to his heart again but gazed at her. 'You're generous, loyal, loving, true…that's what I mean. You're not like other people—'

'I'm just like other people,' she argued fiercely. 'I'm human. *Most* people are loving and loyal, Damon. Most people are generous and honest.'

That was what he needed to learn and it crushed her that he hadn't learned it as he should have, that his life had been so devoid of normal family love.

'I'm nothing special,' she added.

'You're special to *me*!' he bellowed back at her. 'You're more generous, more loyal, more loving than anyone I've ever met and *all* I want is to be near you. You don't value yourself the way that you should.'

But she did now. She did, because of him. That was what he'd taught her. That was why she'd walked away from him. Because she knew what it was to truly love. And that she deserved more than he'd wanted to give her.

'Yes, I do,' she flung back at him brokenly. 'That's why I'm back in Palisades.' That was why she'd left him when it had almost killed her to do so. Because staying would have been an even more painful experience. She wasn't going to settle for less. Not now. Not from him. She couldn't exist settling for less from him. 'That's why I couldn't stay with you. Because I do need…'

The words stuck in her throat as the pain seeped out.

She knew he'd been hurt, but that he couldn't push past it for her? That hurt *her*.

He was staring into her eyes but his face blurred as her tears spilled—hot, fast, unstoppable, stupid tears.

'I'm so sorry, darling, so sorry I did this to you.' He reached out as she tried to turn away from him. His fingers were gentle as he captured her close and wiped the tears from her face. 'Please don't say I'm too late. It can't be too late. Because I love you, Eleni. Do you understand? I love you, I do.' He leaned closer as she remained silent. 'Eleni, please don't cry. Please listen to me.'

Her breath shuddered as she tried to still, needing to hear him.

His hands framed her face and he kept talking in those desperate hushed tones. 'Until you, I had no idea what love was—what it means, how to show it. And I want to love you, so much, but I don't know where to start. I don't know how to make this right. I'm begging you here, Eleni. How do I become the man you need?'

'You're *already* what I need,' she whispered hoarsely, so annoyed that he still didn't get it. 'You're everything I need. Just you. You're enough exactly as you are.' That was what he needed to learn too. 'And you have started.' She pushed past the ache in her throat. 'By showing up. By being here.'

By coming back for her.

He stared at her for a moment and then with the gentlest of fingertips he traced down her cheekbone. She struggled to quell her tremors at his tenderness.

'See? So generous,' he murmured, almost to himself. But then he cleared his throat and leaned that bit closer, his gaze fierce and unwavering. 'I love you, Eleni.'

Once again he said it. What she'd been too afraid to believe she'd really heard. And the words weren't whispered, they were strong, almost defiant.

He shook her gently. 'Did you hear me?'

* * *

Two more tears slowly rolled down her cheeks.

'I am so, so sorry it has taken me so long to figure it out. I miss you like—' He closed his eyes briefly but she'd already seen the stark pain. He opened them to stare hard at her. To try again. 'These past couple of weeks have been—'

That weak scab across her heart tore as he choked up in front of her. He couldn't find the words. She understood why—it was indescribable for her too.

'I know,' she whispered.

A small sigh escaped him. 'I don't deserve it, but please be patient with me. Talk to me. Talk like you did that hideous day you left me. I need your honesty... I just need you.'

She drew in a shaky breath, because she wanted to believe him so much. But she needed to understand. 'What changed? What brought you back?'

'Misery,' he said simply. 'I was so lonely and it hurt so much and I tried to escape it—you—but I couldn't. And finally I got thinking again.' He shook his head as if he were clearing the fog. 'I haven't been able to think clearly since that first second I saw you...it's just been blind instinct and gut reaction—equal parts lust and terror. I'd got *so* defensive and then, when I could finally think, I realised you were right. About everything. But I'd pushed you away. You're worth listening to, Eleni,' he whispered roughly, edging closer to her again. 'When you told me you loved me, I couldn't believe you... I was scared.'

'You don't think I was scared when I said it to you?'

The corner of his mouth lifted ruefully. 'You know my family doesn't do emotions. They do business connections. I want to do more than that, to be more...'

'You're more than that already. You just need to believe it.'

'I know that now. Because somehow, in all this, you *did* fall in love with me.' A hint of that old arrogance glinted in his eyes and his fingers tightened on her waist. 'You do love me.' His chin lifted as he all but dared her to deny it.

But she saw it in his eyes—the open vulnerability that he'd refused to let show before.

'Of course,' she said softly. 'I stood no chance.'

'Just as I stood no chance with you.' His hands swept, seeking as if he couldn't hold back from caressing her a second longer. 'And I'm afraid I can't let you go, Eleni. I can't live through you leaving me again.' He gripped her hips tightly. 'I'm taking you with me. I'm kidnapping you and I'm not going to say sorry for that.' Determination—desperation—streaked across his face.

At that raw emotion the last of her defences shattered.

'You're not kidnapping me.' She sobbed, leaning into his embrace. 'I choose to come with you.' Just as she'd chosen to be with him that first night. 'I choose to stay with you always.' She drew in a breath and framed his gorgeous face with her hands. 'I chose to marry you. I meant my marriage vows.'

'Thank God.' He hauled her into his lap with barely leashed passion. 'I love you. And I promise to honour you. Care for you…always.' He drew back to look solemnly into her eyes. 'It's not just a contract for me, Eleni.'

Her heart bursting, she flung her arms around his neck, kissing him with a hunger that almost overwhelmed her. 'I missed you so much,' she cried.

'Eleni.'

She heard the joy, the pure love in his voice. She felt it in his tender, fierce embrace and in the heat of his increasingly frantic kisses.

'I love you,' he muttered, kissing her desperately. 'I love you, I love you, I love you.'

It was as if he'd released the valve holding back his heart and now the most intense wave of emotion swamped her. Finally the veracity of *her* feelings could flow again. She had complete freedom to say what she wanted. To be who she was—who she'd wanted to be.

His lover. His beloved.

He held her so close, wiping away yet more tears that she didn't realise were tumbling down her cheeks. Opening her eyes, she saw a softness in his strong features that she'd not seen before. She trembled as she registered just how good this felt—how close she'd been to losing him. He'd been gone from her life too long. She needed his touch, his kiss, his hold—*now*.

'It's okay, sweetheart,' he soothed, kissing her again and again as she shuddered in his arms. 'It's okay.'

It was better than okay. It was heaven. And now she clung—unashamedly clung, needing to be so much nearer to him. 'Don't let me go.'

'Never again. I promise.'

But he'd hardly kissed her for long enough when he lifted his lips from hers and rested his forehead on hers, his breathing ragged. 'People are going to see us if we stay here too much longer...a palace car, illegally parked on the side of the road...'

'It doesn't matter.' Her voice rasped past the emotion aching in her throat. 'They know we're passionately in love.'

For real. Not just a fairy tale for the press. She ached to have him again completely.

He read her expression and groaned with a shake to his head. 'We can't be that reckless. And I'm crushing your pretty dress.' He lifted her from his lap, puffing out a strained breath. 'You're Princess Eleni, and this isn't right for you.'

She stilled, a thread of worry piercing her warmth. 'You don't like the palace.'

'I can learn to like it.' He brushed back her hair. 'I can learn a lot, Eleni. I can become the man you need. We can make it work.'

'You're already the man I need. You just need to stay—'

'Right by your side.' He met her gaze with utter surety in his. 'I know.'

Her eyes filled again. 'Where were you planning to drive me to?'

'Back to the boat.' A wry grin flitted across his lips. 'There aren't that many ways to kidnap a princess from Palisades. Damn palace is a fortress.'

She chuckled.

'But the treasure that was locked in there...' His old smug smile resurfaced. 'That's my treasure now.'

'And you're going to keep it?'

'Oh, I am. For always.'

'Then what are you waiting for? Let's get to the marina.'

His face lit up and then tightened in the merest split of a second. 'You can't imagine how much I need you—'

'Actually I think I can,' she argued breathlessly.

His laugh was ragged. 'You're hot and sweet, Eleni.' He swiftly climbed over to the driver's seat and started the engine.

'So, Giorgos and Tony were in on this?'

'I'm afraid so.' He drove quickly, confidently. 'You didn't stand a chance.'

'No?' she asked archly as he pulled into the park by the yacht.

'Believe it or not...' Damon got out of the car and opened her door '...they want you to be happy.'

'And they think being with you means happiness for me?'

'Does it?'

She stepped out of the car and reached up to stroke his face, seeing that hint of vulnerability flicker in his eyes once more. 'It does now, yes.'

He swiftly turned. 'We need to get on board. Now.'

'Are we going to sail off into the sunset?' She was so tempted to skip.

'Not for ever.' He winked at her. 'Palisades needs its Princess but I'll admit I'm going to push for part-time status.' He suddenly turned and swept her into his arms. With that gorgeous effortlessness he carried her across the boardwalk, onto the boat and straight into the bedroom. 'Because she'll be busy with her baby. And meeting the needs of her husband. And she'll be busy drawing and being creative with all the other things she's not let herself take the time for until now.' He paused, holding her just above the bed. 'Does that sound like a good plan to you?'

'It sounds like a brilliant plan.'

It was only moments until they were locked together. He was so close and she stared into his beautiful eyes.

'Take what you want from me, my beautiful,' he muttered. 'Anything and everything I have is yours.'

'I have your body,' she murmured. 'I want your heart.'

'It only beats because of you.' He laced his fingers through hers. 'I wasn't alive until I met you. You're everything to me. I love you, Eleni.'

'And I love you.' She wrapped around him, letting him carry them both into that bliss.

'Too quick,' he groaned, and gripped her hips tightly, slowing her.

Amused and beyond aroused, she tried to tease him. 'But what does it matter? We can go again, now we have all the time in the world.'

'Yes.' Those gorgeously intense eyes focused on her with that lethal desire and her heart soared as he answered. 'We have for ever.'

* * * * *

MILLS & BOON

Coming next month

KIDNAPPED FOR HIS ROYAL DUTY
Jane Porter

Before they came to Jolie, Dal would have described Poppy as pretty, in a fresh, wholesome, no-nonsense sort of way with her thick, shoulder-length brown hair and large, brown eyes and a serious little chin.

But as Poppy entered the dining room with its glossy white ceiling and dark purple walls, she looked anything but wholesome and no-nonsense.

She was wearing a silk gown the color of cherries, delicately embroidered with silver threads, and instead of her usual ponytail or chignon, her dark hair was down, and long, elegant chandelier earrings dangled from her ears. As she walked, the semi-sheer kaftan molded to her curves.

"It seems I've been keeping you waiting," she said, her voice pitched lower than usual and slightly breathless. "Izba insisted on all this," she added, gesturing up toward her face.

At first Dal thought she was referring to the ornate silver earrings that were catching and reflecting the light, but once she was seated across from him he realized her eyes had been rimmed with kohl and her lips had been outlined and filled in with a soft plum-pink gloss. "You're wearing makeup."

"Quite a lot of it, too." She grimaced. "I tried to explain to Izba that this wasn't me, but she's very determined once she makes her mind up about something and apparently, dinner with you requires me to look like a tart."

Dal checked his smile. "You don't look like a tart. Unless it's the kind of tart one wants to eat."

Color flooded Poppy's cheeks and she glanced away, suddenly shy, and he didn't know if it was her shyness or the shimmering dress that clung to her, but he didn't think any woman could be more beautiful, or desirable than Poppy right now. "You look lovely," he said quietly. "But I don't want you uncomfortable all through dinner. If you'd rather go remove the makeup I'm happy to wait."

She looked at him closely as if doubting his sincerity. "It's fun to dress up, but I'm worried Izba has the wrong idea about me."

"And what is that?"

"She seems to think you're going to…marry…me."

Continue reading
KIDNAPPED FOR HIS ROYAL DUTY
Jane Porter

Available next month
www.millsandboon.co.uk

LET'S TALK
Romance

For exclusive extracts, competitions
and special offers, find us online:

 facebook.com/millsandboon

 @millsandboonuk

 @millsandboon

Or get in touch on 0844 844 1351*

For all the latest titles coming soon, visit
millsandboon.co.uk/nextmonth